Praise for Ciji Ware's acclaimed novel *A Cottage by the Sea*

"Not since Anya Seton's classic time-travel/ reincarnation romance *Green Darkness* have I been so entranced by the compelling mixture of history blended with past and present lives. . . . Ciji Ware is a true master at bringing to life a story so fascinating that it should come with a warning—Do not start unless you want to be up all night! . . . Superb!"
—*Romantic Times* (Gold Medal review)

"A deep, complex novel exploring love, betrayal, healing, and renewal in the human heart."
—*Affaire de Coeur*

"A delightful tale with just the right touch of humor, vulnerability, and suspense."
—CHRISTINA SKYE
Author of *Bridge of Dreams*

By Ciji Ware:

Fiction
ISLAND OF THE SWANS*
WICKED COMPANY
A COTTAGE BY THE SEA*
MIDNIGHT ON JULIA STREET*

Nonfiction
SHARING PARENTHOOD AFTER DIVORCE

Published by Fawcett Gold Medal

MIDNIGHT ON JULIA STREET

Ciji Ware

FAWCETT GOLD MEDAL • NEW YORK

A Fawcett Gold Medal Book
Published by The Ballantine Publishing Group
Copyright © 1999 by Ciji Ware

www.randomhouse.com/BB/

Library of Congress Catalog Card Number: 98-96712

ISBN 0-449-00187-3

Manufactured in the United States of America

First Edition: June 1999

10 9 8 7 6 5 4 3 2 1

This novel is dedicated to

the stalwart band of preservationists who stopped an elevated six-lane expressway from being built along the Vieux Carré riverfront in New Orleans, thereby saving a National Historic Landmark from irreparable harm,

and to

Margaret McCullough Clymer and the late Adela Rogers St. Johns, who, together, remind me very much of Great-Aunt Marge,

and, finally, most gratefully to

my friend, Gayle Van Dyck, whose discerning eye is my salvation, and Dr. John Grenner, who believes the secret to life is telling the truth in real time.

A LOUISIANA

THE LaCROIXS
of REVERIE PLANTATION

THE FOUCHÉS
of BAYOU LaCOMB

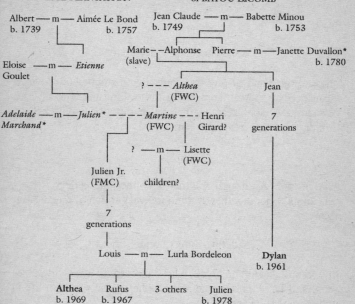

Albert — m — Aimée Le Bond
b. 1739   b. 1757

Jean Claude — m — Babette Minou
b. 1749   b. 1753

Marie – – Alphonse   Pierre — m — Janette Duvallon*
(slave)   b. 1780

Eloise — m — *Etienne*
Goulet

? – – – *Althea*   Jean
         (FWC)

Adelaide — m — *Julien** – – – *Martine* – – – Henri   7
Marchand   (FWC)   Girard?   generations

? — m — Lisette
              (FWC)

Julien Jr.   children?
(FMC)

7
generations

Louis — m — Lurla Bordeleon   **Dylan**
                                                                    b. 1961

Althea   Rufus   3 others   Julien
b. 1969   b. 1967   b. 1978

THE MARCHANDS of
BON CHANCE PLANTATION

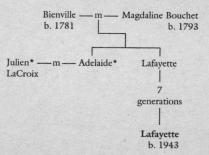

Bienville — m — Magdaline Bouchet
b. 1781   b. 1793

Julien* — m — Adelaide*   Lafayette
LaCroix

7
generations

Lafayette
b. 1943

FWC = Free Woman of Color   FMC = Free Man of Color   * = the same person

GENEALOGY

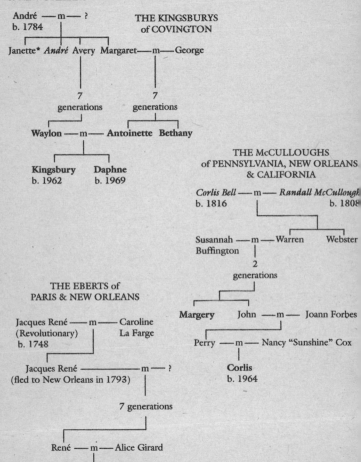

THE DUVALLONS
of NEW ORLEANS

André — m — ?
b. 1784

THE KINGSBURYS
of COVINGTON

Janette* *André* Avery Margaret — m — George

7 generations

7 generations

Waylon — m — Antoinette Bethany

Kingsbury
b. 1962

Daphne
b. 1969

THE McCULLOUGHS
of PENNSYLVANIA, NEW ORLEANS
& CALIFORNIA

Corlis Bell — m — *Randall McCullough*
b. 1816   b. 1808

Susannah — m — Warren   Webster
Buffington

2 generations

Margery   John — m — Joann Forbes

Perry — m — Nancy "Sunshine" Cox

Corlis
b. 1964

THE EBERTS of
PARIS & NEW ORLEANS

Jacques René — m — Caroline
(Revolutionary)   La Farge
b. 1748

Jacques René — m — ?
(fled to New Orleans in 1793)

7 generations

René — m — Alice Girard

Jack
b. 1969

Amy
b. 1965

19th c. story   **20th c. story**

Chapter One

December 20

The trouble with weddings, Corlis McCullough concluded, was that the invited guests could never be sure if they were about to witness the beginning of a wonderful life or the end of everyone's fond illusions—including the bride's.

Corlis slammed the door of the news van and stared up at the venerable Saint Louis Cathedral, its three slate-clad spires silhouetted against the New Orleans night sky. Another day in the Big Easy. Another cream puff story. Another chance to blow her cool over the sorry state of television journalism. And a golden opportunity, after twelve years, to run into Kingsbury Duvallon.

For once in your life, McCullough, don't shoot yourself in the foot!

She glanced quickly around the deserted plaza that fronted the large church. At this predinner hour, Jackson Square was devoid of its usual street performers, chalk artists, and tarot card readers. In the center of the gated park, Old Hickory sat astride his bronze horse, keeping silent vigil over the mighty Mississippi two hundred yards distant. The river churned with paddlewheel sight-seeing boats, the Algiers ferry, and freighters riding low in the water as they plied their way toward the Gulf of Mexico, a hundred miles downstream.

That old, familiar feeling had begun to gnaw in the pit of Corlis's stomach.

Candlelit nuptials. An evening wedding. How chic.

How revolting!

1

She'd started to hate weddings, and she especially hated attending *this* one. The situation that faced her this unseasonably sultry December evening was the one she'd been dreading from the moment she'd arrived from Los Angeles two months earlier to go to work at WWEZ-TV in the fabled Crescent City. However, there was no ducking this assignment.

With a sigh she advanced with her news crew across the expanse of stone paving toward the church's arched entrance, neatly avoiding tripping over the scuffed boots of a wino who was apparently sleeping off the effects of letting the good times roll.

Within minutes Corlis, along with her cameraman and sound operator, was ensconced in the balcony that overlooked the historic structure's vast interior. The seasoned reporter put her mind to the task of calculating the best way to cover this so-called Wedding of the Season—a marriage ceremony that would join two of New Orleans's most prominent old-line families.

Soon, however, Corlis began to calculate her *own* margin of safety. She sternly reminded herself that associate professor of architectural history King Duvallon was merely a groomsman in this wedding tonight. He was also the brother of the bride. At the moment there was no sign of the Hero of New Orleans, celebrated everywhere for putting a stop to misplaced bridge and highway projects, condo complexes, minimalls, and other scourges threatening this southern city's hallowed and revered architecture. Despite Corlis's duty to cover this wedding in the French Quarter, there was absolutely no need for her to get up close and personal with anyone tonight, especially King.

Just dodge this bullet, baby. You can't afford to get fired one more time.

The church's pillared interior was suffused with the golden glow of twinkling lights from two rows of chandeliers that hung from the barrel-shaped ceiling. Parallel lines of eighteen-inch tapers—each ivory candle attached to a pew—marched down the center aisle of New Orleans's famed landmark. The pungent smell of incense collided with the sweet scent wafting from banks of fragrant red and white roses and abundant pine boughs that had been deployed everywhere as part of the Christmas wedding theme. In fact, the bloom-filled church served as a vivid advertisement for Flowers by Duvallon, the firm owned by the bride's family, and the *only* florist ever recommended to bereaved customers by the groom's family, founders of the prominent Ebert-Petrella chain of funeral homes.

This merger must have been in the works since the bride and groom were in kindergarten! Corlis thought with a glance around the cathedral.

"Virgil," she addressed her cameraman, "give me lots of wide shots and some good cutaways of the altar, and some close-ups of the priest . . . and Jack Ebert . . . Daphne Duvallon . . . that sort of thing."

"When do you wanna do your lead-in and the stand-up?" Virgil asked, carefully placing his video camera on its tripod and tightening the screws.

"After the ceremony," Corlis replied. "Let's record an intro and maybe a bridge in front of the church just before we take off, okay? When the guests leave for the reception, I'll stay up here and write the copy while you go down below and grab what you need of the wedding party during the family picture-taking."

Good plan, McCullough. Keep your distance from the almighty Mr. Duvallon.

Virgil Johnson raised his shaved, ebony head from the camera. Then he arched an eyebrow and shrugged agreement with a change of logistics that even *she* knew was completely out of character for her. When had she ever, in the two months they'd worked together, *not* been standing right next to her camera operator, breathing down his neck to make sure he got every damned frame she was going to need when it came time to edit?

She turned to address sound technician Manny Picot. "Be sure you record a nice long stretch of organ music so we can lay it under the action and my voice track, okay?"

"Yeah . . . gotcha," Manny mumbled behind his thick black mustache that bespoke his Hispanic-African ancestry.

Mellow sounds of classical organ music resounded throughout the cavernous space as five hundred of the bride and groom's nearest and dearest continued to file into the church with help from an army of groomsmen.

Corlis glanced down at the best watch she'd ever owned.

Seven-thirty-five. She had purchased it during her heady days as a well-paid, on-air consumer watchdog in Los Angeles. Exactly one week prior to the day she got fired, she'd plunked down an outrageous sum and then was promptly axed for graphically reporting the amount of air pumped into various brands of ice cream. Did she know that her former television station's biggest grocery chain sponsor was the worst offender?

Yes.

Did she overrule the twenty-three-year-old kid on the assignment desk and do the story anyway, despite his warnings that the ad department would kill her?

Yes.

Did she get fired for telling the truth at a moment when she could least afford to?

Yes.

Had she shot herself in the foot that time, too?

Yes.

So, what else was new?

Well . . . there *were* extenuating circumstances *that* time. . . .

Let's not think about that, she told herself. *Just think about getting through the job you came here to do.*

Where the heck *was* Kingsbury Duvallon, anyway? she fretted, peering over the edge of the balcony at the center aisle below. She certainly didn't intend to be blindsided by him—again.

At that moment Corlis heard footfalls coming up the stairs to the balcony, and to her horror, her nightmare suddenly materialized. A dashing, six-foot-tall, broad-shouldered figure, clad in white tie and black tailcoat, appeared like an apparition, not twenty feet from their media outpost.

King looked even handsomer than she remembered, damn it! His stylishly trimmed dark brown mane was a far cry from the close-cropped hair he'd sported when they had both been college students in California. In the shadowed church balcony, his eyes appeared to be a darker shade of blue than when he'd last glared at her while they shouted at each other in the blinding Los Angeles sun. And the engaging grin he'd bestowed on virtually every female member of the UCLA cheerleading squad was nowhere in evidence this evening. In its place, the man's sinfully sexy lips were set in a grim line above a cleft chin that could prompt movie stars to sign up for plastic surgery.

Corlis prayed King wouldn't recognize her after twelve years. After all, her look now was certainly different than it had been in those days. During her tenure as a take-no-prisoners editor of the feminist journal *Ms. UCLA,* she'd adopted a magenta-streaked punk rocker hairdo, shapeless sweatshirts, and baggy jeans, plus she'd been a good twenty-five pounds heavier before the media consultants revolutionized her dietary habits.

Any hope of remaining anonymous was dashed as Corlis became acutely aware that King Duvallon was staring rudely at her across the church balcony. From his glowering expression, he obviously knew exactly who she was. His gaze meandered southward and lingered on the curve of her calves.

Well, to be fair, the man had never seen her legs, now, had he?

King abruptly broke into her reverie asking, "Corlis McCullough, right? My, my . . . I *thought* it was you."

His voice still had its lilting southern inflections, but it had also deepened, and his stare held her glance like a locked-on laser—cool and deadly.

"Hello." She felt her chin jut into the air at a belligerent angle.

Hello? That's all she could manage after twelve years? Not: *Hello Mr. Chauvinist Pig? Hello, you enemy of all women on the planet! Hello, and will you please vacate my balcony?*

"I need to talk to you," King said without preamble.

"Now?" she asked incredulously. "Isn't your sister supposed to walk down that aisle in about two minutes?"

"Exactly!" he countered sharply. "Can you come with me?"

" 'Fraid not," she replied, pointing at her watch. "It's just about show time and I've got a job to do." Then she added archly, "I'm surprised you even recognized me after all this time."

"It's been pretty hard to avoid you," he retorted. "You're on the news every night."

Of course! The ID slug at the bottom of the TV screen. Even *without* the spiky magenta-colored hair and the ill-fitting clothes, how many Corlis McCulloughs were there in the news business?

"I like your hair," he commented abruptly, eyeing her natural brunette shoulder-length mane. Was this an attempted peace offering, or was he just trying to lull her into complacency? He took a step forward and addressed her fellow crew members. "I'd really appreciate it, fellas, if you'd just pack up and go. This weddin's closed to the public."

"Are you kidding?" Corlis asked, amazed by his gall. "Perhaps you aren't aware," she added with forced politeness, "that *somebody* in either the Duvallon or Ebert camps provided our assignment editor with a complete rundown of who's who and what's what at this little pageant! We were sent here by our assignment editor, and *he* wants this story on the ten o'clock news." She crossed her arms in front of her chest and added, "So, I'm afraid leaving is out of the question."

"Well, nobody in *my* family provided you with any press kit. This weddin' is *not* news. We want it to be a private affair!" King repeated, his eyes now slits of steel.

"Believe me," she retorted, "I couldn't agree with you more, but we're here on orders. And, just like twelve years ago," she added with a feigned sweetness that barely veiled her rising indignation, "I don't exactly appreciate your coming up here and telling us—"

"Well, you'd better believe *me* when I tell you, the bride's family wants y'all to just skedaddle on out of here," King interrupted with icy control.

Corlis felt her blood pressure zoom into the stratosphere. What right did this stuck-up character have to interfere with—?

"Hey! Duvallon!" a hushed voice called up from the balcony's stairwell. "Come *on!* They're ready, son! Get down here! *Now!*"

"Excuse me," King addressed Corlis angrily, "but I thought by now you'd have sworn off always startin' World War Three." He turned toward Manny and Virgil. "Get her outta here, will ya, guys?"

Ah . . . the boys' club. Well, forget it, pal, she wanted to tell him. Her TV crew knew perfectly well that in this kind of situation, the correspondent called the shots.

"Look, Professor Duvallon," Corlis replied evenly as she made a renewed stab at keeping her temper under control, "we've been assigned to cover this event. We've been given *permission* by the diocese to set up in this balcony so that we'd have the best view to get the pretty pictures everybody wants," she added, unable to keep the sarcasm out of her voice. "Therefore, we're covering it! So, as we say out west, *adios muchacho*!"

She absolutely *hated* it when she had to roll out her wicked witch routine, but there it was. Their boss, station owner Victor Girard, would crucify her and her crew if they didn't get the story on tape for the late news.

"King?"

It was a woman's voice, and she sounded in some distress.

"Hold on, sugar . . . I'll be right there," King called down the stairwell.

Ever the southern gentleman. "Sugar" was probably the blushing maid of honor that he was slated to escort down the aisle.

"One last time," King said between clenched teeth. "Please *go*!"

"I will," she countered, "if you'd just please go *downstairs* so we could get this thing over with! *Then* we'll go! Scout's honor," she replied, holding up three fingers in mock salute. The nerve of the guy!

For a moment she was tempted to do exactly as King had commanded. Wedding of the year indeed, she fumed silently. Everyone who knew anything about New Orleans had warned her that the place was a small town, but this was ridiculous!

"King!" croaked another disembodied masculine voice.

"I'm comin'!" he muttered. The acknowledged leader of New Orleans's feisty historic preservation movement deepened his scowl, turned on his heel, and strode downstairs without further comment.

Corlis contemplated King's retreating back and suddenly recalled a story she'd once written entitled "Marriage: Legalized Slavery." King and his fraternity brothers certainly had a field day with that one! She found it hideously ironic that they'd run into each other at a *wedding*, of all places!

She turned and gazed down at the elegantly attired throng and, to her shock and dismay, felt a lump rise in her throat.

*Of course this wedding makes you sad. Any wedding would.
Even a wedding as wretchedly excessive as this one. It's per-
fectly normal, considering . . . and it has nothing to do with
Kingsbury Duvallon. Just do your job.*

She blinked hard and leaned over the balcony. There were
three flower girls, two ring bearers, and nine, *count 'em,* nine
shapely bridesmaids dressed in forest-green velvet gowns. All
the groomsmen sported black tailcoats, white bow ties, and
waffled piqué shirts starched to the consistency of corrugated
cardboard. The formality of these eight o'clock candlelight
nuptials and the wedding party's apparel represented the last
vestiges of white upper-class society living in a city where more
than 70 percent of the population was black.

On the assignment editor's story board, tonight's event had
been slugged "Yup Nups." In her mind's eye, Corlis pictured the
wino that had passed out on the church steps, an unfortunate reminder of the city's large homeless population. At a wedding as
obviously expensive as this one, wouldn't a picture of the poor
man slumped against the front of the cathedral be worth a thousand words?

*Forget it, Corlis! No pithy photo essays today. Just your
ordinary puff piece, please.*

She hated to admit it, but the bridesmaids' gowns were
gorgeous. For a brief moment she wondered what it would
feel like to be a bride who knew that, starting tonight, she'd
make a life with a man who would row his oar while she
rowed hers. That she'd have a real home, maybe a couple of
kids someday. Someone to share the good and the bad with,
instead of always being out there on the limb, battling—*what?*
she asked herself bleakly.

Just relax and enjoy the spectacle, she lectured herself. After
all, it was nearly Christmas. Twelfth Night was approaching
January sixth, marking the beginning of the long Mardi Gras
season. Her first Mardi Gras in her newly adopted home! Why
not, just for once, *laisser les bons temps rouler?*

Let the good times roll, indeed! It was about time.

Tonight, the bride, Daphne Duvallon, was to star as queen for
a day. New Orleans film, theater, music, and architecture critic

Jack Ebert was cast in the role of the king, surrounded by pretend courtiers.

Ah . . . but, that's where this fantasy runs amok.

It was a safe bet that no one but she knew that the groom had suggested to her—not four days earlier—that the two of them should visit an intimate little spot he knew for dinner. Following the pretaping of his latest movie review at WWEZ last Tuesday night, Jack Ebert had even proposed that he show her the spectacular view from the cast-iron gallery of his apartment on Conti Street overlooking the French Quarter and the Canal Street skyscrapers towering beyond.

Corlis had declined, of course. She couldn't *stand* Ebert's self-involved pomposity. And she had been sorely tempted to inform the bride of her fiancé's invitation—extended with a lecherous grin on the eve of the creep's own wedding! Shouldn't somebody warn King's poor sister about the kind of guy she was about to marry?

Oh, yeah, good idea. Get real, McCullough!

On the aisle below, Corlis spotted King again, this time among his fellow groomsmen as they assisted the last few latecomers with finding seats in the packed church. She heaved a sigh and tried to ignore the fact that coming face-to-face with Kingsbury Duvallon again had totally unnerved her. If only he knew how much she'd like to do exactly as he'd asked and blow this pop stand!

What a joke. What a waste of time. She *hated* softball assignments like this one. Stories like the Ebert-Duvallon wedding were mere filler. Pap. Air-brained pieces that took the place of news the public *needed* to know. News about the urban ills that bedeviled a place where the unemployment rate was sky-high and the murder rate was close to one a day.

Get off your soapbox, Corlis! Nobody's interested.

A mere thirty-four years old, she thought with a sense of deepening discouragement, she had the journalistic views of a dinosaur. She glanced at her watch again. It was definitely show time. Or it should be. What was the holdup?

Her gaze drifted toward the attractive organist. The information sheet handed to Corlis by the assignment editor noted that Althea LaCroix was a fellow graduate, with Daphne, of the

Newman School uptown, the sole black student in her class, and one of the bride's closest friends. Althea paused, looked off to her right, nodded, and began yet another interlude piece. One of the hungover bridesmaids was probably in the bathroom, being sick.

A heavy whiff of incense reminded Corlis's Scots Presbyterian nose that this was going to be a full-on, bells-and-whistles nuptial mass. She suddenly recalled her great-aunt Marge's spirited family tales about her own Scottish McCullough ancestors floating down the Mississippi in the early nineteenth century to seek their fortune in the celebrated Crescent City. Only her lot of McCulloughs had soon gotten itchy feet and eventually pushed on west to explore the gold fields of California.

Was there such a thing as inherited wanderlust? How many cities had she worked in during the last twelve years? Five? Seven? Now she lived in New Orleans. Once again her gaze swept her surroundings. Had any among her branch of the gallivanting McCulloughs ever set foot in this cathedral before?

Corlis glanced again at the front of the church. She found herself mesmerized by row upon row of votive candles flickering inside ruby-red glass holders, secured by a wrought-iron prayer station located to the right of the nave. For a hundred years or more, these same pinpoints of light must have danced and winked in exactly that spot.

By this time the smell of incense could have choked an alligator. Much to Corlis's amazement, an odd kind of mist began to cloud her eyes, and the warm, ocher-colored walls behind the candles throbbed faintly, as if in rhythm to the timeless wedding music being played softly on the pipe organ.

She felt her own heartbeat slow and take on the cadence of the pulsating walls and the narcotic meter of the stately music that echoed throughout the cathedral's mammoth interior. The edges of her sight suddenly began to gray. To her dismay, she felt as if she might faint and grabbed the balcony's railing to steady herself.

Whoa . . . what's happening here?

"Hey, boss lady," Virgil said, his voice filled with concern, "you okay, sugar?"

No! a part of her brain answered. She was definitely *not* okay.

This spacey faint-headedness she was feeling must be the result of the lunch she'd skipped. There, in the shadows, she could swear that a bride and groom—both appearing distressed— stood rigidly side by side; he in a black tailcoat, complete with a richly brocaded vest, and a stiff white wing collar; she, a plump pigeon in an ivory gown with a V-shaped nipped-in waist and bustle. The bride's dark hair was piled in Victorian curls, while the groom's was parted severely down the center of his head. The vision—or whatever it was—lingered a second longer, and then . . . simply . . . vanished!

"Corlis!" Virgil declared urgently, "you're white as a sheet! Did that Duvallon guy upset you that much? Manny, you got somethin' to drink in your backpack? This girl's 'bout to faint on us."

"I—I'm okay . . . I think . . ." she replied slowly. She was nearly perishing with hunger, she knew that. And the unrelenting aroma of incense had become suffocating. But what in the world had just happened?

Corlis blinked several times as she stared at the red glass votive candles shimmering across the church's wide expanse. Her heart was racing now, and the hand with which she held her microphone had begun to tremble. Had such a brief encounter with King Duvallon, after all this time, caused a full-blown anxiety attack? Maybe thinking about her own stillborn wedding plans to a certain news director in Los Angeles had brought it on? Or, more likely, that antique-looking bride and groom were going to be part of some pageant during the wedding itself. Anything was possible in New Orleans.

"The incense probably got to you," Manny theorized sagely, handing her an unauthorized bottle of beer that he'd extracted from his voluminous backpack. "When I was an altar boy and inhaled too much of that stuff, I used to keel over in a dead faint sometimes durin' High Mass."

"Yeah . . . that must be it," Corlis said weakly, gratefully accepting a swallow from a bottle of Dixie.

Oh my God, I'm drinking beer in church! Damn this voodoo town. I'm really starting to lose my grip!

Finally the organ trumpeted the arrival of the bridesmaids.

Corlis swiftly handed the beer bottle back to Manny and struggled to gather her wits. As the first bridal attendant and her tailcoated escort appeared on the red carpet below them, she commanded sotto voce, "Roll tape!"

Her view of King's reemergence was the top of a fabulous, full head of dark-brown hair. Corlis consulted her notes, which listed the names of the wedding party. Miss Cindy Lou Mallory, the maid of honor—looking buxom indeed in her Empire-waisted green velvet gown—advanced down the center aisle on King's arm. Corlis's gaze drifted from the woman's arresting figure to her glorious head of stunning ruby-colored hair that glowed in a shade that would have made the former Duchess of York reach for the Clairol. When the pair arrived at the foot of the aisle, the voluptuous attendant flashed a knowing bedroom smile at her handsome escort and took her assigned place flanking the priest.

King turned to face the congregation. He stared over the heads of the wedding guests directly at Corlis—and scowled. For a split second she held his gaze, then smiled sweetly in return. He definitely did not look pleased.

For the second time since she'd arrived at Saint Louis Cathedral this evening, her heart began to beat erratically. She didn't want to acknowledge that King unsettled her nerves.

The brother of the prospective Mrs. Ebert shifted his gaze and stared somberly down the length of the aisle. Daphne Duvallon, on the arm of her stocky father, Waylon, appeared at the back of the historic church—he, a perfect fireplug of a man in white tie and tails; she, a vision in graceful folds of white silk and a twenty-five-foot Belgian lace train. As the bride slowly glided toward the altar framed with Doric columns and statues of the saints, Corlis could not deny that the beautiful honey blonde was indeed a breathtaking vision.

However, the groom, Jack Ebert, the mortician's son whose father owned establishments from Metairie to Covington, across Lake Pontchartrain, was an entirely different sight. In Corlis's opinion, nearly everything about the man fell into the medium range: medium height, medium-brown hair, average features, and a medium frame just this side of skinny. His physical appearance was utterly unremarkable, except for his extraordinarily small hazel eyes, along with tiny ears, flat against his head, which brought to mind a potentially vicious rodent. Standing beside his best man and the robed priest, Jack appeared calm and collected, if not mildly detached from the entire proceedings.

But boy could Jack Ebert wield a poison pen! Or computer, Corlis amended silently. She had seen for herself that whatever Jack lacked in on-camera charisma he made up for with the sheer entertainment value of his vituperative prose. His scathing film, theater, and music reviews were legendary around New Orleans. And his critiques of new construction could prompt architects to start designing their own mausoleums. To be honest, Corlis wondered what King's lovely-looking sister saw in the man.

Big bucks, she thought cynically. Daphne Duvallon was a twenty-eight-year-old classical harpist, presently earning her master's in music at The Juilliard School in New York. Like so many old-line New Orleans families, the Kingsburys and Duvallons possessed a proud heritage going back to the early eighteenth century, when Louisiana was a French colony. However, the majority of these formerly prosperous clans had lost their big sugarcane plantations and banking fortunes as a result of the Civil War.

The War of Northern Aggression, Corlis corrected herself silently. For all she knew, the bride's father, Waylon, the proprietor of Flowers by Duvallon, had probably been forced to take a second mortgage or hock the last of the family portraits to pay for his daughter's five-alarm wedding. Or perhaps Daphne needed help paying her tuition. Jack Ebert and his family's chain of successful funeral homes might have supplied a convenient answer to her fiscal problems. Corlis had heard much crazier reasons for getting married—like thinking a divorced television news director in LaLa Land was good husband material, until the moment when a little digging on her part turned up the fact that Jay Kerlin had been divorced *three times*!

Virgil's camcorder whirled softly as the age-old ceremony commenced with the exchange of vows. Corlis marveled at the composed manner in which Jack Ebert recited his promises to

love, honor, and cherish his bride, forsaking all others, till death
do they part.

"And do you, Daphne," the priest intoned, "promise to love
Jack . . . to honor and cherish him, forsaking all others, till death
do you part?"

Corlis gently nudged Virgil's shoulder with the rounded end
of her microphone, their shared signal to focus in for a close-up.
However, both reporter and cameraman were startled when the
bride, instead of answering the familiar question, slowly turned
her back on the priest and her groom and squarely faced the sea
of faces gazing at her from the rows of packed pews.

"First of all," Daphne announced, her voice wavering as
faintly as the pinpoints of light that shimmered on the prayer
station behind her. Members in the congregation began exchanging uneasy glances. "I just wanna say . . . how much I appreciate everything my mama and daddy have done for the
weddin'. . . ." A woman in the front pew wearing a white orchid
corsage began to shake her head vehemently. "In a strange
way," Daphne continued, her voice gaining strength, "I suppose
the person I should thank the *most* is my maid of honor. . . ."

The groom's frozen smile began to wither, and he turned
toward the priest with a look Corlis interpreted as a demand for
holy intercession. As for Cindy Lou Mallory, a stain approximately the same shade of red as her vibrant tresses spread from
her décolletage to her hairline. Among the congregation, heads
bobbed back and forth, and a low rumble of shocked reactions
bubbled up like cheap champagne. Corlis watched with amazement as Daphne Duvallon worked her engagement ring off her
finger.

"You see . . ." she said, her rigid control beginning to disinte-
grate before everyone's eyes, "Jack and Cindy Lou Mallory
don't know it, but I *saw* them makin' out last night. At the
groom's dinner. In the cloak room at Antoine's," she added, her
voice now choked with tears. "Right after the toasts were given,
and we'd all been drinkin' and dancin' for a while! It seems my
maid of *honor*," Daphne Duvallon continued with stony emphasis, "has been havin' an affair with my groom, Jack, here, for
months, while I was in New York!"

An extremely frail-looking elderly woman seated next to

Daphne's mother gave an audible cry and slumped against the shoulder of a middle-aged woman sitting to her left. The seatmate swiftly began to fan her distraught companion with the wedding program, her own features etched in a combination of outrage and dismay.

"So I'm sure y'all can understand why . . ." Daphne forged on bravely, ". . . why . . . I can't go *through* with this. I just *can't*!" she cried. In a lightning gesture, she slapped her engagement ring into the hand of the stunned groom. Then the bride scooped up her twenty-five-foot lace train and nodded emphatically in the direction of Althea LaCroix.

The musician brought her hands down on the organ's ivory keys with a crash. Triumphant recessional music thundered ominously throughout the church while Daphne scored a bull's-eye, dashing her red-and-white rose bouquet against her maid of honor's elaborate flame-haired coiffure.

As suddenly as King Duvallon stepped out from the line of nine groomsmen, a thought hit Corlis like a bolt of lightning.

He knew this was going to happen! That's why he wanted us to leave!

The stunned wedding guests gawked, dumbfounded, as King offered his distraught sister his arm. Within seconds they swept down the aisle and disappeared.

As for Corlis, watching this passion play from the balcony, her journalist's instinct suddenly took over. Pavlov's dog. The bell had rung.

"Follow *me*!" she hissed urgently to her TV crew.

She made a dash for the paneled stairwell as if she were off to cover a fire. Virgil, with his video camera thumping up and down on his shoulder, and Manny, with headphones clamped to his ears, thundered close behind. The panting trio arrived at the arched doors in time to see brother and sister sprinting across the slate paving stones that fronted Jackson Square.

"I'm still rolling!" Virgil shouted as he and Corlis raced in hot pursuit of the fleeing couple. The reporter prayed that her cameraman had caught the shot of Daphne's long train billowing behind the pair like a water-skier's wake.

"Get the hell outta here, you harpy!" King shouted at Corlis over his shoulder as he yanked open the door to the waiting limousine.

She didn't really blame him for his angry reaction, but by this time the adrenaline was pumping. And besides, she considered in some remote portion of her brain, chasing fire trucks was all in a day's work. She'd decide later whether or not she'd actually use this footage.

In the next instant King pushed the bride into the backseat, speedily stowed her long, lacy train inside as if he were gathering an unwieldy parachute, and climbed in after her, slamming the door. A second later the sleek black Cadillac sped away— destination unknown.

"Oh . . . my God!" Corlis exclaimed as she and her crew headed back inside the church in time to see gaggles of dismayed wedding guests leaving their pews. "She *did* it!" she said in an awed tone of voice. "She blew that two-timing creep right outta the water!"

By the time Corlis had broadcast the story of the disastrous Ebert-Duvallon wedding, edited with spine-tingling speed barely in time to make the late evening news, she'd all but forgotten the strange apparition of the Victorian-era bride and groom at the church. It was nearly eleven, and feeling tired, she gathered up her things and left the newsroom.

In the hallway, Larry, the janitor, stopped dead in his tracks when he saw her. He was toting a poster-sized photograph. Corlis gaped at the glossy color image of herself in full makeup and turquoise linen blazer. She looked more like a brunette version of Murphy Brown than she cared to admit.

"Oh, Miz McCullough," the janitor said, shaking his head. For a brief two months, her picture had graced the lunchroom walls, along with those of the rest of the WWEZ-TV broadcast team. "I've got bad news for you, sugar. Mr. Girard done tol' me to take this down."

"Wha—?" Corlis asked, dumbfounded. The *janitor* was delivering this news? "How can I be fired? The story just aired ten minutes ago!"

"Mr. Girard called me on m'beeper. When I called him back,

he was mad as a snake. Tol' me to go right into the lunchroom tonight and—"

"But *why?*" Corlis protested. "That wedding turned out to be an incredible story! The video was fabulous! I thought I wrote it well, and—"

"But, sugar," Larry interrupted patiently, "the tape editor and the director both done tol' me they *tried* to get you to call higher-ups tonight before you went and put that thing on TV."

"Oh, Larry, those guys are always a bunch of wusses in situations like this!"

"Yeah, but sweetheart, if you'd done called the boss, he'd have tol' you that he's Mr. Armand Ebert's second cousin on his mama's side."

"You mean *Victor* Girard, as in the *owner* of WWEZ-TV?"

"That's right."

"You're telling me, then, that the philandering groom's *father*—René Ebert—and my boss, Mr. Girard, are kissing *cousins?*" Corlis exclaimed, and then added in a small, defeated voice, "And so . . . *that's* why we were assigned to cover this particular wedding?"

"I 'spect that's right."

"And Victor Girard, then, was the person who provided the assignment desk with all that inside information about the two 'prominent local families'?"

"I 'spect so, sugar," Larry nodded with a sad, knowing smile.

"Nobody told me that."

"In N'awlings, darlin' . . . all them other white folks'd figure you already *knew.*"

Chapter Two

December 21

Just after midnight Corlis stood on the carpeted ramp that led to the deserted newsroom and surveyed the rows of empty reporters' desks and the news set beyond. The cavernous studio was shrouded in darkness, except for a few lights glowing in the assignment editor's office, whose large picture window overlooked the open floor plan.

Fired!

Again!

Sensations of mild panic and bubbling rage boiled in her solar plexus as she stood holding in her arms a cardboard file box filled with the contents of her desk. She'd been in New Orleans for less than two months and already she'd been canned. Axed. Deep-sixed. Outplaced!

What is it with me? she wondered as moisture rimmed her eyes. *Do I have some sort of Wage Earner Personality Disorder or something?*

For a long moment she gazed around her; then she turned on her heel and fled the newsroom before the security guard arrested her for stealing her own Rolodex.

By the time she arrived at her brick row house on Julia Street, upriver from the French Quarter, the leaden weight that had pressed against her chest as she drove home had become an emotional volcano, poised to erupt. Fighting a lump in her throat the size of a praline, she trudged up the flight of stairs to her living quarters above the photographer's gallery that fronted the deserted street. She balanced the cardboard carton full of her office possessions on one knee while she opened the front door with her key and called out, "Cagney?"

She was startled by the shaky sound of her voice, and distressed when her twenty-three-pound marmalade tomcat didn't deign to appear in the foyer to greet her.

But then, Cagney Cat never came when called. It was a little game he played just to show her who was the boss on Julia Street. At times the feline's red fur, slightly pugnacious attitude, and feisty independence prompted Corlis to think that the four-legged firebrand *was* James Cagney . . . reincarnated.

Forlornly calling out to him one last time, Corlis walked down the hall and dumped the box on the desk in her home office. The small room had been the scullery and broom closet when the building was constructed in 1832, a time when most of the surrounding warehouses had yet to be built. Back then there had been plenty of servants available to scour and clean other people's parlors. As of tonight, however, she couldn't even afford her twice-a-month cleaning woman!

A long soak in a steaming bubble bath did nothing to soothe her soul, nor did the stiff shot of bourbon she downed from a Waterford crystal tumbler before crawling into bed. As she lay in the darkness, unable to sleep, listening to the late-night street noises up and down the old Warehouse District, Corlis had only one thought.

God almighty, what would Great-Aunt Marge say this time?

Would Aunt Marge, a celebrated reporter, consider tonight's broadcast an example of heads-up journalism, or another act of professional suicide? Had Corlis shot herself in the foot—again—or merely fired a volley in behalf of great reporting in a town that was too politically conservative and inbred to tolerate such an act of First Amendment freedom?

Everyone thinks I'm such a tough cookie, a chip off the old block. She reached for a tissue as tears began to spill down her cheeks. *Well, I'm not!*

It was nearly 10:30 P.M. in California. Struggling for composure, she turned on the bedside light. After a moment's hesitation she reached for the phone beside her four-poster plantation bed that no man's form had yet to grace. Margery McCullough's number rang four times before her voice mail picked up. At eighty-three years old, the favorite "sob sister" of the long-deceased newspaper tycoon William Randolph Hearst embraced all the latest electronic gadgets, including a laptop computer that she had purchased for herself when she bestowed a duplicate model on her great-niece as a going-away present.

"You can leave a message here for Margery McCullough," announced a strong, vibrant voice. "I'm either writing my memoirs and ignoring this call . . . or on my other line . . . or I'm out on the town! Your best bet is to leave word you called, and I'll get back to you."

What a woman! Corlis thought admiringly, hanging up without mentioning her most recent debacle. She didn't want her great-aunt to come home to hear about this upsetting news and find it too late to call her back. Exhausted, she turned out her bedside light for the second time and stared woefully at the carved moldings decorating her ceiling, dimly visible in night's gloom.

After what had seemed like hours, Corlis reckoned she'd slept only fitfully, or not at all. At length, when the luminous dial on her bedside clock registered 5:30 A.M., the tears finally burst forth in earnest. Her crying soon prompted a few answering shrieks from a family of feral cats that had long made the back alley outside her bedroom window their nocturnal retreat. Embarrassed by her unrestrained outburst, she stifled her weeping, only to suffer alternating waves of anger and remorse that swept over her in unrelenting succession.

Aunt Marge and I thought my moving to New Orleans was the perfect solution—and look what happened! No job, looming debts, and now a really rotten résumé!

She struggled to sit upright in bed and put her head in her hands. She was thirty-four years old. She'd been engaged once, had worked for six different TV stations in five different cities, and had been fired three times in a twelve-year career for telling the unvarnished truth. Not exactly a great track record.

I bailed out of L.A. so I could get over that rat, Jay Kerlin. I'd hoped I'd make some really good friends here—and maybe even get a life!

A life? What she had on her hands here was a complete disaster!

Corlis leaned against the headboard of her mahogany bed and pounded her fists on the mattress in a fit of frustration.

With sudden determination she threw aside the covers, switched on her bedside light once again, and stood next to her canopied bed. The graceful antique loomed large in a bedroom distinguished by a classic carved marble fireplace and high ceilings. From a drawer in her mahogany highboy, she took out some running clothes, putting on a pair of gray sweatpants and a sweatshirt with the faded blue letters UCLA stamped across her chest. She grabbed a few dollars out of her purse and marched resolutely toward her front door.

It was nearly six when she emerged from her brick building into the moisture-laden morning air and gazed briefly at the globe of yellow light atop the old-fashioned streetlamp. She knew perfectly well that she was taking her life into her hands walking the streets of the Big Easy at this early hour.

So what if she got shot? she mused dejectedly, striding down Julia Street toward the river. At least it would solve her current dilemma—finding another job in a town where she'd already become a public pariah among the city's upper crust.

Fifteen minutes later Corlis cut across Convention Center Boulevard past the towering World Trade Center. She continued along the riverfront in the direction of Jackson Square in the French Quarter, focusing her gaze on the mist rising from the broad Mississippi on her right. When she reached Decatur Street, twinkling crystal lights winked at her from the magnificent magnolia trees that bordered the city plaza across from the Café du Monde, her early-morning destination. Saint Louis Cathedral, the scene of last night's calamity, stood sentinel over the square. The church's triple spires soared heavenward and disappeared into the humid blue-gray fog of early morning, a leaden, murky atmosphere that could easily transform itself into a sultry rain at a moment's notice. A yeasty aroma poured out of a bakery vent nearby.

December in Louisiana.

Dank. Disgusting. Decadent. Delicious.

As she paused to absorb the magnificence of Jackson Square and its gated park, she indulged in a moment to consider how swiftly she'd fallen in love with the physical beauty of New

Orleans—an exercise that only increased her gloom. Who would ever hire her in this town again? Victor Girard would hardly give her a glowing recommendation. Nor would Jay Kerlin at her former station in L.A.

She caught sight of the café's green-and-white awnings, also etched in pinpoints of sparkling lights, and was suddenly reminded that it was practically Christmas, a mere three more shopping days till the twenty-fifth. She'd been kept so busy at WWEZ, she hadn't bought any presents for her few family members in California, to say nothing of shipping them west. And except for Virgil and Manny, she had no one to buy for in New Orleans. At least if she became a fatal crime statistic, walking the streets at this hour, it certainly wouldn't ruin anyone's holiday around here.

Get a grip, McCullough!

Once at the celebrated Café du Monde, she drummed her fingers restlessly on the take-out counter in the courtyard.

"Thank God this place stays open twenty-four hours a day," she said to the clerk while she waited for her coffee. She was starved for conversation with *somebody*.

"Yes ma'am," the clerk said mechanically, handing Corlis the paper cup filled with café au lait.

"Oooh, this feels so nice," she added inanely, grateful for the cup's soothing warmth spreading through her fingers.

"Yes, ma'am." The clerk nodded patiently, handing her a few silver coins and a small white bag containing an order of beignets, diamond-shaped raised doughnuts, without holes, that had been deep-fat fried only seconds earlier and dredged in a thick layer of powdered sugar. After the night she'd had, beignets were the only antidote she could think of to her downward-spiraling funk.

As she took a sip of her pungent chicory-laced coffee while recrossing Decatur Street toward the park, her gaze traced the trajectory of winter sunlight filtering anemically through the verdant trees that bordered Jackson Square.

Gingerly, Corlis trod across the slate paving stones, slick with dew, that fronted Saint Louis Cathedral and encircled the park. On her right the Pontalba Building, with its refined red-brick-and-granite four-story facade—along with its twin across the park on St. Peter Street—embodied the architectural essence of New Orleans. Lacy cast-iron galleries, bedecked with Christmas lights and seasonal swags of pine boughs and glittering decorations, ran the length of both blocks. These elegant buildings were thought to be among the oldest apartments in the New World. A place in the Pontalba offered one of the best addresses and most spectacular views in the entire city.

Well . . . I'll never live in one of those. Not now.

Corlis walked slowly under the Pontalba's arcade and caught sight of the homeless man with the scuffed boots whom she'd nearly tripped over the previous evening. At this early hour he lay curled up against one of the iron pillars supporting the building's metal gallery overhead, a large piece of cardboard crimped over his shoulders. He was snoring peacefully.

A few yards distant, a tarot card reader, swathed in a turban and flowing caftan, was already setting up her collapsible table, staking out a coveted spot to sell her psychic wares when the tourists arose.

"Mornin', sweetheart," she said in a husky voice, startling Corlis from her reverie. "Let me do a readin' for you, sugar. Your luck's bound to change."

"No . . . no, thanks," Corlis replied, walking faster. Farther on, a disheveled-looking young woman, pushing a rusted grocery cart and accompanied by an emaciated hound on a length of rope, wandered in front of the cathedral, cheerfully chattering to herself.

To Corlis's left, a city groundskeeper was shoving a large metal key into the big padlock that secured the park's cast-iron gates against intruders at night.

"Mornin'," he mumbled.

"Morning," Corlis mumbled back, her gaze fastened on the park's magnificent equestrian statue of New Orleans's savior, Andrew Jackson.

In the two short months during which Corlis had lived in Louisiana, she'd become inordinately fond of Old Hickory and the story of his ragtag army. On a mist-shrouded morning like this one, in January of 1815, Andrew Jackson had ordered his motley assemblage of cannon and artillery to attack a superior

British force menacing the city, and pounded them into igno-
minious submission.

The fearless soldier was a man after Corlis's own heart. Like
Don Quixote, Aunt Marge, and other Crusader Rabbits she
could name, he hadn't folded his tent just because the odds were
against him.

*A pathetic amount of good it does a person these days to try
to do the kind of honest journalism I believe in. . . .*

Moodily she walked down the path and drew closer to the
enormous two-story statue that anchored the plaza square.
Would she never learn, she wondered, gazing up at Andrew
Jackson's prancing bronze horse? The Ebert-Duvallon nuptials
was just another story, for pity's sake, like hundreds she'd done
before. Nobody in this town but *she* cared whether or not it told
the absolute, unadulterated truth. And besides, the director and
her editor had tried to warn her to check with higher-ups before
airing the piece, but she had pulled rank.

*And who's going to worry except Aunt Marge and me that I
no longer have a health plan?*

So. Was it worth it? Was the fabulous shot of that twenty-
five-foot bridal train and the moment of truth it symbolized
worth getting *fired* over? Or had the story resonated with
her . . . because Jay Kerlin had been such an absolute heel and
she should have blown him off—just like Daphne Duvallon
blew off Jack Ebert last night—long before she found out that
Jay was two-timing her with Miss Sunny, the weather woman!

*Jeez Louise . . . was the story she did last night journalism, or
had it merely been a case of bizarre revenge?*

Putting such a disturbing thought from her mind, she drank
deeply from her paper cup of coffee and wondered how in the
world she was going to keep up her mortgage payments on the
row house she'd impulsively bought five days after arriving in
New Orleans. At the time, the small down payment seemed
much more sensible than paying rent, but now . . .

Corlis wandered farther down the cement path in the direction of her favorite park bench, clutching her bag of beignets so
tightly, her knuckles turned white. In the distance the cathedral's
pale facade provided a dazzling backdrop for a community
filled with breathtaking side streets and cunning courtyards

that made the place terminally charming and one of the least "American" cities in the country.

Lord, how she'd grown to adore this town! How could she leave New Orleans? But what was she going to do to support her addiction to this city, not to mention pay her outstanding bills?

Utterly dejected, Corlis sat down on the park bench and immediately felt the seat of her pants soak up the dew like a sponge. *"Merde!"* she exclaimed to the pigeons, wondering if, after all the years of French colonial influence in New Orleans, the birds actually understood the French word for *shit*.

Inside the white paper bag, the beignets had grown cold and unappetizing. The words of her former diet coach suddenly rang in her head.

"A minute in your mouth. A lifetime on your hips, Corlis!"

With a sigh she tossed the confections into a trash can nearby and somberly stared at Andrew Jackson's bronze countenance, wondering what Old Hickory would have done in such dire circumstances.

More to the point—what was *she* going to do next?

"What do you call those?" Corlis asked, pointing to a tub full of fragrant white flowers mixed with waxy green magnolia leaves. On impulse she had walked inside the small flower stall a half block down the street from her house, thinking that a bouquet on the coffee table of her living room might boost her lagging spirits.

"Stargazers," the slender young man replied.

"They're lilies, right?" she confirmed.

"Yep . . . the real fragrant kind," the clerk agreed. "Just arrived on the truck a few minutes ago. Those closed ones'll open up as it gets warmer durin' the day, and smell real pretty."

"I'll take a dozen," Corlis said decisively.

Arms full, she trudged up the creaking wooden stairs to her second-story apartment, wondering where could she go after New Orleans. Sioux City, Iowa? Hartford, Connecticut? The idea of moving again and coping with strangers at a new TV station, along with having to abandon beautiful Julia Street, made her want to jump off the Huey P. Long Bridge. By the time she'd opened her front door and walked down the hallway into the kitchen, she'd moved on to another distasteful topic. Since she'd already trashed the cold, uneaten beignets, she forced herself to consider which breakfast item in her refrigerator had less fuzzy green mold on it: the box of Chinese take-home moo goo gai pan or the five-day-old slice of pizza.

Rejecting both, she poured a cup of oatmeal into a saucepan of boiling water and set it on her pint-size stove. The efficiency kitchen had been carved out of another former closet. She put the flowers in a glass vase and wandered into the adjacent living room. She positioned the perfumed stargazers on the coffee table next to her beige linen couch and lay down to rest while she waited for her breakfast to cook. Once again she turned over in her mind the tumultuous outcome of the previous twenty-four hours. Suddenly exhausted from her sleepless night and long walk by the river, Corlis heaved a deep sigh and closed her eyes.

Everything seems such a tangled web! If only . . .

Her thoughts drifted aimlessly as she inhaled more deeply the sweet-smelling lilies in the vase at her side. Conscious of her stomach's rumbling anticipation of the oatmeal warming on the stove, she tried her best to stop itemizing the complications that currently plagued her. In the distance, she could hear the faint hoot of a riverboat. Her thoughts floated further afield like a river craft tugged seaward by the tide. The lilies' cloying perfume seemed to intensify to funereal proportions, filling the room with their overwhelmingly pungent odor.

Whoa! These things really pack a punch! I'll get daisies next time . . .

Corlis sensed her face growing warm. It was as if her cheeks were exposed to a source of heat that caused a flush to fan up her throat. Beads of perspiration broke out on her forehead. The heady scent of the flowers grew even stronger. Their sweetish fragrance actually made her feel queasy. When Corlis opened her eyes, she was startled to see not *one* vase of waxy white lilies—but armloads of snowy blossoms. Their ornate silver containers formed a melancholy phalanx positioned against the opposite wall in a darkened parlor that was lit by a single candelabrum standing sentinel at the head of an open coffin.

And inside the casket's silk-lined depths lay the body of a person whom Corlis McCullough had never seen in her entire life!

Chapter Three

December 21, 1837

A cloying fragrance of lilies filled the room, producing an unsettling counterpoint to the subtle aroma of decay emanating from the corpse. The deceased, in his mid-fifties, was dressed as if for a fancy ball in a formal black suit, a stiff white wing collar that grazed his frozen jawline, and white kid gloves.

On a cherry-wood sideboard a small ivory card with a thick black border had been placed upon a miniature brass easel. In the flickering candlelight Corlis Bell McCullough—of the Pittsburgh Bells, as her mother, Elizabeth, proudly declared—could just make out the freshly printed words.

HENRI GIRARD
Died December 20, 1837
Funeral Services at Saint Louis Cathedral
New Orleans
on Saturday at Noon

Monsieur Girard lay in the luxurious mahogany coffin on a long table in the dining room. Below, on the Rue Royale, Corlis could hear the clip-clop of horse-drawn carriages wheeling beneath windows draped in the solemn black crepe of a house in mourning.

"A fine job," pronounced a voice from a corner of the makeshift death chamber. "Why, a person viewing this body would think that Girard hadn't died of anything more serious than too much rich food and too many glasses of port!"

Corlis felt a congratulatory pat on her taffeta sleeve.

"You've done well, my dear, applying your feminine arts in this emergency." She turned her head and gazed at Ian Jeffries, the man who had extended her the bizarre compliment. His face appeared flushed, even in the dim light shed by the funereal candles. "Thanks to your rouge pots and your excellent choice of attire from Henri's closet, the man looks as if he's merely in a gentle slumber. Even the priest raised no questions when he came to call."

A cold shudder slithered down Corlis's spine, despite the warmth in the parlor where the windows had been shut tight against miasmic drafts off the river.

" 'Twill be a relief, Ian," declared the third member of their little group, "to see this unfortunate man in his tomb . . . and the sooner the better, I say, eh what?" Corlis detected a pulse-pounding strain in Randall McCullough's subdued tone of voice.

She turned away from her husband to stare once again at the body lying still and silent in the casket. She attempted to control the tremors that seized her. The expensive coffin had been hurriedly secured from an undertaker by the name of Ebért. The thin, perpetually smiling little man with tiny eyes and extraordinarily small rodentlike ears had also been the source of the extravagant bouquets of lilies that seemed to scream of the collective guilt shared by all those present.

Corlis felt a sort of dread creeping over her that she couldn't precisely identify. Furthermore, she felt too shaken by the day's events to ask probing questions of her husband lest her inquiries yield answers she didn't want to learn. A loud pounding on the front door abruptly interrupted her train of thought. The hammering rent the air, throwing the three of them into a state of near panic.

"Let me in!" a voice thundered on the other side of the entrance to Henri Girard's magnificently furnished abode. "I demand that you open this door at once!"

"It's André Duvallon!" Randall McCullough declared in a low, rasping whisper, visibly frightened at the prospect of such an unexpected arrival. "In the name of Christ, man! What do we do *now*?"

The pounding increased several decibels.

"All right, all right!" admonished Ian Jeffries, her husband's barrel-chested business partner. He exited the dining room and crossed into the foyer, cracking the door open an inch.

A tall, handsome figure with dark hair and a thunderous expression shouldered Jeffries aside and stalked into the shadowed chamber where Henri Girard lay motionless in his coffin. André Duvallon, Girard's banker, suddenly halted in his tracks and stared aghast at the sight of his boyhood friend silenced by death. A look of pure anguish spread across Duvallon's patrician features, and he advanced a step closer toward the ornate casket. Then he whirled to confront the two men standing nearby, his heavy black cape fanning out in a circle.

"Oh . . . my . . . God! It was *you* who took the body away!" The sound of his accusatory cry reverberated throughout the silent rooms, assaulting Corlis with its palpable suffering. "So, it has come to this! *You* two! Playacting. Making yourself important, when you are the reason this man lies dead in his coffin! You are *scoundrels,*" Duvallon said between clenched teeth, "and I should shoot you both—but of course, you know I shan't," he added in a voice laden with self-loathing. His eyes narrowed as he glanced briefly at Corlis, as if to say, *Have you also somehow played a role in this?*

Corlis was stricken by André's look of disgust mixed with fury and grief.

"M-Monsieur Duvallon . . ." she began in a faltering whisper. "I am so sorry about your friend. So sorry that—"

The stifling air, laced with the sweet smell of the flowers, had begun to physically sicken her. In front of her the room's walls appeared to throb, and the world began to go gray around the edges, transforming the figure of André Duvallon into a ghost in the mist. The next thing Corlis Bell McCullough knew, her knees buckled, and she fell into a dead faint upon the polished cypress floor.

The acrid aroma of burning food had the stimulating effect of smelling salts, rousing Corlis with a start. Across Julia Street, a TV blared through an open window. A block away she heard the electric streetcar loudly clang its bell as it glided down St. Charles Avenue.

What in the world was that?

Abruptly she sat up on her couch. A shudder seized her at the memory of the dead man's waxen face staring sightlessly at the ceiling in a candlelit chamber that overlooked Royal Street in the French Quarter. Everything had seemed so real! That woman had appeared so alive. . . .

What woman?

Corlis Bell McCullough . . .

Now, why would she dream about her namesake like that? The ancestress that Aunt Marge claimed had once floated down the Mississippi on a steamboat while pregnant and suffering from the dreaded yellow fever? Corlis's own temples were throbbing, and she felt as if she were still swimming to the surface of total consciousness.

Suddenly she sniffed the air. Something *was* burning!

"Oh, m'God!" she exclaimed, turning to look over the back of her couch toward the kitchen. "My oatmeal!"

She sprang from the sofa, nearly toppling over the tall vase of sickly sweet stargazer lilies on the coffee table, and groped her way into her tiny kitchen. The room was filled with sooty smoke funneling from a small saucepan irreparably blackened on the top of the electric stove. Corlis grabbed a pot holder, eased the pan into the sink, and turned on the faucet.

A loud hissing sound accompanied an increasing amount of dark smoke that poured from the vessel whose sides were encrusted with the remains of John McCall's Irish Oatmeal. Corlis gazed with dismay at her breakfast while a lingering vision of a coffin, surrounded by vases full of lilies, filled her thoughts. The smoke alarm went off.

"Double, triple *merde*!" she cursed aloud.

She was further startled by a series of agitated chirping sounds and a soft puff of fur rubbing against her calf. She whirled in place and saw Cagney Cat staring reproachfully at the billowing clouds clinging to her twelve-foot-high ceilings. Next the smoke alarm in the hallway began to beep in piercing syncopation.

Corlis made a dash for the tall window nearest her fireplace and pushed up the sash to let the smoke out. In a flash Cagney flew through the open window onto the gallery's wrought-iron hand railing, defying gravity and common sense by padding to the opposite end of the balcony that hung high over Julia Street.

"Come in here, you beast!" Corlis cried over the staccato sounds of smoke detectors. She stuck her head out the window for a welcome whiff of fresh, moist air. Despite this improvement in atmosphere, she felt something akin to hysteria pulling at her throat.

Was she completely losing her mind? she wondered as she observed her tabby sitting precariously on the railing and insouciantly licking one paw. The dream, or vision, or whatever she'd just experienced had seemed so authentic . . . as real as the brief glimpse she'd had of the nineteenth-century wedding couple in Saint Louis Cathedral the previous night.

Corlis pulled her head back inside the room and stared at the vase of white trumpet blooms whose strong, distinctive fragrance now competed with the acrid odor of burned oatmeal.

"California crazy" is what King Duvallon would call her.

What she'd just experienced seemed very different from ordinary dreaming. The scene that had unfolded before her eyes this morning had been more like watching a movie. However, she reminded herself, the events she'd "seen" supposedly had taken place 150 years ago, if they'd happened at all!

Furthermore, who the hell was Henri Girard—the stiff in the coffin?

In her mind's eye she recalled the black-bordered card sitting on the cherry-wood sideboard announcing the date—1837— and the location of Henri Girard's funeral, Saint Louis Cathedral. She suddenly remembered the name of her boss at WWEZ-TV who'd employed and then fired her: Victor Girard.

Girard! The same last name as the dead man!

"Oh, Jesus . . ." she murmured, grabbing her kitchen counter for support. She must really harbor more resentment toward the guy than she realized. But it had all seemed so genuine, as if she really were right there, watching events taking place "live" and in living color in 1837!

Her reporter's training kicked in. She could always look in the city's official birth and death records to see if a Henri Girard had died on that date in New Orleans.

And what if Henri Girard actually existed? What then?

"It was a dream!"

She headed for the gallery to check on Cagney. As she crossed her living room once again, she gazed with a jaundiced eye at the red Persian rug that her great-aunt had described as a precious family heirloom. It had been handed down from the woman whom Marge had insisted she be named for: Corlis Bell McCullough. She and her husband were the only members of the Scottish-American McCullough clan to ever live in New Orleans.

How nice, she thought grimly. *My very own magic carpet.*

She leaned against the window jamb and stared absently down at Julia Street's dew-slicked pavement. Perhaps this strange apparition had been a kind of self-inflicted morality play. Maybe she'd merely dreamed that the man who'd fired her so unceremoniously last night would come to a bad end.

But in a winged collar?

And besides, the dead guy's first name was Henri. Her boss was Victor. Worse yet, in the dream she'd had a good look at the corpse's face. Except for his arched Gallic nose, Henri Girard did not look at all like the man who had just given her her walking papers at WWEZ-TV.

Meanwhile, Corlis began to worry that Cagney Cat might come to an equally bad end if she didn't get him to come back inside. Disconcerted by everything that had happened in such quick succession, Corlis again stuck first her head, then her torso out of her living-room window. She gazed with increasing frustration at the willful feline who remained perched on the gallery's wrought-iron railing.

"Oh, stay out there, for all I care, you big brat!" she declared finally. "I'm going round the corner to the Hummingbird for breakfast!"

At this point, Corlis thought grimly, a hearty meal in her stomach seemed her only hope for putting a stop to all this nonsense! Filled with resolve, she marched down the hallway, grabbed her purse and keys off the bed, and swiftly ran down the stairs and out her front door.

A loud series of short buzzes from the apartment intercom penetrated the fitful, caffeine-laced doze that Corlis had fallen into following her breakfast of pancakes and cane syrup. Whoever was downstairs on Julia Street changed tactics and held a heavy finger on the button.

"All right! All right!" she protested as she padded down the hallway in her sweat socks and pushed the SPEAK button on the intercom.

"Hello!" she barked.

"Corlis McCullough?" A deep masculine voice sounded as irascible as she felt.

"Bin-go!" she said.

"It's King Duvallon. May I come up?"

Corlis sagged against the wall, utterly dumbfounded and dismayed.

"Hello? You still there?"

"What are *you* doing here? What *time* is it? And how do you know where I live?"

"It's nearly eleven A.M. I'll explain all that when I see you."

"Yeah? Well, now isn't exactly the *best* time," she replied, unable to keep the sarcasm out of her voice.

"I'm not surprised you're feelin' out of sorts this mornin'," King replied in his distinct southern drawl. "That's why I decided to stop by. I went for a run down by the river just now, and I got to thinkin' 'bout how yesterday must have felt on your end of things."

"Well, it didn't feel *good*!" she responded, her lips inches from the intercom's microphone.

"Gettin' fired never feels good."

"How did *you* know I was canned?"

"It was in the media column in the *Picayune* this morning," he said. Corlis closed her eyes and groaned. What television station would hire her after this? "Somebody at WWEZ must've leaked it as soon as you aired the story last night," King surmised.

"Yeah . . . your sister's almost-husband is *my* guess. I'm sure

Jack Ebert knows the home telephone numbers of a few media people in this town," she said bitterly. She shifted her weight onto her other foot. "Look, I really don't—"

"Your crew got axed, too," King's disembodied voice interrupted.

"Oh, no . . . right before Christmas?"

"Look . . . can you buzz me up? It's starting to seriously rain out here, and I need to talk to you for a moment."

In a kind of a daze, Corlis watched curiously as her index finger pushed the button that would give King access to the ground-floor hallway, past her neighbor's art gallery, and farther on to a stairway that led to her apartment on the second floor.

As she listened to the hollow sound of King's footsteps on the steps, she glanced down at the rumpled pair of running pants and faded sweatshirt she'd slept in.

Jeez Louise, she felt a mess.

She sprinted the few feet into her bathroom, located off the front hallway, and peered into the medicine cabinet mirror.

I look hideous.

She didn't have a stitch of makeup on, and dark smudges, courtesy of her miserable night, formed sooty crescents underneath her eyes. Before she could even run a comb through her hair, she heard a sharp knock on her front door. She grabbed her hairbrush and made a pathetic attempt to bring some order to her unruly brunette locks. Sighing with resignation, she trudged back down the hall, opened the front door, and beheld King Duvallon in all his glistening glory.

Despite its being December, he was lightly dressed in royal-blue running shorts, a white polo shirt, and a beat-up pair of sneakers. He'd obviously been hoofing it for a couple of miles along the riverfront in unseasonably sultry weather as a storm front moved in off the Gulf of Mexico. Perspiration beaded his forehead. His hair was also damp, and sweat ran in rivulets down his neck and into the black chest hair just visible above his open collar. The short stubble on his face, unshaven since his sister's wedding most likely gave him a mildly roguish appearance. The deep cleft in his chin intrigued her. How did King shave?

"I should have called first," he admitted apologetically. He looked down at his sweat-soaked shirt. "And perhaps I should have showered," he added wryly.

"You're not the *only* one," she said, and then wished she hadn't drawn attention to herself as she observed King give her disheveled garb the once-over.

"As you might imagine, I didn't sleep very well last night." She grimaced. "When I got back from breakfast about seven-thirty this morning . . . I sort of went unconscious. Now I look and feel as if I got run over by a truck." For a moment they stared in silence across the threshold. Then she added quietly, "Why don't you come in and tell me how you knew my address, and why you've stopped by to see *me*, of all people, on a Sunday morning?"

Striding toward the kitchen she asked, "Coffee?"

"Just a glass of water would be fine," King replied.

Corlis knew if she consumed one more ounce of caffeine, she'd probably get the d.t.'s, so she poured herself a glass of water as well.

King glanced around her living room. His slight nod made it seem as if he approved of what he saw—a rectangular salon, graced with a fireplace, ornately carved wooden moldings and twelve-foot ceilings overhead. Two windows, nearly that high, opened out onto the narrow wrought-iron gallery with its marvelous view up and down Julia Street. At that moment a moss-green streetcar glided by, clanging its way through the St. Charles Avenue intersection as it headed uptown toward the Garden District.

Just then Cagney Cat heaved his bulk past the open windowsill.

"Whoa . . . what a big cat!" King exclaimed. "A big, wet cat."

"And not necessarily the brightest," Corlis added. Addressing Cagney, who nonchalantly was rubbing his saturated fur against King's calf, she exclaimed, "You finally come in out of the rain, and look what you're doing to our guest!"

King leaned over and combed his long aristocratic fingers down the cat's back and gently pulled the length of his tail. Cagney *hated* it when *she* did that. However, the infidel stared up at the visitor and began to purr loudly.

"I don't believe it," Corlis muttered, crossing the carpet to close the window against the shower that had begun to spatter the panes.

"I like these rugs a lot," King noted with an appreciative glance at the large garnet-red Persian carpet. A similar narrow jewel-toned runner that had reportedly also belonged to Corlis Bell McCullough graced the long hallway extending from her front door. "They're perfect here."

"Thanks. I take it that you've been in one of these Julia Street row houses before?" she asked, inviting him to sit in the club chair whose beige linen slipcover matched the love seat on which she gratefully sat down. To her utter surprise, Cagney leapt onto King's lap, shamelessly presenting his belly to be rubbed.

"Oh, yes, I've been here before," he said, nodding. He absently stroked the cat's fur as if it were the most usual thing in the world. "As a matter of fact, I spent a lot of time on this street when these places were all flophouses." He glanced around the parlor. "Less than ten years ago, you could have rented a bed in this very apartment for seven dollars a night!"

"*You* used to live here?"

"God, no!" he said, laughing. "I was stone broke when I first came back to New Orleans, but not *that* broke."

"Oh," she said, feeling foolish.

Why in the world is this man in my living room?

"Awhile back," King disclosed, "I was part of a group that went to bat to save this place from the wrecker's ball."

"Someone was going to tear down these gorgeous row houses?"

"Well, they weren't so gorgeous before the rehab, but, yup . . . a developer by the name of Grover Jeffries had big plans for this block. Ol' Grover's hairy pawprint is on most of those high-rises you've probably noticed over on Canal Street."

Jeffries? she thought, startled. *Wasn't that the last name of one of the creepy guys standing around the coffin she'd just dreamed about?* Corlis began to wonder if getting fired for the third time in one's career could actually unhinge a person. She slowly took a sip from her glass of water, trying not to lose her composure. "You mean that guy Jeffries built those steel-and-glass jobs that look like downtown Dallas?"

"You got it."

King pointed in the direction of her ornate fireplace. "A lot of people in this community got together to fight him off. They were able to save this entire block. To restore the facade and make the interior renovations cost-effective, several of the row houses like yours were divided, turned condo for individually owned apartments, while others remained as four-story single-family dwellings."

Another silence.

Finally she said, "Those modern buildings downtown are pretty soulless." She looked at him expectantly.

So? We seemed to have exhausted the pretty-versus-ugly-buildings topic of conversation. Just tell me: Why are you here?

King gave Cagney a sensuous rub on his stomach. Then he looked up at her and declared abruptly, "I'm sorry you got ousted from WWEZ because of your story about Daphne's wedding."

"You *are*?" Corlis replied, astounded. "Weren't your final words to me last night 'Get the hell outta here, you harpy'?"

King grinned. "Did I say that?"

"You sure did. However, I didn't take it personally. You were probably upset by what that creep Jack Ebert had done to your sister, not to mention what Miss Cindy Lou Mallory did to *you*," she couldn't resist adding. She'd heard scuttlebutt from her cameraman that King had been seriously dating the voluptuous redhead. "I expect my TV crew and I were more than just a pesky annoyance."

"Yeah . . . I was pretty upset last night and . . . I wanted to lash out at someone. You were mighty handy."

"I thought you wanted to kick us out of the balcony because of . . . the old business between us," Corlis ventured awkwardly. "But then later I realized that you knew ahead of time that your sister wasn't going to go through with the wedding and you'd just as soon not have that broadcast on TV."

"Exactly," King confirmed. "Althea LaCroix—the lady playin' the organ? She and I were the only ones Daphne confided in right before the ceremony."

"Wow . . . being let in on *that* little secret would have made anybody a bit testy."

"No kidding," King said with a short laugh. "In fact, when I saw the story last night on the news, I was sort of torn between wantin' to strangle you and wantin' to give you a hug for being so alert to what was really goin' on."

"You actually caught the broadcast?"

"Sure did. On the TV in the Old Absinthe House bar," he replied ruefully. "After two old-fashioneds, I must admit. But, still . . . it was pretty amazing. You just let the pictures tell it . . . and you got the facts right."

"Well . . . thanks . . ." Corlis said, blindsided by the compliment.

Silence fell between them once again.

"Actually, I thought the piece you did last night was brilliant."

"You did?" she replied, amazed.

"Yes, I did. Later . . . when I had time to think about it all . . . I realized that when you refused to leave the balcony . . . you were just doin' your job."

"Yup. Like at UCLA."

Now, why did I bring that up? He's trying to be nice, for pity's sake!

This time the silence lengthened to nearly fifteen unbearable seconds.

King shifted his weight as he sat in her expansive club chair and took another sip from his water glass. "Maybe a story like that'll show other brides and grooms that it's never too late to call a halt to a weddin', if you're havin' second thoughts about it. It sure served as a wake-up call for half the groomsmen last night, I can tell you that."

Had King actually been *that* serious about Cindy Lou Mallory? Maybe so, Corlis considered.

"Bailing out is always an option," she murmured, thinking of Jay Kerlin. Well, at least she'd canceled the reservation for the outdoor wedding facilities at the Bel Air Hotel *before* the invitations were mailed.

"And there's somethin' else," King said.

"What?" she asked, alert now for payback time.

"I might have a lead for you on another job."

"*You?* Find a job? For *me*?"

Now she *really* must be dreaming!

Chapter Four

December 21

Corlis stared at King Duvallon in astonishment. "You'd actually recommend me for another broadcasting job in this town?"

Wasn't this the man who, twelve years ago, led his fraternity brothers on a mission to utterly humiliate her and all the other women who wrote and edited *Ms. UCLA*?

"Sure," King said with a friendly shrug. "You're a pro. I could see that last night. And the station I'm thinkin' of is a kind of upstart enterprise here in town," he explained, the hint of a grin playing about his lips. "You ever watch WJAZ-TV? It's nonunion, but they're pretty feisty over there, so the two of you might be perfect for each other." Corlis shot him a look. "They tend to cover stuff around New Orleans that no one else'll touch," King concluded with a blameless expression. "Crusader Rabbit types, ya know what I mean?"

"Don't tell me they're 'cause' TV journalists?" she blurted. "Or one of those vanity TV stations where if you write a check, they put you on camera with your own cooking show!"

"No . . . they have a legit news organization," he assured her. "They're just pretty new in the market, and they're not affiliated with any network yet."

"And nonunion," Corlis repeated glumly. "That means they pay zilch."

"Well . . . it was just a thought," King said, draining his glass while continuing to stroke Cagney Cat's silky fur. "I was thinkin' that after the havoc that the Ebert-Duvallon weddin'

41

wrought in your professional life last night, maybe we—maybe I owed you one."

"Considering our little run-in at UCLA, Mr. Duvallon, don't you think you owe me at least *two*?" she replied archly, then flushed with mortification.

She'd gone and done it again! Given him a zinger when he was being perfectly agreeable. Now, *why* did this man rankle her so? Well, she wasn't herself this morning. Who *would* be, after her miserable night and that awful dream she'd had?

King's generous mouth had settled into a straight line. "I don't think that now is really the time or place to go over ancient history," he said coolly. "You might be forced to hear the other side of the story, and I understand that journalists *hate* doin' that."

"You mean tell the tale of how you and your fraternity broke into our office, plastered the place with 'Keep 'em barefoot and pregnant' posters, stole our logos, and produced a vicious lampoon of our magazine? *That* story?" she shot back. Her dander up, she added, "Or are you referring to the *way* you guys portrayed me on the cover of your bogus edition? Perhaps you've forgotten the awful cartoon of me that you and your buddies hawked all over campus?"

King set his glass carefully on the leather coaster that decorated the mahogany side table next to his chair. "Well . . ." he considered slowly.

"It was . . . humiliating," Corlis replied, staring at her hands, which rested in her lap.

"So was readin' in your magazine about my election as president of my fraternity," he countered quietly. "Didn't the headline of your story start somethin' like 'Redneck Gets the Nod at Sigma—'"

"Okay, okay," Corlis interrupted, holding up her hands in front of her face. "I admit it. . . . . That piece came perilously close to a personal attack. I'd never do that now." She stared at him earnestly. "But that was *after* you guys marched on our offices and challenged the *Ms. UCLA* staff to a naked mud-wrestling contest—and when we *refused*, you kept that twenty-four-hour catcall brigade howling outside our door!"

"Well, at least give me credit for callin' off all that harassment stuff when the sorority across the quad invited us to their swimsuit fashion show that weekend, remember?" King recalled, his lips twitching in a repressed smile.

Corlis shot him a disgusted look and tried not to laugh. Then she shifted her gaze and stared out the window, murmuring, "All those fraternities were *so* disgusting toward women back then. . . ."

"Some of us were . . . pretty disrespectful," King agreed softly. He cocked his head. "But, upon reflection, don't you think gettin' me expelled from school and campaignin' to permanently ban my fraternity from campus was kinda a case of overkill?"

"Well, the same thing might be said of that caricature of me!" she retorted. She added, "But . . . yes . . . I think the whole thing spun out of control. Our side, too."

King pursed his lips and after a long moment nodded.

"You might well be right there, Ms. California. And that cartoon of you *was* pretty vicious." King sought her gaze and smiled faintly. "I expect we've both grown less hotheaded in our old age, don't you imagine?" When Corlis didn't reply, he added swiftly, "Well, maybe *I* have. The military knocked a lot of cockiness outta me, not to mention the attitude adjustment urged on me by a few women marine officers."

"You were a marine?" The man seemed so uptown . . . so patrician. Hadn't his family lived in New Orleans practically since the explorer Bienville plunked down the French flag in the mud in 1718?

"You betcha!" he said, throwing his shoulders back military style. Cagney Cat was startled by this motion and hopped down from King's lap. However, the feline immediately curled his portly body around the man's ragged tennis shoes, resting his furry chin on the toe—and went back to sleep.

"Why would *you* join the marines?"

King grinned and shook his head. "You think I was gonna face my daddy after gettin' his national fraternity banned *forever* from the UCLA campus? Actually, goin' into the service was the best thing that ever happened to me. I came back to Tulane a disciplined studying machine. Like I tell my architectural history students at the university," he added jocularly, "you gotta suck it up if you want to get ahead in this life. But then, you already know that, don't you, Ace?" He rose from his chair and carefully eased his toe from beneath Cagney's chin. "Well . . . I'd better get goin'. Only two and a half more shoppin' days till Christmas."

Corlis rose to her feet as well.

"King?" she said uncertainly.

"Yes, sugar?"

Sugar?

"It was . . . very nice of you to come by here personally and tell me about the job possibility at WJAZ." She visualized the stack of bills awaiting her immediate attention in her broom-closet home office down the hall. She'd been so busy this month, she'd let them pile up. "Is there anyone in particular that I should talk to at the station?"

"Yeah. A guy named Andy Zamora."

"Is he the news director?"

"That, and the station owner, and probably also the janitor. I got to know him when WJAZ covered a big controversy last year on lower Canal."

"Another Grover Jeffries construction project? What *are* you, anyway, the Preservation Police?"

"That happens to be a very accurate description of the work I do," King said, the corners of his lips quirking upward. "Last year I got into a tremendous flap about Jeffries's biggest boon-doggle to date. Have you seen the Good Times Shoppin' Plaza?"

"That hulking, half-finished megamall off Canal Street? Ug-ly!"

"The very one. It went bankrupt six months before you got here, to the tune of nearly half a *billion* dollars. The cost over-runs and the graft—even by New Orleans standards—were off the charts."

"Wow . . ." she said, awed by the size of the dollar amount. "Then how can Grover Jeffries afford to be making any more mischief in this town?"

"This is Louisiana, darlin,' " he drawled. "Ol' Grover and his slick lawyers made sure that in his contract with the city, taxpayers like you and me are footin' the bill for that financial catastrophe—not Jeffries Industries. In the end they couldn't pin a thing on him."

"And WJAZ covered the story as it went along?" Corlis asked with admiration.

"In the beginnin' they were just about the only news outfit that did—that is, until the whole thing blew sky-high and the big stations and the newspapers couldn't ignore it any longer," he said with a hard, angry edge to his voice. "But, like I said, WJAZ's an upstart outfit."

"I wonder if Zamora could also use a pair of crackerjack camera and sound men?"

"Manny and Virgil? I can personally assure you that they'd be mighty grateful for your recommendation."

"How do *you* know?"

"Virgil told me how to get hold of you when I called him this mornin'."

"You're a friend of Virgil's?" she asked, astonished.

"Sugar . . ." he repeated the endearment that Corlis sensed was merely meant to sound ironic, "in some significant ways, New Orleans is a *very* small town. Everybody knows everybody else—you know what I mean?"

"*Now* I do," she replied ruefully, recalling that she had been fired by the *janitor* at WWEZ-TV.

"During the media hullabaloo about the Good Times megamall controversy, I got pretty friendly with most of the TV crews that covered the story. So I know firsthand that Virgil is a very good guy."

"And now he's out of a job, just before Christmas," she said, a bleak expression on her face.

"I'll give Andy Zamora a call when I get back home this mornin'," King assured her as he headed down the hallway, Corlis and Cagney trailing in his wake.

"On a Sunday?" she asked, touched. He must really have a lot of respect for Virgil and Manny.

"Sure, why not?" he replied. Grinning over his shoulder, he added, "I'll tell him he'd better hustle to get a shot at hirin' such a dynamite package deal."

When King arrived at her front door, he turned around without warning, prompting Corlis to back away and inadvertently step on Cagney's paw. The indignant animal emitted a yowl and ran into her bedroom.

"Oh, gosh! Sorry, Cag! Oh . . . do you think I hurt him?" she asked, distressed.

"He's got plenty of paddin'," King assured her as they watched the cat scamper under the bed. "See? He's not even limpin'." Then he peered more closely at the massive four-poster dominating the room. "Well, I'll be . . ."

"What?" she asked, watching him take note of the bed's yellow brocade canopy that spilled down from a top brace decorated with a carved mahogany wooden crest.

"Did you buy this bed in New Orleans?"

"Yes. I probably paid too much for it, but I just couldn't resist. When I sleep in it, I feel like the princess and the pea."

"I have one *exactly* like it in my apartment," he pronounced.

"You're kidding?"

"No, I'm not," he said, advancing a step inside the room.

"Where'd you get yours? From your mother's side of your family or the Duvallons?" she asked, suddenly recalling the scene in which someone named André Duvallon burst into the apartment on Royal Street where a corpse lay cold in its coffin.

"Neither," King replied. "My godfather gave it to me on my twenty-first birthday. Mine was made on his family's plantation, upriver, way back when." He angled his head in the direction of Corlis's bed. "This one probably was crafted by the same slave cabinetmaker that mine was—either at the Marchand plantation or on one of the places owned by a collateral cousin—and the two were handed down to succeeding generations through different family lines. Nineteenth century, right?"

Corlis nodded. "Well, whoever inherited this one must have fallen on dark days, because it was sold at auction in the French Quarter a couple of months ago."

"It's got the exact same carvings that mine does," King marveled, peering at it closely. "Lafayette Marchand had no son to give it to, so I was the lucky guy."

"Didn't he have a daughter?" Corlis demanded.

"He never married."

"Oh. Well, it was nice of him to give you such a beautiful piece of his family's furniture," she ventured lamely.

"I don't think 'nice' quite applies in Marchand's case."

"No?" she asked as she observed an angry furrow creasing his forehead.

"No," King echoed shortly. Then he added, "My godfather went to work for Grover Jeffries a few years back. As his *public relations* adviser," he added, bitter sarcasm edging his voice.

"If Jeffries has such a sleazy reputation, why'd your godfather decide to do that?"

King gave her an appraising stare. "The Marchands are an old, distinguished family, but by the late nineteen-eighties, there wasn't much left of the estate. After the oil bust—ten, fifteen years ago—Laf's law practice wasn't thrivin', either. However, the man knows all the important political players in New Orleans—black and white. So, he transformed himself into a fixer. The very mention of Lafayette Marchand's name has been enough to open many doors for Jeffries in the last ten years. And openin' doors for a wealthy developer can be a very lucrative business in these parts."

"And he's your godfather," she murmured.

"I fired him from that job."

"I'm sorry," she offered simply. "It must be hard for you to run into him all the time, since you make a habit of fighting to save historic buildings from the Jeffries style of urban renewal," she added pointedly. King remained silent, so Corlis thrust out her hand. "Well . . . thanks again for stopping by," she said, feeling unaccountably shy. "And thanks, too, for telling me about WJAZ."

"What are old friends for?" he replied with a wink, his good humor apparently returning. Then he seized her hand and gave it a friendly squeeze. It felt warm and oddly comforting.

"Have a nice Christmas," she ventured.

"*This* year? After that weddin' yesterday? I appreciate the sentiment, Corlis, but I don't think happy holidays are in the cards for the Kingsbury-Duvallon clan," he said, referring also to his mother, Antoinette Kingsbury's, side of his family.

I don't think so either, Corlis concurred silently.

She was suddenly assaulted by a brief unhappy childhood memory of her mother—angry and silent—pushing her out of a dented Volkswagen on Christmas morning in front of her father's glamorous quarters in Beverly Hills. She continued to meet King's gaze, amazed by the unusually dark blue irises that stared back at her. "Well, then," she amended, "I'll just say happy New Year."

"Better," he agreed with a brief nod. A lopsided grin spread across his handsome features. "Happy New Year, Ace. Let's hope it's an improvement over last year—for *both* of us."

Softly shutting the door behind him, she murmured, "No kidding. Bye, now."

She remained standing with her hand on the knob, listening to King's footfalls as he descended the stairs. When she heard the front door to Julia Street close shut, she turned and wandered down the hallway, pausing in the bathroom to gaze at her disheveled reflection in the mirror over the sink.

Damned if King Duvallon didn't look sexier than ever, even in ratty tennis shoes and a sweat-soaked polo shirt! And he actually apologized for the events twelve years ago.

Well . . . he *sort of* apologized.

True to King Duvallon's word, Corlis received a call from Andy Zamora himself, three days before New Year's Eve. After a brief negotiation, she signed a two-year contract with WJAZ-TV on December thirtieth—at a third less salary, and virtually no expense account or perks, except for a health plan.

However, in the immortal words of Aunt Marge, "Beggars can't be choosers." In fact, her elderly relative urged her to take the job with good cheer. "You know the McCullough family motto," Marge advised briskly over the telephone from her condo in California. "Start *now*, and do the best you can!"

Corlis threw herself into her demanding job from the first day she went to work for wiry, plain-speaking Andy Zamora, owner of the shoestring station located in an industrial section of town. She liked Zamora's no-nonsense style, and her instincts told her it was a safe bet that he was a straight shooter.

And besides, she reminded herself, with Aunt Marge's encouragement, she'd made her New Year's resolution: Like the New Orleans Saints football team, she was in a rebuilding phase. She was going to stay put for once, instead of running to the next town, and *this* time she was going to find out why she so often was her own worst enemy.

As for King Duvallon, Corlis had written him a carefully composed thank-you note and half expected to hear from him again, if for no other reason than to inquire how her new job was going.

But she didn't hear from him, and she could only conclude that, despite King's bountiful use of *sugar* and *sweetheart*, he still harbored resentment because of what happened at UCLA.

Well, the Lord knew, she probably retained a few resentments about that incident herself!

Corlis was reminded of that fact when, three months later, she stared at the assignment board in the WJAZ newsroom. She, Virgil, and Manny were slated to cover a story slugged: "New Chair of Historic Preservation Announced March 9/ Noon/ U Campus."

"Who got the big nod?" she asked, her pulse speeding up for reasons she was unwilling to acknowledge. "Not King Duvallon, by any chance?"

"The news release doesn't say . . . but I doubt it's gonna be him," said Zamora, dismissing his friend's career prospects with a shrug. "King was promoted to associate professor last year, but he didn't get tenure. He's still a pretty controversial character out there."

"Really? He teaches architectural history, doesn't he?" Corlis asked, surprised to learn that such a politically correct profession apparently could plunge its practitioners into hot water with the powers that be.

"That's the problem. . . . He's a ferocious public advocate for proppin' up and rehabin' all those rickety buildings around the Quarter and everywhere else in the city. The new department chair they're namin' today will be under the thumb of the architecture school, not the history department, and lots of those slide-rule guys like to tear *down* old buildings in New Orleans and construct very tall glass boxes in their place," Zamora concluded, shaking his head.

"But everybody calls Duvallon the 'Hero of New Orleans,' " she protested. "He's the perfect candidate to head a department of historic preservation. How can they *not* give it to him?"

"Easy . . ." said Zamora. "To fill *this* cushy job, they'll pick some Milquetoast who yaps poetic about pretty buildings but doesn't fight to save 'em the way King does. That way they don't buy trouble from the powerful folks who support their fund-raising round here."

Corlis took a closer look at the news release Zamora had just handed her. "Who's underwriting the endowment to pay the new guy's salary?"

"That's why I like you, McCullough," Zamora said with a satisfied smile. "My guess is *that's* the story. The university's been runnin' in red ink since the oil boom went bust round here, and donations went way down. I was pretty surprised to hear someone's popped for an eight-hundred-and-fifty-thousand-buck contribution for a do-good kinda thing like this."

Corlis whistled softly. "Eight hundred and fifty K. That's a lot of oysters."

"You got *that* right," Zamora said with a cynical laugh. "Somebody's sure gonna get their name carved in granite on a building out there . . ." he drawled. "So far, they've kept it very hush-hush. Should be mighty interestin' to find out *who*."

Some two hundred people jammed the steps leading to the front door of the starkly postmodern steel-and-glass building just off St. Charles Avenue.

God, that place is ugly! King mused, glancing skyward. Absently he wondered if there was such a defense as justifiable homicide against architects and builders who created visually offensive structures. Exhibit A: the supremely undistinguished Graduate School of Architecture looming ahead of him in the misty March air.

At the curb nearby, the side door of a white minivan, WJAZ-TV emblazoned in red letters on the side, slid open. Virgil and Manny, clad in bright yellow rain slickers, stepped from the van. Could Corlis McCullough be far behind? King wondered, strangely gratified by such a possibility.

Several times since Christmas, he'd almost reached for the telephone to call Corlis, but instinct told him to wait. He guessed by now he'd completely gotten Cindy Lou's behavior out of his system, but it had taken a while.

"Whoa!" said Christopher Calvert as all five feet four inches of Corlis McCullough emerged from the van and onto the sidewalk. The Ph.D. candidate who was King's teaching assistant nodded in the direction of the slicker-clad broadcaster. "Isn't that the reporter who did the story about your sister's wedding? I would have bet my green book bag here that no one in this town would have hired *that* little lady again. Do you think she's got a relative at WJAZ?"

"Nope," King pronounced.

"Then how'd she get a job after what happened at WWEZ?" he demanded.

King smiled faintly, "Apparently, she's got friends."

Back in December, Andy Zamora had thanked him profusely for steering this particular group of castoffs in his direction.

"Corlis and that crew are the best in town, and they'll be desperate enough for jobs that I'll bet they'll work for me real cheap!" he'd crowed. "Bless ya, buddy."

When King had received Corlis's prim-and-proper thank-you note, he'd almost given in to his impulse to pick up the phone and ask her to dinner.

Well, now's your chance, Duvallon, he amended silently, discreetly admiring the lady's shapely legs.

He watched with increasing absorption as she pointed her microphone at the satellite dish spiraling hydraulically twenty feet up on a slender pole from the roof of the van. Damned if she didn't look a lot cuter in her yellow slicker than the two burly members of her television crew. Beneath her reporter's rain gear, he caught a glimpse of a sassy slash of red wool skirt that just skimmed her knees. Her brunette hair was tucked beneath the hood of her jacket, a few feathery tendrils curling above her artfully arched dark brows. He'd never taken note of her eyes twelve years ago behind those wire-rimmed granny glasses she'd always worn. Now, thanks to the wonder of contact lenses, he'd noticed when he saw her in her Julia Street apartment in December that her eyes were drop-dead gorgeous pools of sea green and liquid amber, fringed by dark lashes that wouldn't quit.

Man oh man, the woman's eyes could tame a tiger. And those *legs*! He wished he could snap a close-up of them to send to some of his old fraternity brothers. They'd probably fall off their bar stools if they could see what Corlis McCullough looked like now!

He suppressed a grin as he watched her gingerly leap over rain puddles in a pair of saucy sling-back navy heels. Hadn't anyone informed the woman that when it poured in New Orleans, a person needed to keep a pair of galoshes handy? However, considering her sexy ankles, he was glad she'd forgone practicality today.

"Hey, Professor Duvallon!" Chris declared, staring at him curiously. "If we want to get decent seats, we'd better get in there pronto. Look at the size of this crowd!"

The two men joined the throng heading up the brick path toward the large amphitheater that served as a lecture hall during class hours. The university's official news release had promised that at noon "an important announcement regarding a major gift to further historic preservation efforts in Louisiana" would be made at the architecture school.

A fully funded Professorship of Historic Preservation *sounded* terrific. However, King's antennae went up the second he heard that such an announcement was in the offing.

"Did you get Hailey Seitz on the phone last night?" King asked of Chris. The moisture falling from overcast skies had shifted to a Louisiana-style sprinkle—soft and slightly steamy. The Mardi Gras bacchanal the previous week had been celebrated in glorious sunshine. Well, that was New Orleans for you, he thought. If you hate the weather, wait five minutes.

"Professor Seitz said he doesn't know who's being named chair any more than we do."

"Jonathan Poole never returned my calls," King disclosed with disgust. "It's gotta be Poole. Feckless, gutless, lazy, and boring. The perfect choice."

"You know," Chris confided in a low voice in case any colleagues were within earshot, "I can't believe this university would have the gall to pick the guy who *designed* the Good Times Shopping Plaza and whose boss *tore down* four square blocks of historic buildings to put it there!"

"Every time I catch a glimpse of that place, I feel like settin' an alligator after Poole for designin' it, and throwin' a bomb at Grover Jeffries for puttin' it up."

King allowed himself a brief, searing recollection of Emelie Dumas, a retired cook and housekeeper who had worked for his family for thirty-seven years, sitting beside him in a rented truck, numb with shock. The old woman had been coerced into signing the papers allowing for the demolition of her house before King had realized that her entire block was on Jeffries's hit list. He had never forgiven himself.

"Well, at least funding a university chair like this might garner some needed attention to the preservation movement itself," Chris ventured hopefully.

"I wouldn't count on it," King retorted. "Not in *this* town."

Corlis reached back into the van and grabbed her voluminous leather shoulder bag and a notebook from off the seat. She righted herself and prepared to advance on the Graduate School of Architecture building where the news conference was about to begin. Out of the corner of her eye, she caught a glimpse of a gaggle of campus security men congregating in the open green space inside the quadrangle.

"Is there some sort of panty raid expected here today?" she asked facetiously, cocking her head in the direction of the uniformed officers.

"Why, I *hope* so," Virgil replied with a salacious grin as he hoisted his video camera onto his shoulder. "You ready, Manny?"

"Yep," the taciturn soundman replied, angling his freight dolly onto the curb. "Time to rock 'n' roll."

As the trio entered the building's lobby, Corlis caught sight of Professor King Duvallon striding in the direction of the first-floor auditorium. She kept him in her sights as his handsome dark head bobbed above the crowd.

"I'm going to try to line up Duvallon to do a short interview for us after this little show is over, okay guys? See ya in a sec," she said, hurriedly following King's tall, lean figure as he entered through the swinging doors into the hall.

The wide, modern amphitheater was packed with spectators by the time Corlis pushed her way through the milling hordes and caught up with King. Down front, a long table, adorned with a felt banner sporting the school's insignia, was set up on a raised stage. Conferring to one side were university president James Delaney, a few deans, several members of the alumni Board of Administrators, and a few bearded souls dressed in rumpled seersucker suits who looked to her to be terminally nervous members of the teaching faculty.

King, however, was an entirely different matter. His rugged jaw was smooth-shaven, and he was dressed in casual chinos and an open-collared polo shirt bathed in a wicked shade of imperial blue.

"Professor Duvallon!" she called loudly, to no avail. Finally she was able to reach past a couple of people and tap him on the shoulder.

King turned around. "Hey, Ace, whatcha know?" he said, his serious expression breaking into a grin. "Covered a good weddin' lately, sugar?"

"Not lately, *sweetheart*," she replied pointedly. Then she lowered her voice and said, "Ah . . . King . . . do you mind not calling me sugar. . . . It's—"

"You mean you want me to *pretend* we don't know each other?" he teased. "Now, that doesn't sound like the tell-it-like-it-is straight shooter I knew in California! How do you like your new station?"

"It's fine," she replied lightly, not wanting to press her point about his sexist semantics. "However, your friend Zamora works us to death!" She held up both hands and added, "Not that I'm really complaining, mind you. I'm very grateful you opened that door. It's just that I'm running around town like the proverbial chicken with its head cut off, covering two or three stories a day." She took a deep breath. "Did you get my thank-you note?"

"Sure did, sugar," he said. "It was real sweet."

"King!"

"What?"

"That 'sugar' thing again," she muttered, with a glance behind her, in case Virgil and Manny were nearby.

"Oh . . . sorry. This is Louisiana, sweetheart," he said, grinning. "It's just part of the language down here. All the magno-

lias and stuff," he said with a straight face. "But I'll try to remember." He glanced toward the podium and let out a low
whistle. "Mama Roux . . ."

"What?"

"Well, well, will you look who's here?"

"Who?"

"Jonathan Poole and Grover Jeffries." With a slight nod of
his head, King added, "The public-spirited gentlemen who gave
us the Good Times Shoppin' Plaza."

"Jeffries is the same developer guy who almost got away
with tearing down my house on Julia Street, right?"

"The very one."

"What's *he* doing here?" she asked, staring at the barrel-
chested Jeffries, accompanied by his public relations consultant, Lafayette Marchand.

Corlis suddenly remembered another man named Jeffries,
standing by a coffin . . . but she pushed the disturbing memory
away. Instead, she concentrated on the sight of King's estranged
godfather, a tall, patrician public relations adviser whose full
head of silver hair easily qualified him to be a stand-in for Cary
Grant.

"My guess is we'll find out real soon why that scum is here
today," King said grimly. "Nothin' surprises me anymore."

"Can I get your views about this appointment after the announcement is made?" she asked. However, King had abruptly
turned his attention away from her and was surveying the auditorium like a dog scenting danger. "Maybe," he said shortly.
"Let's first see who officially gets the job, okay? 'Scuse me, will
you, sugar? Gotta go talk to some folks."

And before she could reply, Kingsbury Duvallon stalked
down the carpeted stairs and buttonholed a neatly dressed
young black man with a green canvas book bag slung over his
shoulder. Corlis made her way through the crowd to join her
colleagues on the left side of the lecture hall where Virgil and
Manny had squeezed into a vacant spot among a cluster of
tripods and video cameras and had set up their equipment.

A few minutes later the president of the university approached the podium. As soon as he opened his mouth to speak,
red lights bloomed on the battery of camcorders while sound

technicians twirled their dials, setting voice levels for the forest of microphones bristling on the lectern.

"Good morning, everyone," Delaney greeted his audience cheerfully.

Corlis, however, detected a slight nervousness in the way his stubby fingers clutched a stack of index cards. She leaned toward Virgil and asked under her breath, "Heard anything?"

"Just that Grover Jeffries got appointed to the university's Board of Administrators this week."

"Wait a minute! Didn't he go to the University of Texas?" she protested in a low voice. "Why would they make him a governing board member of *this* university? Isn't that reserved for the local bigwigs whose mamas and daddies go back to the year one?"

"This is Louisiana, sugar." Virgil laughed softly. "Could be more to it than we know."

"Why does everyone say 'This is Louisiana, sugar' whenever something really outrageous happens around here?" Corlis groused, remembering that King had voiced the same sort of cynical sentiments. She rolled her eyes heavenward—which garnered a chuckle from both her crew members.

On the right of the platform, next to President Delaney, Corlis spotted the dean of the architecture school. On his left: Professor Jonathan Poole. Next to him sat the former all-American himself, University of Texas graduate Grover Jeffries. Corlis noted that the retired linebacker's slight paunch bore witness to a fitness regimen undoubtedly derailed by too many beers consumed in his corporate suite at the Superdome during New Orleans Saints games. The balding developer, a man in his late fifties, paused to glare at a large section of the audience where King and his teaching assistant had taken their seats. Then he abruptly shifted his gaze to stare at the phalanx of media positioned below the stage. Corlis sensed him lock glances with someone who had just joined the reporters' ranks.

Jack Ebert, the groom so recently spurned at Saint Louis Cathedral, had chosen this event to make his first public reappearance. Thin, brown-haired, he leaned against one of the paneled walls, his slender reporter's notebook open and pen poised. He glanced to his right.

"Well, hello there," he said to Corlis. His small, rodent's ears almost seemed to twitch.

"Hello, Jack," she replied, and appeared preoccupied with the words in her notebook. She'd just as soon steer clear of the guy. Obviously Jack knew that she was the reporter who had produced the now notorious piece about his aborted wedding.

To her surprise, Grover Jeffries offered Jack Ebert a friendly nod from the stage. Then she was mildly surprised to see the developer's brow furrow once again as he shifted his glance to the dapper Lafayette Marchand. The spin doctor had wandered into the press area and stood not three feet from her. Grover Jeffries's hard stare seemed to be communicating to the silver fox, "Keep an eye on those damned reporters!"

Meanwhile, at the podium, President Delaney cleared his throat for a second time and nodded in the direction of a university sound technician whose job it was to record this event for the school's archives.

"We, at this university," he declared formally, "are delighted today to announce a most generous gift . . . a gift that will bestow on this institution another jewel in its crown, so to speak." Delaney seemed to gather confidence as he continued to read from his note cards. "The Graduate School of Architecture is the grateful recipient of an eight-hundred-and-fifty-thousand-dollar donation to endow a chair of preservation architecture. . . ."

A scattering of applause and low murmurs of appreciation percolated among the crowd.

"We are indebted, indeed," Delaney continued, raising his voice a notch, "to such civic-minded citizens as our benefactor, Mr. Grover Jeffries, who—along with the board of directors and stockholders of Jeffries Industries—has so selflessly—"

There was a loud gasp from certain sections of the auditorium. Shuffling began to erupt in the tiers of seats where most of the students were sitting. Corlis wondered absently if videotape was sensitive enough to pick up the electricity that suddenly charged the air. President Delaney looked over the restless audience with an air of uncertainty. Then he plunged ahead, continuing to read from his prepared text.

"Mr. Jeffries has so selflessly given an endowment to fund a professorship dedicated to the teaching of historic preservation at our architecture school."

Suddenly a loud voice from the lower right side of the auditorium rent the air.

"Sellout!"

Corlis looked to see who was protesting this turn of events in such a ferocious and public fashion. An instant of dead silence permeated the hall, only to be followed by an avalanche of other voices joining in: "Sellout! Sellout! *Sellout!*"

However, the loudest voice, soaring like an avenging angel over the chanting chorus, belonged to the person who had initiated the uproar—none other than associate professor of architectural history Kingsbury Duvallon.

Chapter Five

President Delaney glared in the direction of the acrimonious outburst led by a member of his own faculty, doggedly chose to ignore the hecklers, and continued to read from his prepared notes.

"We are also proud to announce that one of New Orleans's most respected architects, and an adjunct professor here for many years—Jonathan Poole—will have the honor to be named the first Grover Jeffries Professor of Historic Preservation, and—"

This accolade proved too much for the majority of students. Hisses spewed into the air like escaping steam. Corlis lightly tapped Virgil on the shoulder, signaling him to swivel the lens of his video camera from the podium to the auditorium.

"Sellout! Sellout!" the students continued to chant.

By this time King was on his feet, the sound of his deep voice ringing out in the hall.

"Before this university officially accepts this *tainted* donation," he thundered, "I would like to ask Mr. Jeffries one question!" The crowd instantly quieted as rows of faces turned to look expectantly at the speaker. "Is this endowment derived from the profits you made demolishin' historic buildings all over New Orleans, sir?"

His words hung in the air for all to consider. Grover Jeffries, however, neither flinched nor provided an answer to the question, but rather stared stonily toward the rear of the auditorium.

President Delaney spoke up sharply. "Sit *down* and have the courtesy to allow me to—"

King ignored the demand and continued to address the developer in a scathing tone of voice. "I am speakin', Mr. Jeffries, of that half-built monstrosity, the Good Times Shoppin' Plaza. So, I ask you again, sir: Did the money you're givin' to endow this so-called Professorship of Historic Preservation come from the *profits* of your construction company . . . a company that has systematically laid waste to this city's treasured store of historic buildings?"

The color had drained from Grover Jeffries's face, only to be replaced by a flush of crimson that subsequently bloomed in his cheeks. Once again President Delaney barked from the podium, "I would ask you, Professor Duvallon, to *sit down* and be civil enough to allow me to continue!"

However, King advanced a few steps closer to the podium where the array of VIPs sat onstage, faces frozen. "I say to *all* of you," he declared, bristling with outrage, "that if you *think* this donation's gonna buy Mr. Jeffries, here, the right to bulldoze the rest of Canal Street to build his god-awful high-rises, then I suggest you consider the wishes not only of the preservation community but also of the poor people whose houses have been flattened to build that fatuous boondoggle of a megamall. A project that's in danger of bankrupting this town!"

"I am ordering you to *sit down*, Professor Duvallon!" President Delaney insisted, pounding on the podium with his fist.

King turned around and addressed the entire audience sitting behind him. "I charge that this is a most *cynical* attempt by Grover Jeffries and the downtown business interests represented by his henchman, Lafayette Marchand, over there," he added ferociously, pointing to the silver-haired public relations man standing on the sidelines, "to make it *appear* that Jeffries and his ilk are interested in historic preservation. He's tryin' to lull everybody into thinkin' he and his cronies are the *good* guys . . . and make us forget about the Good Times Shoppin' Plaza fiasco and the irreplaceable historic buildings he demolished! He thinks that as long as he *looks* like Mr. Philanthropist, paperin' over his past sins with dollar bills by gettin' this university chair named after him, lots of folks will forget about the *real* issues at stake in this city!"

"Where's Security?" Delaney shouted. "Get Campus Security!"

Meanwhile, King turned around again to confront the phalanx of dignitaries who were staring at him with various expressions of horror and dismay.

"And what truth is there to the rumors, Mr. Jeffries," King exclaimed loudly, "that your company has some *other* big ideas about tearin' down a lot more historic buildings along Canal Street? We all hear you've got some mighty big plans concernin' a twenty-eight-story *hotel* you'd like to construct on the site where there are a whole raft of buildings that have stood in the six-hundred block for a century and a half!"

The exit doors on both sides of the auditorium suddenly burst open, and a dozen campus security men, plus several members of the uniformed New Orleans Police Department, streamed into the hall. President Delaney glanced first at Grover Jeffries, who appeared near a fit of apoplexy, then pointed in King's direction. "Him!" was all he said.

Undeterred, King shouted to the audience, "Our sources warn us that already on the drawin' boards are a number of *other* mammoth projects for central New Orleans." He swiftly glanced to his right, where a wedge of officers was advancing toward him. "If we don't reject this offer of dirty money the university is accepting to offset their own red ink, then Grover Jeffries, Jonathan Poole, and Lafayette Marchand will *lay waste* to the historic landscape for at least another decade! We've got to *stop* them!"

Before King could open his mouth again, an officer barked to his uniformed companion, "Arrest this man for disturbin' the peace and trespassin' on private property!" The security guard reached for one of King's wrists. King ignored him and glared at President Delaney.

"I have a constitutional right of free speech and assembly!" he shouted. "I am a teacher of architectural history and historic preservation *at this university*! Acceptin' this money and namin' a professorship after Grover Jeffries, of all people, is an insult to—"

"Get him out of here!" Delaney yelled at the arresting officer. *"Now!"*

After this, pandemonium broke out. King was quickly hand-cuffed and hustled out the side door, surrounded by the campus police. While the camcorders whirred, the students and faculty in the audience were in an uproar, crowding into the aisles of the lecture hall and surging toward the stage, nearly engulfing President Delaney, the dean of the architecture school, and Grover Jeffries himself.

The sound of high-pitched whistles pierced the air as another brigade of campus police officers and NOPD's poured down the aisles of the auditorium, roughing up anyone who was unfortunate enough to be standing in their way. The CEO of Jeffries Industries cast a ferocious glare in the direction of Lafayette Marchand, as if to indicate that this entire fiasco was his fault.

Corlis shouted into Virgil's ear, "Are we still rolling?" When the camcraman nodded affirmatively, she exclaimed, "Then keep following Duvallon and get some good shots of them putting him in the squad car! I'll go see if I can nail an interview with Jeffries about his reaction to this ruckus. Meet you here in ten minutes, okay, champ?"

Virgil and Manny made a beeline for the side door. However, by the time Corlis turned back to the stage, President Delaney and his benefactor were just disappearing through an exit door that slammed shut with a bang.

Holy moly! Corlis thought, her heart pounding from the excitement. That King Duvallon is *something else!*

"Good job, McCullough," Andy Zamora said gruffly, nodding at one of a bank of television sets installed at the far end of his office at WJAZ.

Corlis leaned wearily against the door jamb, sensing the adrenaline draining from her body now that the mad dash to get her story on the evening news was finally over.

"Thanks," she said shortly. Then she asked, "Got a minute?"

"Sit." Zamora gestured toward a chair opposite his desk. "While I was on the air, a voice-mail message came in from the star of our little show today."

"No joke? King sure got out of jail fast."

"No, he *didn't*," Corlis said. "In fact, King wanted to know if I'd go up to Central Lockup and bail him out."

"And?"

"That's all he said," she replied, puzzled. "Now, why wouldn't he ask someone in his family to do a thing like that?"

The news director leaned back in his chair with a thoughtful expression.

"Well . . ." he considered slowly, "his sister, Daphne, is back up north, finishin' at Juilliard and layin' low, after her weddin' blew up. His favorite aunt Bethany, doesn't drive. His grandmother, Mrs. Kingsbury, is eighty-five, and slightly gaga. And I've heard tell that King's never been on the best of terms with his mama and daddy. Plus, I 'spect he wants to advance his cause with *us*. Get his story out through the media. He's obviously gonna fight this endowed professorship deal," Zamora concluded.

"Well, it's a great story, Andy. President Delaney calling in the campus cops and the NOPD to arrest a member of his own faculty is bound to escalate the level of protest against Jeffries Industries, don't you agree?"

"Sure will." Zamora threw his pen down on his desk. "Okay, McCullough, I'll authorize you to bail Duvallon out of jail—but *only* if the bond is under three hundred dollars. And get a receipt. I'll call our company lawyer and get a judge to set his bond."

"Great," Corlis promised, standing up.

"But fork over the money *only* if King'll talk—for the record—*on* camera."

"Just getting him to talk *off* the record about being manhandled by the cops at the behest of his own university should certainly help us advance the story."

Zamora shook his head firmly. "He's gotta talk *for* the record—*on* camera," he repeated sternly. "And the interview's got to be exclusive to WJAZ. We air it, and *then* he can talk to the other stations if he wants to. Tell him that's the deal. Otherwise, keep your pocketbook zippered with your WJAZ money *inside*, do you understand?" Corlis nodded her agreement. "Do you think he'll do it?" he asked. "Talk on camera, I mean?"

"Oh, he'll talk," she assured her boss breezily.

However, Corlis was not at all certain that King would speak on the record. But if he declined her request for an on-camera interview, she had an alternative plan: She'd bail him out of jail on her own nickel and get him to talk *off* the record, just for background and not for attribution. Corlis reckoned he must be a fountain of information on the byzantine political scene in New Orleans—and she was determined not to fall into any bear traps again covering *this* story!

Corlis smiled jauntily at her boss and headed for the door, humming under her breath, "It ain't necessarily so. . . ."

Once outside the nondescript brick building that housed WJAZ, she walked toward her Lexus, which she had unceremoniously parked adjacent to a Dumpster overflowing with fast-food remnants and empty bottles of Dixie. She swiftly flipped on the air-conditioning and waited for the car's interior to feel less like a convection oven, musing that she'd been too Californian and too shell-shocked when Jay fired her in L.A. to give up her status-symbol luxury car. Now she'd give anything to own a vehicle whose payments didn't rival the mortgage on her New Orleans apartment!

She shifted the car into gear and nosed out of her parking space. With a growing sense of excitement, she began to consider the elements of this classic David-and-Goliath story: a wrangle between a fearless professor of historic preservation and a pugnacious developer. She figured there was probably a lot more to the recent altercation than had been revealed publicly, especially if Grover Jeffries had his beady little eyes set on tearing down more historic buildings along Canal Street in order to build a high-rise hotel. A huge project like that might provide jobs and publicity that would be irresistible to the local politicians.

Yep, she thought, joining the stream of rush-hour traffic heading out of the city, the controversy had "juice." And it didn't take a rocket scientist to predict that King Duvallon was in for the fight of his life.

"City of New Orleans . . . central jail . . . how may I direct your call?" said the voice on the other end of Corlis's cell phone.

She leaned against her car's sumptuous leather headrest. The loan payments might be killing her, she considered briefly, but a Lexus certainly provided her a comfy traveling office.

"My name's Corlis McCullough, from WJAZ-TV," she explained to the operator as she sped up the ramp to I-10. "I received a phone page from this number."

"Oh! Hi, Corlis!" the operator exclaimed with easy familiarity. "I see you all the time on TV! Imagine! Now I'm talking to you *in* person!"

"Hi there," Corlis said, trying to sound gracious despite her constant amazement that the viewing public considered people they saw on the tube their old friends. "By any chance, can I speak to a prisoner? He called me about an hour ago. His name is Kingsbury Duvallon."

"Oh . . . Professor Duvallon!" the woman said in an admiring tone of voice. "We don't get many prisoners in here like *him*, I can tell you that! Is he a friend of yours?" she asked wistfully.

"Well . . . kind of," Corlis replied, feeling awkward to be answering the woman truthfully. "I covered the big uproar at the university today. I think Professor Duvallon is calling me about that."

"I'm real sorry, sugar, but I'm afraid he can't come to the phone. The prisoners are havin' supper. A judge just set his bond, though," she added helpfully.

Corlis thanked the operator and was about to hang up when she blurted, "Can you get word to him that his message got through to me? Tell him I'm coming down to the jail?"

The operator's voice sounded muffled, as if she'd put her hand over the telephone mouthpiece for privacy's sake.

"I will if I can . . . or get somebody else to, okay, sugar?" A brief pause ensued. Then the operator asked, "Can you get me a WJAZ T-shirt, or one of them cute rain ponchos I've seen you wearin'?"

"Will do," Corlis agreed instantly. "Leave me a voice mail at the station with your home address . . . and thanks for telling Professor Duvallon I'm on my way. You've been very nice." Then she pushed the END button on her cell phone and stared out her windshield at the bumper-to-bumper traffic, lost in thought.

Kingsbury Duvallon was still in jail. He'd decided to call WJAZ and asked for her. What a lucky break! Or was it?

For the better part of a half hour, Corlis fought evening rush-hour traffic all the way up I-10, exiting to Broad and Tulane Avenues. Just before six-thirty, she parked beside a deserted curb in the city complex that included the criminal district court, police headquarters, and Central Lockup.

While securing her car door, she gazed across the street at the gray, cinder-block construction that housed the jail. What a perfect architectural example of form following function, she thought grimly.

Postmodern brutal.

The building was so sterile and devoid of ornamentation that it looked as if it could also have served just as well as an auto body shop. Once inside, Corlis concluded that the linoleum floor and turquoise plastic seats were the lobby's most attractive features. A window with a large BAIL BONDS—PAY HERE sign beckoned. She approached a barrel-chested clerk and inquired about the process of springing Associate Professor Kingsbury Duvallon out of the clink.

"Judge Bouchet says that'll cost you three hundred dollars to get him released, ma'am," the clerk announced. "You pay in cash, traveler's checks, or a Western Union money order."

"Right. Got it," Corlis replied, digging into the zippered compartment of her leather shoulder bag for the cash that WJAZ issued its reporters, along with their pagers and cell phones, for precisely these sorts of emergencies. She'd pay the money first and find out afterward if King would agree to an interview. If he wouldn't go on camera, she'd simply have to reimburse the station.

Ten minutes later King emerged through a door that led from the holding tanks. A day's growth of beard shadowed his chiseled jaw. For a split second she imagined what he'd look like in a towel, shaving in front of a mirror, and was immediately chagrined by the power of such impure thoughts to stir her imagination.

The prisoner halted at the threshold, a pleased look spreading across his features.

"Hey! California! This is great. I got your message that you were comin' here, but I never thought you'd get here so fast!" He strode across the linoleum and enfolded her in a bear hug.

She was startled by this effusive display but allowed him to hold her in his arms for several seconds longer than necessary, merely because it felt so good. Then she took a step back and cocked her head to give him the once-over.

"Hi, jailbird," she drawled. "You owe me three hundred bucks." She lowered her voice and said in a stage whisper, "That is, unless you're willing to do an exclusive on-camera interview. Then it's on WJAZ."

"Ah . . . I see. You want me to tell your viewers all about the barbaric torture methods I endured in here, is that it?"

"Did you get roughed up?" she asked, taunting him lightly. She guessed from his hearty nature that nothing had happened. As a matter of fact, he looked handsomer than ever with a five o'clock shadow darkening his face.

Cut it out, McCullough. This is business, remember?

"Nobody roughed me up, but the food's lousy here. In New Orleans, *that's* news, I suppose."

"Look, King," Corlis said, "all I would like is for you just to give me some idea what it was like in there, and what you and your supporters intend to do next, now that you've thrown down the gauntlet. *Speaking* of which," she added swiftly, "how come none of your friends or a family member came to bail you out?"

"None of them had three hundred in cash handy, and besides, it's more fun havin' *you* do it, sweetheart," he shot back.

"Yeah . . . sure," she scoffed. "Let's not forget that the president of the university you *work* for has had you arrested and thrown in the brig, soldier. What's your response to all this? Are you going to resign?"

"Hell no!" he said, laughing. "Like some Yankee said up north, 'I've just begun to fight!' "

"So . . . will you say all this on camera?"

"Depends on what you ask me when the cameras are rollin'."

"Well, just so you know," she added apologetically, "it's your pal Andy Zamora's edict to offer you the bailout in exchange for an exclusive on-camera interview. If you talk to us first . . . after the piece airs on WJAZ, then you can tell your story to whomever you like."

"Don't worry . . . I'll give you an interview 'bout some of what you want to know," King replied obligingly, "but I'll also pay you back the bond money. They don't take American Express in this place," he joked, "and I didn't have that kind of cash on me when I was arrested."

"If you want to pay your own bond, that's totally up to you. It's WJAZ's nickel," Corlis said, shrugging.

"I wouldn't care if it were Grover Jeffries's nickel," he replied, looking at her steadily. "No special interests pay *my* way, and I'll talk to whomever I choose, whenever I choose, Mr. Z."

"I'm impressed," Corlis said in a slightly mocking tone, and, privately, she was. "But here's the deal about the interview," she persisted. "I need something substantive to get Zamora's attention. Can you advance the story any and let me air the interview before you talk to other reporters? Like, do you feel President Delaney's latest move is a strategy to shut you guys up and threaten your jobs?"

"As a matter of fact, I *do* have a few thoughts about that. I also have a great line about lyin' down in front of bulldozers, should Grover Jeffries decide to threaten to demolish any more historic buildin's in New Orleans. But first," he said, chucking her lightly under her chin, "you gotta feed me. Supper here was inedible."

"Food first. Then we talk?"

"You betcha."

He tucked his hand under her elbow in a courtly fashion, and added, "But first, do you mind if we swing by your place and let me take a shower?"

"*My* place!" she said with mild shock.

He rubbed the dark stubble on his jaw. "I feel—and probably smell—pretty ripe. And I'd just as soon not deal with certain members of my family who are bound to be callin' me all night, or layin' in wait for me at my place," King disclosed. "And there's another reason."

She reminded herself of Aunt Marge's number one edict: a reporter should never get palsy-walsy with a news source—and allowing King, naked, into her bathroom definitely fell into the even-the-appearance-of-intimacy category.

"Oh? What's that?"

"You live on Julia Street, correct?"

"You know that."

"Haven't you ever noticed who your neighbors are?"

"Yeah. Sort of," she replied, mystified by his line of questioning. "All those art and photographic galleries on my street . . . plus, I occasionally run into people going in and out of the row houses next to me—that is, on those few nights when I get home before dark."

"Ever run into anyone at 604 Julia Street, near the river end of that block?"

"King! You make me feel like I don't have a life! Okay . . . so, tell me . . . *who* lives at 604? Cindy Lou Mallory?" she quipped, and then could have bitten off her tongue.

"Hardly. She's your *Town and Country* Garden District type of girl. Seriously, Ace . . . haven't you ever noticed the discreet little sign that says 'The Preservation Resource Center of New Orleans'?"

"Oh? Yeah! Now that you mention it. I just never paid attention."

"Well . . . here's your chance. I need to check in there and find out about any late developments."

"Sounds good to me," Corlis replied, salving her conscience somewhat, since allowing King to take a shower at her house was merely in the line of duty. "Could we shoot the interview there . . . at 604? I'll call Virgil and Manny on my cell phone and get them over there in an hour."

"Tomorrow we shoot the interview," he countered firmly. "Tonight we eat and drink wine."

"And tomorrow you also show me the historic buildings on Canal Street you think Grover Jeffries has slated for demolition, agreed?"

"All *that* for merely bailin' me out of jail when I'm payin' you your money back?" he said with mock dismay. "You're one tough cookie, McCullough."

"No, I'm not. But do we have a deal?"

"Deal," he agreed. "Now get me outta here."

In the end, Corlis ran around the corner to the Hummingbird and picked up a big take-out order that included gumbo and corn bread while King made use of her shower and the pink plastic razor she used on her legs.

Arms full, she used her heel to close her own front door and was mildly unnerved by the way her breath caught when she heard King's deep baritone singing behind the closed bathroom door.

"Blue eyes . . . baby has blue eyes . . ." he warbled in a fair imitation of Elton John's classic melancholy love song. His loafers were parked beside the white upholstered chaise longue in her bedroom.

Corlis continued down the hallway, through her living room, and into the small kitchen, where she deposited the paper bags containing their dinner. As each minute passed, she became increasingly affected by King's masculine presence, which seemed to permeate every nook and cranny of her home. She heard the shower water turn off and, after a few minutes, the door to the bathroom open.

From the hallway she heard King chortle, "Well . . . hello again, big guy! You are by far the *largest* ol' tomcat I've ever seen. I *love* that orange fur! Come here, you . . ."

Corlis peered around the corner. King stood at the threshold of the bathroom with one of her big, fluffy white towels wrapped around his trim waist. The hefty feline looked up at him with a worshipful stare the likes of which Corlis had never witnessed in the animal's entire life.

And for good reason, too, Corlis thought, swallowing. King looked *great* in just a towel. Who needed Calvin Kleins?

"I . . . uh . . . I'm sorry if he's bothering you," she said. "He usually ignores everyone—especially me—so you should consider that adoring gaze a high compliment."

"What a specimen," King said, laughing as he bent down to rub Cagney's belly, which the cat had made completely accessible by flopping on his back and extending his four paws straight into the air. King appeared totally unselfconscious to be standing, nearly naked, in his former adversary's hallway.

"I don't believe this," Corlis murmured. "He's turned to putty in your hands."

After a moment King rose to his full height and said, "I'll just throw on my clothes. You must be famished, too. How's the gumbo?"

"Totally fabulous," she replied. "I'll go heat it up."

"Great. I'll be right out," he promised, and padded toward her bedroom with Cagney Cat trotting obsequiously in his wake. "Mind if I use your phone to let some folks know I've escaped prison?" King called over his shoulder.

"Sure . . . it's right beside the bed. Be my guest."

If he was steering clear of his family, she wondered who would he be calling.

No concern of yours, dearie. You're just covering a story, remember?

"Yeah, yeah, Aunt Marge . . . I hear you!" she muttered under her breath.

Chapter Six

March 9

In Corlis's bedroom, the telephone next to her massive four-poster bed rang before King could pick up the receiver to make his calls. By this time, however, Corlis was standing in her tiny kitchen on a step stool, attempting to retrieve a seldom-used soup tureen in which to serve their main course.

"Damn!" she muttered, holding the unwieldy piece of crockery in her arms. "King? Can *you* get that?" she called out.

She gingerly backed down the kitchen stool, speculating that Andy Zamora might be trying to get in touch to see whether or not she'd gotten King to agree to an interview. She set the large bowl gently in the sink to rinse off dust that had undoubtedly made the trip with her from California. She turned on the water full blast, swiftly soaped and rinsed the ceramic interior, and tipped it upside down, expecting to be summoned momentarily to the telephone. From the depths of her bedroom, she heard King chuckling. Tea towel in hand, she walked down the hallway toward the sound of male laughter.

She leaned against the door frame and whispered curiously, "Who *is* that?"

King, still wrapped in his bath towel, sat on the edge of her bed, grinning. He put his palm over the mouthpiece and said, "It's your aunt Marge. . . ."

"Aunt Marge—?"

King laughed again at something Corlis's great-aunt said, and nodded. "Yes, ma'am . . . I'll surely tell her to do that. Absolutely." He cupped his hand over the receiver again. "When I told her my name, she said she thinks you and I have some sort of a New Orleans connection, way back when, and she wants you to check it out," he disclosed with an amused look on his clean-shaven face.

On King's chest a nap of dark hair spread across an expanse of muscle groups harking back to his days as a U.S. marine. Now that she stood only two feet away from him, she concluded that the former soldier would have done his drill sergeant proud. Even ten years later Corporal Duvallon had a fabulous body, drat it!

"Now, why would Aunt Marge think that you and I were— "

"She found the name Duvallon in a diary written by an ancestor of yours who lived in New Orleans before the Civil War. Here," he offered, holding out the receiver. "She wants to tell you about it."

"R-Really?" Corlis stammered, reaching for the phone. "Aunt Marge? Is everything all right?"

"Fine, fine!" Marge McCullough said briskly. "Is that the Hero of New Orleans you e-mailed me about? The one you got the authorities to throw out of UCLA?"

"The very one," Corlis said, turning to face the wall so that King would have some privacy while he dressed. "I'm preparing for an interview with him tomorrow," she said by way of explaining the reason a man was answering her home phone after nine o'clock at night. "What's this about Corlis Bell's diary? "

For years Aunt Marge had referred to a journal, kept locked in a safe-deposit box, that the original Corlis—née Bell— McCullough had penned.

"Well, remember awhile back, you told me all about the disastrous Ebert-Duvallon wedding, and about that builder— Grover Jeffries, you said his name was? Didn't you tell me that he was the person who once tried to demolish your apartment on Julia Street to build some big old post office substation?"

"Yes," Corlis replied as strange, unsettling sensations began to flutter in her chest.

"Well, for the longest time, I kept thinking about what a terrible thing that would have been if that beautiful building of yours had been destroyed. Then I happened to be at the bank today, and suddenly the name Jeffries went dingdong in my head!"

All her life Corlis had never ceased to marvel at Marge's steel-trap memory, which was even more remarkable now, considering the woman was in her eighties.

"Don't tell me you found somebody named Jeffries in the diary?" she demanded apprehensively, recalling the strange scene—or whatever it was—of a man named Jeffries who, along with Corlis Bell and Randall McCullough, stood beside the corpse of somebody named Henri Girard.

"Yes!" Marge exclaimed excitedly. "I'd asked the people at the bank to get my safe-deposit box, and you'll never imagine what I found out! I couldn't wait for you to go check your e-mail . . . so I thought I'd just call you."

"Well . . . what did you find out?" Corlis inquired, acutely aware that, behind her, King had just zipped up his trousers and was donning his polo shirt.

"In the diary it mentions that there was an *Ian* Jeffries who went into business with Corlis's husband."

Ian Jeffries? Oh my Lord!

Corlis could feel her heart start to race.

"Are you sure the diary says Ian?" Corlis asked weakly.

"I'm looking right at it!" Marge insisted tartly. "He and Corlis's husband were involved in some sort of business venture there in New Orleans . . . sometime in the late eighteen-thirties or forties, from what I can determine. I've just sort of skimmed through it."

"That is . . . just . . . pretty . . . weird," Corlis said faintly.

"And here's something even stranger, considering who just answered your phone!" Aunt Marge said enthusiastically. "There was a banker named Duvallon that apparently was mixed up in the enterprise . . . as in *King* Duvallon!" Marge added with a note of triumph in her voice. "I asked that nice-sounding young man if his family had ever been in the banking business, and he said he thought maybe they were, but he'd look into it to know for sure."

Corlis heard King sit down on the end of the chaise longue across the bedroom and start to put on his shoes and socks. She didn't dare look at him. This woo-woo stuff was seriously starting to get to her!

"Amazing," was all she could manage, gripping the receiver with both hands.

"Well . . . as I said, the name Jeffries just kept ringing in my head," Marge reiterated. "May I remind you, dear, I was born in 1913. My great-grandmother was Susannah Buffington McCullough, the woman who had married Warren McCullough."

"You've lost me, Aunt Marge."

"Oh, *you* know! The little boy born on the Mississippi to Corlis Bell on their journey south from Pittsburgh? Well, I remember *her*—Granny Susannah—telling me that your namesake, who was, of course her mother-in-law—"

"Wait a sec!" Corlis interrupted. "Let me get this straight: Corlis Bell McCullough was *your* great-grandpa Warren's mother?"

"Right. His wife, my great-grandmother Susannah, was told by the original Corlis *herself* that the McCulloughs and the Jeffrieses were practically run out of New Orleans over some big scandal or something," she said, chuckling. "I do so love a juicy story!"

"Especially ones that involve family skeletons, right, Aunt Marge?" Corlis commented dryly.

"I hadn't read that diary in fifty years, and I'd forgotten some of the details. And also, isn't the *Duvallon*-McCullough connection astonishing?"

"To put it mildly," Corlis said, glancing over at King.

"I'll go dish out the food, okay?" he whispered.

Corlis nodded and allowed him to walk out of her bedroom before she said to her aunt, "And, the Jeffries-McCullough connection is pretty wild, too."

"Where'd that Grover Jeffries come from originally?" Marge inquired.

"Texas."

"Oh," the older woman sighed, sounding disappointed. Then she brightened. "Of course, the other Mr. Jeffries—Ian Jeffries—could have been run out of New Orleans *to* Texas, along with the McCulloughs, and this Grover Jeffries character is a descendant who moved *back* to Louisiana."

"Jeffries isn't a particularly unusual name. It's a long shot," Corlis concluded.

"Want me to have the diary photocopied and I'll send it to you?" Marge asked cheerfully. Then she paused when her niece didn't reply. "Or maybe you're too busy to indulge your old aunt in the family genealogy fetish?"

"Ah . . . no . . . of course not, Aunt Marge. I'm fascinated by this genealogy stuff. By all means, make me a copy and send it along."

Fascinated—and not a little spooked!

"Wonderful! I'll sign up to get the Elder Ride people to take me to the photocopy place when I can spare the time," Marge said, sounding pleased.

"Xerox away. I'd love to read the diary. By any chance," she asked warily, "did you come across the name of Corlis's husband?"

"She's none too complimentary about *him*!" Aunt Marge pronounced with a good deal of enjoyment. "Let me think a moment. . . ." There was a pause, and then Marge's voice rang breezily through the wire. "Here it is. His name is Randall. Randall McCullough."

"Oh, boy. . . ."

"What's that?" Marge asked.

Corlis leaned against her bedroom wall. She raised her free hand to her temples and began to rub the taut skin in a circular motion.

Just then an egg timer sounded on Marge's end, producing a loud ping in the background. The elder McCullough was a true Scotswoman, thrifty to the core.

"There's your timer, Aunt Marge," Corlis noted obediently. "Send me a copy of the diary, and we'll keep in touch by e-mail." She almost dreaded the possibility there might be hard evidence, like this family journal, that could back up her recent bizarre experiences. "Is your computer working all right for you?" she asked, changing the subject. "No trouble getting on-line?"

"Love it, love it, love it!" Marge replied with hearty enthusiasm. "I'm up to the point in my memoirs where Hearst gave me twenty-five cents in 1934, and sent me into downtown Los

Angeles to write a story about women living on skid row in the depths of the Depression."

"How long did you have to stay there?" Corlis asked, awestruck, as she always was when her great-aunt described her early career.

"A week," Marge replied blithely. Then she added unnecessarily, "The city streets weren't quite as mean as they are today, of course, and money went a lot further in those days, you know."

"I'll bet it did," Corlis said, again picturing the bills she had let pile up on her desk. "But even so, it's got to be a great story, Aunt Marge. Keep writing, okay? And you take care, y' hear?" she said in an approximation of King's southern drawl.

"And *you* enjoy your interview with Mr. Duvallon," Marge replied. Corlis could almost see her great-aunt wink at her phone receiver in her Westwood condominium, high atop Wilshire Boulevard. "He can't be as bad as you've made him out to be. Just remember, Corlis, fairness and accuracy are our primary missions as reporters. Love you, darling."

A classic exit line by Margery McCullough, she thought, replacing the receiver.

She left her bedroom, sniffing the air appreciatively. A wonderfully rich scent of exotic herbs and spices wafted from the front of the apartment. Smiling to herself, she set off down the hallway to investigate precisely what sort of folly an ex-marine could get into in her kitchen. Much to her pleasure, she found King dutifully reheating the gumbo on the top of her stove.

"Where'd you find that pan?" she marveled, silently recalling the charred saucepan she'd been forced to discard after she'd burned her oatmeal a couple of months back.

King pointed to the step stool and then to the top of her kitchen cabinets. "Tucked way, way up there. I take it Ms. McCullough doesn't do too much heavy-duty cookery?"

"As in *never*," she replied, "but you sure seem to know what you're doing." She peered over his shoulder and caught a fragrant whiff of the bubbling gumbo, a spicy concoction that contained a variety of shellfish, okra, chicken and/or sausage, depending on the mood of the chef at the Hummingbird.

"I ought to be able to reheat gumbo!" King laughed. "After all, I was a cook in the marines."

"You were a *cook*?" she exclaimed. "I'd have thought you'd have made officer before you were through."

"I'd just gotten thrown out of a prestigious university, remember?" King reminded her as he spooned steaming stew directly into two large bowls, ignoring her soup tureen. "I'd defied family tradition by goin' out west to school. After I was booted out, I didn't exactly have a file of glowin' recommendations, not to mention a diploma, to get into any officers candidate school."

"Why did you decide to go to college in California in the first place?" Corlis asked, ignoring his reference to being ejected from UCLA thanks to her.

"Let's just say my parents and I agreed we both needed a break," he explained shortly. "How 'bout you set the table in there?" King suggested, nodding in the direction of the living room, where a small dining table stood next to the wall opposite the fireplace. "I would have done it myself, but I didn't know where you kept your linens."

"My *linens*? Straw place mats are about it, Chef Duvallon," she replied, opening a drawer to retrieve silverware and the necessary implements for the dining table. With her booty in hand, she paused suddenly in the middle of the Persian carpet and turned to face King, who followed a few steps behind carrying the two filled soup bowls.

"I think I *did* overreact," she announced.

King halted his forward progress halfway across her living room.

"Place mats are fine," he assured her mildly. "You're a busy lady. Who has time to iron, right?"

"No!" she protested. "I mean about my getting you kicked out of UCLA and launching the petition drive to get your fraternity permanently banned from campus."

King gazed at her for a moment, then grinned.

"You *definitely* need to get somethin' into that stomach of yours, sugar," he declared, indicating with a nod that she should quickly set the table so he could unburden himself of the hot soup bowls.

"King!" Corlis objected, swiftly laying down the place mats and silverware. "Haven't you been waiting twelve years to hear this?"

"Since I never thought I *would*—no. I haven't been waitin'," he replied. Then he shot her a mischievous look. "But I do confess, it's mighty nice to hear those faintly apologetic words emanatin' from your luscious lips." Corlis felt her cheeks flush. "Thank you," he added before she could reply. "And if the truth be told, gettin' thrown out of UCLA was probably the best thing that ever happened to me."

"Oh, come on now," she chided. "Isn't that going a bit too far?"

"No . . . I'm serious," King insisted. "If I'd done everythin' just as my mama and daddy wanted me to, I'd be some nose-to-the-grindstone lawyer in an old-line firm housed in some godawful high-rise on upper Canal Street somewhere, and I'd be absolutely miserable! No, sugar," he said, pulling out a dining-room chair and indicating that she should sit down, "our little set-to twelve years ago put me on a much better path."

"How so?"

"When I got expelled, my parents cut me off without a cent," he explained, taking a seat to her left. "Not that they had much family money anymore, mind you, but I had to completely earn my own way after I got out of the marines." He took a bite of gumbo and continued, "While I was still in school, I started volunteering for various historic preservation groups around town. Those folks changed my life."

"I take it you decided early on not to become a lawyer," she said, spooning the hot gumbo into her mouth.

"I sometimes wish now that I had added those skills to my quiver," he said ruefully, "but no . . . I became fascinated with the history of the architecture in the South. It tells so much about the past . . . right there in wood, stone, and mortar."

It tells so much about the past. . . .

"It sure does," she agreed emphatically. Then she volunteered cautiously, "You won't believe it, but my aunt Marge found reference to an *Ian* Jeffries in the McCullough family diary. That's why she called me tonight."

King raised an eyebrow. "That *is* pretty amazing. And the name Duvallon was also mentioned, she told me," he said thoughtfully.

Corlis hesitated briefly before plunging ahead with a question that she'd been longing to ask all evening. "Have you ever had any . . . ah . . . untoward . . . experiences when you've worked with old buildings?"

"What do you mean 'untoward'?" he said, glancing up from his soup to stare at her intently.

"Well . . . ah . . . you know! Weird stuff . . . like . . . well, like—"

"You mean seein' ghosts, or hearin' things that go bump in the night?"

Corlis felt her jaw tighten. She honestly couldn't determine if his question meant he thought her a fool, or—worse yet—demented . . . or if he really wanted an answer.

"Well . . . sort of," she ventured. "More like having a sense of . . . well . . . of the *people* who once lived in a certain time, and . . . as if you could envision exactly how certain places must have looked in the early days . . ."

"Have you seen somethin', Ms. Reporter?" he asked quietly. Corlis kept her eyes glued to her bowl of uneaten gumbo as a silence lengthened between them. "Well, *have* you, sugar pie?"

"Have *you*?" she countered. "Ever?"

"Once. At least I think so."

"You *have*?" she asked, relieved. She was astonished that a former member of the U.S. Marine Corps would admit to such an un-macho thing. Then, to her horror, she suddenly felt her eyes growing moist.

"Corlis?" she heard King say, his voice filled with concern. "What's the matter, sweetheart?"

"Oh, thank God you *said* that," she whispered in a strangled voice.

"Called you sweetheart?" he asked, puzzled.

"No," she said, flushing again.

"Oh!" he grinned. "You mean what I said about once seeing somethin' I couldn't explain in an old house?"

"Yeah . . . the ghost thing," she said, surreptitiously wiping her eyes with her paper napkin. "Because I've truly wondered since the first day I saw you in New Orleans at your sister's wedding, if maybe . . . just maybe . . . I was starting to go stark, raving mad."

King abruptly stood up from the dining-room table and strode across the Persian carpet into Corlis's minuscule kitchen.

Jeez Louise, Corlis thought, *I hardly know the guy and now he must think I'm a loon!*

King removed the top to her bottled water jug and poured the liquid into a glass. The next moment he'd returned to her side and handed it to her.

"Here . . . drink this. You're white as a sheet."

"Like I've seen a ghost?" she replied with a rueful smile. She obediently took a sip, relieved that at least he hadn't branded her an out-and-out crazy woman. In fact, she was amazed to see an expression of genuine empathy play across his features.

"Well, *I* sure got the jitters when I thought I'd seen one."

"*You?* Where was that?" she demanded.

"One time, when I was still living with my folks at our family house on Orange Street, in the Lower Garden District. The place was built in 1842 by the Kingsburys, in the period when the Americans were trying to show off to the French—who'd excluded them from purchasing real estate in the Quarter—that they could build beautiful houses, too."

"And did you determine what it was you thought you saw?"

"Not really," King said, shaking his head. "It was just a strange sense I had of someone bein' in the parlor," he allowed. "I thought I saw a . . . kind of a *shade* glide by, reflected in a big mirror hangin' over a chest of drawers." King picked up his spoon once again and commenced eating a mouthful of gumbo. "The family lore has it that some early family member supposedly put a bullet in his head for reasons that have been lost over time. There's always been talk that his ghost hangs around the liquor cabinet in the parlor, hopin' to get a handout!"

Corlis couldn't help laughing, relieved that King was speaking so candidly.

"Did you pour him a mint julep?"

"Now, *that* would have been a good idea," he said, smiling. He shrugged. "People who work with old buildin's experience this sort of thing all the time."

"Truly?" she said. "We're beginning to sound just like those weirdos on *Unsolved Mysteries*!"

"Well . . . what did *you* see?" King asked matter-of-factly.

Corlis heaved a sigh and shook her head.

"Look," she temporized, hesitating. "I was under a lot of

stress last year . . . and I get terrible headaches if I go too long without eating. Maybe I just—"

"What did you *see*?" he repeated gently.

"I—I'll tell you about it sometime," Corlis said, feeling untethered and prone to weeping for some strange reason.

"You said you've been under stress," he noted. "You mean, changin' jobs, leavin' your family . . . and makin' such a big move across the country?"

"Well . . . that . . ." she admitted, "and . . ." She paused briefly, then plunged ahead. "I called off a wedding last year, just like your sister, Daphne."

"You did?"

"Yes . . . only it wasn't quite such a last-minute thing," she said with a little laugh, though his startlingly blue eyes were boring into hers. "The invitations had stamps on them, but thank God, they hadn't been mailed. Then I did a geographical."

"A geographical? You mean, move here?" She nodded affirmatively. "I'd call that stressful, all right." Then he asked, "How'd the groom take it?"

"To tell you the truth, I think the son of a gun was relieved."

"Why do you say that?"

"Because Jay Kerlin and I worked together and our television ratings were slipping. The media and marketing consultants sent out from New York strongly recommended that he hire a va-va-voom blonde to anchor the six o'clock news, instead of me."

"Ouch," King said, setting his spoon down and listening intently.

"Two months before the wedding," Corlis related with a rueful expression, "Jay started getting pressured to demote me back to general assignment reporter—or they'd have *his* head as well. Then I found out he'd lied to me." She toyed with her spoon, making circles on the surface of the rich gumbo, laughing shortly. "Turns out he'd been married three times before. He just forgot to mention *two* of his ex-wives. But then, to be fair, marrying me would have been a dumb career move."

"What a wonderful business you're in," King commented.

"No kidding." She was faintly embarrassed to have revealed so much personal information to her old enemy. "So, you can see . . . with this woo-woo stuff on top of everything, I guess I need a bit longer to process it. Can you understand that?" she said, her voice tight with an emotion she didn't quite understand but felt compelled to hold fiercely in check.

"Sure," he replied quietly. "Sounds like you've had quite a year. We both have." Then he reached across the table and touched her hand—a gesture that sent an amazing jolt up her arm. "Look, Corlis . . . who knows if these kinds of paranormal experiences are real? If it makes you feel any better about this woo-woo stuff, as you call it," King reassured her kindly, "real estate agents deal with this phenomenon a lot in a place as old as New Orleans. I even know a guy . . . a Jesuit who left the priesthood and took up sellin' houses. Well, he gets called on all the time to do space clearin's whenever somethin' strange comes up."

"Space clearings?" She was acutely aware that King's hand remained on the dining-room table, an inch away from hers. "You mean like exorcisms?"

"Sort of . . ." King said, nodding and taking a sip of water. "Nothing as dramatic as that movie . . . but I've had a couple friends of mine call him in when they bought old places that they were gonna to fix up, and then had bizarre things start to happen."

"And what does this 'space clearer' *do*?" she asked, amazed that two perfectly sane people were having this sort of a conversation. "Has he hung out a shingle as a New Orleans ghostbuster?"

"Dylan? Oh no. It's done very much on the hush-hush. Like I said, he just comes over and clears the space."

"Of *what*?" Corlis persisted. "*How*?"

" 'Entities,' he calls them. Meditates at the site. Says prayers . . . lights white candles . . . burns small bundles of herbs to purify the atmosphere—that sort of thing."

"Sounds very Californian," Corlis noted archly.

"Space clearin' started long before the New Age was declared out west, darlin' girl," King chided her. "It's an ancient Chinese custom . . . you know . . . feng shui?"

"Is that the stuff where the Chinese orient hearth and home to face certain directions they think are lucky?"

"Somethin' like that," King confirmed with a grin. "It also

has to do with gettin' rid of evil spirits, or bad vibes—or whatever you want to call 'em. It's a practice that's been around for thousands of years."

She was fascinated by King's knowledge. "Besides the . . . entities, what else is he clearing out?"

"He clears places of any negative energies that can flow from the buildin' itself . . . or the land it sits on, and even from artifacts, like an old sword, or a piece of antique jewelry—anything that was around when unhappy events or trauma occurred." King cocked his head at an angle. "Haven't you ever had the experience of walkin' into a place and wantin' immediately to turn around and get the hell out of there?"

"Sure," Corlis nodded. "Bad vibes." Her thoughts went immediately to the closed, oppressive parlor on Royal Street with the corpse of Henri Girard lying still and sinister in its coffin. And then, of course, there was the evening just before she got fired. "Do *I* know about bad vibes," she declared ironically. "One night I arrived unannounced at Jay's apartment in the Hollywood Hills to confront him about having those three ex-wives, and guess what?" she asked rhetorically. "There was Miss Sunny, the blond weather girl, wearing a filmy peignoir and being served a romantic candlelight dinner on a dining table that Jay and I had bought together for our new home! I, of course, gave him what-for and broke off our engagement, right then and there. You could have lit a fluorescent bulb with the negative vibes flying around that room!"

King scrutinized her closely and then said, "Wow. What a guy."

"What a guy," Corlis concurred.

"You know, maybe you should meet Dylan sometime . . . and ask him about space clearin' yourself. He's a hell of a nice man and has some amazin' stories about the situations he's been called in on to consult."

"So you think he's really legit?" Corlis asked.

"You mean . . . is Dylan sane? Not a crazy?"

"Not a con artist?" she declared skeptically. "A lot of people who say they're mediums or claim to have occult powers are charlatans, out for people's money."

"The guy was formerly in the *priesthood*," King explained

patiently. "He's completely sincere. But who knows if any of this stuff has merit? *You're* the one who's seein' things, remember?" He leaned toward her with a mischievous leer. "Now, why don't you tell Dr. Duvallon exactly what's been botherin' you, my dear? Where have you seen spirits flittin' about?" He glanced around her living room. "This place is pretty old. Gotta have a lot of stuff lurking in the shadows," he added in sepulchral tones.

"King!" Corlis said with a shaky laugh. "As I said before, it's probably just my bad habit of working long hours and not eating regularly." She gave him a sidelong glance. "But I wouldn't mind meeting this guy. Might make a good story for WJAZ . . . a real estate agent that doubles as a ghostbuster. What's his name again? Dylan . . . what?"

"Dylan Fouché," King replied, "and I'd appreciate it if you didn't make a complete mockery out of him," he added lightly. "He's a friend."

She protested, stung by his accusation. "I would never fry a source if what they told me was off the record!"

King gazed at her from across the dining table and said quietly, "No, I don't think you would, Ace. Well, anyway, one of Dylan's ancestors founded an order of African-American nuns in New Orleans. The Fouchés are a very traditional black-Catholic family in these parts. Somebody in nearly every generation joined a religious community."

"Why did he leave the priesthood?"

"When you meet him, you'll see that Dylan marches to a *very* different drummer," King shrugged. "The priesthood wasn't the right fit for him, but he's a tremendously decent fellow—and a first-rate real estate agent. He's a huge supporter of the Live in a Landmark program where people who fix up derelict historic houses get some tax breaks."

"I'd really like to be introduced to him sometime, and you have my word, King, I won't do anything to publicly ridicule his work as a . . . space clearer. I'd just like to talk to him. Could you arrange it?"

King glanced at his watch and stood up from the dining table.

"Piece a cake," he said. "Let me help you with these dishes, and then, do you want to go with me to the Preservation

Resource Center down the street? I need to check in, and we can decide on a good spot to shoot the interview there tomorrow—after I show up in court at nine and get a stern verbal warnin' from Judge Bouchet."

"You seem pretty sure of all that," she said suspiciously.

"This is New Orleans, darlin', " he said, poker-faced.

"Is Judge Bouchet some cousin on your mama's side?"

"Close. My paternal grandmother's brother-in-law."

"How did I know that?" she asked rhetorically.

As they quickly tidied up the kitchen, Corlis found herself surprised by the odd sensations she experienced merely standing next to King at the sink. They were only inches apart, and suddenly she had a fantasy of using her dish towel as a lasso and pulling that long, lean body toward her to feel its comforting length pressed against her own—as it had been when he'd greeted her with a big hug at Central Lockup earlier.

Whoa, McCullough! The guy was merely saying hello. The next move on your part is not jumping on his bones! He's a news source, remember?

"I'll just let the rest of these dry on the drain board," she said abruptly, hanging her dish towel on a nearby hook.

Five minutes later, they walked down the block, halting at an overhead fanlight window mounted above a white Georgian door. King held it open for her as she entered a modernized interior of a building that had been constructed two decades before the Civil War. In the main room, stripped-brick walls and track lighting provided a cheerful work space where a few late-night stalwarts hovered around a computer.

After introductions were made all around, King's teaching assistant, Christopher Calvert, beckoned to them. "Hey, you're not going to believe what Grover Jeffries filed with the City Planning Commission this afternoon," he said.

"Let me guess," King said, furrowing his brow in a study of mock contemplation. "He's applied for an order to demolish."

"What else is new?" Chris said, shrugging. "Can you guess what for?"

"The Selwyn buildings on Canal."

"Right," Chris confirmed with a gleam of admiration in his eyes.

"And he wants a zonin' change to nullify the historic district designations for the block he wants to develop."

"You got it. Can you tell me what he intends to build on that site?" Chris asked.

By this time others in the office had ceased their chatter and were listening intently.

"Our Grover Jeffries wants a use permit to put up a twenty- or thirty-story hotel."

"Okay, Professor . . . tell me something else. How did you *know* the specifics of all that?" Chris demanded while the others emphatically nodded their heads.

"The Boston Club," King revealed coolly. "Why do you think I keep my membership current in a place where everybody prides himself on havin' ancestors who were in New Orleans when it was a genuine swamp? Believe it or not, I heard about this proposal in the men's room two weeks ago," he disclosed, smiling with bitter irony, "but I was hopin' it was just talk. A company called the Del Mar Corporation wants to team up with Jeffries because they think he's got city government wired. They're apparently bettin' that he can ram the project through, despite its sittin' smack-dab in the middle of a designated historic district." King squinted at the computer screen. "What I *didn't* know was that Jeffries Industries would move so fast on this project."

"No wonder ol' Grover wanted that eight-hundred-fifty-thousand-dollar gift to the university announced this week," Chris Calvert said angrily. "With something like this, he's gonna *need* some good friends downtown."

King shot a glance in Corlis's direction that said, *Get it, now?*

"And no wonder the powers that be wanted to throw me in jail and harass the rest of you," King noted dryly.

Chris said, shaking his head, "You know, from what we've been hearing around town today, Grover Jeffries has put on about as much pressure as you can to try to get this thing jammed through fast."

"Wait a minute, wait a minute," King cautioned soothingly. "We don't know what role the Selwyn family plays in all this. After all, they've been in New Orleans a very long time and have owned those buildings for more than thirty years. Remember, *they* have to agree to the Del Mar Corporation's little schemes."

"The Selwyns have already sold the property," Chris announced, pointing to the screen.

"To whom!" King exclaimed. Corlis leaned forward to have a look.

"Ah . . . *finally* a piece of information you *don't* know!" Chris exclaimed. "The entire block has been sold recently to some entity held offshore, or in Delaware, or someplace. We haven't been able to track it yet."

"The sale's already a done deal?" King demanded, making no effort to hide his dismay. Corlis was yearning to jot down what she was hearing, but she chose, instead, to concentrate so she could remember everything later.

Be a fly on the wall! That's when being a reporter is the most fun . . .

Aunt Marge was always right about such things, Corlis thought. If she began taking notes, King and the others would start to censor themselves.

"Sure looks like the Selwyn sale's gone through," Chris confirmed.

"I wonder if the Del Mar group bought out the Selwyn family by makin' them an offer they couldn't refuse," King mused.

"Possibly," Chris said, nodding. "And even if we succeed in slowin' this project down, King, I wouldn't be surprised if suddenly we have an unexplained three A.M. fire in the six hundred block of Canal. This is a huge project. Millions of dollars involved. *Lots* of jobs at stake."

Corlis observed the steely look of determination in King Duvallon's eyes.

"At the risk of soundin' a tad dramatic—and I only speak for myself, mind you," King announced, glancing at his colleagues in the room, "but I swear to y'all, I will lie down in front of the damned bulldozers and get hit by the wreckin' ball *right* between my eyes before I'll let those buildings on Canal Street become a pile of rubble."

Chapter Seven

March 10

Virgil pointed his television camera lens in the direction of a row of three-story buildings facing Canal Street. The facade was a roof-to-sidewalk expanse of dingy, weather-beaten woven aluminum that stretched nearly a city block.

"This is *it*?" Corlis asked, unable to conceal her disappointment.

"That's right," King nodded.

A big metal *S*, denoting that a family named Selwyn once owned the buildings, loomed overhead at the entrance to the ugly structure.

"*These* are the next batch of buildings the preservation crowd want to save?" she asked, incredulous. "Didn't this style of architecture go out with sweatbands and tie-dyed T-shirts?" she demanded, silently recalling a wedding picture of her parents taken in 1961, in a field, on the edge of a cliff that overlooked the Pacific Ocean. In the photo her mother's skimpy dress and her father's short-sleeved shirt sported matching appliquéd sunflowers. To Corlis's way of thinking, the outdated style of the Selwyn buildings was equally tasteless and, like her parents' marriage that had ended bitterly, deserved to be forgotten.

Corlis glanced at her watch. She was feeling pressured to dispatch her crew to their late lunch break following a long morning of work. Today's skipped meal was typical; there just hadn't been time to grab a bite anywhere en route. Earlier, in front of the half-completed Good Times Shopping Plaza, she and the crew had interviewed King about his earlier arrest. He had, indeed, been fresh from his municipal court appearance, where, as predicted, he'd gotten off merely with a stern warning from Judge Bouchet. Immediately the foursome embarked on a tour of the abandoned hulk, located a few blocks from the river.

Before they entered the unfinished structure, King handed Corlis an unmarked envelope.

"For you," he said.

"What is it?" she asked.

"WJAZ's bail money. I got it back this mornin', so . . . *you* get it back."

She smiled at him and said, "Man of your word. Thanks."

"Thank *you*, sugar," he replied.

Corlis rolled her eyes heavenward and shook her head in silent resignation. King cast an amused glance at Manny and Virgil, who were looking on with unabashed curiosity. "Oh," he said solemnly. "Sorry 'bout that 'sugar' thing."

Later, when her crew had wandered off to shoot "B" roll background shots, King led Corlis inside the bankrupted megamall project. She noticed King pause and stare in silence at a section of a vast wall that flanked Tchoupitoulas Street.

"What are you looking at?"

"The house of a friend of mine once stood here." He balled his hand into a fist and struck his padded flesh with force against the new building's wall made of poured concrete. "Right *here*!"

"Who was it?"

"The nicest ol' lady you'd ever want to know," he said, his voice tight. "In fact, I call her my black mother. She cooked and cleaned for my grandmother for more than thirty years."

"And *this* was the exact spot where her house stood?" Corlis asked, touched by an intense sadness.

"Emelie's family'd lived for generations here in a little Creole cottage. In less than five minutes, the whole thing was a pile of rubble. She ended up warehoused at her son's place, upriver, in a room that used to be the laundry porch."

"God . . . that's awful!"

A few minutes later their group had exited the looming, half-finished structure. King's mood soon improved. They'd strolled up Canal Street in the direction of the Selwyn buildings and the woven aluminum facade. By this time Corlis was gazing at the unsightly structure, shaking her head.

"This block doesn't do a thing for you, huh?" King asked with a faint smile.

"No!" Corlis declared bluntly, pointing at the rusted screen that soared three stories over their heads. "I don't get it, King. Why get all upset about demolishing a place like this? Let's face it . . . a lot of folks, including *me*, would call this a major eyesore."

"Oh, ye of little faith," he admonished, shaking his head in mock disgust. "C'mon . . . let me show you somethin'."

"You guys can take off," she directed her crew, "and I'll meet you back at the station by four o'clock."

In her opinion, there *was* no story here, and she wondered silently how King's passion for saving buildings could extend to this monstrosity.

"Now, just cool your jets, California," King urged. He bid the crew farewell and led the way toward the glass and metal-edged revolving doors, also part of the 1960s-era makeover. He halted before entering the building and dug into his briefcase, pulling out a large flashlight. "Stand right here." He placed his free hand on her shoulder while pointing his light and shone it between the three-story-high woven screen and a series of older brick and stone structures to which the screen was attached. "Now, look straight up there . . ." he directed, waving the beam of light on two feet of airy space that divided the original buildings from the aluminum facade.

"Look *where*?" she demanded, craning her neck.

"Right *there*," he replied. "Can you see? Those are the buildings' original Doric columns . . . fifty-four of 'em, I think . . . supportin' the second story above them."

Corlis squinted. "Oh . . . wow . . ." An impressive row of fluted columns holding up a stately arcade marched all the way down the block—behind the aluminum screen—as far as she could see. "They're *beautiful*!"

King waved his flashlight higher above their heads. "This stupid screen that the Selwyns erected to 'modernize' the place in the sixties casts the upper floors into really deep shadow, but you can get a glimpse of the original windows with their granite lintels. These eleven buildin's were once part of a complex of *twenty-three* row houses, with commercial shops on the bottom floors and livin' quarters on top. The entire structure was built in 1840 to look kinda like a Greek temple." Excitement tinged his voice. "Sadly, over the last one hundred and sixty years, twelve row houses have already been demolished."

"What were the shops downstairs used for originally?" she asked, awestruck that this phenomenal beauty had been disguised so long.

"They started out as a commercial center for cotton and sugar merchants," King explained. "We know that there were also tailors and women's hat shops and even a saddlery in here . . . with rather elegant livin' spaces built above on the third and attic floors."

"They're just gorgeous," Corlis murmured, reaching between the multistory screen and the building to touch a granite column. "It's almost as if all this aluminum, hideous-looking as it is, kept them *protected* from the elements for decades. Look how smooth and unpitted the stonework is!"

"Exactly!" He lowered his flashlight and smiled benignly at Corlis, adding, "There's a lot more research to be done to find out who built 'em."

"And now they're on Grover's hit list?" she murmured. "What a crime."

"Most people *don't know* what beauty exists behind this aluminum screen. My guess is Grover wants to move fast before anyone figures it all out, and Lafayette Marchand is helpin' to smooth the way, the son of a bitch! The two of them have been busy settin' the stage for twenty or thirty stories of steel and glass to replace what's been sittin' on this land for a century and a half."

For a moment Corlis chewed her lower lip in thought, then asked, "What do you think the chances are of finding a few direct *descendants* of the original owners who might still be living here in New Orleans?"

"Well . . ." King considered slowly, "you could look in the files at the city's buildin' department. They go pretty far back, and maybe you could find the names of the people who were the drivin' forces behind constructin' the place, back in 1840. You could also check out the earliest deeds for the property to see who's listed as the first owners."

"All that stuff's public record, isn't it?" she said enthusiastically. An idea had begun to form in her mind that would be more intriguing to WJAZ's viewers than the usual one-minute-fifteen-second takeout about another bunch of buildings threatened by the wrecker's ball. "What are the buildings like inside?"

"Want to have a quick look?" he inquired, glancing at his watch. "Unfortunately, I've got to be at a meetin' at the Preservation Resource Center in half an hour, but I can at least give you a sense of what the interiors looked like in the old days."

He gave a push to the revolving glass door and followed her inside to a small, dingy lobby. Shabby ceramic tile lined the walls and ceiling, an interior feature that must have been installed about the same time as the homely metal exterior.

"The place looks pretty deserted," Corlis noted, her voice echoing throughout the lobby as they walked along.

"A lot of the businesses housed in this block closed down. One or two ambulance-chasin' lawyers and a few accountants still lease the upper floors."

King placed his hand lightly under her elbow and guided her to his left and through a fire door. Instantly she was transported into another era. A long, dimly lit corridor met her gaze, flanked by waist-high wooden wainscoting that ran the length of the hallway. Door frames on both sides were decorated with wood-carved medallions studding each corner. Paint the color of lemon curd curled from most wall surfaces, and the single lightbulb hanging from a broken fixture overhead cast eerie shadows in their path.

"This wing is completely abandoned now," he said. "Fortunately, this particular section still retains much of its original construction and ornamentation."

Suddenly the sound of a telephone ringing startled them both.

"Oh, heck . . . is that *me*?" she asked, fumbling in her purse for her cell phone.

"No, it's my mobile, I think," King said as he rummaged inside his bulging leather briefcase. "Hello?" He shook his head. "The static's terrible! Hold on a sec, will you?" He apologized to Corlis, " 'Scuse me, sugar. I'll just step out into the lobby and see who this is. Be right back, okay?"

Well, there goes lunch, Corlis thought wistfully, resigned that King wasn't likely to break himself any time soon from his habit of calling everyone of the female persuasion "sugar." She silently concluded she'd simply have to grab her customary doughnut and coffee before she went to edit the story Virgil had shot earlier that day. Walking farther down the hallway, she ignored her incipient headache, which was verging on something more serious.

King's steps faded in the distance as Corlis absently ran her fingertips over a carved wooden door on her right, leaving her hand covered in dust. When she cracked the door open a couple of inches, a sudden cool draft of air raised the hairs on the back of her arm. Inside she discovered an anteroom with curtainless windows where a small rusted heater stood in a corner, along with an old lead-lined sink and sideboard. Beyond she caught sight of an arched entrance, swathed in darkness. The dank and dismal place might have been, most recently, an old laundry room or perhaps a photographer's darkroom, she speculated. Slowly she advanced toward the archway. Peering through the gloom, she could see a shadowed stairwell against the wall on her right that led to a second story. In the air Corlis could swear she smelled a faint aroma of natural gas.

"This old place is probably a death trap," she muttered, turning to leave.

Then she glanced toward the landing, conscious that her head had begun to ache in earnest, a sure signal she should eat something. She dug into her handbag, hoping for a chocolate bar. No luck.

Suddenly she was startled by the sound of angry voices. The words that floated toward her were indistinguishable, but loud enough to let her know an argument had started.

Curious, she took another step toward the archway that led into the second room. Her eyes slowly became accustomed to the light, as if someone had mysteriously turned up a dimmer switch. In the anteroom the sink and heater had vanished, and in their place a small brocade love seat stood against one wall, illuminated by a two-tiered gas chandelier. Corlis stared at the ceiling, mesmerized by the lighting fixture's faceted glass icicles, winking overhead.

Gaslight?

She walked through the archway into the larger space that was sparsely but elegantly furnished. A silver tray filled with calling cards stood on a mahogany piecrust table. Whereas a moment before the windows in both rooms had been bare, now midnight-blue velvet curtains etched with gold braid and tassels cascaded in graceful folds down the wall. The carved oak stairs were carpeted in a rich floral pattern, while the surface of the walls fairly pulsed with paint the color of cinnabar, accented by white wooden moldings and trim.

She mounted the first few stairs and felt a familiar pounding in her chest. The railing felt solid beneath her hand, and the sound of voices could distinctly be heard from behind a closed door at the top of the landing. Corlis felt herself drawn to the top of the stairs. . . .

The closer Corlis Bell McCullough came to the second-floor landing, the more the May heat intensified. Her instincts were to flee back down the stairs and out into the sultry air blanketing Canal Street. However, spellbound by the sound of a ferocious female voice shouting from behind the paneled door, she remained paralyzed on the landing.

"Julien LaCroix! Stop this at once!"

Next she heard the sound of some object being thrown against a wall.

"Damn you both!" shouted a male voice in reply.

"Julien!" The woman's voice went up a notch. "I simply cannot permit this! Control yourself! It is outrageous that you should barge in like this . . . especially *now*!"

"I suppose you expect me to leave my callin' card, like Etienne —or Henri Girard—once did?" The man's words were laced with both fury and the pain of betrayal. "I am the *father* of this infant son, Althea Fouché, and I demand to hear from Martine's own lips how she could have kept from me knowledge of my family's involvement!"

"Julien . . ." another voice, soft and pleading, protested weakly. "You are no gentleman to be behaving this way. You must go at once." Then, in a husky, conciliatory tone, the woman added, "We will talk when I have regained my strength. I promise you. Return in two days' time and I shall——"

"You shall do *what*?" he shouted. "Erase all that has happened? Mend what cannot be mended? Martine, you two have *lied* and *cheated* and *deceived* us all! I suppose you were in league with Randall McCullough and Ian Jeffries all along, weren't you?"

"Never!" Althea exclaimed.

"Well, believe me, those two blackguards will be run out of New Orleans forever, if I don't kill them first!" Julien threatened savagely. "And your daughter, Lisette, will never forgive you when she learns of your treachery!"

Corlis Bell McCullough inhaled swiftly and stepped deeper into the shadows on the landing.

"Lisette will understand that what was done was done for her future and her brother's future!" countered the woman whom the man had addressed as Althea. "The McCulloughs were in league with you and Ian Jeffries to wrest this land from Martine, and all the while, you protested your love for her!"

"I did love her! I *do* love you, Martine," the man cried in anguish, "but you never revealed the truth about Henri and my father! And you never told me that André Duvallon——"

"All you really wanted was the deed to the Canal Street property," interrupted Althea. "My daughter may not be bold enough to say it, but I shall! You've behaved like a cad!"

"Julien?" asked the softer voice identified as Martine. "What could you expect me to do under the circumstances?"

Before Corlis could duly consider what was being said about her husband and Ian, the door across from where she stood in the shadows was yanked open. She swiftly retreated farther down the hallway just as a figure in a dark tailcoated suit and vest and starched white collar suddenly appeared on the threshold. Behind him in the dimly lit chamber, a golden-skinned woman lay with her back propped up against lacy pillows piled high on a garnet brocade chaise longue. A tiny baby lay sleeping in her arms, amazingly deaf to the angry exchanges by the adults.

"Julien——" the new mother beseeched.

"I cannot answer for what I might do, Martine, if I remain here a moment longer!" declared the distraught visitor.

"Then go!" ordered Althea, who stood dressed in a floor-length russet gown at the foot of the elegant chaise.

The young man, whose dark mustache contrasted sharply with his pale, perspiring complexion, cast a withering glance at the light-skinned, middle-aged Negress. Althea glared back at him. Martine brought her hands to her face. Her amber eyes were luminous with tears that began to spill down her cheeks.

Ignoring Martine's show of emotion, Julien abruptly stormed out of the room and down the staircase. Again Corlis flattened herself against the wall. However, the tormented young man appeared oblivious to her presence.

Althea strode toward the open door, the hem of her taffeta bustle sweeping across the sitting room's plush Persian carpet. She scowled at Julien's retreating back. Then she flung shut the door with a resounding bang.

Corlis jumped as if someone had trod on her toe, startled by the sound of screeching brakes as a cacophony of angry motorists on the street honked their horns in frustration.

Bewildered, she turned on the landing and gazed at the small anteroom below, now plunged into darkness. She was astonished to note that there was no sign of the man called Julien LaCroix, and no gas-illumined crystal chandelier hung suspended overhead. Nor was there any longer floral carpeting on the stairs.

There was, however, a faint whisper of natural gas floating in the air.

Or was it merely mustiness? Corlis asked herself, gazing doubtfully at the old heater, which looked as if it hadn't had a working pilot light in decades.

The room was bare of any furniture, and the only light filtering into the deserted chamber came from the outer hallway's naked bulb glowing through the half-opened door to the corridor.

"Corlis? *Corlis!*"

As if through a fog, she recognized the deep timbre of King Duvallon's voice calling her name. By this time a splitting headache pounded behind her eyes. And as had occurred at Saint Louis Cathedral during the Ebert-Duvallon wedding, Corlis actually felt as if she might faint.

It had happened *again*!

She had been a witness to another tumultuous event in a time period in which her ancestor Corlis Bell McCullough had lived! But what were people named Fouché and LaCroix doing here?

She suppressed a small gasp of recognition.

Fouché? As in Dylan Fouché, the real estate broker who King said doubled as a ghostbuster?

None of this made a bit of sense.

Man, oh man . . . I definitely better start taking time out to eat lunch!

"Hey, California! Where are you?"

More to the point, Corlis thought, leaning weakly against a wall of peeling crimson paint, where have I *been*?

"Corlis!" King called, more insistently.

"Here," she replied, amazed that she could even speak. "I'm in *here*!"

She clutched the banister in a death grip and descended the steps. Then, decidedly shaky, she moved beyond the archway and through the anteroom toward the half-opened door. An overwhelming sense of relief flooded through her as she caught sight of King Duvallon's tall, broad-shouldered figure advancing down the hallway. She sagged against the door jamb and breathed deeply of a fresh supply of air.

Suddenly she felt like hurtling herself against King's chest and resting her cheek on his flamboyant striped tie, just to confirm that he really was a live human being. She raised both hands and rubbed her temples with her forefingers, as if to erase the images of a furious young man in starched collar and tailcoat, a woman recovering from childbirth who reclined on a chaise longue upholstered resplendently in ruby red, and the angry Althea who had practically tossed the male intruder down the stairs!

Althea!

Wasn't Althea the name of the African-American woman who was Daphne Duvallon's best friend and who had played the organ at her wedding? How utterly bizarre! It had been the *white* man in the tailcoat who had been addressed as Julien *LaCroix*. And why had the distraught characters on the second floor repeatedly referred to people named McCullough, Jeffries, and Duvallon?

Corlis watched silently as King drew nearer her side.

"Sorry that took so long," he apologized.

"How long *did* it take?" she asked abruptly.

"The phone call?" King responded, looking at her curiously. " 'Bout five minutes. Why?"

"Oh . . . nothing."

King regarded her closely. "You okay, sugar?" he asked. "You look a little pale."

Once again Corlis glanced at the bulb above their heads.

"I think there might be a small gas leak somewhere around here," she said, looking over her shoulder. "I've suddenly got a bear of a headache."

"Really?" King asked, concerned. "I'll give a call to the gas company and have them check it out."

Corlis shook her head. "I probably just need something to eat. I skipped lunch." She looked at him expectantly and said quickly, "Oh, but you have a meeting to go to, right?"

"That's what the phone call was about," King said cheerfully. "It's been postponed till seven-thirty tonight. The guerrillas at the PRC have fanned out, gatherin' information we need to fight Grover's order to demolish and petition for a zonin' change in the historic district."

"Guerrillas?" she echoed, wondering if there was a half-eaten bag of corn chips left in her car.

"That's what I call the volunteer troops at the PRC."

"Oh . . . yeah, right . . ." she said vaguely. She glanced down at her watch. "It's almost three o'clock. I have forty-five minutes till I *have* to start editing my piece back at the station."

"Don't worry," King said. "In New Orleans, a good meal is seconds away. Want to go to Uglesich's for a quick po'boy?" he asked. "I've got my car outside. It'll take us three minutes to get there."

"I've left my car down near the Good Times Shopping Plaza."

"I'll drive you back to yours after lunch."

"But I'm buying, okay?" She suddenly felt uncomfortable with her unprofessional behavior. "It's strictly business. I want to talk about why you want to preserve these buildings. I can put it on my expense account."

And maybe somehow I can figure out the reason I keep seeing folks who look like they belong in a Broadway production of Showboat!

She'd think about this disquieting episode later, she counseled herself. If she stopped now to consider what had just happened, she truly *would* lose her mind—or keel over in an embarrassing swoon.

Corlis bit her lip and asked awkwardly, "Is Uglesich—is it an expensive restaurant? I do have to remember that I'm working for WJAZ now."

"Trust me," King said, laughing, "you and your expense account can afford it." He gently seized her elbow and guided her down the shabby corridor and out into the full light of day.

True to his word, King made a quick call to the gas company, then whisked Corlis to her desired destination: lunch. He soon turned his battered green station wagon into Baronne Street, a rather nondescript area adjacent to the downtown business district. He pulled in front of a weather-beaten clapboard structure whose peeling cream-colored paint was reminiscent of the shabby interiors on Canal Street. He pointed to the slanting roofline and a series of wooden brackets that braced the roof of the small restaurant.

"The width and the gradual slant reflects West Indian influences," he explained. "A lot of immigrants from Haiti and Cuba came to New Orleans after the slave revolts in the late eighteenth and early nineteenth centuries, and brought these architectural styles with them. In fact, in the French Quarter a lot of the buildings are more Spanish influenced than French!"

"Makes sense to me," Corlis commented. "But no more lectures on architectural styles, Mr. Preservation. Feed me, please."

Within minutes Corlis sank her teeth into her first po'boy sandwich at Uglesich's and thought she'd died and gone to heaven. King leaned back in his chair and appeared to be greatly amused while she groaned with ecstasy.

"Oh . . . m'God," she said with her mouth half-full. "What *is* it? The mayo? The fried oysters? The crispy bread? It's the best thing I ever ate in my *life!*"

"You ever had oysters Rockefeller at Galatoire's?" he demanded, alluding to one of New Orleans's premier restaurants in the French Quarter.

"No," she mumbled, licking a dollop of mayonnaise from the corner of her mouth.

"Then you are not an authority, yet, on the best thing you ever ate in your life."

"Mmmmm," was all she could reply.

"At the risk of lecturin' an expert," he said, glancing at his watch and suddenly becoming all business, "would you like to know the most efficient way of going about researchin' the history of those Greek Revival buildings?"

Corlis nodded emphatically and took another bite out of her sandwich. She peered at the remains of King's po'boy. "You gonna eat that?" she asked, leaning into his shoulder.

"Be my guest," he replied, a faint smile on his lips.

Corlis already felt her spirits rising. Nothing like feeding the brain ambrosia, she thought happily. Perhaps the little vignette she thought she'd witnessed on the second floor of those old derelicts was just that: a hallucination caused by food deprivation and too many weird aromas floating in the New Orleans air! At least she hoped that's what it was.

But what about the corpse? she asked herself. And the couple at the cathedral? Missing a few calories couldn't possibly be the cause of all this bizarre behavior!

Just don't think about it!

"My team's just scratched the surface lookin' into the history of the Selwyn properties," King disclosed. "Remember, we only recently got wind that Grover Jeffries has been sniffin' round about a possible development project in the block."

Corlis swallowed a bite of his sandwich and asked, "What have your guys found out so far?"

"Not much. We just don't have the staff to go diggin' up the entire historical background of every building that's in jeopardy. The Historic New Orleans Collection at the Williams Library, on Chartres Street in the French Quarter, is another place you could check out. That is, if you're *really* interested in tracing the descendants of the original builders and owners."

Would those libraries also have birth and date records going back to the early eighteen hundreds? Corlis wondered. Perhaps she could look for the names Henri Girard or Julien LaCroix. . . .

Forget it!

"This sounds like a pretty big project," she said slowly. Zamora was decent, but he was short-staffed and had a newscast to fill each night. "Would you be willing to show me the ropes about this specialized kind of research?" she asked. "At least get me started by introducing me to the librarians and city archivists? It could save a lot of time."

King regarded her with an appraising stare. Instinctively Corlis could read in his glance her very own thoughts: This story was bound to throw them into close proximity—and neither of them knew if this was going to be a good or a bad thing, considering their past. On the other hand, if she took into account the fluttering sensations she was experiencing suddenly, her anatomy, at least, was voting yes on this particular research project.

"Sure," King said finally. "I'll point you in the right direction." He glanced at his watch. "Can't do it today, though."

She, too, glanced at her watch. "Oh boy, me neither! I've got to get back and cut the piece we shot!"

"I'll drive you to your car," he offered.

King made as if to push back his chair in the noisy restaurant, then paused. "I'm afraid I can't meet you at the library till later in the week. Tomorrow I have meetings at the PRC all mornin' and have a class to teach in the afternoon."

"You know?" she commented thoughtfully. "You preservation folks are pretty fearless, aren't you?"

"Have to be. In the preservation biz we have to take it to the mat and pull the trigger all the time," he said matter-of-factly. "If we don't keep up the pressure, these priceless buildings come down and they can never be replaced."

"Tell me something, Professor," she asked. "You've just been arrested on order of the university's president. All this protest- ing stuff can't be good for the career aspirations of someone like you, on tenure track. Aren't you worried that the school's going to can you?"

"Sure," he said with a shrug. "But, you, of all people, should understand a thing like this. It's happened to *you* often enough, hasn't it?"

"You had to remind me," she said, rolling her eyes.

"Even so, you do your thing anyway, don't you?"

"Yep. But still, in the middle of the night I've been known to worry about the old mortgage payments," she admitted. Then she laughed. "I *worry*, but you're right. I do what I have to do, no matter what."

"Same for me," he said.

"Hmmm," was all she replied.

"What does 'hmmmm' mean?"

"It means I admire that."

"Well, me-to-you, sugar."

She regarded him for a long moment before plunging ahead with something that had been bothering her for some time.

"Let me ask you this," she proposed, and paused. She gazed at him intently. "It's way off the subject, but there's something I want to know." She hesitated again, then asked. "Were you the one who actually drew that insulting cartoon of me for the lam- poon edition of *Ms. UCLA*?"

"You mean the one on the cover, showin' you sittin' at a typewriter?"

"Yeah . . . where I look like a gargoyle with grotesquely fat legs," she reminded him.

King hesitated, as if he were checking his answer for air leaks before speaking. "No . . . I didn't draw it."

Corlis waited. Her reporter's instincts told her that wasn't the complete story.

"However?" she pressed.

"I gave my buddy Fred Barber the *idea* for it."

"I see." She continued to look at him steadily. "That was pretty mean," she said at length.

"It surely was," he replied soberly. "I'm sorry for it now. It must have hurt when all the other students ribbed you about it."

Corlis gazed into his eyes and allowed the moment to sink in.

"Mama Roux!" King said with a droll smile. "Those po'boys sure do pack a punch!"

Corlis glanced down at her empty plate and flushed. "It's not the po'boys. I realize now that I owe you a genuine apology for the way I behaved, too."

"Look, sugar, that goes both ways. As I think back on that whole affair, I can honestly say that I'm ashamed to have been a party to such a personal attack." He gave her legs an appraising, sidelong glance. "And besides, if you'd only worn skirts like the one you've got on today, I'd have known that caricature of you was *so* inaccurate," he added in a teasing drawl.

"Well . . . thanks . . . I guess," she replied uncertainly. "Ah . . . look, King . . . I don't mean to still sound . . . doctrinaire, or anything, but . . ." She paused once again, then blurted, "I *really* don't think you should call me 'sugar' so often." A smile tugged at King's mouth, but he remained silent, apparently enjoying her struggle for words. "We're just two people involved in a story together, you know? Just two professionals . . . who are . . . ah . . . professional, and—"

"Sure. As I said before, down here it's just a manner of speech. A habit. Like sayin' 'dude' in California, I suspect. No offense meant."

Corlis sensed that he was both teasing and serious.

"None taken," she replied, striving to make her tone light.

King rose from his chair and glanced around the crowded restaurant. "Well . . ." he suggested, pulling back her chair, "we'd better get goin'."

"You're right," she agreed, noting the time. "This is going to be the deadline from hell today. Oh!" she exclaimed. "I still have to pay our check!"

"Lunch's on the house."

"It can't be!" she said, exasperated. "I *have* to pay. It's an ethical thing! I—"

"Oh, now sug—Ace, don't worry about it. It's a present. To both of us."

"Lunch? But why?"

"I saved a couple of buildings in this neighborhood," King

shrugged. As they left the restaurant, he added, "Professional courtesy, y'know?"

Corlis was about to continue her protest but merely heaved a resigned sigh. "I don't have time to argue."

And within minutes King's dented station wagon pulled up next to her car, double-parked, and escorted her to the Lexus.

"Pretty snazzy, there, California. Very nice paint job," he added, opening the driver's door for her.

"Spoils of war," she answered as she slid behind the wheel.

She turned on the ignition. "Thanks for sharing your po'boy!"

Flashing a grin, he replied, "Glad you liked it." Then he cuffed her gently on the chin. "You take the best of care, now, okay, Ace? See ya on TV."

Chapter Eight

March 11

Corlis found herself with a couple of free hours in the afternoon of the following day and made her way to a complex of buildings at City Hall, on Poydras Street, where New Orleans's building records were housed. By three o'clock, she was installed at a bare, steel-legged table at the end of a row of ten-foot-high metal bookcases. Acres of books, ledgers, and accordion-pleated portfolios ran the length of the basement where the oldest archives were kept at a temperature that felt to be subzero. A check of the 1830 census records produced an "H. Girard, bachelor" living on the Rue Royale. Thanks to a helpful clerk, several bulging, dust-clad files now crowded her desk, identified by handwritten labels penned in a spidery script that declared them to be residential records of the:

700 Block of the Rue Royale
1750–1850

At number 728 Royal Street, in the French Quarter, the owners of record were listed in chronological order, including a name that had caused her heart to pound erratically.

Henri Girard, merchant. Deceased December 21, 1837.

Here was proof: The corpse in the opera clothes had truly lived—and died. Corlis ran her forefinger along the line that listed his long-forgotten name.

Next to the files for Royal Street, the archivist, at Corlis's request, had deposited on her desk another startling collection of stiff manila folders. These contained permits, plans, maps, and correspondence relating to building construction during the first half of the nineteenth century in the burgeoning American Sector. One file, in particular, riveted her attention.

600 Block of Canal Street
City of New Orleans
1803–1850

Corlis's thin linen suit jacket did little to protect her from the blast of air-conditioning overlaid with dank, musty air. She hunched her shoulders against the advancing current and briskly rubbed her upper arms in an effort to warm herself.

For two more hours she sifted through a mountain of documents on her desk. Several provided startling glimpses into the nineteenth-century origins of the screen-shrouded buildings that now figured in the controversy over Grover Jeffries's endowment of the university professorship. Corlis's labors yielded the plot map number of the buildings that had indeed been constructed around 1840 in an area of the city where little development had taken place before. With this in hand she hoped to trace their ownership by consulting early editions of the City Directory. If she were able to *link* those feisty nineteenth-century entrepreneurs—whoever they may have been—with their modern-day descendants still residing in New Orleans, a television story about the battle to prevent the demolition of those Greek Revival beauties would be more powerful.

Another blast of air-conditioning wafted from the overhead vents. Corlis shivered again and reached for the accordion-pleated file folder for the 600 block of Canal Street. With the ease of a seasoned researcher, she stacked the papers to one side, flipped open her slender reporter's notebook, and made a systematic inventory of the subject matter the documents contained before she started the daunting task of reading the pages one by one.

She glanced at her watch. It was a quarter to five. The city archives would be closing any minute now, so she'd have to come back when she could steal some time away from her regular reporting duties. Swiftly she began sequestering the old documents in their proper containers. As she handled the aged material, a distinctive scent of mold rose to her nostrils—a blend of dust and odors from centuries past.

Far off in the distance, she thought she could hear the muted sounds of the river—a steamboat hooting, signaling its imminent departure from the Toulouse Street Wharf, or perhaps a massive freighter was heading downstream toward the Gulf of Mexico, sounding its warnings to smaller craft passing by.

Not possible . . . the city archive is too far up Poydras Street to catch the sounds of river traffic. . . .

Corlis picked up a fragile-looking plot map labeled with the date 1838. A grid of brown lines depicted the perimeters of the *carré de la ville*, now called the Vieux Carré—the Old Quarter, now the French Quarter. On the left-hand side of the grid, a street identified as Canal clearly denoted the open area of land as it appeared a few years before the Greek Revival structures had been built. Even earlier, in the eighteenth century, the property in question had apparently been part of a former plantation bordering the first town settlement. By the early 1830s, it had been ripe for development, thanks to an influx of newcomers from northern American territories and especially from Kentucky, following the Louisiana Purchase in 1803.

For some peculiar reason the map's singularly earthy scent and the paper's fragile texture began to produce odd, tingling sensations coursing up Corlis's arm. Mesmerized by the document, she traced with her forefinger the outline of the 100 block confines of the French Quarter, bordered on the downriver side by Canal Street. She rested her nail on the two-dimensional rendering of the old dirt levee that she had read somewhere had been constructed after 1718 to prevent the Mississippi River from overflowing its boundaries and flooding the tiny outpost.

Sounds of life on the waterfront became louder, and she found herself imagining tall-masted ships and long, sleek barges riding low in the water, poled by muscular slaves to destinations along the riverbank. Her fingers grazed the spot where the map's elegant calligraphy marked the area presently known as the Toulouse Street Wharf that had served as a dock for the latest in sail and paddle wheel technology.

Like Showboat. *Like in the days when the original owners of those beautiful buildings on Canal Street traded sugarcane and cotton and shipped their products to buyers around the world . . .*

Corlis's hand clutching the antique map began to tremble, and her vision blurred. The sketch of the old levee holding back the river water swam before her eyes, and then, just as suddenly, it appeared to take concrete shape. Her breath caught as she watched the barricade's mounded black, loamy soil—pungent and warm—miraculously rise to a height that allowed a wonderful view of a three-masted ship on the wide Mississippi. The vessel was slowly making its way through a thicket of other wooden masts toward a dock bustling with robust stevedores. Members of the crew waited at the railings for the order to throw lines overboard so they could secure the graceful deepsea craft to the shore.

"Oh my God!" Corlis whispered hoarsely as a wave of panic began sweeping over her.

It's happening again!

"When do you plan to tell Julien about the deed to the Canal Street property?" Randall McCullough inquired of Ian Jeffries.

Jeffries, a portly man of medium stature, was fashionably dressed in chocolate-colored trousers with a matching tight-bodied coat, neckcloth, and opalescent breast pin. He stood on the wharf in the warm April sun and gazed speculatively at the variety of ships and river craft moored near the riverbank, six vessels deep.

If one wasn't privy to the truth about the underhanded rogue—as McCullough and his wife, Corlis, certainly were—Ian Jeffries presented the reassuring demeanor of a successful man of business. For all the world he seemed a New Orleans "comer" in the parlance of a city recovering nicely from the money crisis of the previous year, and the earlier devastating cholera and yellow fever epidemics of 1832–33.

"Will you broach the subject of that Fouché woman's damnable trick while Julien remains here in New Orleans, or wait till you both get to Reverie?" pressed McCullough.

"For mercy's sake, Randall!" admonished Corlis before the

plump-faced Jeffries could supply an answer to her husband's question. "Poor Monsieur LaCroix's bound to be far more upset to hear of his father's stroke and Henri Girard's death than that his father's fool partner has deeded over a few acres of company land to his mistress in his will!"

"Hush, Corlis!" Randall McCullough said crossly. He cast his wife an admonishing grimace, wishing for all the world that he'd refused to let her come along on this dangerous mission.

"Don't you hush *me*!" she retorted.

Hoping to intimidate his wife of four years into silence, McCullough continued to glare at the woman whose small stature belied her assertive, inquisitive nature. Who could have imagined, he mused with mounting irritation, that such a slip of a thing could have survived yellow fever on their journey down the Mississippi River, or that she could have produced a healthy baby boy before the flatboat had even pulled up to the very wharf where Julien LaCroix and his bride of one year would soon be disembarking?

"You overstep yourself to speak of subjects that do not concern you!" he scolded.

"Nonsense, Randall," Corlis retorted. "Why are you and Ian making so much of such a small parcel, when the LaCroix family owns—"

" 'Tis not for you to determine what is of importance here, or what Ian and I should say to Julien—or even *when* and *where* we should say it!"

Randall allowed his glance to rest briefly on his wife's thickening waist, concluding that Corlis had become even more irritable and plain speaking during this second pregnancy. In another month he would insist that she completely withdraw from polite society.

Ignoring his scowl, Corlis turned to Randall's new partner. "Ian," she appealed, "the poor gentleman's been abroad for more than a year now. 'Tis my opinion you will alienate Monsieur LaCroix if you press your own cause too soon. The man will be deeply shocked to hear—before he's barely set foot on Louisiana soil, mind you—that his father is without the facilities of speech or movement, and that the plantation's affairs are in such terrible disarray."

"Not to mention Henri Girard's mishandling of Reverie's cotton and cane sales here in the city," Ian Jeffries added grimly.

"Suicide was too good for 'im, I say," Randall muttered grudgingly.

"Randall!" Corlis rebuked him sharply, glancing over her shoulder. "If anyone were to hear you . . ." She stared at her husband, aghast, unable to disguise her disdain. What a blustering fool he was, she thought silently. The worst of their Scottish race!

She glanced momentarily at his broad chest and muscular shoulders. She recalled with some embarrassment now how drawn she'd been to this mercurial man in the beginning of their unorthodox relationship. How foolhardy, indeed, had she been to risk her virtue within the circle of the brawny arms of a carpenter. Randall McCullough had been hired by her banker father to build the family mansion in Pittsburgh. Six weeks of her impetuously succumbing to the man's infamous charms had predictably rendered her *enciente*. Within a fortnight of the discovery that she was expecting a baby, she'd become the hapless bride in a hasty wedding ceremony. By summer's end she was floating south down the Ohio, and ultimately the Mississippi River, only to wind up in this steamy bog that was New Orleans.

Corlis made a valiant attempt to ignore the heat as she shifted her glance away from Randall. She wondered what strange malevolence had taken possession of both her husband and his building partner, Ian Jeffries. The two men had met on that intolerable riverboat full of tricksters and gamblers that had whisked them down the Mississippi in the autumn of 1834. Jeffries had boarded the craft at the Reverie plantation's dock en route to New Orleans, and the two Scotsmen had come together like beaten eggs. Yet as partners they hardly had the common sense of one man. Their elaborate schemes to strike it rich in this busy port had so far come to naught, and in fact, they might well have resulted in an arrest for out-and-out extortion.

Her husband, Randall—together with Julien LaCroix, the restless son of prominent plantation owner Etienne LaCroix—and Ian Jeffries had concocted elaborate plans for capitalizing on the boomtown atmosphere that currently held New Orleans in its grip.

Corlis vowed silently that as soon as they accumulated enough money, she would insist that they board one of these ships to the California territories. There, she was sure, they would find land and prosperity in a place where the weather wasn't so insufferable!

However, before Corlis could conjecture any further on the likelihood of Jeffries & McCullough Builders making a fortune and moving farther west to milder climes, Ian Jeffries demanded her attention. He pointed out two figures that were standing on the deck of the three-masted clipper, now securely moored to the wharf by thick lines of woven jute.

"Ah!" Ian cried, "I do believe that's Julien, standing near the gangway . . . and isn't that Adelaide by his side?"

Corlis squinted against the sun's glare at the sight of a stocky, dark-haired woman in her mid-twenties attired in an elegant morning dress with a bell-shaped skirt, in the latest Parisian style, made out of a fabric known as pongee. Corlis's mother, Elizabeth Bell, had owned a similar woven raw silk garment, and it had cost upward of a hundred dollars!

Would Adelaide LaCroix, née Marchand, even remember her? Corlis wondered nervously. She'd been among the nobodies at the enormous wedding ceremony held in Saint Louis Cathedral last year to celebrate the joining of the two powerful plantation families. The church had been packed to its arched and gilded ceiling with well-wishers, and the overpowering scent of incense, Corlis recalled with a shudder, had caused her sensitive nose to twitch wildly. She'd nearly swooned right there in the pew.

As a bride, Adelaide Marchand had appeared to be abjectly miserable, standing at the altar dressed in crisp white taffeta cinched tightly at the waist, with sleeves as round as Chinese lanterns. Her groom was the debonair Julien LaCroix, whose bold wagering and legendary amorous exploits were whispered about behind fluttering fans in elegant sitting rooms and double parlors throughout New Orleans. The pair, distant cousins— with their matching raven hair and amber eyes—had known each other since babyhood. On the joyless occasion of their wedding, they had stood woodenly beside each other at the altar, looking more like brother and sister than soon-to-be husband and wife. And from the dour expressions on both their countenances, they appeared as ready for a squabble as any two siblings could be.

"Come!" ordered Ian Jeffries, interrupting Corlis's wool-gathering. "I want Julien to see that we are here on the wharf," he added urgently, striding toward the ship as the roustabouts lowered the gangway with a loud bang. "I want Monsieur LaCroix to appreciate that 'tis we who've come to greet him— and we who have been looking after his interests during his long absence, eh, McCullough?"

Or rather, keeping some unholy secrets while looking after your own interests, Corlis mused.

"Aha!" exclaimed Ian Jeffries to his partner. "The gangway has been secured. Follow me!" he commanded his companions.

"Corlis," Randall McCullough warned her with a scowl, "I ask that you smile prettily . . . and keep your mouth *shut!*"

"You cannot be serious!" exclaimed Julien LaCroix explosively. In the heat of his words, a shock of dark hair fell across his perspiring forehead, and he banged his balled fist against his cloth-covered knee. Then the twenty-eight-year-old heir to Reverie plantation glanced irritably around Hewlett's, a café on St. Louis Street. The public house had become a principal watering hole for the city's merchants and brokers, who transacted much of their business under its hospitable roof.

"I'm only too sorry to tell you, Julien, that your ledgers will confirm the whole sorry tale I've just related to you," Ian Jeffries said dolefully.

Julien was now thankful that Ian Jeffries and his partner, Randall McCullough, had urged him to leave Adelaide with the freckle-faced Mrs. McCullough at the LaCroix house on Dumaine Street. The men then repaired to Hewlett's and a table in the corner where their unpleasant discussion was unlikely to be overheard.

"And my father?" Julien asked, pausing to down a strong shot of the greenish-colored absinthe in hopes it would fortify him against further dismaying news. "Can he not speak at all?"

"We thought it best to prepare you, sir," Randall McCullough chimed in gravely. "He can neither speak nor move since the paroxysm struck. He and his nurses have apparently devised some system of eye blinking to make his simple wishes understood."

"Mon Dieu!" Julien said, lowering his head into his hands. Then he raised his eyes. "And my father's partner, Henri Girard? Has he carried on with our plans?"

Randall looked to his partner for guidance.

"I'm sorry to have to tell you . . ." Ian Jeffries said quietly, "but Henri has died. Just before Christmas, it was."

"Dead?" Julien repeated, dumbstruck by this second revelation. "Yellow jack? When I was in Paris I read that the fevers in Louisiana were especially wicked last year."

"No, Julien," Ian answered slowly. " 'Twas not yellow fever. Some say heart failure, or a diseased liver, perhaps. . . . No one was quite sure."

"But Girard was relatively young!" Julien protested. "A good ten years junior to my father."

"The man did enjoy his port—often to excess, I'm told," Randall McCullough noted tactfully.

"Fortunately his personal affairs were in reasonably good order—such as they were," Jeffries allowed. "Most of the financial problems currently plaguing your family firm are recent. There was a money shortage at the banks last year. Then the dual tragedy of your father's illness and Girard's sudden death left your family's business rudderless these last months."

"We did our best, sir," McCullough added modestly, "but as mere outsiders . . ."

He allowed his words to drift off. No one had to define the social gulf that existed between the French Creoles and the "upstart Americans" in Nouvelle Orleans.

"I am most grateful to you gentlemen for all you have done to help my family in such trying circumstances," Julien said quietly, staring pensively into his glass.

"I'm sure, now that you've returned," Ian proposed smoothly, "there are other matters we can assist you with—"

"And what of our strategy to expand up Canal Street?" interrupted Julien, nodding emphatically. "Did that go as planned?"

Ian Jeffries and Randall McCullough exchanged uneasy glances.

"Something untoward has happened, Julien," Jeffries ventured.

Each man waited for the other to speak.

"What?" Julien demanded. "Out with it! What other disaster must I confront my first day back in New Orleans?"

"There is a document on file in the courts that states that both your father and his partner jointly deeded over the Canal Street property just before Girard died."

"What!" Julien replied, dismayed. "To whom?"

"The tract where you'd hoped to start your own business venture now belongs to a woman named Martine Fouché."

"Who?" Julien exclaimed, confused.

"You've never heard of her?" inquired Randall McCullough with a look of surprise.

"Never in my life!" Julien snapped. Then he paused. "Ah . . . yes. I do remember her. She was Girard's quadroon mistress," he said finally with an air of weary resignation. "I only vaguely recall her name now, because my father's partner virtually never appeared in public with her, nor allowed her to parade through the *carré de la ville* alone—even to the dressmaker's. Henri was rather eccentric in such matters." He set his glass down sharply. "But why in St. Cecilia's name would my father and Girard grant her the deed to such valuable property? They knew of my hopes to expand our cotton and cane export operations." His eyes narrowed and his gaze shifted from McCullough to Jeffries.

"It was vastly puzzling, to be sure," Randall McCullough murmured politely.

"Well, we shall see if Mademoiselle Fouché has legal title to that plot or not, won't we?" Julien said with a peevish glare at his companions.

"Your . . . your father apparently co-signed the deed, Julien," Ian Jeffries revealed reluctantly. "It's a legal transaction, indeed, I'm afraid. Randall and I took the liberty of having your lawyer, Monsieur Marchand, look into it."

"A *female* is granted title to land that was always, by rights, to be *mine*?" Julien said, his voice rising. Nearby patrons glanced curiously at their table. "It's patently against the law!" he spat, abruptly lowering his voice. "Surely even my brother-in-law knows *that*!" he added, alluding to Lafayette Marchand, an attorney known for his love of horses and gambling and his disinclination for legal work, except when it came to protecting the Marchand family interests.

"Martine Fouché—and her mother, Althea—are Free Women of Color. Althea was emancipated in her youth by *her* patron, Marius Fouché, your neighbor upriver. Therefore, Mademoiselle Martine Fouché was indeed legally granted the deed to that prize piece of LaCroix land on Canal Street," Ian Jeffries said slowly. "She showed me both documents herself."

"*You* two have been privy to all these family matters through your exchanges with Negroes?" Julien demanded, his face growing flush with irritation. "By what right—"

"We felt it a duty to try to get to the bottom of these unorthodox transactions, Julien!" Ian interrupted.

"As I'm sure you are aware," Randall McCullough hurriedly assured Julien, "Lafayette Marchand might not agree with your plans to use your wife's funds to expand your warehouse operations on Canal Street, and we did not wish to inquire of *him* such sensitive information in your behalf."

Julien LaCroix appeared somewhat mollified. However, neither he nor his companions referred again to Julien's scheme to tap into his wife's inheritance to finance such a potentially risky venture as doubling the size of LaCroix & Girard's operations.

"It is just that these are very *private* matters," the young planter said in a low voice. "*Family* matters." The patriarchs of white French families like the Marchands and LaCroixs had little social interaction with American immigrants like Jeffries and McCullough. However, all three gentlemen sipping absinthe at Hewlett's were members of a younger generation, eager to lay claim to the new prosperity along the rich Mississippi Delta. A vibrant, burgeoning economy based on sugar, cotton, steam power, and cheap labor beckoned to those smart enough to seize the opportunities that were there for the taking, no matter what their family background.

"Of course," murmured Jeffries, with a show of deference to LaCroix's proud heritage. "I can certainly understand why you are distressed by this current state of . . . affairs. But I assure you, Julien, this will prove to be a mere setback. Randall and I have employed the utmost discretion to get to the bottom of all this for you. We, too, have an important stake in the development of the Canal Street holdings," he reminded him differentially, "and, besides, we—"

But Julien LaCroix was barely listening.

"I cannot *believe* my father would be party to such incredible transactions as these—virtually giving away the Canal Street property to his partner's *mistress* . . . and a Negress in the bargain!" Julien shook his head angrily and then signaled to the barman that he required another drink. "Did this happen before or after my father's present indisposition?" he demanded of Jeffries. "Perhaps Girard pressured him in his mistress's behalf? Are you sure it is Etienne's bona fide signature on the deed, or perhaps it was made under duress, or when he was ill?"

"The date on the documents attests to the fact that the property was transferred . . . ah . . . *before* your father fell ill and his partner died," Jeffries replied with considerable delicacy.

Julien allowed this information to sink in for a moment. Then, compressing his lips in a thin, tight line, he said grimly, "Well, gentlemen . . . we shall soon *see* what kind of female could have plied her wiles with Monsieur Henri Girard in such fashion as to accomplish this astounding feat!"

Near the Rue des Ramparts Julien stood in the gathering twilight and stared at the little one-story white house with green shutters. It was only one of a dozen small, charming dwellings that lined the street and offered sanctuary to a remarkable class of women that everyone in New Orleans knew about, but of which little was ever discussed.

He'd long been aware that his own father had kept a series of lithesome young black women under his "patronage"—a practice known as *plaçage* spoken about only among men and *never* even alluded to in mixed company.

Hell! Etienne LaCroix had even turned over one of the young ladies for Julien's own pleasure and amusement on the day he'd turned eighteen.

Claire Languille.

Julien had found her lovely—and utterly avaricious. He'd soon grown weary of her whining and her petty schemes to separate him from as much of his money as she possibly could. He withdrew his favors and sought relief for his strong libido among the denizens of a brothel on Girod Street.

Adelaide, Julien's bride of one year, had been aware since her girlhood of the disturbing practice of *plaçage*. It was an unhappy reality in the social fabric and family life of New Orleans. What galled his wife the most, he reckoned, was that these beautiful coffee-skinned young rivals of the white women of Adelaide's class could rarely be branded prostitutes in the way of their sisters on Girod Street.

It was known that Julien's own grandfather had sired children with a full-blooded African woman on Reverie plantation, producing a passel of mulattoes. The female offspring, in turn, had found protectors among his father's generation of white planters, with the product of these liaisons dubbed *quadroons*—so named because they were one-fourth African. Their rearing had often been identical with that of white girls, some having been schooled in French and in the finer things in life. Others were even sent by their ambitious mothers—who had prudently secreted away the funds to Paris for "finishing"—so that they would be able to bargain for even better situations upon their return to New Orleans. Some 45 percent of all members of the black race in New Orleans were now counted among the *gens de couleur libres*, Free People of Color. A class unto themselves, the quadroons and octoroons refused to socialize with other blacks. Some had arrived at such heights as to own cotton and sugar plantations themselves, along with the slaves to run them. Other free blacks had made their mark in literary circles. Some were celebrated musicians, merchants, and even real estate brokers. The less educated assumed the vocations of barber, tailor, carpenter, mason, and upholsterer, or supplied the city with game and fish. Free People of Color published their own newspapers, attended the Orleans Theater in the second tier, and supported the opera with the same reverence for, and knowledge of, music as the whites in the audiences.

Julien ignored the passersby hurrying along the Rue des Ramparts after their day's work and reflected upon all he had discovered in the short time he had been back in the Crescent City. He had made it his business to unearth the fact that Martine Fouché, a quadroon herself, had given birth to a child by her white patron behind the walls of that charming cottage. Many such octoroons like little Lisette were likely to be given their freedom in their father's wills. Eventually thousands moved north, where they—or their children—passed for white, and melted into urban societies whose members were unsuspecting as to the origins of these newcomers.

No, Julien reminded himself. The woman residing in the green shuttered cottage on the opposite side of Rampart Street was no common whore. Martine Fouché was likely to have been reared as gently as his wife, Adelaide, herself, and for the same purpose: to attract a white man, preferably rich, who, in exchange for sexual favors and her bewitching company, would protect this light-skinned damsel from the storms and hardships of life.

Julien remained rooted on Rampart Street contemplating the tidy cottage and its adjacent sidewalk, or *banquette*, as the French preferred to call it. Squinting in the fading sun, he suddenly thought he spied a shadow move behind the curtained window and began to speculate as to what Martine Fouché would be like. He wagered that she would be quite a different personality from his wife Adelaide, who had thus far been little interested in exchanging *her* sexual favors for much of anything, now that she had achieved the status of wife. To be fair, neither he nor Adelaide had been under any illusion that theirs was more than the classic arranged marriage among white Creole families. Even granting that, their long honeymoon abroad had been an utter disaster.

Yes, Martine Fouché was most likely to be a very different breed than the high-strung Adelaide Marchand LaCroix.

Julien began to theorize as to the nature of the quadroon's relationship with her elusive patron, Henri Girard. If that fool Girard hadn't eaten and drunk himself into an early grave, this type of sub-rosa liaison might have lasted a lifetime. More often than not, however, as in the case of his father, Etienne LaCroix, the novelty and passion of these arrangements wore off soon enough. Then these discarded sweethearts—whose chiseled bone structure often resembled that of their white fathers, and whose rich, café au lait complexion reflected the skin tones of their African-American mothers—received a bequest sufficient to maintain the former mistress in comfortable style or to set her up in business. Half the hairdressers in New Orleans were former concubines of his father's contemporaries, and their light-skinned children were routinely given their freedom as part of the "final arrangements."

But to grant a woman, whose mother was a former slave, if you please, an *entire city block*, ripe for development, was unheard of!

Julien's fingers pulled his starched collar away from his neck; sweat was trickling in rivulets down his chest.

Damn this Martine Fouché! Had she practiced some insidious form of *voudou* on poor Henri Girard? What puzzled Julien even more was that Etienne LaCroix—his own *father*—had been a party to this outrageous turn of events! Now, due to Etienne's severe indisposition, the patriarch would forever be a *silent* partner.

"Well, Mademoiselle Fouché," Julien said aloud, striding away from the cottage's narrow front door, "until tomorrow, then. And I assure you, *ma chére,* you shall not cast any spells on *me*!"

Chapter Nine

March 23, 1838

"Café, monsieur?" Althea Fouché murmured, "or perhaps *un peu du croissant*?"

"Coffee, please, but nothing else, thank you," Julien replied. He found himself inordinately surprised at the well-furnished parlor of Mademoiselle Fouché's tastefully appointed Creole cottage.

He glanced around the room at the whitewashed fireplace with its French enameled ormolu clock taking pride of place on the mantel. A rich sapphire-and-white Persian carpet graced the cypress planked floor. Through a set of French doors, Julien glimpsed the inviting chamber beyond and a corner of a bed's carved mahogany footboard and its white matelassé quilted counterpane. The dwelling's furnishings were undoubtedly selected by the mistress of the house, but bought and paid for by profits from sugarcane and cotton sold through the Reverie plantation's exporting company, LaCroix & Girard.

"Martine will join us in a moment," her mother informed him demurely. "We had word, of course, that your ship had docked this week, but she was not expecting your call at quite such an early hour, monsieur. You must forgive my daughter while she prepares her toilette."

Julien immediately realized that he had just been reprimanded oh so gently for his intrusion. Oddly, he felt properly chastised, rather than outraged, by Althea Fouché's impertinence.

"The coffee is excellent, Madame Fouché," he said as a peace offering to ameliorate the imposition of such an early appearance.

"Why, thank you," Althea replied coolly, not relinquishing her hold on the situation.

Julien heard the rustle of skirts sweeping across the carpet and once again shifted his glance to the French doors leading to the nearby bedchamber. A slender young woman dressed in a gown made of stiff black bombazine, nipped in tightly at her minuscule waist, advanced into the room. Her straight blue-black hair was pulled severely to the nape of her swanlike neck and fastened without a ringlet in sight.

Why, she's dressed in mourning. . . . Imagine! Just like any fine Creole lady whose life companion had passed away.

Julien noted that Martine's face was a perfect oval, except for the graceful narrowing of her chin. Arched brows, as inky a shade of blue-black as her hair, framed wide-set amber eyes that were the same color as the coffee he was currently sipping from a thin porcelain cup.

The young woman looked to be twenty-six or twenty-seven. She had slightly flaring nostrils and a generous mouth—both subtle reminders of her African origins. And like her sister quadroons, her high cheekbones, shell-like ears, and delicate bone structure could be credited to her French and Spanish ancestry.

Even so, Julien was only vaguely aware of these lovely features, for what had captured his unwavering attention was Martine Fouché's glorious golden skin and her lustrous hair. The woman who stood but a few feet from his chair eyed him with cool, confident grace.

"Monsieur," she murmured, "welcome home to New Orleans. May I convey my condolences for the ill health of your father?"

"We share other sorrows, I have come to learn," he said, rising to his feet deferentially, a move that he found most startling for a man who had come to this house intending to rattle sabers and take no prisoners on the subject of the Canal Street lands.

"Ah . . . you refer to poor Henri," Martine said softly. She motioned vaguely that he should resume his seat as she took one of her own on the stiff, Empire-style silk settee. "He was, perhaps, suffering far more discomfort than anyone suspected, including my mother and me."

"But he was not so indisposed as to have neglected his duty to you, mademoiselle," he said pointedly. "My men of business inform me that my father and Monsieur Girard have gifted you with a plot of land on Canal Street, within view of the river."

"That is so, monsieur," Martine concurred, accepting a delicate porcelain cup of coffee from her mother's hand. "It was, of course, exceedingly generous of them."

"Exceedingly."

Julien watched her bring the lip of the cup to her own, marveling at her bright, even teeth.

"You are distressed by this gift to me, monsieur?" Martine inquired softly.

"I have no quarrel, mademoiselle, that Monsieur Girard has provided for your future, as well he should have," Julien began. He wondered, suddenly, where his hostesses had sequestered Henri's ten-year-old child, Lisette.

"My mother and I are relieved, then, that you concur with your father and Monsieur Henri's bequest to me," Martine replied, meeting Julien's gaze steadily. "We, like you, I suspect, would wish to avoid any unpleasantness over such matters."

"But of course," Julien hurriedly assured his hostess. "Life is full of *tristesse* as it is, wouldn't you agree? My father's helpless condition—not being able either to speak or to move a toe or finger—attests to this, *n'est-ce pas?*"

"But yes . . . that is certainly true," Martine said, nodding her graceful head.

Julien gently set his coffee cup on the table next to his chair and held Martine's unwavering gaze.

"I would like to suggest to you a way in which we both could feel fully satisfied that our interests were considered."

"And that is . . . ?" Martine asked quietly. Julien sensed immediately a change in the timbre of her voice, a kind of watchful wariness. She was clearly a pragmatist, *une femme de couleur libre* who knew, certainly, that despite her elevated status as a nonslave, her fate rested ultimately on the goodwill and fair-mindedness of white people. Even so, Julien had to admire the way in which she appeared unafraid to stand her ground.

"I do not think my father and Monsieur Girard were aware how very much I had counted on founding my own small business within our larger enterprise of LaCroix & Girard," he noted carefully, "nor that the Canal Street property had figured prominently in that plan."

"I would know nothing of such matters, monsieur," Martine murmured.

"Of course you wouldn't," Julien agreed gently. "Therefore, I would like to offer to exchange the property on Canal Street for land or money that would perhaps be of equal or greater value, in Faubourg Marigny," he proposed, studying Martine's expression. "I have thought to expand our sugarcane and cotton export business on Canal."

"I see." Martine nodded. She cast a glance in her mother's direction. Althea Fouché merely cocked her head and remained silent. "Well, monsieur," she said, smiling faintly, "that is a very generous suggestion, and if you would be so kind as to permit me, I shall think on it for a while." Her smile broadened, allowing him another glimpse at her beautiful, even teeth. Julien suddenly felt his heart swell at the sheer loveliness he saw shimmering before him. "Perhaps you will return and we can speak of it again," Martine suggested with an enigmatic smile.

Mademoiselle Fouché was by far the most entrancing, most seductive, most alluring woman he had ever laid eyes on, including the famed professional courtesans he had sought out in Paris. The day he had said his vows to Adelaide in front of God and half of New Orleans assembled in Saint Louis Cathedral, he had sworn that his whoring, rabble-rousing days were at an end. He did not dislike his second cousin twice removed. He had enjoyed her company when they were children.

However, the physical side of marriage had revolted Adelaide. Night after night she'd declined to share his bed, pleading sick headaches and a myriad of similar indispositions. So Julien had found himself in Paris's most exclusive brothels. Now he faced the golden-skinned Martine, who had been raised since babyhood to a life of pleasing men—white men. Surely she had never shied from complying with Henri Girard's carnal needs. After all, Girard had certainly enjoyed nearly a decade of—

Girard is dead, Julien reminded himself. By eating and drinking to excess, the foolish man had forsaken this poor girl, her mother, and her child. Perhaps, he thought with sudden inspiration, he would offer *himself* to sweeten this proposed trade of the Canal Street property for a possession more suitable to a woman of color. And besides, this beautiful creature would surely welcome a new protector, one who could shield her little family from an uncertain future, clouded by threatened lawsuits and possible unpleasantness. As for Julien, a permanent arrangement with a woman as appealing as Martine Fouché would avoid the rigors and risks of patronizing the strumpets on Girod Street.

For the moment Julien LaCroix determined to say no more to Martine about exchanging the land once owned by LaCroix & Girard. He could well afford to wait. In fact, all manner of delicious anticipation flooded through him, lifting his heart and stirring his groin.

Martine Fouché was a breathtaking and totally unexpected surprise. Put in his path, amazingly enough, by a series of misfortunes.

One man's misfortune is another man's good luck.

The thick mantle of gloom under which Julien had lived began to dissipate for the first time since he had stood in front of the stern priest in Saint Louis Cathedral. Then, for no reason he could fathom, in his mind's eye he imagined the figure of Henri Girard lying in a coffin, cut down in his prime.

How tragic to die so unexpectedly, Julien mused, and to have indulged in such apparent gluttony when the man had everything to live for . . . and when he had Martine Fouché awaiting him in this warm and inviting cottage.

A mere seven-minute walk from the impressive, iron-balconied LaCroix town residence located on the Rue Dumaine, he considered happily, within earshot of the sounds of the river traffic and the tall cathedral's sonorous bells.

"It is most kind of you to extend an invitation for me to return to this delightful home you have made with your mother and daughter," Julien pronounced warmly as a plan began to evolve in his mind. "Upon my next visit, I shall send word in advance, to assure myself that I do not impose . . ." he added with appropriate deference.

"It is you, Monsieur LaCroix, who are most kind," Martine

replied with a sidelong glance that Julien found highly provocative. "My mother and I look forward to our next rendezvous."

Julien spared a glance for the formidable Althea LaCroix and knew, instinctively, that she and her exquisite daughter would prove to be women to be reckoned with.

Randall McCullough studiously avoided his wife's critical stare and instead gazed directly into the pier glass, concentrating on securing his stiff white tie at the proper angle. Outside the window, the clip-clop sound of horses' hooves pulling a carriage was muffled by the spring rain that was coming down in veritable sheets and splattering in a staccato tattoo against the glass panes.

"I feel perfectly well, Randall," Corlis Bell McCullough announced in a sharp tone, "and I am still able to fit into my ball gown. So, I fail to understand why I cannot—"

" 'Tis unseemly for you to leave this house, that's why!" he responded irritably. "A woman in your advanced condition shouldn't be traipsing about at night in the rain. And besides, Ian and I will have a chance this evening to speak privately with Julien LaCroix, without that interfering lawyer, Lafayette Marchand, hanging about."

"And how is that?" she asked, curious in spite of herself.

"Marchand has gone upriver to visit his sister for a few days."

"I wouldn't judge Julien's brother-in-law as interfering," Corlis commented. "I heard from my dressmaker, who's a friend of Marchand's tailor, that he's not at all anxious for Adelaide's inheritance to be invested in some scheme to enhance the Canal Street property, should Julien ever secure it from Mademoiselle Fouché. I can certainly understand that point of view," she added, arching her eyebrow meaningfully.

"I will thank you not to interfere with my business dealings, Corlis," Randall said imperiously.

"Even if the money you're investing in this latest scheme came from the sale of my family's diamond jewelry?" she asked accusingly. Her husband maintained a stony silence as he eased his black cloak onto his shoulders. "If you ask me," Corlis continued, undaunted by his dark expression, "I think 'tis right decent of Mr. Marchand to visit poor Adelaide LaCroix and try to cheer her up a bit. The poor thing's had to nurse Julien's father night and day, for pity's sake, while her husband gads about town!"

"You know nothing of these matters," Randall said loftily, "so I would appreciate it if you did not speak as if you did."

"Well . . . what I do know," she responded with a tight, tart smile, "is that three gentlemen dressed up in fancy clothes on a sodden night like this—but without their wives on their arms—can only be making their way to one destination."

"And that is?" Randall said, glaring at her to hide his chagrin.

"The Salle d'Orleans," she retorted, "and don't think I don't know it, even if poor Adelaide LaCroix pretends to be dim as a post about these things!"

"No decent woman talks about a place like that!" Randall declared self-righteously.

"Ah . . . but supposedly decent men like you go there, don't they, Randall McCullough?" she responded, angrily putting her hands on her expanding waistline. " 'Tis nothing but a glorified slave mart, that's what the Orleans Ballroom is! And as a white man, and a Scots Presbyterian to boot, you should be ashamed to be seen there. Business matter," she pronounced with disdain. "My stars!"

And with that she flounced out of the bedchamber and refused to bid her husband farewell when he departed for the night.

The exterior of the Orleans Ballroom was not in the least imposing. However, Julien never ceased to feel a rush of anticipation when he entered the nondescript building whose mammoth interior was adorned with elaborate crystal chandeliers, expensive paintings and voluptuous statuary—a hint at the sumptuous array of womanhood invariably on display there.

The walls of the room were remarkable for their inlaid and paneled woods and a floor made of three layers of pure cypress and a layer of oak—said to be the finest anywhere for dancing in the United States. The chamber was also noted for its lofty, ornamented ceiling and balconies that overlooked the gardens at the rear of Saint Louis Cathedral.

Julien had always found it ironic that New Orleans's holiest sanctuary was within a stone's throw of an establishment devoted to white churchgoing gentlemen, blessed with means and social standing, to select black mistresses in full view of their peers.

And what a selection there was tonight!

Julien lounged against the richly paneled wall, awaiting the arrival of Randall McCullough and Ian Jeffries. He allowed himself the pleasure of drinking in the alluring sight of bright-colored satins, rustling taffetas, velvets, and richly embroidered watered silks, the expensive laces and the astonishingly low-cut bodices of the women whose charms and favors were available—for a price. Burnished golden skin was in evidence everywhere, making this gathering unlike any in southern Louisiana.

Julien surveyed the elegant room full of gorgeously attired people, reflecting that the Free People of Color certainly raised beautiful daughters, well schooled in French and poetry, and the arts of carnality. As he watched the coquettish looks flashed in his direction, he knew that behind the discreet flirtatiousness exhibited by those whose charms were on display this evening lay a deadly serious purpose.

Free Women of Color were forbidden by the Code Noir, the Black Code, to marry either their own slaves—which they prized as much as did their white counterparts—or the slaves owned by white men. And of course, it was unthinkable and illegal for them to marry into the white race. As a result, free black men and women could establish legitimate families exclusively among their own free ranks.

The only other choice was to increase their coffers by offering the most exquisite of their young women, in quasi-permanent "arrangements," to white men of wealth and status who, in turn, would endow yet another generation of light-skinned blacks with freedom for the children of those unions, along with money and support.

This system—*le plaçage*—was destined to perpetuate itself as long as arranged marriages among the most prominent white families were reinforced by a religious dogma that forbade divorce. Love, or even lust, seldom entered into marriage between whites, Julien thought sourly, considering his own unhappy union with Adelaide. Sheer monotony, if nothing else, in Louisiana's prim and proper white households was the principal cause of the continued success of the Quadroon Balls.

"Ah . . . Julien . . . there you are!" exclaimed Ian Jeffries, interrupting Julien's reveries. The blustery American strode over to LaCroix with Randall McCullough following in his wake. Both men were, as was Julien himself, smartly fitted out in opera attire. "We were held up by the rain and an absolute jam of carriages at the front entrance." He lowered his voice and added discreetly, "Have you seen her yet?"

Julien was about to answer when he glanced up at the balcony above them.

"Ah . . . yes," Julien said on a low breath. He was surprised to acknowledge to himself the relief he experienced at the sight of Martine Fouché, who had indeed made an appearance at the ball. These last weeks she had politely declined his repeated requests for a meeting to discuss all manner of proposals he was ready to extend to her. Bouquets of flowers, bottles of champagne, and, finally, a beautiful porcelain figurine he had bought in France had accompanied the notes delivered to her door. As far as Julien was concerned, a six-month bereavement was quite enough for the dazzling mademoiselle. He had proposed they meet on this neutral ground where they could discuss "matters of great import to us both."

Tonight, thank heavens, Martine Fouché was highly visible. She had stationed herself in the balcony and was sipping a cordial from a crystal glass while speaking quietly with her mother. The young woman's lustrous black hair was swept up and fastened with a brilliant garnet. Her gown was of midnight-blue watered silk, only a shade lighter than the black bombazine she had worn the last time he'd seen her. The garment, whose muted color signified her recent loss, was utterly without ornament but exquisitely cut and fitted to her perfect shape. Martine's beauty and simple elegance attracted the attention of every person in the room.

Yet she was standing alone upstairs with only her mother for company.

Nearly all thoughts of the Canal Street property had fled

from his mind. He would make his proposition known concerning that particular matter at another time, he assured himself. It was suddenly clear that intimidation of any sort was not the path to securing all of his goals. His principal intent tonight, he realized, was to get past Martine's mother and speak with this stunning young woman alone.

"Gentlemen," he addressed his two male companions, "I've decided another approach would be more conducive to our ultimate aims than the one for which I summoned you here. Why don't you explore the card rooms and avail yourselves of the libations and appealing company while I make my presence known? I'm sure you can amuse yourselves while I have a word with Mademoiselle Fouché."

The two men exchanged puzzled glances and then drifted off toward the card rooms where boisterous games of faro were known to erupt into duels at a moment's notice. Meanwhile, Julien found the stairway and made his way toward Martine. Yet, he hesitated to approach immediately, sensing that Althea Fouché was preparing to depart, perhaps to find a liveried manservant to refill their refreshments. Biding his time, Julien stood behind an ornamented pillar and waited.

When Martine was finally alone, he stepped forward and said in a calm, low voice, "Good evening."

"Oh!" Martine said with a little gasp. "You startled me!"

"That was not my intention," he said, smiling. "May I renew your cordial?"

"Ah . . . but no, thank you. Maman is seeing to that." She cocked her head and added, "But then, you knew that perfectly well, did you not, monsieur? What is it you would like to talk to me about? The Canal Street property, is it?"

The woman was obviously not easily hoodwinked by flattery—nor cowered by threats. Julien hoped his face wasn't flushing as he gazed steadily into her brown-gold eyes. "Not at all. . . . I was merely hoping for permission to call on you tomorrow."

"You find daylight more propitious for a business discussion?" she asked, a wry smile playing at the corners of her mouth. He marveled at her perfect use of French and her elegant syntax. Had she studied in Paris? There were so many things about this fascinating woman he wished to know.

"I was not thinking of business at all. I was hoping that perhaps one day soon, we could stroll by the river with your daughter, Lisette. I am told she is going to be a beauty, like her mother."

"Ah . . . monsieur . . . what clever ploys you enlist in your behalf," she said, her smile broadening into one that was half coquette, half proud *maman*. She heaved a sigh and opened her fan, waving it near her delicate chin in a graceful, languid motion. "To praise the daughter first is quite endearing to a doting parent such as I. And you are right. I would enjoy escaping the confines of my cottage for a brief while."

"Would eleven tomorrow morning suit?" he ventured boldly. The ballroom below them appeared to sparkle even more brightly, now that Martine nearly had agreed to a rendezvous.

"Let me inquire of Maman," she replied evenly, glancing over his shoulder at Althea, who approached, now accompanied by a gloved servant carrying a silver tray with two glasses. "If that hour suits her as well, we shall make a happy foursome, *n'est-ce pas?*"

Move. Countermove.

Julien knew he was engaged in a game of chess that would require all his wits.

The servant bowed and departed while the two women quickly conferred.

"We would be delighted, monsieur. Eleven o'clock tomorrow, then?" Martine murmured. "And now, please do not feel you must keep us company. I'm sure you and your two gentlemen friends had some other notions of entertainment in mind this evening. *A demain,* then."

Until tomorrow indeed.

Before dawn Corlis Bell McCullough heard a carriage draw up in the road, and then a deep voice ordered the driver to wait below, on Julia Street. She reached for her dressing gown at the foot of her four-poster bed and slid her bare feet onto the cool, bloodred Persian carpet.

Muted masculine voices echoed in the gaslit stairwell, and

she could only hope her husband and his companion would have a care for four-year-old Warren, dozing in his cot on the other side of the bedchamber.

She tiptoed to the bedroom door and opened it a crack, staring into the hallway just in time to watch Ian Jeffries and Randall enter the apartment and walk arm in arm past her bedroom and into the darkened parlor.

"Let me just turn up the gaslight, Ian, and then I shall pour you another brandy!" she heard Randall exclaim jovially, his words slightly slurred.

Her husband was drunk, a condition that was probably matched, brandy for brandy, by that scoundrel Ian Jeffries! She had no doubt that the two men and Julien LaCroix had had a high old time of it at the Quadroon Ball.

Corlis wondered that she felt no jealousy at the thought of her husband having congress—polite or otherwise—with those exotic young women at the Salle d'Orleans. Well, she mused bitterly, as far as she could determine, all women were slaves, whether members of the black race or white! Even when they possessed their own property, money, and jewels, their wealth was inevitably placed under the management and control of the male members of their families.

She glanced down at her thickening waistline. A second infant would make an appearance after less than four years of marriage. In the end, females were mere prisoners of their gender, she concluded glumly.

We have the babies . . . and in that tells the tale. . . .

Corlis gently pushed the bedroom door open a few inches wider and advanced stealthily down the hallway in order to hear more clearly the men's conversation.

"But don't you fear, Ian, that the black bitch is going to reveal to Julien our role in the demise of Henri Girard?" Randall demanded. "I thought surely our waiting would be at an end tonight, but if LaCroix's behavior at the ball is any proof, he seems beguiled by that she-devil!"

"Julien is beguiled," Ian replied gruffly. "We accompanied him to the Orleans Ballroom to put a wee bit of muscle into her exchange of the Canal Street property, and look what happened!"

"Julien ends up paying court to the jade like some lovesick fool!" Randall concluded, aggrieved.

"It was a revolting display!" Ian agreed, his words beginning to slur in the manner of his companion.

"These Frenchies are the devil's own, don't you think? Can't trust 'em as far as you can throw 'em."

"Well, we missed our opportunity to get the land ourselves," Ian mused, "but I'll be damned if I'll lose out on the opportunity to serve as the builder of that property."

"Just remember, Ian," Randall warned. "If Martine keeps the land, the bitch will never hire us to build on it after what happened with Henri. And if we should try to force her hand, she might tell Julien just how her patron died and why Etienne LaCroix is currently in a state of decrepitude!" Corlis recognized the panic edging her husband's voice. He was, at heart, a complete coward. "Really Ian," Randall continued, almost whining with anxiety, " 'twould be utter folly to risk involving ourselves without Julien in our camp—"

"Calm down, man!" Ian interrupted irritably. "If, perchance, Martine is stupid enough to accuse us of anything regarding Henri, we shall maintain that she is a lying, devious slut. We'll say that you and I were merely attempting to prevent Girard from deeding land to her that, by rights, was to be given to Julien upon his return from France."

"Other than through Martine herself, is there any way Julien could learn of—"

"No," Ian said shortly. Corlis heard the sound of liquid being poured into glasses. "Fortunately for us his father remains silenced and paralyzed." There was a moment's quiet emanating from the front parlor while Corlis assumed Ian Jeffries took a long draught from his replenished glass of brandy. "Let that be a warning to you, Randall," he advised loftily. "The folly lies in allowing one's emotions to run rampant. Julien's father became enraged about events and promptly suffered a fit of apoplexy. Julien now is ass-over-teakettle about a shopworn quadroon. Keep a cool head, my man!" Ian added with pompous certitude, "That's the way to success!"

"I don't know," Randall countered doubtfully. "We're playing a very dangerous game."

"Of course, 'tis dangerous. That's how the game is played! Look, McCullough, if you are not prepared to put it all on the line with me, we can end our partnership here and now!"

"That's not what I meant," Randall protested hastily. " 'Tis just that it's all a bit dicey, what with Martine Fouché now a wild card as far as young LaCroix is concerned. Surely you see the peril . . . to us both? Should anyone learn that we—"

"I see it!" Jeffries intervened gruffly. "I see it well enough." The man was thoroughly inebriated and full of self-importance. "But as we both know by now, everyone in New Orleans has his or her price. Or they wind up dead."

Corlis's mind was racing. She leaned unsteadily against the wall, wishing heartily that she had not left the isolation of her bedchamber or heard the exchange between her husband and Ian Jeffries in her front parlor.

She had learned just enough to comprehend how the baffling pieces of a certain puzzle were beginning to fall into place. She now dreaded to consider the real reasons Henri Girard had met such an untimely end, or why she had been ordered to employ her powder puff and rouge pot to make it appear as if the handsome forty-seven-year-old bachelor had died of natural causes.

Corlis turned and retreated to her private sanctuary, leaving her husband and his partner to continue their drinking until, undoubtedly, they both passed out in the front room. In the darkness of her bedchamber, she listened to the even breaths of her young son asleep in his cot and pondered whether she dared warn a stranger named Martine Fouché. Wasn't the poor woman more than likely to come to an unhappy end if she stood in the way of the partnership of Jeffries, McCullough, and LaCroix?

The skies were clear of the downpour that had pounded the roof of the Orleans Ballroom the previous evening, at times nearly drowning out the orchestra. Today the promenade along the levee was swept clean of its usual debris, and the heavens were a pale blue. A temperate April breeze lifted the frilly edges of Martine's and Althea's parasols as Julien and his female companions strolled along the busy waterfront.

A ten-year-old girl with dark hair skipped ahead of the threesome, the ruffles of her dress rippling in frothy waves as she played with her new puppy, oblivious of her elders.

"Monsieur LaCroix, you've been too clever," Martine scolded gently. "Obviously I cannot possibly deprive Lisette of the dear gift you brought in its own beautiful basket. Yet it was not necessary. We hardly know you, monsieur."

Martine's mother nodded in grim agreement but remained silent.

"But it gives me great pleasure to bring your little girl such a gift," Julien replied mildly. "After all, she has so recently suffered the loss of her father, and I thought the puppy might give her something to take her mind off the tragedy that befell her . . . and you."

Martine arched her brows ever so slightly. "I think there was more on your mind than poor Henri Girard's sad fate, but let us not talk of such *tristesse*. Perhaps you have good news of your father? Has he shown any signs of improvement?"

Julien was taken aback at Martine's familiarity with the health of his family member. She seemed intimately acquainted with the difficult situation faced by everyone at Reverie: the patriarch of a vast business enterprise who could neither move nor speak.

"My father's condition, unfortunately, remains the same," he disclosed indulgently, "but thank you for inquiring." Martine and her mother obviously considered themselves equals, perhaps the result of her long association with his father's business partner, who had been privy to all LaCroix family affairs.

Just then the puppy began to yap insistently.

"Maman!" Lisette said, retracing her steps. "He won't stop barking. Why is he so upset?" she asked worriedly. She stared up at Julien with large blue eyes flecked with brown and edged by coal-black lashes.

Passer blanc . . .

Why, she could pass for white!

"I do believe your puppy is hungry, Lisette," Julien said with a smile. "He's only a little baby and eats quite often, I am told, while he's growing so quickly." Nonchalantly he addressed Althea. "My cook packed some food, chopped meat and scraps and such. It's in the basket we left at the cottage. . . ."

He deliberately allowed his sentence to dangle suggestively while the puppy continued his loud demand for food. Julien purposefully had kept the poor thing off its rations prior to his arrival at Rampart Street. He needed to create an opportunity to be alone with Martine Fouché.

"Maman!" Lisette said, her voice full of motherly concern. "We must go home at once and feed my puppy!"

A flash of disappointment clouded Martine's smooth, elegant features. He had gambled that she would have grown restless during these last days of her official mourning and would be looking forward to this outing. To Althea he said, "Pity, though. . . . I so wanted to show Mademoiselle Fouché the beautiful clipper ship anchored a bit farther down the quay."

His scheme worked. Martine put her slender hand on her mother's silk sleeve.

"Maman, would you consider taking Lisette back to the cottage with the puppy? I would so enjoy continuing our stroll beside the river."

Althea made no attempt to disguise her displeasure at the suggestion. However, after a moment she nodded in agreement, and she, Lisette, and the new puppy headed off toward Rampart Street.

When they were out of sight, Julien took a step closer to Martine's side and smiled. "That little rascal played his part to perfection," he chuckled. "I couldn't imagine how else to have a moment alone with you, my dear. I shall, indeed, escort you to the clipper ship, but first, may we sit a moment in the Place d'Armes?" he asked.

Martine turned her graceful head to stare at him, her full lips parted slightly in surprise. Her delectable white, even teeth contrasted fetchingly with her honey-colored mouth.

"Why, Monsieur LaCroix, I—"

"Please call me Julien," he urged, guiding her toward the public square in front of the cathedral. He boldly seized her hand, his pale white fingers entwined with her golden flesh.

"Monsieur," she temporized, yet she allowed him to gently pull her to his side and sit down on a wooden bench.

Julien was seized by an overwhelming desire to touch her face, her hair, the pulse fluttering at the base of her throat. He reached toward her and gently grazed the back of his fingers against the smooth plane of her high cheekbone.

"So incredibly lovely," he murmured.

"I would ask you not to do that," she said stiffly. She gathered her skirt's ink-black bombazine in her hand and said, with anger edging her voice, "I am still in mourning, Monsieur LaCroix, and this is a public place. I would ask you to show proper respect!"

Julien was shocked by her blatant reprimand. As she abruptly turned to face him, he studied her beautiful features, which were tensed for combat.

"Was your relationship with Henri such a love match?" he asked with icy dispatch as a stab of unaccountable jealousy for a dead man clutched at his vitals. His original mission had been merely to gain her confidence in order to reclaim the Canal Street property. Suddenly his ulterior motive had become his primary one—to claim Martine Fouché.

"My relationship with Monsieur Girard was a very private one," she replied with unmistakable hauteur. "I do not wish to discuss it with a stranger."

Julien allowed his hand to skim down Martine's slender neck and rest lightly on her shoulder. He gazed openly at the rise of her bosom swelling beneath the tight bodice of her dress. She lowered her glance in an unspoken demand that he remove his hand.

"Let us speak frankly, dear Martine. Henri is not with us any longer, is he?" Julien said quietly. "He has departed this world due to selfish, unhealthy habits that have deprived his loved ones of his company, is it not so?" Martine's eyes widened in reaction to his harsh pronouncements, but she remained silent. "And now he's left you with a deed to some valuable land but no protector. How very unwise of him."

Martine stood up and stepped angrily away from him. Julien would wager that if she had been a man, she would have challenged him to a duel, right on the spot.

"Are you threatening me, Monsieur LaCroix?" she demanded, her voice low and shaking with fury. "If I don't submit to your advance, you will somehow strip my legacy from me? Is that what you are about?"

Julien took her measure warily. What was he doing? he demanded of himself. He was neither accomplishing his goal of persuading her to trade her property nor luring her into his bed!

"I am merely stating the facts of the situation," he replied, attempting to sound calm and in control.

"The *facts*, as you so delicately put them," she countered, tapping the tip of her closed parasol into the dust near his polished half-boots, "are there for all the world to see in the deed that has been signed by your own father and Monsieur Girard and properly witnessed!"

He quickly rose from the bench as she turned abruptly toward the facade of Saint Louis Cathedral. In another instant he knew he would lose all possible chance to woo her, let alone persuade her that he would honorably exchange her land on Canal Street for property of equal value.

"Martine . . . I'm—I'm sorry," he faltered. "You misunderstand my intent! I—"

But Martine Fouché was in no mood to listen to a man whose actions she had found highly insulting. She looked over her shoulder and stared unblinkingly into his eyes. "Good day, *monsieur!*" she declared. And with that, she strode quickly across the open plaza and entered the cathedral.

After a moment's astonishment Julien hurriedly set off, arriving at the entrance of the church only steps behind her.

"Martine!" he called after her, ignoring curious pedestrians passing by. "Wait! I must talk with you." Once inside the cathedral, he was forced to pause near the door to wait for his eyes to adjust to the church's sepulchral interior. "Martine?" he whispered hoarsely. "I acted like a cad. Martine! Where are you?"

He caught sight of a black-clad figure disappearing like a ghostly apparition inside the confessional booth. Meanwhile the bells in the church's tower tolled the noonday hour, reverberating solemnly in the belfry directly above his head.

As the carillon stilled and the normal sounds of the bustling *carré de la ville* resumed in the Place d'Armes, Julien wondered with a bleakness that reached into his very soul if he had not lost all chance of capturing the favors of the proud, enigmatic Martine Fouché.

Chapter Ten

March 11

The sound of church bells faded in Corlis's ears and, in its place, she heard an insistent beeping noise coming from her electronic pager.

Her heart still pounding, she glanced around in complete confusion at the dimly lit basement and its rows of ledger books and file folders stowed in metal shelves in the underground city archives. Then she gazed at the 1838 diagram of New Orleans spread on the desk in front of her. Warily, she leaned forward and squinted at a faded green square identified as "Place d'Armes" on the map, located in the center of the hand-drawn grid, known in modern times as the French Quarter. When was the name Place d'Armes changed to Jackson Square?

There, drawn on the yellowed map, was the miniature, two-dimensional sketch of a three-spired church, complete with bell tower, and the words "Saint Louis Cathedral" written beneath in spidery nineteenth-century script.

"What in the *world* just happened to me?" she declared aloud, then glanced around to see if anyone was close enough to hear the ravings of a madwoman who had somehow been thrust back into a crazy time warp where the human subjects of her historical research were running around, *live* and in living color!

As far as she could determine, reincarnation this definitely was *not*! But what in blazes was *causing* these little paranormal junkets back in time? And all to the same destination: New Orleans, immediately prior to the time when King Duvallon's treasured Canal Street buildings had been constructed. Even more astounding, each of these exotic episodes—or whatever they were—was lasting longer and becoming more detailed. Clearly she couldn't blame this most recent blast from the past on her missing a meal, or on some wild figment of her imagination!

Corlis rubbed her throbbing temples with the tips of her fingers and speculated briefly about the ancestress she'd been named after—Corlis Bell McCullough. She hurriedly made a note on the yellow pad as a reminder to confirm more details about the husband of the original Corlis.

Was there any way to prove that the opportunistic blowhard Ian Jeffries could be a forebear of *Grover* Jeffries? And most astonishing of all, Corlis realized, staring fixedly at the antique map, in *this* particular visitation, she had accessed a past that had not always involved Corlis Bell McCullough *directly*. Perhaps her progenitor merely provided "the way back."

Without warning, panic flooded her solar plexus and made her feel faint with anxiety. This kind of thing simply couldn't be happening to *her*, of all people! She'd been known her entire career as a hard-core skeptic, more than a little cynical and, in her line of work, *always* on the lookout for charlatans who claimed to have paranormal experiences. In fact, she had long prided herself on being able to detect a fake a mile away.

Corlis deliberately inhaled a calming breath as she scanned the deserted archive. She noticed that her skin had begun to feel that now familiar clamminess that always accompanied these visitations, along with the perspiration that suddenly beaded her forehead. A pang of nausea swept over her.

Suddenly her beeper went off a second time. She studied the telephone number displayed on the tiny screen. She could only determine from its familiar prefix that someone who lived in the French Quarter was trying to reach her. Her watch said it was five o'clock, exactly.

How strange! she thought, biting her lip in concentration. If she'd fallen asleep, she'd only dozed a few minutes. But *had* she merely fallen asleep? Then she sat upright in her chair. She certainly wasn't going to find the answer just sitting in *this* dank place. She rose to her feet but was forced to steady herself by leaning against the desk until her vertigo abated. Cautiously she stashed the rare documents into the proper folder to await her next visit and made for the exit just as the basement archive closed for the day.

Sure as shootin', I don't want to be shut up in a place like this all night!

With a brief nod to the security guard in the lobby, she ventured outdoors, eager for the privacy of her car. Right now, Corlis thought with single-minded determination, her only goal was to find out who had sent her an electronic summons from the "real world"—and had thereby, inadvertently, bid her return from the nineteenth century.

"You can leave a message for King Duvallon, Jitters, or any of the preservation guerrillas, after the tone. Have a decent day."

Corlis leaned her head against the back of her luxurious leather driver's seat and inhaled slowly, then held her breath for a count of five and exhaled. Her masseuse in L.A. had taught her this technique for "finding her center."

King had called her. From his house. After business hours.

Oh boy, Aunt Marge. What do I do now?

A million questions swirled in her head as she quickly pushed the END button on her cell phone to avoid saying something foolish into King's answering machine.

If she considered Kingsbury Duvallon just a source—like any other she dealt with day in, day out—she wouldn't be feeling so giddy over the simple fact that he'd called her . . . would she? And what if she disclosed to him what had just happened to her in the city's basement archive? How could a mere acquaintance like King Duvallon be the only person in the universe that she'd trust with this bizarre information?

Corlis slowly shook her head in dismay. Why, she wondered bleakly, did she absolutely *yearn* for this former adversary to put his arms around her and tell her she wasn't going crazy?

You know the rules, McCullough. You're covering a story. No fun allowed.

With all the money at stake—not to mention the politics— the controversy brewing over the demolition of those buildings on Canal Street could be big.

Very big. You've got to keep everything between you and King strictly professional!

For years Aunt Marge had drummed "the code" into her: "If the relationship between a reporter and a source begins to get personal, dear, the reporter either has to confine herself exclusively to contact during business hours and when other people are around—or take herself off the assignment," Aunt Marge declared. "There are no ifs, ands, or buts about this, darling girl."

Just then her mobile phone sounded.

"Hello?"

"Well . . . I'll be!" A deep voice chuckled. "I actually got you in person! Where are you, Ace? It took all my spies to track down your cell number."

"King!" Corlis exclaimed. "How *did* you find me? This thing is as classified as a Pentagon safe phone!"

"Can't reveal my sources," he said smugly.

"Virgil again. I gotta talk to that guy."

"Got somethin' very interestin' to show you."

Corlis could hear the excitement in his voice.

"Yeah? What?"

"As I said, I've got to *show* you."

"Well . . . okay," she said doubtfully. "Where do I have to go to see this mysterious whatsus?"

"My place."

"What?"

"I had the librarian at the Historic New Orleans Collection make two copies late today—which I just picked up on my way home. How 'bout comin' over for a drink first, and we'll have the unveilin'. Then we can grab a bite at a little neighborhood place I know round the corner."

"What *kind* of unveiling?" she asked suspiciously. "And copies of *what* ?"

"What's the matter, Ace? You goin' cold on this story?"

"No! In fact, I've been doing a little digging on my own . . . in the basement of City Hall."

Not to mention a little time-traveling!

"That's great, sugar!" he said enthusiastically. "Are you in your car right now?"

"Yes. Parked just off Poydras," she said as she stared into her rearview mirror, wishing she'd washed her hair that morning.

"Get yourself to the Quarter, on the double. I'm on the corner of Dauphine and Ursulines. The gate'll be open, so you can park in the courtyard."

"Okay . . ." she agreed uncertainly, "but I don't know about dinner."

"We'll talk about it when you get here. I promise that I'll remove from the house all signs of my ever havin' been a member of a fraternity. Bye now."

Corlis took the longer route to King's place to give herself time to steady her nerves. She needed a few more moments to recover after her latest rendezvous with an unsettling historical cast of characters.

At dusk on this cloudless March day, shafts of soft topaz light suffused the atmosphere as she drove down Decatur Street. On her right, the sluggish Mississippi had turned into a ribbon of molten gold as the sun began to fade along the narrow streets of the French Quarter.

It was all so beautiful, she thought. She was filled with a savage adoration for the elegance and decadence of the city. Its culture and crime. A place where the best and worst of humanity mixed it up at Mardi Gras and at Jazz Fest, in the churches uptown, and in the bars along Bourbon Street. A place that made a person deliriously happy—or suicidal.

Once on Dauphine Street, she quickly spotted two wooden gates that were magically swinging open as she approached, their sage-green hue inviting against the house's warm, toast-colored stucco walls. Above the first floor a lacy wrought-iron gallery was supported, at intervals, by pillars of matching iron filigree. Enormous shaggy ferns cascaded from hanging pots along the stylish balcony. Corlis steered her car into the courtyard and parked between King's battered station wagon and a late-model navy-blue Jaguar convertible. A fountain embedded in the far wall splashed musically.

There were no two ways about it. The place was gorgeous!

Meanwhile the gates behind Corlis's car closed automatically. She glanced to her left, and there, standing in an exquisitely molded wooden doorway, framed by large shutters painted the same sage-green color as the gate, was King Duvallon, smiling broadly.

"Good goin' findin' this place," he complimented her. "But then, you're Ace Reporter McCullough, right?"

Corlis squeezed out of the driver's side, careful not to bump the Jag's pristine paint job with her car door.

"Wow . . . this is fabulous!" she exclaimed, taking in the picturesque courtyard with its exuberant sprays of magenta bougainvillea. "Who's your neighbor?" she said with an admiring glance at the classic lines of the other car.

"Fortunately, I don't have any," he said.

Corlis halted halfway to the door. "You live here on your own?"

"Yup."

"And y*ou* own the Jag?"

"Yes, ma'am," he replied in his best military manner.

"But what about that beat-up Ford station wagon you drive all over town?"

"That's my weekday car." He shrugged. "This one's for special occasions."

"Oh," she said in a small voice. She glanced up at the intricate ironwork crowning the classic French Quarter house. "At the risk of being nosy, do you actually *own* this incredible place?"

"With a gentle assist from the Whitney Bank . . . but, yes, I own it," he said with a wry smile.

So much for the struggling academic. But hadn't she heard that the Kingsbury and Duvallon clans lost most of their money and property in the years following the Civil War? What was with the fabulous car and the unbelievable house, she wondered, as she followed King down a short hallway, its walls hung with large ebony-framed color photos of Mardi Gras parades of years past. Things were *definitely* not exactly what they seemed to be!

"Don't tell me this was a derelict building once upon a time?"

"You're lookin' at the first person brave enough to sign up for the Live in a Landmark program," he said. "When I first saw this place, it had half a roof and virtually no plumbin' that worked."

And it must have taken a bundle to make it look like this! Just where did a humble professor get that kind of dough?

At the end of the hallway, Corlis found herself gazing with amazement at a spacious, airy room that had obviously been assembled from several smaller ones that had existed in the building's earlier incarnation.

"Oh no . . ." she groaned, her gaze absorbing the sight of a clutch of computers stationed around the room. "You aren't running a telemarketing scam out of here, are you?"

King put his head back and laughed. "Boy, you really *have* covered every swindle known to man, haven't you?"

"Just about," she agreed. "But what *is* all of this?"

"I've turned the downstairs level into an open space with three distinct purposes," he explained, making a sweeping gesture. "This area is where I prepare for my teachin' chores," he said, pointing to a desk built into a wall lined floor to ceiling with bookshelves overflowing with leather-bound volumes and antique building artifacts enclosed in glass display boxes—including a huge hand-forged iron nail and a cracked and peeling carved wooden rosette that probably once graced a mantelpiece.

"And that area?" Corlis asked, gesturing across the room.

"The other part over there serves as a kind of war room for the preservation work I do." Two desktop computers and a laptop rested on a six-foot-long tavern table. A round conference table, piled high with documents, stood under a square-paned window framed by large wooden shutters inside and outside. Against one wall was a photocopier, and next to it, a large, slanted desk for architectural drawings.

"Very high-tech in a very old building," Corlis commented, impressed.

"It's a good example of what we in the preservation biz call 'adaptive re-use.' Restore the exterior to its original look and renovate the interior for modern use."

"Pretty amazing," she murmured. Looking around, she asked, "And the third office?"

King pointed to an alcove on his right, where she glimpsed yet another desktop computer.

"I'm what you might call a socially conscious, self-directed financial investor," he said, faintly self-mocking. "I spend about a third of my time researchin' and managin' my personal portfolio. And then I spend some of the profits on things I believe in."

"What do you mean? You buy stocks and bonds?"

"I invest mostly in mutual funds and trade in the stock of small start-up companies in the tech sector."

Corlis surveyed the large room appreciatively. "Well, whatever you've been doing, Professor, it must have worked!" she declared flatly, recalling the sixty-thousand-dollar automobile parked in the courtyard next to her own car.

"It did," he replied with a rakish grin.

"I thought most of you New Orleans blue bloods were broke."

"That's certainly true for most of the Kingsbury-Duvallons."

"Except *you*," Corlis said pointedly. King merely shrugged and smiled modestly. "So, don't tell me you started with five dollars and parlayed it into millions? I *hate* when I hear that kind of thing," she said, only half joking.

"You're not too far from the truth," he admitted. "When I came back from the marines, my grandfather Kingsbury had just died. There were some U.S. Savings Bonds that had been bought in my name when I was born and left in a safe-deposit box for twenty-odd years. It didn't add up to much, but I educated myself a bit about finance in my early twenties, and was lucky enough to learn 'bout computers fairly early on. In fact, I believed in the digital revolution back in the eighties and invested here and there in companies I had faith in."

"Microsoft?" Corlis asked glumly.

" 'Fraid so," King said with an apologetic grin. "And surprise, surprise! Most of the nineties proved to be the hottest stock market since the nineteen-twenties. If you're not greedy, it's easier to guess right about when to collect your winnin's and get out."

Corlis exclaimed on a long breath, "This is unbelievable! Who'd ever suspect? That banged-up Ford station wagon . . . those ratty old tennis shoes?" Then she narrowed her gaze. "So tell me: Why do you pose as a slightly impoverished professor?"

"I like my privacy."

"Hasn't the secret leaked out by now? Surely your old girl-friend, Cindy Lou, must have figured out your net worth."

King raised an eyebrow. Corlis could see that he was both amused and taken aback by her candor. "I've grown kinda choosy about who I invite over. And people who gossip 'bout me don't get invited back."

"Well, I'm duly honored to be here tonight," Corlis said with a slight bow. The truth was, she was flabbergasted to learn that a man as obviously well off as Kingsbury Duvallon worked as hard as he did and risked as much as he had for causes he believed in. "And don't worry," she assured him with a mischievous smile, "your secret is safe with me." She teased, "Why, Professor Duvallon, I bet you even keep gold bars in your sock drawer!"

"Nope," King said, laughing. "I have much more interestin' things to do with my money."

"Like what?" she asked, wildly curious. Then she flushed with embarrassment, recalling his remark about treasuring his privacy. "Hey, I *am* pretty nosy. It's an occupational hazard. What I just asked is none of my business."

"I'll tell you 'bout it sometime," he replied mildly, adding, "off the record, of course."

"I think your whole *life* must be off the record!"

"I think you're very perceptive. Now, let's go on upstairs."

"Why?" she asked nervously. "Is what you wanted to show me up there?" It occurred to her that all her assumptions about the Hero of New Orleans and his preservation movement were suspect. She really didn't know the guy at all.

"Somethin' else first. Follow me."

Without further conversation, King led the way up a flight of plushly carpeted stairs. They arrived at an elegant foyer paved in black and white marble squares that opened onto one of the most tastefully appointed living rooms she'd ever seen in her life.

"Wow!"

"Nice, isn't it?" he commented quietly. "Most of this buildin' dates from 1795, reconstructed after a terrible fire that destroyed an earlier house built in French colonial days."

"*Nice* doesn't quite cover it," she said, admiring the stunning Empire-style furniture.

The walls of the large front parlor were painted a rich buttery gold. Facing Dauphine Street were a pair of sage-green French doors that opened onto the wrought-iron gallery Corlis had admired from the courtyard. Framing the doors, burnished brocade drapes cascaded in sweeping folds and pooled on the parlor's polished wood floor. Illuminated on the wall opposite hung a magnificent gilt-framed portrait of the Madonna and Child. To Corlis's right was a white marble fireplace, topped by a large gilded rectangular mirror, and above it, another luminous landscape depicting eighteenth-century Venice. An enormous chandelier hung overhead, its myriad crystal-laden branches dripping, amusingly, with brightly colored green, gold, and purple beads—necklaces tossed to crowds from floats during Mardi Gras parades long past.

"It borders a bit on the rococo, but it's very New Orleans, so it suits me," he said with a laugh as he watched her reaction.

"This place looks like an Italian *palazzo*," Corlis said, awestruck.

She turned slowly in place, noting the finely upholstered chairs and an inviting mahogany-and-dark-green brocade chaise nestled into a corner, begging for someone to doze over a good book. And everywhere were intriguing pieces of small sculpture: a carved wooden religious figure; a bust of a helmeted knight, a waist-high bronze statue of a whooping crane standing on one leg. Beneath her feet stretched a rich Aubusson carpet woven in deep tones of gold, red, and green.

"Do you want to see my bed?" King asked.

"*What?*" Corlis gasped.

"My bed," he repeated patiently. "The one that's exactly like yours."

"Oh, the bed," she echoed inanely. "The four-poster. Sure."

King led the way down another hallway and into a spacious room with highly polished parquet floors set in a herringbone design. A gloriously carved chest of drawers stood against one wall, and in the corner was a graceful cane-seat plantation chair.

Dominating the high-ceilinged interior was a massive bed with four chiseled wooden posts the thickness of a man's thigh—identical to Corlis's own bed on Julia Street. Heavy hunter-green silk brocade side curtains and a waterfall of ivory mosquito netting hung from a mahogany canopy. Taken as a whole, it was hands down the most romantic bedroom she had ever seen, and it boggled her mind to realize that it was created by a former U.S. marine!

"Tell me again. . . . Who gave you the bed?"

"Lafayette Marchand, remember?"

"Ah . . . yes . . . the godfather you disowned," she murmured. "Did his family have a plantation, too?"

"At one time, ages ago. But I think I remember him sayin' that the bed was actually made on the LaCroix plantation."

"LaCroix?" she echoed faintly. "As in Althea LaCroix? How is that possible?"

She realized, however, that it was *very* possible. Who knew better than she that Julien LaCroix had had a yen, in the nineteenth century, for the daughter of a Free Woman of Color named Althea Fouché? Did Martine Fouché eventually succumb to Julien's charms and take the LaCroix family name at some point?

King said, "Well, accordin' to Lafayette, the white LaCroixs, who owned the big Reverie plantation upriver, and the Marchands were connected through marriage somehow—as most of the old New Orleanian families are, y'know."

Corlis remained silent about the wedding between Adelaide Marchand and Julien LaCroix. Nor did she mention having witnessed, through some unexplained means earlier that day, the argument Julien LaCroix had had with Martine Fouché. Instead, she gazed at the bed and its silk curtains hanging gracefully from the carved wooden canopy overhead. Perhaps Julien had gifted his would-be lover with a bed that he'd directed his cabinetmaker to copy from others already furnishing Reverie? Which one of them—King or her—was sleeping on furniture that had belonged to the unfortunate Adelaide Marchand LaCroix and her disaffected husband, Julien—and which one in a bed that had been made for a beautiful courtesan?

"Well . . . back to business," she said finally. "What else did you want to show me?"

"We have to go back downstairs to the office, but first let me get you a glass of wine."

"Ah . . . no thanks. Better not. I have to do some . . . writing tonight," she evaded.

King glanced at her curiously and asked, "Do you work *all* the time, Ace? Don't you take time off once in a while to have a little fun?"

It was a legitimate question, she acknowledged silently. When was the last time she'd had fun? she wondered.

"Oh . . . the hell with it," she exclaimed, removing her sling-back heels and carrying them in her hand. "These things are killing me. Do you have any merlot?"

"How's a bottle of Sunstone? I stocked up on some California wines today, just for you."

"You did?" she asked, touched. "Sunstone's a *fabulous* wine! It's from a little winery near Los Olivos, north of Santa Barbara. I *love* it!" She smiled at him. "You're just full of surprises, Professor. Sunstone. Wow."

Within minutes, wineglasses in hand, King and Corlis returned to the downstairs office, where he opened a large cardboard tube and unrolled a pair of architectural drawings.

"Have a look at this," he said, placing them on the conference table with a flourish. "The librarian at the Historic New Orleans Collection is a regular Sherlock Holmes."

Corlis padded in her bare feet to his side and bent to peer over his shoulders. "The Selwyn buildings?" she asked, her glance taking in the sketch of horse-drawn carriages and an omnibus full of men sporting top hats and women holding parasols—*just like the one Corlis Bell McCullough had been clutching the day she'd stood on the levee, waiting for Julien and Adelaide LaCroix's ship to dock!*

"This was done around 1842, we think," King declared, nodding, "a year or so after the buildin's opened for business. All twenty-three original sections of the block can be seen in this sketch. See the commercial enterprises on the street level?" He pointed at signs that denoted a haberdasher, a milliner, and a large dry goods shop, among others. "Many of these merchants lived above their own establishments in fine style." He pointed out an insert drawing on the lower left corner. "One section on the back of the block that faces Common Street apparently housed a saddlery, a ladies' dress shop, and the offices of cotton and sugarcane merchants who were exportin' products grown on plantations upriver to buyers all over the world."

As the hair on the back of her neck lifted slightly, Corlis murmured, "Look at that. . . ." She pointed to a sign sketched above one doorway. "It says LACROIX AND COMPANY—EXPORTERS OF COTTON AND SUGARCANE. LaCroix . . . as in your bed."

And mine, she considered silently.

Her gaze shifted from the drawings to King's face, alight with enthusiasm.

"What a sleuth you are, Ace. I didn't even notice it."

This is the building where Julien LaCroix stormed up the stairs into the private living quarters of Martine Fouché . . . the building that may have been constructed by Ian Jeffries and my own ancestor, Randall McCullough!

"It's just all too weird," she said.

"What is?"

"Nothing," she said, embarrassed. "Have your preservation guerrillas come across any more documentation about who built these?" she inquired, doing her utmost to appear calm. "Names, other than LaCroix, that I could trace to see if any descendants currently live in New Orleans? I think our television viewers might relate more personally to the case being made for preserving these buildings if they could see them in terms of human connections to the past—and not just in terms of saving the bricks and mortar."

"Smart cookie," King agreed. "And a good place to start is to talk to the librarian who found this for me. I'll give her a call and tell her what we're lookin' for."

"I can call her," Corlis countered. She gathered up her purse and set her wineglass on the table. "Thanks a million for the lead," she said in her most professional tone. Then she turned and asked, "By the way . . . who's Jitters?"

King gave her a measured look and said, "You mean the 'Jitters' mentioned on my phone message? Why didn't you leave word when you called earlier?"

Busted!

Corlis could feel herself blush.

"I . . . ah . . . had another incoming call right then, so I hung up and took it," she fibbed. "Well, who *is* Jitters?"

"A kitten that I rescued from a Dumpster just after Christmas. Meeting Cagney Cat inspired me, I guess."

"Where is he?" she asked, looking around the room again.

"He's still a scaredy-cat . . . very jumpy. He's probably beneath the bed upstairs, hiding out."

"Hence the name Jitters."

"You got it."

"That reminds me, I have to go home to feed my cat," she said, avoiding his piercing look.

"From what I've seen of Mr. Cagney, that boy could afford to miss supper occasionally. You, on the other hand, could use a good meal. Let me take you to dinner."

At that moment she knew if she held his gaze an instant longer, she would throw herself against his well-muscled chest and ask to be served breakfast in bed. However, ignoring his invitation, she said, "Cagney wouldn't thank you for suggesting he skip dinner." Despite her best intentions, she looked directly at King, nearly drowning in the dark-blue pools of his eyes. After a pause she heard herself saying, "You do know, don't you, that I'd really love to have dinner with you?"

"Then do."

"We can't. I mean, *I* can't."

"Why ever not?"

"You've been involved in enough controversies around here to know why."

"Maybe," he admitted slowly, "but I want *you* to tell me why."

"King!" she protested. "You're not being fair. You know perfectly well why."

"All I know is a conflict of interest exists if there's a personal relationship between reporter and source. Our dinner would be strictly business, sugar."

She cocked an eyebrow. "Then why, after I repeatedly have asked you not to, do you continue to call me sugar and sweetheart and darlin'—not to mention Ace!" She held up her half-empty wineglass. "And if it's just business, why am I having a glass of wine with you with my shoes off—*in your home*?"

King gave her a measured look and seemed to admit defeat.

"Because . . . there might be *more* than business goin' on here, am I right?"

Without a word she quickly slipped on her shoes, shouldered her bag, and glanced around the office regretfully. "I'd better be on my way."

After a long, awkward pause, King said quietly, "Let me walk you to your car."

Before she turned to leave, Corlis saluted him with her rolled-up 1840s rendering of the threatened Selwyn buildings. "Thanks a lot for this."

King escorted her to the courtyard entrance of the house and pushed the button to activate the gates. Meanwhile Corlis quickly opened her car door and slipped into the driver's seat.

"Last chance," he said, ambling toward her over paving stones surrounded by springy green moss. "Sure you won't have supper with me?"

For a long moment, Corlis reconsidered his proposition. She also took into account the unholy attraction she was feeling toward this man—an allure she could no longer ignore.

Honest reporters don't carry on personal relationships with their sources.

"I really appreciate your asking me," she said earnestly, looking up at the devilishly handsome figure leaning against her car. A person *could* drown in those blue eyes, she thought. "But as long as I'm assigned to this story, and you're a player in the piece, I can't accept any invitations. Do you understand?" she asked, trying to keep the pleading tone out of her voice.

"Ace, you're somethin' else," he said. He flashed her a grin. "But *you* have to understand: This is Louisiana, darlin' . . . so it's kinda hard for a poor southern boy like me to follow every single rule you Yankees set down."

"I'm not a Yankee!" she retorted. "I'm a westerner."

"That's probably why I like you so much," he replied, composing his features into a deadpan expression. "I always knew you had that pioneerin' spirit. Wanna meet at the library tomorrow mornin', 'bout eleven o'clock? I can show you the ropes."

Corlis shot him a doubtful look, then laughed. "It's business, right?"

"Absolutely. Just business." Then he leaned a fraction closer and added, "But right now, we're both off the clock."

Without warning he leaned inside the car, cupped her face between his hands, and kissed her soundly on the lips. And instead of pushing against his embrace, she could only marvel at his wickedly sensuous assault on her nervous system. Even worse, her only desire was to open the car door and follow him up to the magnificent bedroom at the top of the stairs.

McCullough, you are certifiable!

At length, King took a step back and stared down at her with an unmistakable gleam of triumph in his eye. "Now you take good care of that cat of yours, sugar pie . . . and sleep tight."

Chapter Eleven

March 12

The next morning, Corlis stopped off at the city's historic records building on her way to her scheduled meeting with King. Once inside the archive, she opened a nearby window and allowed plenty of fresh air to waft through the basement where rows of shelves were bulging with old documents.

She was leaving nothing to chance.

After inhaling deeply she found herself smiling.

Then she swiftly began to scan the accordion-pleated folder containing papers that chronicled the history of the 600 block of Canal Street. She searched for any documents relating to the original owners and builders of the twenty-three structures that had once been on the site.

"Bingo!" she whispered when she found the signature of one "Ian Jeffries" affixed to the building plans submitted to the city in 1839. Stunned to have located what she was looking for so easily, she stared at the yellowed document for several minutes.

"Glory, glory," she murmured. Her heart began to race while she fingered the brittle paper. Beneath Jeffries's sweeping penmanship, the foreman on the project had also signed his name: Randall McCullough.

Corlis leaned back in her chair and slowly shook her head in disbelief. It unnerved her to think that she had somehow accessed her ancestor's life. Were these signatures proof positive that some sort of system was at work whereby descendants of people with "unfinished business" got to rub shoulders generations later—as sort of a cosmic joke—just to see what would happen? Or was this evidence that the modern-day Corlis McCullough was going bonkers?

She scribbled the reference to the aged building permit into her reporter's notebook. Then she returned the file to its proper folder and headed for the exit in order to keep her appointment with King on Chartres Street.

Corlis eased her car into a narrow parking space in the crowded French Quarter and did her utmost not to think about the beautiful balconied house on Dauphine and Ursulines streets—or King's unexpected ten-alarm kiss. Did she dare tell him about the extraordinary linkages she kept uncovering between people she now knew—or knew of—in New Orleans and long-deceased figures involved in the buildings on Canal Street? For the moment, at least, she decided she would keep what she'd learned this morning to herself, lest she stretch King's faith in her sanity too far.

The Williams Library was located in the heart of the Quarter in a turn-of-the-century courthouse built in the beaux arts style. The grand old building had been restored and refurbished as a state-of-the-art specialized archive.

Talk about your adaptive re-use! Corlis thought admiringly as she reached the second floor and walked through brass-studded leather-upholstered doors into the main reading room. The lofty chamber was built to a majestic scale, with high ceilings, fanlight windows, and long, mahogany library tables resting on a richly woven gold-and-navy carpet. She immediately spotted King leaning casually against the reference desk, speaking in a low voice with a middle-aged woman with dark close-cropped hair.

As for Professor Duvallon, today he sported a dark-green polo shirt and freshly pressed chinos, a combination that subtly complemented the richness of the library's decor.

"Hey, Ace . . . whadcha know?"

I know that I'd better ignore that kiss last night, Mr. Preservation!

King swiftly introduced her to the director of the library. Corlis's gaze shifted to several bulging files resting on the librarian's desk. "Have you two found any more documentation about the people who built the six hundred block of Canal?" she inquired with a growing sense of excitement.

"I've pulled together some material King asked me to research," the librarian replied. "Perhaps you'll find something in this folder that will head you in the right direction." She smiled. "In fact, I think you're both in for a few surprises."

"How so?" King asked, intrigued.

"I don't want to spoil your fun, but I will say this—at least three of the co-owners were Free People of Color, and two were women."

"Incredible!" King exclaimed. "As early as 1840?"

"Remember, King," the librarian said, "most people are surprised to learn that at least forty-five percent of all blacks in New Orleans at that time were *free*—not slaves."

"About how many people is that, do you know?" Corlis asked.

"Well . . ." the librarian said, glancing at some figures she had jotted down. "There were some thirty-three thousand blacks, so . . . that means about eighteen thousand of them were classified 'Free People of Color,' and many of them owned slaves themselves."

"Then my chances of tracing descendants of the original owners—black and white—might be pretty fair," Corlis said. "It'd be great if I could get some modern-day family members to talk about their heritage on camera."

"That certainly places the historical value of these structures at a much higher level than any of us had guessed, don't you think?" King suggested.

"I think this information makes them *very* important," the librarian whispered. "These were among the very first black-owned businesses in the entire United States. Not only that," she added, keeping her voice low in deference to other library patrons, "a few Scots-Irish merchants, a Jewish businessman named Jacob Levy Florence, and several other merchants whose names I still have to pin down, were also co-owners in this block."

"It sounds like what we have here is a sort of Rainbow Coalition of nineteenth-century entrepreneurs," King declared.

"Including some women," Corlis interjected triumphantly, and clamped her hand over her mouth in embarrassment.

King looked over at her, amused. The librarian ushered them into a small conference room.

"Even Paul Tulane was among the consortium," the librarian said, pointing proudly to a monograph in her file that described the life of the Anglo-American merchant who had founded the prestigious university on St. Charles Avenue uptown.

Corlis felt a frisson of excitement. "Could you tell me the names of the two women owners you mentioned?" she asked, and ignored King's gentle poke to her rib cage.

The librarian flipped open the file folder once again and scanned a typed list.

"So far, I've only found the name of one woman whom I can confirm was a bona fide owner: Livaudais . . . Celeste Marigny Livaudais."

"Oh . . . interesting," murmured Corlis. Oddly enough, she was vaguely disappointed not to hear the librarian pronounce the name Martine Fouché.

C'mon, McCullough. Be thankful you're not the voodoo lady you thought you were. Forget all that stuff! Concentrate on getting a story on videotape that Andy Zamora will let you broadcast on TV!

Just at that moment Corlis's telephone pager, attached to the strap on her leather shoulder bag, produced the familiar series of short pips.

She peered at the tiny screen. "Oh, Jeez Louise," she sighed, noting the number printed in electronic dots.

"Gotta go cover a fire?" King asked.

Corlis nodded resignedly. "I wish," she replied, making a face. "The symphony's annual luncheon at the Pontchartrain Hotel starts in twenty minutes . . . a real softball event, as we say in the news biz," she added for the librarian's benefit. "Virgil, my cameraman, is wondering where I am," she said, pointing to her pager.

King picked the file folder off the conference table.

"Thanks a million for the photocopies," he said to the librarian, "and let me know if you turn up anything else." To Corlis he added, "I'll walk you to your car."

The warm, faintly humid March temperatures outside forecast the sultry summer heat that everyone in California had predicted Corlis would find insufferable. As they advanced down the sidewalk, a fast-talking teenager attempted to thrust into her hand a short, bamboolike stalk of sugarcane with a free, cellophane-wrapped piece of candy and a card attached by a piece of red yarn.

"Patti's Praline Pleasure Palace. Best in N'awlings, darlin'!"

"I'm *not* a tourist!" she protested, noting the salesman made no attempt to offer any of his wares to King. "I live here!"

King chuckled and pointed to a long line of people standing patiently by a restaurant door, waiting for K-Paul's Louisiana Kitchen to open for lunch.

"*There* are your customers, Remy!"

"She's such a pretty lady!" Remy declared with a broad grin. "I can always *try*, can't I, Professor?"

"You know that guy?" Corlis whispered, amazed as King gently clasped her by the elbow and guided her past the youthful huckster and around a couple dressed in matching shorts and tops that declared "Been to New Orleans—Got This Stupid T-Shirt."

"Oh, Remy's a real character around here. He and his sister Patti have been in the Quarter for years, sellin' pralines like their mama and grandmama before 'em."

"There's my car," Corlis announced. King leaned against the Lexus while she dug in her purse for her keys. He raised his forefinger to his lips, reached toward her, and gently tapped her on the nose. "Now that you and I have concluded our business meetin' today, I'd sure like to—"

"King!" Corlis protested, alarmed by the magnetic force drawing her dangerously close to his side.

He continued to hold her in a riveting stare until he said, finally, "You take care, y'hear?"

Corlis had reason to remember King's words when she and her television crew made a quick pass, with camcorder rolling, through the ballroom jammed with well-dressed symphony patrons having lunch at round linen-covered tables decorated with elaborate floral centerpieces. The "culture vultures," as the movers and shakers of the New Orleans classical music scene were known, had turned out en masse to raise money for an orchestra that struggled to survive in a town renowned for jazz.

"This is a nonevent," Virgil commented under his breath.

"I'd say it's worth about a seventeen-second voice-over and call it a day," Corlis agreed. "Let's blow this pop stand."

"Is that any way to treat one of our fair city's most hallowed institutions?"

Corlis turned to identify the source of the soft southern voice laced with disapproving irony that had just whispered in her ear.

"Jack."

"Hello, Miz McCullough." A hank of Ebert's straight sandy hair skimmed the tops of his pale brows above eyes the color of chlorinated pool water. "Better not let Bonita Jeffries hear you say that."

Damn, but this is a tiny town! Corlis thought. Grover Jeffries's well-placed donations over the previous decade had landed his wife the presidency of the symphony board and earned her some social clout in the bargain.

"In TV land, seventeen seconds on any subject is a lot of time," she replied flippantly. "How are you, Jack? Heard about your new assignment with *Arts This Week*. Congratulations."

"Thanks," Jack said shortly. "I'll be takin' a look at the personalities as well as cultural institutions in New Orleans. The magazine's top management has given me carte blanche."

"Good for you," Corlis said with false enthusiasm, wondering if her nose was growing longer, like a female Pinocchio.

"They especially want me to cover architecture," he said with a faint smile.

"So I heard. Sounds like Beth Worthington gave you a broad mandate," Corlis murmured, speculating where this conversation was leading.

"Has WJAZ still got you coverin' the controversy at the university?"

Corlis shrugged nonchalantly. "The professorship named after Mr. Jeffries? That's pretty much died down, don't you think?"

"It may heat up," Jack said importantly. "Someone told me that there may be a big Jeffries project afoot for the Selwyn properties. You heard anything more 'bout that?"

"The Selwyn buildings?" Corlis echoed. "What kind of project?" She loved playing dumb for a guy too lazy to do his own research.

Jack gave her a hard look and shook his head. "Some hotel or apartment house, or somethin', over on Canal. Who knows if the rumors are true? I just thought you might have heard the same rumbles round town that I have."

"What rumbles are those?" she asked innocently.

Jack pulled back the left sleeve of his white linen suit. His attire was matched by the pale warm-weather clothing worn by two-thirds of the men in the ballroom—which made the gathering appear to be a convention of Colonel Sanders clones. "I guess there can't be much to the gossip if *you* haven't heard 'bout it," Jack noted evenly. "Well, my watch says I'm on a deadline that's comin' up mighty shortly. Better get a move on. Nice seein' you, Corlis."

Yeah. I'll just bet.

Corlis had a deadline of her own and soon headed back to WJAZ to record the voice track on today's story about the symphony. An easy day, she thought gratefully. By five-thirty she was headed down Canal Street, wondering if Cagney Cat had deposited any remains of birds or mice on her wrought-iron gallery today.

Her car came even with the ugly aluminum screen that masked the Selwyn buildings. On impulse she headed for an empty parking space in front of the large metal *S* that hung over the entrance. Through the windshield Corlis drank in the block's amazing transformation since its construction in 1840. As she sat in her car, she pictured the stately columns that she knew stood behind the false front. Her mind drifted to the black-and-white rendering King had given her that revealed the buildings as they had appeared around 1842.

From the front door of the building, white-collar workers exited in groups of two and three. At this time of day no one would notice if she indulged in a little detective work. She locked her Lexus and strode toward the entrance. Once inside the dilapidated lobby, she headed for the rear of the buildings to see if she could determine where some of the nineteenth-century commercial establishments had once done business.

Within minutes she emerged from a back door onto Common Street, to discover that the unsightly aluminum screening extended on only three sides of the city block. On the Common Street side, the buildings were faced with painted brick, enhanced with Boston-granite piers and lintels around windows matching the ones she'd glimpsed behind the front facade. Nearby an exhaust fan from an eatery called Miss Pearl's Saddlery, an establishment whose sign declared it specialized in "Authentic Louisiana Cuisine," pumped the odor of pancakes and cane syrup into the sultry afternoon air.

The Saddlery! That must be where a shop selling harnesses and carriage equipment once existed.

Corlis could feel her adrenaline starting to pump. Just then a large black woman in a floral caftan was escorting a looselimbed teenager out the restaurant's front door.

"Now, Remy, you go on outta here! My customers want *pancakes* and *cane syrup*, not those fake pralines you and yer sister push on everyone. Go on, bother somebody *else*!"

"These pralines are real *good*, Miss Pearl!" Remy retorted with an injured air. "Just the sugarcane sticks are fake!"

"I don' care. On your way, boy. I don' want my customers filled up with candy 'fore they even order their *meal*! Now, scat!"

Corlis tried to suppress a smile as Remy, quickly recovering his dignity, sauntered toward her to display his wares. His face brightened when he recognized her. "Hey, pretty lady! You Professor Duvallon's friend, right? Didn't I jus' see you two, over front of K-Paul's, on Chartres?"

"That's right," Corlis said, nodding.

"Here, " he said swiftly, shoving into her hand a bogus piece of sugarcane with a praline wrapped in cellophane and attached by a piece of yarn. "Have one. Patti's Praline Pleasure Palace. Best in N'awlings, darlin'."

"So you say," Corlis said doubtfully, examining the round, sugary confection studded with a golden pecan.

"My sister'll kill me if I don't give 'em all out. Here. Take two. Now I can go get me a soda!"

And before Corlis could protest, the young man strode confidently down Common Street and turned the corner toward Canal.

Curious, Corlis removed the cellophane from one of her "gifts" and began nibbling on the edges of the sugar disk that smelled faintly like maple syrup. She strolled past Miss Pearl's Saddlery toward a wooden door that was practically hanging off its hinges. A solitary row of sooty windows, set a few feet below the roofline, indicated that the decrepit wood door marked the entrance to a former warehouse or storage area. She reached for the knob and easily pulled open the door.

Inside, shafts of light from the windows overhead illuminated dust motes floating like fireflies. Corlis immediately felt a sneeze gathering, the result, she concluded, of layers of grime permeating the large empty space. Her eyes grew more accustomed to the dim light as she gazed around at the enclosed area.

She took another bite of her praline, inhaling its sweetish aroma laced with the earthy scent of the nut in its center. She was relieved to observe that it wasn't a sickly cloying smell like that of the day lilies, but rather had the fragrance of lush, flavorful honey. She ran her tongue over its sugary surface. It felt sticky to the touch.

Like sugarcane!

She glanced at a pile of shredded decaying burlap bags. Could this be the site where Julien LaCroix had finally established his warehouse, thus expanding his crop exports from the Reverie plantation? The warehouse space obviously had been used until fairly recently.

Her heart quickening, Corlis raised the praline to her nose and took a deep whiff—an action she instantly regretted. The scent intensified until it took on the smell of burning caramel. The cool, darkened warehouse grew inexplicably warmer . . . and warmer . . . until Corlis thought she would expire from the heat. Suddenly she became aware of the sound of flames crackling nearby, flames so hot, they roasted the very atmosphere.

Why in the world would anybody be lighting fires in temperatures as scorching as these?

"My stars, I don't think I've ever been so hot in my life!" Corlis Bell McCullough exclaimed. Tendrils of damp, pale red hair remained plastered to her moist forehead as she waved a lace fan across her flushed face to no avail. "Who'd ever think it could be this hot in *autumn*?"

Across from her in the carriage, her husband, Randall, and his partner, Ian Jeffries, barely grunted in reply. The two men, their eyes closed, rested their heads against the padded walls inside the swaying fiacre. Outside, the unrelenting heat of summer had continued unseasonably through this October day. Corlis could see it shimmer off puddles of stagnating water that dotted the road beside the riverbank. Despite last night's downpour, insufferable temperatures blanketed the countryside on either bank of the Mississippi.

"Imagine, lighting fires in weather like this!" she complained, gazing at the crackling orange flames that licked the length of a vast field of sugarcane to their left. The acreage had been recently shorn of stalks that were once above nine feet tall. In recent days hordes of Negro slaves had fanned through these forests of bamboolike foliage and leveled them, piling razor-sharp fronds with long round stems into a line of waiting wagons.

Randall McCullough opened one eye. "That's what Roulaison is, Corlis," he said with an edge of condescension. "They burn the fields like this each October. I would have thought you'd quite enjoy seeing what takes place on a large plantation during the cane-grinding season."

Well, I would have, if it weren't so blasted hot, you fool!

In Pennsylvania the leaves on the trees would be turning red and gold, as the autumn weather grew more wintry. . . .

Her dressmaker had told her about this festive time of social gatherings, dances, and candy pullings on plantations like Reverie. The great house's tall brick chimney stacks could be seen up ahead between a massive double line of moss-draped oaks. At this stage of the harvesting process, the cultivated lands bordering the entrance to the West Indies–style mansion were wreathed in thick black smoke that billowed high into the heavens. Ashes rained down everywhere, coating their carriage and the horses that pulled it, and layering the air with suspended soot. The resulting smudge transformed already intolerable temperatures into a Hades that she found nigh insupportable.

She wrinkled her nose as the remnants of raw cane melted in the field fires. Ian Jeffries's own nose began to twitch and he shifted in his seat.

"Why, it smells just like crème brûlée!" he chortled. "It raises my hopes that the food served at Reverie should be first-rate."

Slaves a few short yards from their carriage continued to torch stubble on terrain that would soon be replanted. This thrice-yearly cash crop was making Louisiana planters like Julien LaCroix and his invalid father, Etienne, rich beyond their wildest dreams.

As their vehicle rolled on, Corlis caught sight of a large metal grinder whose crank was being turned by a cow encased in a leather harness. The unfortunate beast's fate was to walk in endless circles in the blazing sun around the freestanding apparatus.

"Poor old thing!" Corlis muttered sympathetically.

Randall opened an eye once again. "He'll be well fed when he's through with his day's work," he commented. "Inside that grinder the harvested cane's being pulverized. See that juice spurting into the large wooden barrel beneath the spout?" he added with an air of smugness. A recent conversation with Julien LaCroix at the Old Absinthe House bar had resulted in the three of them being invited to Reverie for the festivities. "Called 'white gold,' it is. . . . Worth a fortune, and if you tasted it right now, it'd be candy-sweet!"

Why, oh *why* couldn't Randall and Ian involve themselves in *this* sort of enterprise, rather than their risky building schemes? she fretted silently as both men closed their eyes once again. She supposed that she should feel flattered, as an American, to be included in such private celebrations as this year's Roulaison, hosted by the LaCroixs, a French Creole family infamous for their clannishness. But then, Julien LaCroix appeared to be a forward-thinking young man with modern notions concerning business ventures that could only be achieved with the support of such go-getters as her Randall and his building partner, along with their banker, the dashing young André Duvallon.

Corlis was overwhelmed by a sense of melancholy whenever she recalled the delightful evening she had once spent as Monsieur Duvallon's dinner companion. Neither of them had mentioned the death of Henri Girard, or André's emotional outburst in front of the coffin in the parlor on the Rue Royale. In fact, she admitted to herself, at the dinner party two months afterward, he had seemed genuinely interested in her description of her former life in Pittsburgh.

Corlis stared out the coach window, recalling André's compelling blue eyes that were the color of the midnight sky. His manner held none of the hauteur she'd experienced from most native New Orleanians since arriving in Louisiana. Even her French Creole dressmaker—a retired harlot who was, after all, merely a quadroon—had somehow made her feel awkward and inferior.

Before long, Reverie's wide veranda and large, slanting roofline hove into view. Several servants waited on the steps to greet their approaching carriage, but thus far no member of the family had emerged through the majestic front door to bid them welcome. Corlis was actually looking forward to becoming better acquainted with Adelaide LaCroix, though goodness knows, Julien's young wife would probably snicker at her American guest behind her back the minute Corlis employed her own unpredictable use of the French language.

Well, at least I haven't let myself become a fat pigeon, as Adelaide has, she thought with some satisfaction, glancing down at her waistline, now restored to its normal girth following the birth of Webster two months previously. Suddenly Corlis wished she'd never agreed to the hiring of that dark-skinned girl to mind the babies during their sojourn to Reverie.

Her breasts ached with milk that she would have to expel as soon as she could steal a moment of privacy. Why had she allowed her husband to talk her into abandoning her children like this? "Randall, do you think Yolanda will have the sense to send a message to us out here if something goes amiss with the children?"

"Now, what should go amiss?" Randall muttered. "Oh, do be quiet, Corlis. You worry about everything."

"Only a fool wouldn't worry, married to a man like you," she retorted in a hoarse whisper. "I certainly worry about what you've done with my *jewelry*, Randall McCullough!" Her sense of indignation was suddenly reignited regarding their recent contretemps over the valuable sapphire necklace, earrings, and bracelet that her parents had given her when she turned sixteen. She had discovered this latest loss when packing earlier in the day, only to learn that Randall had taken her precious possessions from her jewelry case without permission. "I expect you to redeem all those items of mine immediately."

Randall opened both his eyes this time. He glanced across the coach at his sleeping partner and then glared at his wife. If they had been alone, Corlis thought he actually might have struck her.

"And I expect *you* to keep a civil tongue in your head," he hissed.

Corlis held his angry gaze for a moment longer, then turned to look out the window again, just in time to see a snake slither across the road. Its coppery skin had been singed by the flames burning in the scorched field. Fortunately the horses didn't see the disgusting creature, but Corlis felt a shudder of revulsion.

Oh, dear God . . . I cannot abide this scalding swamp!

She wondered, feverishly, how she could possibly extricate herself from the life she had unwittingly chosen when she had succumbed to the brutish charms of a man whose fate was now inextricably linked to hers. Every time she gazed at a full moon, she pulled down the shade so she wouldn't be forced to reflect on the moonlit night when she had allowed her father's lowly carpenter to—

Spilt milk! Think about something else. . . . Think about André. . . .

Despite the banker's encouragement, and despite the earlier sale of her diamonds, not one of Randall and Ian's building schemes had gotten off the ground. Severe flooding last spring delayed or waylaid their plans at every turn. The men had grown desperate to strike a bargain with Julien LaCroix regarding construction on Canal Street. And now even André hinted that he was having difficulties raising enough financing for partners who possessed little solid collateral beyond Corlis's sapphire jewelry, long pledged, it would seem, to a shady moneylender on Girod Street.

Randall tapped her rudely on the shoulder, startling her from her reverie.

"I'm warning you, Corlis," he threatened under his breath,

"I'll tolerate none of your uppity airs." Their coach was now a mere fifty yards from the columned mansion embraced by a canopy of ancient oaks. Her husband nodded brusquely in the direction of the portly young woman who had just stepped across the threshold and stood on the veranda, her hands clasped below her ample bosom. Even from this distance Corlis judged that Adelaide LaCroix's white dimity gown and bustle gave their hostess the unfortunate appearance of an overstuffed freshly laundered pillow. "I'll expect you to behave your charming best toward Julien's wife," Randall ordered sternly. "We need you to find out from her if Julien's genuinely committed to our constructing this damnable building for him—or, rest assured, you'll never see your precious sapphires again, do you understand?"

"Don't be a fool!" she retorted in a low voice, refusing to be cowed by his bullying behavior. "I'll wager you that Adelaide LaCroix has not one whit of influence over her husband, and I truly doubt the woman troubles herself with the details of his business affairs."

She knew perfectly well that Adelaide, like Adelaide's mother-in-law, Eloise LaCroix, was content merely to spend the money her family earned from the sale of sugarcane and cotton on the latest Paris fashions, fine furniture, beautiful chinaware, and rich food—if Adelaide's ample girth was any indication.

And besides, Corlis thought, frowning, as far as she was able to discern, Julien LaCroix hadn't even secured the Canal Street property yet. The building firm of Jeffries & McCullough could draw up as many plans as they liked. Young Monsieur LaCroix would not engage their services until he'd persuaded the mysterious Martine Fouché to sell or exchange her legacy. And from what Corlis had gathered from her talkative dressmaker, Annette Fouché—Martine's cousin—Julien's chances of accomplishing *that* feat were most unlikely.

No, she considered unhappily, her eyes drawn to the moss spilling in silent cascades from the oak branches above their heads, Randall and Ian's fortunes did not appear particularly promising.

Corlis sat forward in the carriage, aware that the back of her gown was soaked in sweat. Not a breath of air stirred in the trees or across the blistering cane fields. This nightmarish trip to Reverie plantation, like so many of her feckless husband's schemes, was bound to be another exercise in futility.

Well, there was no help for it, Corlis thought morosely. They were marooned in Louisiana for the foreseeable future, and she might as well make the best of it. At least, she reflected, smiling to herself, she might once again be fortunate enough to draw André Duvallon as her charming dinner companion.

Chapter Twelve

October 29, 1838

Night had fully descended on Reverie. The graceful plantation house was suffused with the mellow glow of candlelight in every room, along with gaslit globes illuminating the front parlor. Corlis Bell McCullough and the other Americans were gamely coping with the myriad of silver utensils and a forest of crystal stemware set for the many courses of food and wine.

Meanwhile Julien LaCroix peered into the large sitting room, now cleared of all furniture, to confirm that the musicians were in place and ready to commence playing. Much to his satisfaction, the pianoforte was positioned in front of the unused fireplace. To the right of the keyboard instrument, a gilded harp stood silhouetted against the chamber's lemon-yellow walls. A violinist and several other musicians in this small orchestra conferred about the order of music to be played at tonight's ball.

In the adjacent dining room the guests continued to linger over a sumptuous dinner that had included turtle soup, creamed oysters, fried catfish, and bowls of fragrant, steaming rice—a meal that had begun in the late afternoon following a day in which Julien and his staff had supervised activities in the cane fields that marked the conclusion of the harvest. A low murmur of voices and the clink of porcelain cups on saucers signaled that coffee and liqueurs would soon give way to dancing.

"Ah . . . Monsieur LaCroix," the music master hailed Julien. "*Bonsoir.* All is in readiness."

"Yes, Monsieur Grammont," he murmured. "Thank you. I

170

wonder, though, if there'll be much dancing in unseasonable weather such as this."

The face of the short, rotund musician was beet red and his cravat thoroughly wilted due to the sultry temperatures that had not lessened, despite the setting of the sun. It might as well be July as October, Julien thought irritably. When *would* this heat abate?

"Ah . . . but of course they will!" Grammont said cheerfully. "In the winter we Creoles dance to keep warm. In the summer, to keep cool."

"And in the autumn, with no relief to the heat in sight?" queried a booming voice from the threshold of the nearby foyer.

Julien's tall, handsome brother-in-law, Lafayette Marchand, strode into the ballroom with the confidence of a bachelor who—along with his equally good-looking friend and cousin, André Duvallon—would soon be much in demand as a partner to a bevy of unattached young ladies. Marchand had abundant dark hair, and his starched white shirtfront gave him the air of a man who had only seconds earlier been released from the care of his personal valet.

"If the love of dancing among this group is any indication, Julien, your guests will never see their beds tonight," Lafayette declared with a confident smile.

"I predict we shall be playing for seven hours or more, Monsieur LaCroix," Grammont agreed jovially.

"Would you care to make a wager on that prediction?" Lafayette proposed suddenly to Julien, drawing him to one side.

"Blessed Saint Cecilia!" Julien replied tiredly, pointing to the casement that stretched from floor to ceiling. "You would be willing to wager which raindrop first slides down that window over there."

"I am certainly willing to bet you concerning *one* particular subject, my dear Julien," Lafayette Marchand said in a low voice that held a note of warning. "I would hazard a guess that a certain lovely lady who dwells on Rampart Street will never exchange her hard-won land on Canal, no matter what you offer her," Lafayette declared. "Even if you offer *yourself* into the bargain, as I suspect you might."

Julien was blindsided by such bold impertinence voiced by

his wife's brother. How in blazes had the man acquired such intimate knowledge of his business affairs, to say nothing of his growing obsession with Martine herself? Julien quickly sensed that he must reign in his temper now, before he was pushed to the boiling point.

"Don't be an ass, Marchand," he replied coolly, hoping that the scales being played by the music master and his cohorts at the far end of the chamber masked their hostile exchange.

"Ah, then," Lafayette replied with a mocking air, "I am happy to have some reassurance that you will not pledge any more of my sister's legacy in the service of foolhardy building schemes outside the *carré de la ville*, such as the one I heard bandied about earlier by you and those uncouth Americans drinking absinthe in your back parlor."

Why, the blackguard actually had been *eavesdropping* on his conversation with Jeffries and McCullough!

Julien forced himself to ignore his brother-in-law's latest insult. The sound of chairs scraping along the floor in the next room alerted him that the rest of his guests would soon be descending upon them.

"May I suggest, Marchand," Julien replied in as pleasant a tone as he could muster, "that you relieve yourself of any anxiety you may have concerning LaCroix family affairs and confine your concerns to the amount of your losses at the horse track?" he added, unable to curb his ire. "Though you may be my wife's brother, that gives you no special status here at Reverie, as far as I'm concerned. If you continue to stir the pot between Adelaide and me, you may find yourself no longer welcomed here as a guest. Now, if you will excuse me." He strode up the wide, curving staircase with two specific missions in mind—the first of which was to escape Lafayette Marchand's highly irritating presence.

Etienne LaCroix lay motionless and mute in a darkened room lit only by the pale rays of a harvest moon filtering through the window. Julien cracked open the door and beheld his father, still as a corpse. He was lying alone, as he had for the past year, in a massive four-poster whose wooden canopy, draped in blue silk brocade, extended from the top of the mahogany headboard over half the bed.

Maisie, the cook's assistant, was in the process of gathering up the bowl of puréed rice and milk she had been attempting to feed her patient.

"Was he able to eat anything?" Julien whispered to the slave, who had belonged to his family since her birth.

"Not very much, Mr. Julien," Maisie replied softly with a discouraged nod in the direction of the half-filled bowl she held. "I'll just take these things downstairs. My Albert's gonna sit with Mr. Etienne tonight, with everybody else so busy wi' da party. He'll be up soon's I tell him to."

"Thank you, Maisie," Julien said. "Tell Albert I greatly appreciate his watching over Father."

"I surely will, Mr. Julien," Maisie said, smiling faintly. "You take care now, y'hear?" she added with the easy familiarity of someone who had long ago played pirates and hide-and-go-seek with him on the banks of the Mississippi as it meandered through Reverie's fertile acreage.

Julien drew up a cane wicker chair beside his father's bed and stared at the man who had given him life, but very little in the way of parental affection. Etienne LaCroix had ruled his son's existence with a determination that had left Julien unsure which thoughts were his own and which had been put there by the almighty patriarch. Well, by God, Julien thought, staring at his father's sallow, sunken cheeks, *it's time for the son and heir to begin making some decisions on his own!*

Etienne suddenly opened his eyes, almost as if he had detected Julien's rebellious frame of mind. The old man's head remained stationary, but his eyes shifted to stare at Julien with an intensity that was positively unnerving.

"Good evenin', sir," Julien said, addressing his father in the manner he had been taught since he was a child. "I bring you greetings from all your guests downstairs who asked to be remembered to you."

Etienne continued to stare at Julien, who shifted uncomfortably in his chair.

"Father, can you hear me? Blink once if you understand what I just said . . . that your guests send you their warmest regards."

He waited. The chamber was filled with the sounds of the ticking clock on the bedside table and the chatter of night locusts buzzing outside the tall windows that opened onto the second-story gallery.

To Julien's enormous relief, Etienne LaCroix found the energy to blink. Once.

"Yes, you understand me," he cried, relief flooding over him like water that sluiced through the rice fields downriver.

While part of his brain began to formulate the best way to approach the subject uppermost on his mind, Julien described the colorful scene taking place downstairs. He gave an account of the successful conclusion to this autumn's cane harvest, the food-laden tables welcoming the thirty guests entertained this night at Reverie, as well as the dancers poised to cavort in quadrilles, polkas, and two-step waltzes across the polished cypress floors to the music produced by Monsieur Grammont and his fellow players.

His father kept his lifeless eyes, the color of gray-blue slate, riveted on his son's.

"And I expect, Father, that the profits this year should exceed any we've been privileged to enjoy, which means . . . ah," he added delicately, "that warehouse space in New Orleans to store our hogsheads and those of neighboring plantations will be scarce."

He allowed this statement to hang in the air, hovering above the finely embroidered linen coverlet pulled up to his father's chin. Once again Julien shifted in the woven reed chair he had drawn up beside his father's bed.

"You know, Father," he said, as if a thought had just occurred to him, "it might make quite a lot of sense if we approach . . . ah . . . if we inquire of Henri's . . . friend, Mademoiselle Fouché . . . whether she might be willing to trade that property that you and Henri deeded her for something *else* of equal value. That way we could build a larger warehouse nearer the wharves and—"

Etienne LaCroix's eyes suddenly widened and his mouth twisted into a grotesque grimace. His lids began to open and close in rapid succession.

Blink, blink. Blink, blink. Blink, blink.

No! No! No!

Julien stared at his father as his own outrage began to bubble up, a match for the unspoken fury that the titular head of the LaCroix family expressed in a silence so deafening, it roared in Julien's ears. As usual, Julien thought bitterly, Etienne *had* to be in control, *had* to rule with an iron fist, even from the living grave this well-appointed bedroom had become! Not once had his father ever embraced any of his ideas, or even complimented him for having them. Not once had the man given any indication that his only son would one day assume the mantle of family leadership.

Julien's mind was awhirl, his thoughts a seething cauldron of slights, affronts, and contempt that his father had exhibited toward him his entire life! Julien had been forced to swallow his sire's scorn and utter disregard whenever he'd tried to introduce modern methods or suggested alternative ways to cultivate the LaCroix land in this new age of steam power.

Etienne now narrowed his eyes in a soundless declaration that seemed to his son to seethe with hatred.

Blink, blink! Blink, blink! Blink, blink!

No! You will not undo what Henri and I have done! No! No!

Julien jumped to his feet and stood beside his father's bed, his hands balled into tight fists. It was all he could do to keep himself from smashing his father's face—or better yet, yank the soft feather pillow from behind Etienne's greasy yellowed hair and push its plush linen surface against his father's nose and mouth.

What did the Canal Street land mean to the man at this stage in his life? The property couldn't have mattered very much to his father, if he had been willing to allow Henri to deed it over to the slut that his partner had kept on Rampart Street.

Martine.

Julien soundlessly retracted his epithet. Martine Fouché was no slut. She was the most beautiful, voluptuous, entrancing woman he'd ever met, and he now wanted her with the same passion and single-mindedness that he wanted the Canal Street land.

And by God, he would have *both*!

Martine would eventually see reason, especially if he wooed her—as he ardently wished to do—and gave her property or funds of more than the value of her bequest.

"Tomorrow I shall prepare a document that I want you to sign that states you did not intend to deed over that Canal Street land," he declared, staring down coldly at the helpless shell his father had become. "That at the time you signed the deed and witnessed Henri's will, you had been dosed with an excess of laudanum and did not know what you were about."

In response, his father's hollow cheeks sucked in against his teeth as if he'd tasted the foulest tincture Dr. LeMoyne could dispense. Julien, however, ignored this obvious sign of displeasure and continued in a low voice.

"This statement, signed with your *X*, shall provide Mademoiselle Fouché with something comparable on Rampart Street, and—"

Blink, blink!

No! You may not void that deed!

Julien realized with sudden dread that Etienne LaCroix would fight until the very moment when he breathed his last. The old tyrant would never do the decent, graceful thing and transfer his empire to the next generation, even if *not* doing so meant leaving his hard-won legacy in a shambles of idiotic transactions and mismanagement endorsed by that gambling roué, Lafayette Marchand!

"No? You do not wish to sign? Well, dear Father," he said with bitter resentment, "we shall see about that! One man's *X* will appear as good as another's! I shall have the Canal Street land, and you and Lafayette Marchand won't be able to do a single thing to stand in my way, you paralytic *bastard*!"

Before he could complete his tirade, he heard the rustle of silk skirts.

"Dear God in heaven, Julien, how dare you call your poor, sick father a . . . a—that terrible word you just uttered."

Julien's young wife, plump as an overfed partridge, filled the doorway leading to his father's sickroom. Her face was still pretty, in a dumpling sort of way—all rounded cheeks and clear skin, though the point of her chin now melded into a fold of flesh that slanted toward her lacy collar, with no definition of a neck in sight. Her breasts had grown enormously in the year they'd been married, almost in direct proportion to the amount of whipping cream and chocolate eclairs she had consumed vo-

raciously at their dining table. When he made love to his wife—
or attempted to—he did his best to whet his appetite by imagining those lolling pillows of flesh to be mounds of freshly
churned butterfat, turning to silky cream that he could suck dry.

Much to his amazement, he suddenly felt a stirring in his
groin as a result of such licentious thoughts. He turned his back
on his father and strode to his wife's side.

"He's being difficult, as usual," he said impatiently. "It's time
we stopped treating him as if he were the Etienne LaCroix of
old. The man's unable to speak or think." He stared at his wife's
enormous taffeta-cloaked bosom. For some reason he yearned
to bury himself in its fleshy folds and forget the burdens of running a huge plantation with no true authority at his command.

"Etienne is perfectly lucid," his wife countered, her shifting
eyes communicating her discomfort at the suggestive way in
which he was regarding her bodice. "Why were you shouting at
your father? The guests might hear," she admonished him
prudishly.

"I don't give a damn about our guests!" Julien said, reaching
with his right hand to cup her silk-clad breast in his palm. "I
need a drink."

"Albert can fetch you one," Adelaide replied stiffly, staring
beyond his shoulder as if she were examining the wallpaper on
the opposite side of the bedchamber. "He's downstairs." Julien
gazed at her impassive expression. Partly as an experiment to
gauge his wife's reaction, he provocatively pressed his thumb
against the nipple faintly outlined beneath the silken fabric.
"Julien!" she protested, her voice edged with anxiety. "Stop
this!" She cast a frantic glance at the still form staring at them
from the bed. "Your *father*!"

"Stop?" he asked, palming her other breast with his free
hand and ignoring Etienne's silent, oppressive presence. "Why
should I stop? Does this not give you an ounce of pleasure, my
dear wife? Or this?" His thumbs massaged his wife's bodice in
rhythmic circles, and he felt himself grow hard beneath his
trousers.

"No, it doesn't," she retorted, taking a step backward. "Your
behavior revolts me!"

"And when I kiss you?" he inquired, the anger he felt toward his father rising like a gulf tide surging up the river. "I've been told by certain mademoiselles on the Champs Elysées that I do this quite expertly . . ." he murmured, pulling her roughly to him in an agony of frustration. His mouth found hers closed and clamped tight against her teeth. Adelaide had rebuffed his polite advances for months now. And polite or not, this evening would only prove to be more of the same—a state of affairs that goaded him to insinuate his tongue between his wife's lips.

"Julien!" she spat. She pushed hard against his chest, her stout arms galvanized with sudden strength. They broke apart, both panting from exertion. "How dare you!" she said, her massive bosom heaving in indignation.

"And how dare *you*, madam," he replied with as much dignity as he could summon under the circumstances. "How dare you close your bedchamber door to your husband all these months! Have you a problem you would like to share with me?" he mocked. "Or perhaps you fear it will be *I* whose ardor will evaporate, should I see you naked as the unappetizing pig you've become!"

"Julien . . ." she cried, her eyes suddenly welling with tears. "Why are you so angry? Why are you—"

"Angry? Loving? Respectful? Patient?" he asked in quick succession, the heat of barely leashed fury staining his cheeks. "It matters not what face or feeling I present before you, Adelaide. You are no wife to me, and since our dreadful honeymoon, you hold little attraction for me, beyond a mere receptacle for my lust. And now," he said with loathing, both for her treatment of him since their wedding night, and the humiliation he had long suffered at his father's hands, "I do not even desire you as *that*."

And before Adelaide could respond, the heir to Reverie plantation bolted past his bride of less than two years, charged down the back stairs, and out the kitchen door. In a blind rage he made his way for the dock. His path was illuminated by the harvest moon that shone down from a clear night sky onto the swiftly flowing water that coursed toward New Orleans and the Gulf of Mexico.

* * *

The sensation of bachelor André Duvallon's hand upon Mrs. Randall McCullough's back felt sinfully delicious as they whirled around the dance floor.

One-two-three . . . one-two-three . . .

Corlis thrilled to the seductive rhythm of the small orchestra playing music for the daring new dance from Vienna, the two-step waltz. Not since her marriage had she been so physically close to an unmarried man in a public place, and she found it delightful, even if the underarms of her pale green gown were sopping wet. If only the dancing could go on forever, she thought dreamily, as her long silk skirts glided gracefully across the surface of the parlor's polished cypress floors. If only she had met a man like André *first . . .*

"Your auburn hair is like fire," André said softly, glancing at the top of her head with a grave smile as he expertly avoided less agile couples twirling around the converted ballroom. "It's rather like you, my dear Corlis . . . full of light and heat and vibrancy."

At dinner they had agreed to call each other by their first names, although Corlis knew she should never have condescended to André's bold suggestion. She glanced at his ink-black mane and yearned to tell him how handsome he looked. A light, giddy feeling had taken possession of her, almost as if someone other than the daughter of Elizabeth and Enoch Bell, of the Pittsburgh Bells, were cavorting at Reverie plantation's annual Roulaison. Randall and Ian had retired to the side veranda, smoking cigars and talking business as best they could, considering the sorry state of their spoken French. For his part, André had been an absolute dear and insisted that he and Corlis converse in English.

The music ceased, and Monsieur Grammont announced that the favorite activity of the sugarcane harvest was indeed about to get under way outside on the veranda.

"The taffy pull will commence in five minutes!" the conductor declared, and was greeted by applause and a burst of excited chatter from the crowd.

"Is it acceptable among you Creoles for a distinguished banker to take part in the taffy pull?" Corlis asked laughingly of

André, doing her utmost to mask her nervousness at the unexpected warmth and tingling anticipation that continued to flutter in her abdomen.

"Ah, the taffy pull," André murmured. He leaned forward and whispered conspiratorially in her ear, "It provides us with a perfect opportunity to explore the plantation, *n'est-ce pas?*"

Without waiting for her response, André offered Corlis his arm. "If you accept my invitation to take a stroll instead," he suggested with a mischievous glint in his eye, "it will save those lovely hands of yours from blisters. And besides, we even might find a breath of fresh air in the cool of the oak grove."

Without replying, she clasped his proffered arm and strolled along with the guests surging past the front door and into the warm evening air. The atmosphere outside was redolent with the scent of pink jasmine blended with a lingering aroma of burning sugar from the cane fields surrounding the house.

As the animated partygoers chose sides for the taffy pull, Corlis and André wandered, unnoticed, down the broad front stairs onto the grass. Initially Corlis hesitated to place her satin slipper on the ground for fear of snakes. However, André appeared unafraid of such encounters and guided her down a gravel path in the direction of one of the *garçonnieres* that were attached to both sides of the main house. These solid brick structures, Corlis had been informed by a servant who had introduced herself as Maisie, were additions that had been built by Etienne LaCroix to accommodate visiting bachelors so that they would not be tempted to wander down the halls of the mansion where the daughters of the family slept.

André's hand slid down Corlis's arm until he enfolded her right palm with his left one. He nodded at a swing that hung suspended on ropes from atop a high branch of an enormous oak whose verdant canopy loomed a hundred yards from the house.

"Shall I show you the best way to cool yourself in a climate like this?" he asked.

"I cannot fathom 'tis possible ever to be cool again," Corlis retorted good-naturedly, "but I am willing to keep an open mind on the subject."

"Come," he commanded, striding off toward the towering oak with Corlis in tow.

He stood behind a wooden swing seat attached to two hemp ropes that had been secured to a stout branch high over their heads. André placed his hands on either side of her waist.

"Now, sit down, hold tight, and I shall send you floating to the heavens, *ma petite,*" he said, his lips nearly grazing her ear as the strange, tingling sensation Corlis had felt while dancing surged once again.

Silvery shafts of moonlight penetrated the sheltering branches of the oak tree as she pointed her dancing slippers to the skies. She leaned back like a delighted child and allowed herself the freedom of soaring toward the thick foliage, her toes grazing the moss that hung in graceful shrouds from above. Her senses seemed alive as never before. Higher and higher she flew, and for a moment she hung at the edge of the world, then fell backward with such a rush, she thought she would surely crash to the earth.

However, each time André was stolidly behind her back, waiting to push her ever higher, allowing her to partake of a pleasure so pure that it seemed as sweet to her as all the romantic novels she'd ever read secretly as a girl. She heard herself squealing with joy like a five year old, and then she began giggling uncontrollably.

Without warning, André's arms were wrapped around her waist, abruptly halting her flight. She was panting with exertion and allowed herself to settle her back against the starched expanse of his dress shirt.

"I feared that I would lose you in the heavens," he said, and his lips brushed against her ear a second time.

"My stars, but that was fun!" she exclaimed between gulps of air. She tilted her head skyward and met his warm, smiling gaze. "May I do it again?"

André chuckled and shook his head regretfully. He came around the swing to face her and offered her his two hands to pull her to a standing position.

"I think we might soon draw the unwelcome attention of the taffy pullers."

"Oh," Corlis replied, feeling admonished like a naughty child.

"So, let us remove ourselves from their sight," André suggested gallantly, leading her deeper into the shadows near the door to the *garçonniere*.

He pointed to a slatted wooden seat where they both could sit down.

"That was a lovely ride," Corlis said, self-conscious now that a married woman could have behaved in such an abandoned fashion. "Thank you," she added primly. She gazed toward the main house as a burst of merriment erupted from the two teams engaged in the taffy pull on the veranda. "I would expect that many young ladies will look forward to dancing with you when the winning side triumphs over there."

"Not as much as I look forward to dancing with you again," André said solemnly.

Corlis shifted her gaze and stared into his eyes, wondering if there wasn't a glint of amusement lurking behind thick, dark lashes that any woman would envy.

"I will soon retire, I think," she said slowly. "I find all this exertion in such humid temperatures quite enervating."

"It can be difficult for northerners to adjust here," he replied agreeably. "How have your husband and his partners found building their projects in such a climate as this? Does it greatly slow their progress?"

"They've managed to complete the commissions they've received so far," she answered, sensing that André was not merely indulging in idle chitchat. "Ian's slaves do the labor, of course, while Randall supervises," she added pointedly, wishing to make it clear to Julien's banker that her husband wasn't a common hod carrier.

"So, they haven't had the opportunity to construct any large projects as yet?" André inquired.

Why was he asking about business when there was such a lovely moon overhead?

"The Canal Street development seems a likely possibility," she ventured cautiously.

"Ah . . . but of course," André agreed. "Let us hope that will come to pass."

"With your participation, I trust," Corlis declared softly, amazed at her daring for raising such a delicate subject.

"Your husband must be eager to start work on this project."

"They are eager, naturally, to be a part of this worthy effort and to offer their building expertise," she replied.

"And their own funds?" André asked. "Would your husband and his partner wish also to join in the financial partnership that may be formed to make this development a reality?"

Corlis envisioned her sapphire necklace and earrings basking in the window of the pawnshop on Girod Street, and felt her ire rise.

She was not fooled by André's seemingly innocent query. "I am merely Randall's wife," she said carefully, summoning a demure smile to her lips. "I know little of such complicated matters." She tilted her head at what she hoped was a fetching angle and added, "I do so hope that you and Monsieur LaCroix will be able to . . . ah . . . smooth out the financial details so construction can begin." She suddenly desired to know, as much as Randall McCullough did, whether Julien was serious about this project or not. "Do you think you will succeed?"

"Julien's role . . . remains to be seen," the Creole banker replied obliquely.

"As his personal banker, are you not privy to his intentions? Will he regain control of the Canal Street property, do you suppose?" she asked boldly.

"I am not at liberty to say, my dear, inquisitive *amie.*"

And at that moment Corlis determined that the dashing André Duvallon was not necessarily enamored with her auburn hair but rather with what he could learn from her about her husband.

Apprehensively she glanced toward the darkened end of the veranda where orange points of light glowed intermittently, a sign that Randall, Ian, and their male companions were still smoking their cigars. It certainly wouldn't do for Randall to observe her deep in conversation with a banker who later might refuse to offer the funding they required to stay in business.

She noticed that André was also observing the cluster of men conferring on the porch. Now that he had exhausted his quest for information, clearly he would prefer to be among their company, rather than hers.

Damn the man's gorgeous blue eyes, she thought dolefully. Nothing in this blasted swamp was ever what it seemed.

"I do believe, André," she said in a fair imitation of the blushing magnolias that she'd observed conversing earlier with the handsome bachelor, "that I would greatly appreciate something cold to drink right about now, wouldn't you? Would you be so kind as to escort me to the house? And then I will leave you to the adoring young ladies who breathlessly await your return to the veranda."

No longer arm in arm, she and André strolled down the gravel path in the direction of the beautiful house, its stately windows aglow in golden candlelight.

What would become of the children if Jeffries & McCullough didn't get work? She and Randall simply couldn't keep up the pretense of the successful young couple from the North for very much longer.

She envisioned her little ones asleep in their cots on Julia Street. With all her soul she yearned to be far from this graceful mansion where she sensed that most of the smiling faces and the polite conversations she had overheard tonight masked a labyrinth of treachery and betrayal.

A few minutes later André Duvallon clasped his goblet of plantation punch and politely inclined his head in a gesture of farewell.

"Well, if you insist you must retire, do let me relieve you of that," he urged, accepting her half-full glass with his free hand and setting it aside. Corlis nodded in polite response as they walked in silence toward the curving staircase.

"Good night," she said simply.

Then she turned away from her escort, delicately lifted her long skirts, and began ascending toward the guest wing. She heard the sound of the handsome banker's footfalls as he retraced his steps across the parquet foyer. She glanced over her shoulder in time to observe him stride past the wide front door to join a cluster of die-hard merrymakers talking and laughing on the shadowed veranda.

When she reached the landing, she gazed down the long, carpeted hallway and wondered bleakly if she would be able to find the bedchamber assigned to Randall and herself. And even if she did, she would then be faced with the daunting task of escaping from her stays and corset without assistance.

Suddenly a strange noise drew her attention.

On her right a door stood slightly ajar. From inside, she was startled to hear the muffled sound of someone weeping inconsolably. For a moment she hesitated and then pushed the door open a few inches wider. A large mound of white dimity, edged in ruffles, lay heaving in the middle of a massive four-poster plantation bed. Corlis blushed scarlet, thinking that she had stumbled upon a most indelicate scene. Then she realized with a start that Adelaide LaCroix had flung herself onto the middle of her mattress and was crying her eyes out.

Corlis's satin slippers moved silently across the Turkish carpet that nearly filled the large high-ceiling bedchamber. A large armoire took up one wall and a mirrored dresser the other. Portraits of LaCroix ancestors stared vacantly at each other across the room, indifferent to the young matron's distress.

"Hello . . ." Corlis whispered, feeling uncertain about what to do next, or even how to address her haughty hostess. Should she call her Adelaide or Madame LaCroix, considering the sobbing woman's present state of disconcerting dishabille? She placed a gentle hand on the trembling shoulders of Julien LaCroix's unhappy wife. "It's Corlis . . . Corlis McCullough. Can I help?"

Adelaide abruptly ceased her heart-wrenching lament but did not respond beyond burrowing her bloated, tear-stained face more deeply into the quilted silk coverlet.

"You poor dear," Corlis ventured. "What has happened?"

Adelaide gave a little gasp and rolled over on her back. Stifling another sob, she awkwardly managed to pull herself to a sitting position on the bed and dabbed her eyes with a lacy linen handkerchief. She reached for a glass on the bedside table and took a deep draught of its milky green liquid. An aroma of licorice wafted across the coverlet.

Absinthe.

The devil's own drink, Corlis had heard it called. The national libation of France. Its aficionados and detractors alike credited its fiery contents with producing a veritable state of altered consciousness in those who imbibed more than a single glass.

Adelaide's glass was nearly empty, as was the bottle that stood next to it.

"He's . . . g-gone to her!" Adelaide wailed, her words slurring as her voice rose to a pitch that would set dogs to barking. "He thinks he'll . . . g-get the property back from . . . that . . . woman!"

Corlis retraced her steps to the bedroom's threshold and firmly shut the door leading to the hallway. Then she returned to Adelaide's bedside and enclosed the woman's pudgy hand between her own slender ones.

"Let's get you to bed, shall we?" she asked gently. "Why not let me summon your maid?" The poor woman was obviously beside herself.

"No! No!" Adelaide shrieked, shaking her head fiercely. "Don't c-call for her! I c-can't *bear* that woman." She leaned her tear-stained face close to Corlis and whispered hoarsely, "Maisie's *Julien's* friend! He's probably . . . probably had his way with her since . . . since they were practically children!" she cried garrulously. She brought the glass to her lips once again and took another gulp of its greenish contents. "Med'cine," she noted with a slight hiccup.

Corlis barely succeeded in retrieving the tumbler from her hostess's hand before Adelaide flopped backward on the mattress. "Oh . . . Madame LaCroix," she chided gently.

"C-Call me Adelaide," Julien's wife sobbed, reaching for Corlis's hand again. "You're a n-nice wo-man," she said, her speech thickening. "Even if you are from Pennsyl-vania. S-Sit here!" she pleaded, her eyes fluttering closed while she patted the mattress beside her. "Keep me com-pany till I fall asleep. . . ."

Adelaide's plump cheeks exhaled an enormous sigh. Even so, her hand did not relax, and she held on tightly to Corlis.

"That's good," Corlis whispered soothingly, relatively certain that the woman would soon pass out. "Just go to sleep now. Things won't seem so dire in the morning."

That's what people always said, but it was never true. Life for the McCulloughs was dire indeed.

"I don't really *care* . . . if he has her . . . you know what I mean?" Adelaide said suddenly, startling her companion. "It would actually be of some relief to me."

Has *who*? Corlis wondered. The servant, Maisie, or some other woman Julien had gone off to see? She thought suddenly of the owner of the Canal Street property—Martine Fouché. Annette—her dressmaker—spoke of the *placée* in the hushed tones of an acolyte. It was highly probable that Adelaide LaCroix's husband had deserted her tonight for Martine's cottage on Rampart Street.

"In fact, if he *is* with her, it would be easier all round," Adelaide commented in a tone drenched in self-pity. "It's jus' . . . jus'. . ."

She began weeping again.

"Hmmm," Corlis responded, absently patting the woman's plump hand in what she hoped was perceived as a kindly gesture.

"Julien's such a fool, though," Adelaide mumbled. "He's always . . . always been a fool . . . about such things. Thinks he knows the whys and wherefores, he does. Ha!" Adelaide expelled an unpleasant snort. "But I know . . . *I* know so . . . so much more about Mademoiselle Fouché than *he* does. Ha . . . ha!" The woman's laugh sounded like a witch's cackle. "Isn't that ironic? I know what Julien *doesn't* know. . . . I know how she's pretended to—" Adelaide flung the crook of her arm over her eyes and pursed her lips in a pout. "Oh, well. . . . What does it matter . . . ? What does *anything* . . . matter?" she murmured piteously.

The next thing Corlis knew, Adelaide's heavy breathing became the labored exercise of a drinker falling into an alcoholic stupor. Corlis waited. Except for the sound of the woman's inhaling and exhaling, the bedchamber was now silent.

And then it became patently obvious to Corlis that Adelaide Marchand LaCroix had, indeed, passed out.

Chapter Thirteen

October 30, 1838

"Faster, Albert!" Julien shouted at the glistening black back of his father's slave. The muscular servant had been poling the pirogue downriver, hugging the shore, for more than half an hour now. "Ten picayunes if we arrive in New Orleans in under three hours!"

Julien had commandeered Albert from his father's sickroom and ordered the manservant to the Reverie dock to take him to the Crescent City. From this moment on, Julien didn't give a damn if Etienne LaCroix's bedpan got emptied on time or not!

Julien seized the other pole that lay inside the long, narrow boat and added his efforts to the enterprise. A spooning couple had claimed the deck of the small steam packet tied up to the dock for their trysting place, prompting Julien to make for the pirogue instead. The pole's smooth, rounded wood felt good in his hands. The murderous rage that had propelled him out of the house and away from his wife began to abate. Soon the steady poling of their small craft fell into a soothing rhythm.

Place . . . push . . . pull away. Place . . . push . . . pull away.

He had discarded his frock coat, removed his collar, and rolled up the sleeves of his dress shirt. Sweat shone on his forearms and trickled down his chest, as cooling air brushed against his skin. The moon, a large, luminous disk that hung suspended in the night sky, served as a last memento of this year's Roulaison.

Thank God cane cutting was over, Julien thought. Perhaps by

188

next harvest Etienne LaCroix would be in his grave, and as his son and heir, he would be—

He felt himself lose the rhythm of his stroke and, as a result, nearly pitched into the surging river. Albert glanced over his shoulder and frowned.

"Sorry," Julien said shortly. He waited, watching Albert's movements intently, and rejoined the stroke.

Place . . . push . . . pull away . . .

Althea Fouché had already ordered their household slave to serve the coffee and croissants for breakfast when she heard a sharp knock on the front door. Martine, who sat at the pianoforte fingering a Chopin étude she had learned in Paris, glanced at her mother with a puzzled expression. Then she instructed Elfie to see who it could be at the ungodly hour of ten in the morning.

"A Monsieur LaCroix, ma'am," Elfie reported in a low whisper as she gestured toward the half-opened front door.

Martine and Althea exchanged looks of astonishment.

"Mon Dieu!" Althea exclaimed under her breath. "Why would that man come here without first leaving his card? And on a Sunday!" she added indignantly.

"Please inform Monsieur LaCroix that I am not receiving visitors at this time," Martine said sotto voce. It was the truth, she thought distractedly. She was still wearing her loose-fitting bed gown made of sheer white lawn and her flowing bed jacket of the same thin cotton, decorated with ruffles around the collar and cuffs. "Be very polite!" she warned Elfie sternly. "Tell him that perhaps he might call next week at—"

"But next week would be too late!" a voice declared from the door.

Martine and her mother turned to stare incredulously at the intruder. Julien LaCroix had advanced into the parlor. He handed his walking stick and top hat to the round-eyed Elfie and made a slight bow.

"Monsieur . . ." Martine temporized, rising from the piano bench near the wheeled trolley on which their breakfast had been laid. "As you can see, we are not dressed properly to receive you."

"It is of no consequence," Julien said, gesturing as if to sweep her objections aside. "At Wednesday's ball at the Salle d'Orleans, the beautiful Martine Fouché's many admirers will be dueling over the opportunity to become her protector. I wish to advance my cause early, and more privately," he added, lifting Martine's slender hand and bending over her honeyed fingers. Then he turned and performed the same gesture of respect to Althea.

"Monsieur LaCroix, this is neither the time nor the place—" Althea began.

Julien maintained possession of the older woman's hand and smiled confidently. "What better time or place to put our cards directly on the table?" he asked. "I shall not make a long story of why I have come here today." He smiled faintly, his trim mustache and intense eyes riveting. "I would be deeply honored to become your daughter's patron and to establish a bank account in her name with funds ample enough to provide for her, yours, and dear Lisette's complete comfort."

Althea and her daughter traded startled looks. Then Martine's mother pursed her lips and cocked her head in the bargaining stance routinely adopted by the mother of a desirable quadroon.

"Since we are to place our cards squarely on the table, monsieur," Althea declared skeptically, "I must make mention of the Canal Street property toward which you have employed every device possible to wrench from my daughter's possession. How does it figure in this *generous* offer you are making?" Her slight tone of sarcasm was not lost on Julien.

"What of Canal Street?" he replied with a shrug. "I have thought at length on that particular subject," he continued slowly, turning to face Martine. "I had preferred to exchange it for something of equal or greater value, but that apparently is not satisfactory to you. I propose, then, to become an investor of sorts, joining with others, including you, Martine, if you will allow it. I offer to take the initiative, along with my banker, André Duvallon, to raise the funds necessary to build on the land. I will, of course, participate in any profits—but then, so will *you*, in even greater measure."

Julien was acutely aware that Martine and her mother had taken in every word. He had just made the kind of offer no other suitor was likely to put forth: his full financial patronage of the little Fouché family, *plus* his willingness to allow Martine to keep her property in her name without a court challenge. In addition he was willing to buy into the project by supplying the capital necessary to build on the site.

"And what benefit do you hope to derive from this, monsieur?" Althea asked, her dark-brown eyes alight with interest.

"A hundred years' lease on the warehouse I propose to build at the back of the property, fronting on Common Street, on the downriver end of the block."

He watched the faces of Martine and her mother, noting their surprise. He was a bit surprised himself that he had come up with such a profitable solution. Albert had indeed managed to get him to New Orleans in under three hours. At dawn's light Julien had taken a long walk from the wharves up to Canal Street and along Common Street to the rear of the large, open tract that Martine now owned. There was plenty of room for a large warehouse at the back, as well as for a block of row houses flanking Canal Street, with commercial spaces allotted to the first floors under an arcade.

He could already envision the entire development—built in the popular Greek Revival style—and he wagered that the fledgling firm of Jeffries & McCullough would dearly love to undertake such a commission at a rock-bottom price. Others were bound to want to participate. His mind was churning with the names of young men who might wish to become partners in such a project: the merchant Paul Tulane, for one. William Avery of Avery Island was another possibility. His banker, André Duvallon, had informed him that Jacob Levy Florence was always eager to get in on such forward-thinking projects. Even Celeste Marigny Livaudais, a Creole doyenne who had played the silent partner in many an investment in the city, would clamber to be part of this effort.

The Canal Street project would represent the *nouvelle* New Orleans, the blending of cultures that the commerce-crazed Americans had brought about, whether his father approved or not!

"And you are willing to put all these grand promises in writing?" Althea asked with a sidelong glance at Martine.

"Oh, indeed I am," Julien replied softly. "Signed and witnessed in as legally binding an agreement as the deed Henri Girard drew up for Martine." He then turned his full attention to the woman for whose sake he would grant such largesse. "On my journey downriver last night, I thought deeply on this subject of our potential liaison, Martine," Julien said. "You may be surprised to learn that I have experienced a revelation," he continued in a tone that had become both serious and somber. "I wish us to be *equal* in all things," he declared, his voice suddenly throbbing with an emotional intensity that astounded even him. "In business, of course, but in our personal relations as well. It is the only way for us to proceed."

Martine's eyes widened and her voluptuous mouth parted a fraction. For a long moment she gazed at him in silence, her chin lifting slightly, a sign that she questioned the sincerity of his unorthodox declaration.

"Let us remember, monsieur, that I am the granddaughter of a slave," she replied at length. "And though my daughter, Lisette, has blue eyes and pale skin, we are of African descent, sir. White men—especially white men who are also French Creoles—are apt never to forget that reality. Henri did not make such grandiose statements as to equality, and neither ought you. It is better to be absolutely honest in such affairs."

Her eyes bore into his, and whatever secret card he might have been tempted to play later in this game was no longer of any value.

"I may have behaved in a grandiose manner to you previously," he said, amazed at how naked he felt before her piercing gaze. "Yes, Martine, you are a woman of African blood . . . but I have found, to my regret, that the blood in one's veins is no guarantee of tenderness, compassion—or a capacity for love. Yet, I believe you have those capacities flowing in your veins—as do I."

"And your wife?" Althea asked in a steady tone of voice. "What of her? Has she no capacity for . . . tenderness?"

"Ah . . . yes . . . Adelaide," Julien murmured. "Let us speak plainly. Unfortunately—and for reasons that I cannot fathom—

she has, from our wedding day, found the intimacies of the married state utterly repugnant. And it is *love* I desire to have in my life. Love and loyalty. As a LaCroix, I have allowed others to deprive me of it for too long." Martine arched a perfect eyebrow but remained silent. "You are startled to hear me talk of love, not commerce?" he asked, gazing from mother to daughter. "But we are French, are we not? And since I returned from Paris, I have found, to my surprise, that I long for love in my life and am willing to give it back in full measure, my dear Martine. I have lived without it my entire life, and when I see the wreckage it has wrought, I am compelled to remedy such an unhappy state of affairs if I can."

"Monsieur LaCroix," Althea began firmly.

However, Julien ignored the presence of the domineering older woman. Instead, he seized Martine's hand and pressed it to his lips.

"I humbly ask you to allow me the privilege of coming to your home and taking you as my full partner in life, as well as in commerce. And for this," he said, gently stroking the honeyed skin of Martine's cheek with his pale fingertips, "I shall honor and keep you always—till death do us part."

His father would not order his life anymore, Julien thought with a flush of triumph, visualizing the helpless condition to which Etienne LaCroix was now consigned. There was no need to wrest the land from Martine by forging his father's mark on legal papers. He, Julien, was finally free to seize what would make him happy . . . what would give him exquisite pleasure, in fact. He was now free to run the Reverie enterprises as he saw fit. At long last he was at liberty to live in whatever fashion and among whatever company he chose. And as far as society and the old buzzards in their black cassocks lurking about the confessional booths at Saint Louis Cathedral were concerned, let them be damned!

From this day forward, Julien swore, as he removed his family's gold crest ring from his finger and placed it on Martine's, he would give himself to love.

Lisette Fouché's blue eyes were round and full of questions. She stared into the mirror at the reflection of her grandmother as the older woman secured the youngster's thick black braids with white satin bows. She caught a glimpse of their two valises, filled with the clothes they would need on their trip to the little family cabin on the banks of Lake Pontchartrain.

In the parlor, the little girl could hear the murmuring voices of her mother and the dark-haired gentleman with the black mustache and kind eyes to whom she had curtsied a half hour earlier. Monsieur LaCroix had given her the adorable puppy some months back. This day she watched the gentleman pull out a raft of official-looking documents. As soon as her mother and Monsieur LaCroix began signing them, sitting side by side on the velveteen sofa, Grandmother Althea took Lisette firmly by the hand and steered her into the tiny bedchamber they shared at the back of the cottage.

And now that the ordeal of braiding Lisette's hair was nearly accomplished, the little girl summoned the courage to ask, "Why are we going away, *Grandmère?*"

Her grandmother flashed one of her rare smiles and replied, "To give your *maman* and your new papa some time to themselves. Listen for the carriage to pull up front, Lisette. Monsieur LaCroix has sent his very own landau to take us to the cabin."

"How long will we be away?" Lisette asked in a small voice, feeling homesick for her mother before she'd even stepped out of the cottage onto Rampart Street.

"Only a short while," Althea replied reassuringly, patting her head. "We shall be back in the city long before Christmas."

"And will we visit—"

"No!" Althea interrupted sharply. "I told you earlier, Lisette!" she reprimanded her granddaughter. "You are not to speak of him now, especially when Monsieur LaCroix is visiting us. And as for Henri Girard, he is in his grave, so he will not know if we pay our respects or not! You are to forget about all of that!"

"But he was my father," Lisette exclaimed rebelliously. "They were both so kind to me!"

"That is true," Althea conceded, holding her granddaughter's chin and staring fiercely into her startled eyes. "But for your mother's sake, and for our future, all that must remain in the past, and not ever spoken of from now on! It would upset Monsieur LaCroix to be reminded of that . . . that friendship. You must promise me, *ma petite!* All depends upon it!"

Lisette saw something in her grandmother's eyes that the older woman had never exhibited in her life: fear.

"But I don't understand," she whispered.

Althea Fouché pulled Lisette protectively against her silk bodice and cupped her head between her brown hands, her fingers digging into her granddaughter's tightly braided hair.

"Perhaps sometime you will . . . but not today. Now do as I say and be a good girl. It's for your future, too, Lisette."

And with that her grandmother swiftly closed their two valises and seized Lisette's pale hand in her darker one. She gently led the child to the door of the bedchamber. Then she turned and strode toward a portal that led to the back garden.

"But what about *maman*!" Lisette exclaimed in a hoarse whisper. "And Monsieur LaCroix? Mustn't we be polite and say good-bye?"

"It is best if we just depart quietly," Althea said brusquely. "Come, Lisette, the carriage has pulled up to the *banquette* outside. I'll carry the valises, and you run along and fetch your puppy from the back garden and take him round to the front. We must leave your *maman* and Monsieur LaCroix in peace."

In Martine's bedchamber, ivory candles cast an umber glow from matching brass sconces that hung on either side of a small, unused fireplace. The surrounding whitewashed walls gleamed with a patina of burnished gold as twilight fell across the massive mahogany bed—a recent gift from Julien, built and carved by the talented chief carpenter at Reverie plantation.

Out on Rampart Street a few people clustered on their front stoops, chatting quietly, hoping that a cool evening breeze would waft up from the river six blocks away. Occasionally a carriage wound its way down the narrow road, its harnesses jingling in a musical counterpoint to the clip-clop of the horses' hooves.

Two porcelain cups of coffee sat on a silver tray, growing cold, despite the sultry weather penetrating the cottage's thick walls. Julien filed the documents they'd signed earlier into a leather pouch and reflected soberly on their contents. The papers described his unorthodox personal and financial relationship with Martine Fouché—a partnership that would scandalize most of New Orleans, should people ever hear of the finer details.

Beautiful Martine had affixed her signature with a sure, steady hand. Now she lay languidly upon a flaming-red brocade daybed.

She was his. Signed. Sealed. And delivered, intact, upon a silk chaise longue.

Or was it the other way around? he wondered joyfully, pouring two glasses of champagne into delicately fluted glasses. Julien's gaze was drawn to the graceful curve of Martine's right hip.

God . . . how he wanted her. The mad, wonderful thing of it was—he could *have* her! Tonight. Tomorrow . . . and always.

She was a Free Woman of Color. She could enter into a contract like any citizen. She had agreed in writing to allow him to be her patron. He would support her and her family in return for her exclusive favors. One of the documents they had just signed had guaranteed that any progeny of theirs would be named LaCroix. They would build the Canal Street development together—she supplying the land, and he, much of the capital—and share in its profits.

Julien heaved an enormous sigh and smiled broadly at Martine. Her lips curved slightly in response. However, her eyes held the kind of wonderment that he realized his own must be reflecting.

When had he fallen in love with her? At what precise moment had her welfare come to be as important to him as his own? He had begun this strange liaison with the sole purpose of returning the Canal Street property to his control. He still wanted that surely, but he also now wanted something else just as much: a sane life. A life where he was wanted, accepted for who he was, rather than merely tolerated.

Had no other white man in Louisiana seen that there was an alternative to the horrific bonds that strangled the life and joy out of men forced by economic necessity to wed unhappily? Yes, other men had entered into *plaçage* . . . but not in the fashion he had this blessed day.

The difference, he realized with a profound sense of gratitude, was that he deeply admired Martine Fouché. During the weeks of their negotiation over the documents they had cosigned tonight, he had come to respect her.

He stared intently at Martine's fine bone structure, amazed by these new, radical thoughts that were spinning through his brain. He saw in Martine's high cheekbones and straight nose the firm foundations of her young daughter's burgeoning beauty. He already loved Lisette. Martine was gentle and kind, as he hoped he would always try to be. She was interested in music and poetry. She passionately wanted to build and own something grand—as did he—and be beholden to no one, except to those she trusted.

And it would appear that he numbered in that company. She had willingly signed the documents forging their new partnership this day. The only thing that had stood in their way had been their color. Remove that difference in one's heart and mind—and then they could be of *one* heart and mind. It was an incredible concept! And look at its power, Julien considered humbly, to change the quality of his life.

Glory of glories, he thought with rising excitement as he glanced around the warm, inviting cottage. . . . He had a legal right to come to this tasteful, welcoming haven whenever he might wish! And right now, he reflected, rising to his feet and walking toward the chaise longue while carrying a glass of champagne in each hand, he wished never to leave.

He handed her the fluted stemware.

"To us both," he said softly.

Martine smiled but did not repeat his toast. She was still a bit wary, as he would certainly expect her to be. She, far more than he, knew the cruelty that existed outside the thick walls of her tiny cottage. She probably knew firsthand how white men did not always fulfill the promises they made. She sipped delicately from her glass and then smiled more broadly.

"It's wonderful."

"That it is," Julien agreed, taking a seat at the bottom of the chaise longue next to her silk-shod feet.

When he had finished his champagne, he set his glass on a

nearby table. First he carefully removed Martine's right satin slipper. And then the left. Lightly resting his hand on one of her ankles, he drank in the sight of her sipping the golden liquid as he fingered the sheer fabric of her bedclothes. Slowly, languidly, he began to rub his thumb in concentric circles around her ankle, and then slid his fingers up her calf.

Martine sipped the last of her champagne and set the glass aside. She continued merely to gaze at the ministrations of his hand, then lifted her eyes to reveal the effect his actions were having on her.

"Monsieur . . ." she murmured, her lips tilting upward in an appreciative smile.

"Julien," he reprimanded her softly. "Please, Martine . . . call me by my Christian name."

"Julien," she repeated in a low, husky voice. "Would you enjoy our moving over there?"

Julien glanced at the large bed, a duplicate of the beds to be found in sleeping chambers throughout Reverie plantation. In fact, he and Adelaide had been given an identical one as a wedding present from his father.

"Perhaps . . . later . . ." he murmured, pushing from his mind the woeful memory of his wedding night with Adelaide. "For now, I am exquisitely happy to be just where I am—with perhaps this exception." He moved farther up the chaise. "May I touch you, Martine?" he asked solemnly. She nodded, smiling faintly. His fingers grazed her right breast, and he heard her swift intake of breath. "There? And . . . there?"

She cupped her hand over his and pressed his fingers more firmly into her own flesh. "No one has ever asked before they touched me, Julien," she said, and he thought he saw tears prick the corners of her eyes.

"Oh, my darling Martine . . ." he replied, pulling her lithe golden body into his arms, "I will always ask. I ask because I want you to know how much I desire you . . . how much I wish to—"

But Martine put a slender finger to his lips to still his words.

"And may I tell you, too, what I desire?" she inquired, gazing intently into his eyes. "Is *that* permitted as well in this revolutionary relationship you have sworn we are to have, Julien LaCroix?"

Julien was somewhat taken aback by her assertiveness. And then he laughed aloud. She was testing him, testing his sincerity. She probably always would. "And what would you have me do this very second?" he retorted with a mocking smile.

"I would have you take me to bed," she said simply, pointing to the enormous bed and its lustrous silk hangings. With no warning she leaned forward and began to kiss him with an intensity that swelled like the scent of night-blooming jasmine on a sultry breeze. With the instincts of a jealous man, Julien suspected that the fervor of her embrace was an attempt to blot out memories of other candlelit evenings in this very boudoir.

"And you do not fear the ghost of Henri Girard lurking in this chamber?" he asked soberly. He heard her breath catch and felt her stiffen in his arms.

"Why say such things?" she chided, pulling away from him.

"Perhaps because . . . I . . . am . . . jealous," he replied ruefully.

Martine looked him squarely in the eyes and declared, "Let us be done with the subject once and for all!"

"I doubt it's such a simple thing—"

"I would not have entered into this agreement unless I could come to you willingly, Julien," she reproved. "I mourn Henri's passing—yes," she added, slipping from his embrace and gliding toward the silken coverlet that she proceeded to pull off the mattress and throw to the floor. "But we will never achieve any type of union if you remain jealous of a ghost!"

Julien was startled by the ferocity of her words—and pleased. He strode swiftly across the room and enfolded her in his arms, pressing her voluptuous form against his chest.

"Do I dare tell you how much I've longed for this?" he murmured into her dark hair. "Do I dare reveal how empty this part of my life has been . . . this linking of bodies?"

"This is all so strange," she whispered, wrapping her arms around him willingly, "that you should say such things about yourself to me . . . that you—"

"I know why Henri wanted you to be safe, and why he gave you the land," Julien interrupted in a low voice as he began to kiss her lips, her cheeks, her ear. "He knew the secret to happiness, too! He knew that by giving freely to you, he would get back a hundredfold."

Again he felt Martine stiffen in his embrace.

"Please! I beg of you, Julien," she murmured hoarsely, "do not compare yourself with Henri! He was a dear, sweet man, but you are totally different from each other. . . . Let us have only two people here, in this bedchamber. Just Julien and Martine! It is our only chance for the happiness we both desire."

"I'm sorry . . ." he said humbly as she pressed her body hard against his. "I have so much to learn of these things. . . ."

"And so you do," she whispered seductively, inserting the point of her tongue into his ear. "And I am skilled at teaching you whatever you wish to know. . . ." Her throaty laugh bubbled. "As an example . . ." She deliberately pressed her torso more firmly against his, moving her hips rhythmically. "This is what can excite a woman, Julien . . . yes! That's right! Not wild, unbridled motions that you thought the whores of Paris would find manly."

"Why, mademoiselle . . . I am truly shocked," he said with a mocking smile.

"It is an art to slowly heat both partners to the boiling point," she persisted, reaching between them and guiding his hand to lightly stroke her. "So few men realize that . . ." she whispered as her hips continued to undulate slowly, building to a torturous tempo that drove Julien nearly mad with longing.

"Oh . . . Martine," he whispered on a low breath. "Is it your belief, then," he murmured, "that if a man takes time to stir his partner's fires . . . he will be repaid in full measure?"

"But of course!" she murmured, playfully brushing his hands aside to allow her own gentle exploration. "You feel it already, do you not, Julien? You are an apt pupil, monsieur," she added, in a mischievous tone of voice.

And then they fell effortlessly upon the wide expanse of mattress. Slowly, and with agonizing deliberation, they removed each other's clothing, article by article, until they lay naked in the golden light cast by the flickering tapers overhead.

Martine stretched out next to him on her side, her head cradled in the palm of her hand. The long, slender fingers of her free hand played delicately up and down his torso, wandering dangerously close to his groin, where his desire for her was ferociously evident. Her long nails sent delicious chills to the very base of his spine. He longed to smother the length of her with his own body, but something in her manner, in the entire direction that their union seemed to be heading, stayed his actions. Instead, he allowed her the freedom and the time to make her own explorations of his skin, his contours, the very essence of his physical self. And in doing so, he learned much about her tender sensibilities . . . her generosity of spirit . . . the way in which she gave, as well as received.

And then, to his joy and amazement, she began kissing him on the same spots where her hands had been lightly caressing him. Excited currents coursed through him like the surging, flowing waters he encountered on the frantic trip downriver to New Orleans.

In one gloriously fluid movement, she was hovering above him, a golden-skinned angel with long, glistening hair that gathered like a ring of black fire about her shoulders and singed the voluptuous curve of her breasts. With touching dignity she seized the object of her desire and placed it at the entrance of her most secret self. "May I?" she asked quietly, her mesmerizing caramel-colored eyes staring boldly into his own.

He reached up, placing his palms on either side of her narrow waist above hips that flared in perfect proportion to her magnificent, full breasts. Slowly, confidently, he pulled her toward his pelvis. He inhaled deeply of her warm scent.

"*Jesu!*" she cried, closing her eyes as she sank on top of him and flung her arms around his shoulders. "There are things, dearest Julien, you have mastered brilliantly."

"You are the inventive one," he protested softly. "I never did . . . exactly this . . . before in my life."

"No, *cher?* Neither have I. Not precisely . . . this."

And then the river on which they sailed ebbed and flowed in rhythmic swells, like the spring tides along the Delta—strong and unstoppable—until the moon rose. Not the full harvest moon, but nearly so. Shafts of golden light played across their tangled bodies lying contentedly in a bed that had been carved by skilled black craftsmen for the pleasures of their white masters.

As for Julien and Martine, they were oblivious to all but the sound of each other's breathing and their serene drift toward sleep.

Chapter Fourteen

March 12

Without warning, a motorcycle backfired on Common Street.

"Whoa!" Corlis cried, harshly jolted back to the present.

Julien and Martine—in bed!

Corlis seriously began to wonder if she was becoming some sort of paranormal Peeping Thomasina!

She raised her eyes and absorbed the sight of the deserted warehouse's gloomy interior. Then she glanced down at her hand. In it she held a half-eaten praline. The candy's sweetish aroma was the last thing she remembered before the panorama at Reverie plantation and the intimate scene that had transpired in Martine's little cottage on Rampart Street.

How could she have witnessed all that? How would she know about the most personal thoughts and emotions belonging to people who lived more than a century ago? Even her ancestress Corlis Bell McCullough herself wouldn't have been privy to the secrets she had seen.

Corlis was shaken, and not a little aroused, by the memory of the passionate lovemaking. Except for King's brief kiss in the courtyard of his house, it had been a long time since she had been touched intimately by a man. Furthermore, she hadn't merely *seen* these visions in the French Quarter and upriver, she'd *inhaled* them. The smell of burning sugarcane fields came back to her in a rush.

Scent!

Bubbling molasses. Lilies. Incense. Mold and decay.

203

What if a particular fragrance or aroma had the power to trigger deeply ingrained *memories* in people linked by family ties and through associations originating in the distant past?

Corlis suddenly recalled a book that her mother had given her once for Christmas. It had been entitled *Aromatherapy and the Mind.* To be polite, Corlis had glanced at it and later stored the volume on her shelf as yet one more example of a gift that her mother would have preferred someone give *her*. In the preface, however, Corlis vaguely recalled the author postulating that "scent offered a direct route to the unconscious." The question was: *whose* unconscious?

A dozen images collided in her mind's eye of a house that recalled *Gone with the Wind,* a heavy-set woman in frothy crinolines sobbing on a quilted mattress; and a beautiful quadroon with come-hither eyes, languidly stretched out on a bloodred chaise longue.

Corlis shook her head. A dust-laden shaft of light illuminated the wooden door that opened on to Common Street. Normal life was taking place just outside the building, so how had all this happened to her? And for what purpose? To what end? What if the explanation for all this was nothing more complicated than that she was going out of her mind?

She suddenly made a beeline for the warehouse exit. Flinging open the door, she stood on the sidewalk in the descending March dusk, enormously grateful for the sight of ordinary motor traffic. She leaned weakly against the exterior of the brick building, reassured somewhat by its feeling of solidity, and gave concentrated thought to the possible causes of such out-of-body experiences.

She knew Aunt Marge would ask rhetorically: *What do various pieces of evidence have in common?*

Cautiously, Corlis raised the praline to her nostrils and inhaled, as she had earlier. The smell of exhaust from the cars going by overwhelmed the candy's distinctive sweetish odor. She was grateful when the world around her remained in place. Yet *something* had happened to her inside that warehouse! The book that her mother had given her said that one's sense of smell, of all the five senses, had the greatest power to stir the memory, stimulate one's feelings, or create a mood. What had happened to her *this* time went far beyond *that*!

She set off down Common Street toward her car, mulling over each bizarre experience she'd encountered since December. She dug into her shoulder bag for her car keys and recalled with growing amazement that these connections to the past had not always been linked to her having skipped a meal, as she'd first surmised.

It all got back to *scent*!

To be sure, the powerful odor of incense during Daphne Duvallon's wedding at Saint Louis Cathedral had seemingly produced a pair of unhappy newlyweds whom Corlis now deduced had been Julien LaCroix and Adelaide Marchand. Then, on the morning she'd put a vase of stargazer lilies on the coffee table next to her couch, she'd suddenly found herself in Henri Girard's flower-decked parlor, where the poor man was laid out in a mahogany coffin in the presence of Ian Jeffries and her very own McCullough ancestors!

She began to tick off the other instances where individual aromas had triggered these bizarre "trips."

The faint odor of natural gas had assaulted her inside the Canal Street buildings on the day that King had given her a private tour. The next thing she knew, in the glow of a gaslit chandelier, Julien was storming down the staircase of Martine Fouché's elegant new town house.

And, of course, it had been the musty odor of the old map showing New Orleans in 1838 that had whisked her to the dusty wharves on the banks of the Mississippi where a three-masted ship returned the LaCroixs from their honeymoon in France.

Corlis inserted her car key in the driver's-side door and was overwhelmed by an increasingly familiar stab of anxiety. Her heart was thumping erratically in her chest, and her palms felt clammy. Although she prided herself on her self-sufficiency, she was forced to admit that these visions had simply gotten too much for her to cope with alone.

She slipped behind the steering wheel, rested her forehead on its curving surface, and took a deep, unsteady breath. King had been remarkably empathetic, but she felt foolish revealing any more of this crazy stuff to him. Especially since he was her *key* source in the ongoing story at WJAZ.

If she told her boss, Andy Zamora, about seeing visions, he'd probably put her on psychiatric disability. And if Aunt Marge learned about this, the veteran reporter would be prompted to fly to New Orleans to check things out for herself—a risky proposition for an octogenarian. As for Corlis's parents, they were both utterly useless in a situation like this.

Suddenly the name Dylan Fouché popped into her thoughts, the dropped-out Jesuit priest King had told her about. The man who dabbled in ghostbusting and clearing buildings of un-wanted "entities." Although Dylan Fouché didn't know it yet, he was already *part* of this strange saga. And besides, Corlis considered with a surge of hope, the former Father Fouché was the only person she could imagine who might possibly possess the tools that could get her out of this jam.

Just then her pager sounded.

"Oh, pul-eeze!" she groaned out loud, recognizing the tele-phone number displayed on the tiny screen. She was ten min-utes late for her taped interview with King and his preservation guerrillas.

Fortunately, the videotape session at the Preservation Resource Center went smoothly. Once concluded, Virgil and Manny effi-ciently packed up their television equipment in the deserted of-fice while Corlis and King returned various pieces of office furniture to their proper positions around the reception room.

"Well . . . do you think you can use any of that?" King asked expectantly, pointing to Virgil's camcorder.

"Andy Zamora's gonna love your statement about being will-ing to lie down in front of Grover Jeffries's bulldozers to save those buildings," she teased. Corlis was fairly confident her boss at WJAZ would eventually put this segment on the air. She'd proposed a three-part package that would lay out for the viewers various sides in the controversy brewing over plans to downgrade the zoning of part of the historic district in the Canal Street area: jobs created by tourism versus jobs created by con-struction projects.

King gave her a knowing look. "Thought you'd like that," he said dryly. "Well, Ace, it's just after eight. Feel like grabbin' a bite?" With a wink in Corlis's direction, he turned to the televi-sion crew. "You guys wanna join us?"

"We're not off the clock till ten," replied Manny with regret.

"Besides, we just got paged," Virgil added, hanging up an office phone. "Some woman has accused the head of the police Anticorruption Committee of accepting a bribe. Zamora wants us just to grab a sound bite of her making the charge from her front stoop."

"Now, isn't that nice?" deadpanned Corlis.

"This is N'awlings, sugar," observed King with a droll smile.

Virgil hoisted his tripod onto his broad shoulder and said to Corlis, "When we go back to the station later tonight, I'll put this tape cassette in your mailbox with all the other stuff we shot today, okay, boss?"

Corlis nodded and turned to look at King as Virgil and Manny headed out the door. She was hungry. And she was worried.

"Let's eat," she proposed.

"Are you actually sayin' you'll have dinner with me?"

"Under certain conditions, the rules say it's okay. It'll be a business dinner in a public setting. I've a few more things I'd like to ask you about."

King's lips spread into an engaging grin that contained the barest hint of the conquering hero.

"Ever been to Galatoire's?" he inquired.

"Always wanted to, but never quite got there." It was embarrassing to admit that she'd never indulged herself at one of New Orleans's landmark restaurants in the French Quarter.

"Well, you will tonight," he said, glancing at his watch again.

"Do you think we can get in? It's always packed when I go by there."

"Oh, we'll get in."

"Okay . . ." she replied, not sounding convinced. Then she blurted, "Can we ask Dylan Fouché to join us?"

"Dylan Fouché?" King replied, surprised. Then he gazed at her narrowly. "Okay, Miz Reporter. Out with it! What's goin' on? Is this piece you're doin' gonna make us preservationists look like a bunch of wackos?"

"No," Corlis protested. "My wanting to meet Dylan isn't about the Selwyn buildings. . . . Well, I mean, it's not about the controversy. I just thought tonight might be a good opportunity for you to ... ah ... introduce me to your friend." She shrugged, hoping to appear nonchalant. "I might even do a profile on him sometime."

King gave her a long, hard stare, then seemed to be satisfied by her answer. "What *does* it have to do with?" he pressed quietly.

"Maybe I'll tell you after I meet Mr. Fouché and ask him a few questions," she said obliquely.

"Is the purpose of your meetin' him to make sure *you're* not wacko, Ace?" Corlis gave him an irritated look and nodded in the affirmative. "Well . . . my, my . . . this is gettin' mighty interestin'," King said. "Let me give him a call."

The boisterous crowds of tourists along Bourbon Street in the French Quarter were moving in undulating swarms, choking the sidewalks and the blocked-off street.

King seized Corlis's hand and headed for the unassuming entrance to Galatoire's, one of New Orleans's restaurants spoken of in the same reverent tones by food lovers as God is by parishioners who worship in Saint Louis Cathedral, a few blocks away. To her surprise, a dapper waiter attired in a black suit, crisp white shirt, and jaunty bow tie immediately welcomed them inside the high-ceiling dining room. He indicated by his enthusiastic wave that they should advance across the black-and-white-checkered floor into the crowded, noisy restaurant. Overhead, fans whirred as they threaded their way through the plethora of café tables covered in snowy white linen.

"Ah . . . Monsieur Duvallon," the waiter said in accented English, his arms extended toward King as if he were a long-lost friend, "how good to see you again!" He unabashedly gave Corlis the once-over. Then he seized her right hand and gallantly bowed. "And a good evening to your lovely companion."

"Cezanne," King replied, inclining his head, "I'd like you to meet Corlis McCullough. Can you get us a table?"

"But of course!" Cezanne exclaimed as if his feelings had been injured. He cast another curious look in Corlis's direction. "You are on television, *non?*" Corlis nodded affirmatively, and Cezanne beamed at King. "Ah . . . now I am *also* zee personal waiter of a TV star!"

And with that he marched with an air of importance across the thronged dining room to a small table for two. It was one among several positioned against mirrored walls framed at intervals with carved white-painted moldings. The waiter pulled out a bentwood straight-backed chair that looked straight out of a Toulouse-Lautrec painting. He indicated with a courtly nod that she should sit down. With equal gravity, he provided the same service for King.

Just then two men rose from a table a few feet away and headed straight for them.

"Oh, great," Corlis muttered to King. "Our two favorite people—Jack Ebert and Lafayette Marchand." The pair paused beside their table.

"I can see you two are obviously workin' overtime," Jack said with a cynical smile that insinuated their rendezvous was purely personal. "I expect you both heard that Marchand's boss has just announced plans for a wonderful new hotel on Canal Street." He cocked his head to one side and asked King, "Are you preservation folks gonna oppose it?" King responded to the query with a cool glance. In the ensuing silence Jack turned to address Corlis. "And what about you? Has King already persuaded you that Grover Jeffries is the Darth Vader of the Evil Empire?"

Marchand put a steadying hand on his dinner companion's shoulder.

"Miz McCullough is widely recognized for her fine reportin'," Lafayette Marchand said pleasantly, "and I'm sure she'll get the facts made public on both sides of this issue," he admonished Jack. "Please call me, Corlis, if I can assist you in any way. And y'all enjoy your meal," he added with a courtly bow, and propelled the television critic out the restaurant's front door. Meanwhile their waiter hovered nearby.

"Zee usual starter, Monsieur Duvallon?" Cezanne inquired politely when the two men had departed.

Corlis was having difficulty concentrating on anything besides her uneasy feeling that it was sheer bad luck to be spotted at a glamorous restaurant by King Duvallon's principal nemeses. Would Marchand, especially, believe that King was just a source?

Was he merely that?

Be honest, now, McCullough.

The waiter smiled benevolently at Corlis as she placed her order for a glass of merlot. "I will be zee envy of everyone tonight!" Cezanne declared. "Monsieur Duvallon brings only special friends to Galatoire's, is that not so?"

Corlis wondered how often King and Cindy Lou Mallory had sat at this cozy table.

Lafayette Marchand and Jack Ebert have a right to be suspicious! I'm becoming a jealous fool—for no reason! The man merely kissed me once through a car window!

Cezanne retreated while she carefully smoothed the large linen napkin the waiter had placed in her lap, and tried to recover her equilibrium.

King glanced at his watch. "Dylan Fouché is going to join us for dessert. I thought I'd introduce you two, have some coffee, and leave you folks alone to get acquainted."

The man had the most uncanny ability to sense exactly what she needed, when she needed it, she thought with a rush of gratitude. However, when it came right down to it, she wasn't even sure what she would say to someone like Dylan Fouché. She wondered what the former priest's reaction would be when she told him about Martine Fouché, she thought with some trepidation. Would he recognize the name from his family tree? And if Martine had really existed, would Dylan be amused—or offended—to have counted among the generations of pious Fouchés a courtesan of mixed blood beholden to a nineteenth-century white planter?

Cezanne arrived with a ramekin filled with steaming oysters Rockefeller.

She sensed King watching her closely as she tentatively dipped a small cocktail fork into its creamy mass. Sliding over her tongue was a magical mix of spinach, garlicky buttered bread crumbs, and a mysterious flavoring she'd never tasted before.

"Oh, dear God!" she gasped, "I think this is the best thing I've ever eaten in my life!"

"You said that at Uglesich's about your po'boy sandwich," he reminded her, chuckling.

"That's true . . . but I never ate *this* before!" she protested. "What, in addition to the garlic, *is* that incredible flavor?"

Cezanne had remained by their side and was grinning happily. "It's a flavoring known as *herbsaint*," he said, giving its French pronunciation with a great gusto. "A kind of liqueur . . . you know . . . like calvados or curaçao."

"Well, it's just fabulous!" Corlis exclaimed, her fork suspended halfway to her mouth.

"The dish was named in 1899 for John D. Rockefeller," King explained, glancing at Cezanne for confirmation. "At that time, he was the richest man in the world, and it was the richest dish in the world, so, the name seemed apropos."

"Ambrosia," Corlis sighed, taking another bite and settling back in her chair with a contented smile.

"Wait till she tastes zee crabmeat Yvonne!" Cezanne declared confidently. "She'll never let you bring her anywhere but Galatoire's!"

"Cezanne, you are somethin' else!" King admonished the waiter blandly. Cezanne merely smiled with an air of satisfaction and backed away.

The crabmeat entrée was equally mouthwatering. Corlis had nearly forgotten about her request to meet Dylan Fouché when an unusually tall, reedy man in his thirties, dressed in a crisp, seersucker suit and bright pink silk tie, crossed the restaurant to their table. In his lapel was a fresh carnation the same pastel shade as his tie. To Corlis he handed a long-stemmed red rose, surrounded by frothy green ferns and Queen Anne's lace, and wrapped in cellophane with a fuchsia bow.

"Stars receive flowers . . ." Dylan declared with a flourish, "so this is for you. I admire your work on television, Miz McCullough."

Corlis hardly noticed his offering, for she was staring at Dylan's pale-brown complexion, high cheekbones, mildly flared nostrils, and generous mouth. His features seemed to her near carbon copies of those possessed by the glorious, golden-skinned Martine Fouché—whose image was now indelibly burned into Corlis's memory.

To cover her astonishment she quickly glanced down at the

table and fingered the cellophane wrapper protecting the rose. "This is . . . beautiful. It's really . . . very nice of you. . . . I—"

Dylan deposited his lanky, impeccably tailored body into a chair and flashed a wide, gleaming smile at her across the table.

"Well . . . King says you've been seein' things."

"Nothin' like bowling the lady over with your finesse, Fouché," King declared with mild irritation. Then he looked at Corlis with an expression of concern that she might think he'd broken a confidence. "I certainly didn't describe events in that way to this character. I just mentioned you'd come across some unusual experiences that you have *not* described to me in any detail, but that you'd like to discuss with . . . an expert. Is that an accurate summary?"

"No need to defend yourself to Miz McCullough, King," Dylan intervened, his lips quirking upward slyly. "I'm psychic, remember?" To Corlis he added, "Between what little King, here, told me over the phone, and meetin' you just now, the remark about your seein' things just popped out."

"Yeah, right," King admonished. "You'd better watch that impulsive nature of yours. She's a mighty savvy reporter. You could blow your cover."

"Naw . . ." Dylan said with a dismissive wave of his hand. "This lady's also trustworthy. Just a little impulsive herself, right, Corlis? It's gotten you into some trouble in the past, I'd wager."

"I can vouch for that," King volunteered with a crooked smile. Corlis ignored the wisecrack, uneasy that Dylan Fouché could virtually read her thoughts. Her table at Galatoire's had unaccountably turned into the Mad Hatter's tea party! King pushed his chair back. "Well . . . I'll leave you two together," he announced, rising to his feet. "Dylan, can you see the lady home to Julia Street?"

"Julia Street? How divine. That's perfect!" Dylan exclaimed.

"Why do you say that?"

"Well . . . don't you feel right at home?" Dylan asked mischievously.

"Yes . . . but—"

"We'll talk about all that later," Dylan assured her with a breezy wave of his well-manicured hand. "Okay, gorgeous," he announced to King. "Leave us to it." He turned just in time to catch Corlis's double take in response to Dylan's endearment. "Such a tragedy for the gay community that Kingsbury Duvallon's straight—but then, all the better for *you*, isn't it, Miz McCullough? You've changed your mind about this guy, haven't you?"

Corlis was flabbergasted by Dylan's accurate observations. She felt naked and exposed by what he had just said in front of King, and promptly flushed scarlet.

King gave Cezanne the high sign that they'd like to pay the check. To mask an unexpected stab of regret that King was leaving, Corlis reached beneath the table and retrieved her shoulder bag.

"I can put this on my expense account," she announced emphatically. Then she immediately wondered if Andy Zamora would think it "strictly business" to pay for oysters Rockefeller at Galatoire's.

"That's very sweet of you to offer," King replied swiftly, "but *I* asked *you* to dinner, remember?" He grinned at Dylan. "Thanks for respondin' to my call so quickly," he said. He patted the real estate broker on his well-tailored shoulder. "It's nice to know that she's safe with you, buddy."

"Safe as a nun," Dylan replied, breaking into laughter at his own joke. "Oh, by the way, King, I think I've found a buyer for that dilapidated property on Girod Street."

"Really? That's great news."

"You wanna play angel again?" Dylan asked. "It's a young schoolteacher and his wife who's a social worker. They've got money for the down payment, but it's their first house and the bank, well, *you* know——"

"Send me the paperwork," King interjected, "and I'll let you know."

Dylan looked at Corlis. "Now, *that* place's gonna need space clearin', big-time!" he chortled. "Used to be a brothel, way back when. But, as is my custom," he pronounced, placing his hand over his heart with mock solemnity, "I wait till I'm called. Bye, sugar," he added affectionately to King.

"So long, Dylan. Remember, now," he cautioned good-naturedly, "I'm countin' on you to make sure the lady gets back to Julia Street, her aura intact."

Corlis took a deep draught from her freshly poured cup of coffee. She watched King pay their check and make his way out of the restaurant while she considered her host's unusual brand of private philanthropy. When she returned her attention to her new dinner companion, Dylan Fouché was in the act of poking his fork delicately into a slice of key lime pie. Suddenly Corlis recalled the milky-green absinthe quaffed by the distraught Adelaide LaCroix as her husband fled into the arms of Martine Fouché.

Dylan looked up from his dessert and stared fixedly at Corlis with eyes that were the most amazing amber color—just like Martine's. Their golden translucence held her in his gaze, and she felt, instantly, that she could tell him anything. Just like to a priest.

And she did.

Chapter Fifteen

March 13

It was a few minutes after 1:00 A.M. before Dylan and Corlis glanced at the clock on her mantelpiece. They'd been talking for hours. One flight below on Julia Street, the neighborhood of warehouses and art galleries had grown quiet—except for the occasional truck driving past and turning left onto St. Charles Avenue, where moss-green streetcars glided by with decreasing frequency as the night wore on.

She had been relieved when Dylan took her description of the world of Martine Fouché in stride. He'd stopped teasing and now sat with a serious expression on the love seat in her parlor, sipping a third cup of strong, black Café du Monde coffee from a dainty white-and-gold porcelain demitasse.

"Have you ever heard of this kind of thing happening to people before?" she asked anxiously, having described at some length the details of the strange series of visitations she'd experienced since Christmastime. To her chagrin, Dylan shook his head.

"Oh, I've heard of many individual experiences along these lines," he assured her, "but I don't think I've ever encountered anyone like you who had such a long-runnin' and varied picture show!" Then he added in a surprisingly grave tone of voice, "Now, you'd tell *me*, wouldn't you, m'dear, if you were in the habit of smokin' funny stuff or poppin' pills?"

"Yes, I would—and no, I'm not," she replied stiffly.

"Well . . ." he drawled, "you're from California, so I hope you understand why I feel I have to ask."

215

"Yes, Father Fouché," she said with an edge of sarcasm. Then she gave him a frustrated look. "Sometimes, Dylan, it can be very difficult to tell when you're serious and when you're putting me on."

"That's one of the reasons my bishop and I thought it wiser for me to leave the orthodox priesthood and find some other vocation, like real estate."

"Well, do you think you could give me some clue about what could possibly be going on here?"

"I can try to explain it," he said, "but this time it'll be *your* turn to see if you believe what I'm tellin' you."

"Try me," she said, kicking off the high heels she'd worn to Galatoire's. She sat, feet curled up under her on the large club chair opposite him.

Dylan glanced around the parlor and slowly rose to his feet.

"This is as good a place to start as any," he said. "You were lyin' on this couch where I'm sittin' now, correct, when you suddenly found yourself starin' at a dead body in a coffin a couple of blocks from here in the French Quarter?"

"That about describes it . . . yes," Corlis nodded.

"Well . . ." he said slowly, "let me start at the beginnin'." He swept his arm in an arc over his head and declared, "The atmosphere contains not just the air we breathe but also energy, invisible in the same way that ozone is. The friction generated by material objects moving around on the planet, actin' and reactin', creates the electrically charged energy." He looked at her closely. "With me so far?"

"I think so," Corlis replied thoughtfully. "Are we also talking 'auras' as part of that energy?"

"That's a piece of it—yes."

Corlis nodded. "At UCLA I covered a story once where scientists in the botany department used special cameras to photograph the energy given off by the leaves of plants, energy they called auras. Ever heard of that?"

"Sure! Kurlian photography? A visible record of an invisible phenomenon in nature. Same kind of thing," Dylan said approvingly. "The energy floatin' around everywhere ranges from the very low level to very high energy . . . up to, some would say, *spiritually refined* energy. Certain places on our planet play host to very high levels of this energy. Sedona, Arizona, for example, is considered a place of refined energy. Delphi, in Greece, is another."

"The idea of sacred sites, you mean . . . like Stonehenge in England? Those are places of spiritually refined energy?"

"Precisely," Dylan agreed. "Well . . . there are those of us who believe that the energy activated by everything that ever happened in a particular place goes out in ripples, like the effect of a stone being dropped in a pond. The energy put out by people—their actions, reactions, conversations, arguments, kind words, moods, and the essential emotional atmosphere they create—has to go *somewhere*." He pointed at the wall behind her chair. "It gathers inside structures . . . on the walls . . . on the floor . . . invisibly clingin' to the ceiling of buildings, especially. Even furniture, objects, plants, and pets give, receive, and store up energy. Therefore, the interaction of what takes place in very old buildings like this one gets *imprinted*, in a sense, into the very fabric of the wood and mortar."

"Wow . . ." Corlis breathed. "What a concept!"

"Cool, isn't it?" Dylan said with a smug smile. "Repetitive patterns get *deeply* imprinted. . . . Events accompanied by strong emotions or trauma are recorded the most intensely."

"So, are you saying that what you end up with over the years are kind of like psychic cobwebs clustered inside buildings . . . or at places like the battlefield at Gettysburg, where there's just a *sense* you feel that a lot of people suffered and died at that spot?"

"Exactly," Dylan nodded. "Think of it as concentrated clumps of static energy—unseen to the naked eye—that can accumulate in all the corners. A residue, if you will, of psychic debris that gathers over time, and this state of affairs can be especially true inside really old buildings like this one."

Dylan became lost in thought as he gazed steadily, first in one direction and then another.

"Well . . . ? *What?*" Corlis demanded. "Are you saying you can feel leftover tension and—what do you call it—psychic debris in *this* particular room, for instance?"

"I not only feel it, I can *see*," he declared calmly. "The stuck energy in this place of yours stands three feet thick off the walls and feels like psychic molasses. There must have been a lot of mental and emotional anguish goin' on here since—when were these row houses built?"

"I think King said 1832."

"Even in the lives of people with the normal ups and downs of livin', that accounts for a lot of Sturm und Drang takin' place within these walls. Births, deaths at home; arguments, physical struggles . . . It can generate plenty of psychic caca," he joked. Then his expression grew serious. "However"—he glanced at her strangely—"I believe you, particularly, would be able to pick up on the energy that's congealed around here, and in other old places around New Orleans."

"Why me?" Corlis asked apprehensively.

"Because I think you were drawn to New Orleans and to buyin' this house for a reason," Dylan replied. "And you've probably guessed by now what that is."

For a long moment Corlis remained silent. Then she said, barely above a whisper, "The minute I saw this place from the street . . . it felt familiar. . . ."

"The dates are about right," Dylan said, nodding. "Didn't you tell me earlier tonight that the first Corlis McCullough was in New Orleans around that time? She could have been a visitor in this room at some point and left her energy imprinted. Perhaps you, her direct descendent and her namesake, simply picked up on it like those extra-sensitive cameras at UCLA you described. Like it or not, Miz Show-Me-the-Facts," Dylan said gently, "from what you've just recounted to me, you obviously have some psychic abilities of your own."

"Oh, go on!" she protested.

"No, I'm serious. People inherit blue eyes and bowlegs, don't they? Have you ever thought that perhaps it's possible for DNA to pass on—just like blue eyes or brown hair—a few lastin' memories to generations of the McCullough clan, and you simply have an unusual ability to tune in to them?"

Corlis lay her head against the back of the club chair and closed her eyes.

"Oh, wonderful. Just what I need. Inheriting some old relative's memory bank!" Then she opened her eyes to look Dylan squarely in the eye. "For some reason, I'm sure now that Corlis

Bell McCullough *lived* here, in this very apartment," she said quietly, silently recalling her vision of a young mother padding down the hallway to eavesdrop on a conversation between Randall McCullough and Ian Jeffries that took place over brandy and cigars in a New Orleans parlor more than a century earlier. "I just know it." Then she tossed a petit point pillow at him and declared, "I want you to space-clear this place—pronto—and then I want to forget all about this weird nonsense, once and for all!"

Dylan caught the pillow and laid it carefully on the love seat beside him. "From what King told me about you, I figured you might want to do somethin' like that," he said with a short laugh. He unfolded his long legs and stood to leave.

"You're going?" she said with alarm.

"It's late, sugar," Dylan said in a tone of familiarity, as if they'd known each other for years.

"You mean you won't help me?" Corlis protested. She sprang to her feet. "You *have* to help me," she pleaded. "I mean, I don't exactly know if I *believe* all this stuff you're telling me . . . or the stuff I've been telling *you*, Dylan, but I'm at my wit's end!" She began pacing in front of her fireplace. "It's starting to affect my work . . . my judgment . . . my *life*! Please—"

"Now, calm down, sweetheart," Dylan said soothingly. "I'll do a space clearin' for you."

"You will?" She was filled with an enormous sense of relief. "Thanks," she added in a small voice. "I guess."

"But what I'll be doin' takes some plannin' and preparation," he warned.

"What will you do, exactly?" she asked. "This doubting Thomasina wants a full-bore *exorcism*—okay?"

"All right!" he said, laughing. "But, I don't just snap my fingers and say 'Abracadabra! Entities, beat feet outta here!' " he protested. "I need to make some arrangements. . . . I need my equipment."

"What kind of equipment?" Corlis inquired doubtfully. "This isn't voodoo or anything, is it?"

"Look, now," Dylan said, gently chiding her. "You asked me for help, and that's what I'm tryin' to do." He looked at her closely. "You're not accustomed to askin' for help, are you, darlin'?"

Corlis was startled by the directness of his question, and something in his voice hinted he already knew her answer.

"No," she admitted, surprised by how meek she sounded, even to herself.

"Well . . . it's about time to seek some shelter in the storm. You could use it. I'll see you around noon, okay?"

Corlis nodded, thankful he'd agreed to return.

"And before I get here, I want you to vacuum and dust, throw away the garbage and empty all the wastebaskets. Tidy up any clutter in that office of yours. It makes less work for me." Corlis looked at him questioningly. "Less extraneous stuff for the built-up energy to cling to," he elaborated.

Just then Cagney Cat sauntered into the living room and rubbed sensuously against Dylan's pants leg. Dylan reached down and vigorously scratched the cat's back near his tail. "It's okay if this guy sticks around tomorrow. He'll adore it."

She felt like giggling at the notion of Cagney Cat, assistant ghostbuster. She escorted her visitor to the front door, with her feline trotting along behind. Dylan leaned forward and bussed her on the cheek. "See you at noon tomorrow."

"Thanks," she said. "I don't understand very much of this, but I'm grateful you don't think I'm a mental case."

"Naw . . . I think it's pretty amusin' that a person like you should be havin' things like this pop up in your life right now," he avowed, his golden-brown eyes twinkling slyly.

And before Corlis could react, Dylan strode down the stairs and walked out the front door into Julia Street. To her amazement, Cagney meowed plaintively. The cat turned on his paws, dashed down the hallway, and scampered into the front parlor. Corlis quickly followed and was startled to see him leap through the open window and onto the iron gallery's hand railing, balancing there precariously, exactly as he had the morning she'd burned the oatmeal. The twenty-three-pound feline appeared to focus his complete attention on Dylan Fouché while the former priest got into his car and drove off. Then Cagney closed his amber eyes and went to sleep, seemingly undisturbed by the thirty-foot drop to the pavement below.

As for Corlis, she didn't even attempt to call him to come inside. Instead, she quickly got ready for bed and prayed for a dreamless sleep.

Dylan appeared at the stroke of noon. He was dressed in a pair of jeans and a T-shirt that sported an image of Pete Fountain blowing his clarinet and the words "Jazz Fest '93" embossed over his narrow chest.

"I thought maybe you'd be wearing a black cape," Corlis teased, leading the way down the hallway toward the front parlor. He paused at the door to her office and glanced inside.

"Very neat and tidy," he said approvingly. "Good girl."

Cagney Cat, who'd been asleep on the love seat where Dylan had sat the previous evening, opened his eyes, stretched languidly, and hopped down onto the Persian carpet. He trotted over to Dylan and rubbed his side vigorously against the man's pants leg.

"Hey, buddy . . . how ya doin'?" Dylan drawled. Cagney chirped ecstatically, arched his back, and flopped onto the floor, wanting his stomach rubbed. "What a guy," Dylan said, laughing. He gave the cat's vast tummy a playful pat.

He set down the briefcase he had brought with him and took out, among several items, two small, leafy green bundles wrapped in twine. He retrieved sticks of incense, a few white candles, a salt shaker, and a bouquet of small daisies.

"What are those?" she demanded, pointing at the green bundles the size of cucumbers.

"Trussed-up sage, with some rosemary mixed in," he informed her. "When this particular herb burns, it helps cleanse the air of psychic pollution."

"You don't say?" Corlis commented, deadpan. "I hope the smell doesn't send me back to the Crusades."

Ignoring her, Dylan continued, "The candles, salt, and incense aid in consecratin' the space for higher, healthier purposes."

"And what are the flowers for?"

"They're offerings to the guardian spirits of the house and to the earth it sits on."

"Whatever," muttered Corlis, suddenly feeling as if she was getting in way over her head with this woo-woo routine.

"Thanks for your enthusiasm and support," Dylan replied wryly. "Do you want to purify the objects in the rooms as well?"

"What do you mean, 'objects'?"

He pointed to the floor. "These Persian carpets, for instance, have a thick crust of psychic crud."

"This is getting a bit too much for me, Dylan. Those rugs are vacuumed every week!"

"Well, somebody's extrasensory cooties are still clingin' to it, sunshine! It's got the imprint of a couple of very nasty, greedy folks all over it!"

Corlis thought of the grasping Randall McCullough and his partner, Ian Jeffries.

"Okay! Okay! Clear the rug, and anything else you see lurking around here. But let's just *do* it," she added apprehensively, "and get it over with."

Without further conversation Dylan snapped the heads of the daisies off their stems and arranged them in three small dishes around lighted candles. He stuck the incense in several holders and lit them as well. Then he asked Corlis to place the offerings around her house—in the parlor, in her bedroom, and the third dish in her tiny kitchen.

Methodically he removed a gold crest ring from his pinkie finger, his watch, his belt with its metal belt buckle, and the metal coins from his pockets and put them inside her refrigerator. He pointed to a flat gold necklace Corlis wore and asked her to take it off.

"Metal attracts energy," he explained when she had returned to the front parlor. "It acts as an electrical conductor, which would be counterproductive."

"Right," Corlis agreed doubtfully.

"Let's both wash our hands in the kitchen sink."

"Aye, aye, sir."

Next Dylan took off his shoes. "I hope you don't mind. I get a better feel for how well I'm clearin' the space of negative energy if I walk around the place barefoot."

"Be my guest," she nodded. "My shoes are the first thing I take off when I come home."

He crossed the parlor and pushed open the two large windows that fronted the ironwork gallery facing Julia Street.

"The energy needs a place to go," he explained. "It can travel through solid objects, but I like to invite it to dissipate and diffuse into the larger atmosphere outside.

"Sounds perfectly sensible to me," Corlis said. The truth was, everything that had happened since Dylan arrived seemed surreal.

He then took her hand and led her down the hallway toward the front door. To her surprise, they continued down the stairs and stood beside the closed entrance that faced Julia Street.

Dylan paused, shut his eyes, and indicated with a gesture that she should do the same.

"Try to quiet your mind," he said softly, and began inhaling and exhaling in deep, even breaths. "Silently petition for help with our cleansin' enterprise here today."

"You mean pray?" she asked, feeling uncomfortable even uttering the word.

"Whatever," he murmured. After a few minutes matching Dylan breath for breath, she felt an unaccountable sense of calm and serenity settle into her chest. "Now open your eyes and stand sideways, like I am. Hold your hand nearest the front door a few inches away from it . . . like this."

Corlis did as she was instructed.

"Follow me and begin to stroke the energy field of this door."

"Do *what*?"

"Every solid object has an energy field, remember?" Dylan reminded her. "Pretend you're pettin' your cat, only not touchin' him. Stroke the area near the wall and mentally commit your intention to connect spiritually with your home for the purpose of purifyin' your livin' space of old, negative energy generated by past traumas that took place here. Be *receptive*, Corlis," he urged. "Listen to what the house has to say to you."

"I feel kind of silly," Corlis dared to whisper.

"Don't waste your energy feelin' silly," he gently reprimanded. "Use it instead to feel the magnetic pulsations left over from the people who lived here before you did."

Chastened, Corlis did as she was told. Amazingly her palms and fingertips began to tingle slightly, and she began to sense a force field flowing around her hand. She followed behind Dylan as he moved counterclockwise along the walls on the ground floor. The sensations she was encountering reminded her of everything from the feel of fine cobwebs to an impression that she was handling thick, sticky molasses—just as Dylan had described earlier.

"Some places feel hot, some cool," she marveled.

"And some sensations will be pleasant, others, not so pleasant," Dylan commented softly. "You may even feel dull aches in your bones or a zippy, tinglin' feelin' in your palms."

Abruptly he began to shake his hands briskly.

"What are you doing?" she whispered.

"Riddin' myself of the energy I'm pickin' up as I travel around the perimeter of the lower floor. This place is loaded with it."

As an experiment, she sharply gave both hands several hard flicks of the wrist and was gratified to feel the weird sensations course through her fingers and out the tips.

When Dylan arrived at a corner of the room, he raised his hands slightly above his head and clapped downward to the level of his waist, increasing the intensity of his clapping as he got closer to the floor.

"What *are* you doing?" she demanded in a low voice.

"Clappin' out the bad energy stickin' to the nooks and crannies," he explained matter-of-factly, as if his actions were the most normal in the world. As they trudged upstairs to the second-story apartment, Dylan commented, "The livin' room, the bedroom, and the kitchen are the most important places for us to work on clearin' out bad stuff. And don't let me forget the closets and cupboards."

Corlis followed in Dylan's wake around the entire apartment, making a good-faith effort to suspend her normal critical faculties and just go with the program, as he was urging. To Corlis's astonishment, she realized that all the while Cagney had been following them from room to room.

When the three of them entered her bedroom, Dylan moved toward the wall behind the huge four-poster and began to clap in sharp, even motions. For no reason she could fathom, a flood of emotion suddenly began to well up in her chest. The next thing she knew, tears were streaming down her cheeks. Worse yet, she felt wracking sobs filling her throat. She saw in her mind's eye a picture of King's handsome face—only it *wasn't* King's at all. It was André Duvallon with blood streaming down his cheeks.

"Breathe! Breathe in and out . . . *big* breaths!" Dylan commanded, watching her closely. "That's a girl. . . . Let it go. . . . Let the tears come if they want to. . . . It'll help the energy move on out. . . . It will pass, I promise you."

"I—f-feel so s-stupid!" Corlis wailed. "I'm not feeling s-sad for myself. . . . It's for . . . it's like—"

"Lettin' go? Something passin' through?"

"Yeah . . . s-sort of," she stuttered. "It's as if s-something sad that happened here was leaving . . . dissipating or something. I dunno. This is pretty crazy, Dylan," she gulped, flashing him a watery smile while reaching for a tissue from her bedside table.

"No . . . it's good," he said quietly. He put an arm around her shoulders and gave her a warm squeeze. "Take another deep breath. How are you feelin' now?"

Corlis looked around her bedroom and suddenly felt a strange lightness come over her. Then she grinned. "It feels *good* in here!"

"All clear?" Dylan asked, beaming beatifically.

"All clear!"

Corlis dutifully threw salt into the corners of every room, as instructed, and followed Dylan throughout the apartment with a lighted sage-and-rosemary bundle laced with juniper berries in her hand. As its pungent, medicinal aroma filled the atmosphere, she remarked in a low voice, "It smells like someone's getting ready to cook a turkey!"

"You mean . . . like Thanksgivin'?" he said pointedly.

"Are you reminding me to show a little gratitude?" she replied meekly. "For being able to purify this place?"

"Might be a good idea, oh ye of little faith."

On their third round of the building, Dylan brought a small bell out of his briefcase. On the ground floor he rang the bell once and paused to listen to its pure, clear tone. Then he walked the perimeter of the downstairs foyer, ringing the bell at intervals.

"Visualize all the spaces fillin' with shimmerin' light and sound," he commanded with quiet intensity as he continued on his rounds. "This will create a protective shield of pure, vibrant light." Then Dylan drew a horizontal figure eight in the air with the bell. "It's the symbol of eternity," he declared with absolute conviction. "It tells the spiritual energy to keep goin' round and round this protective ring we've constructed." He turned suddenly and rang the bell over her head, as if to enclose her in its pure, tinkling sound.

"What are you doing?" she protested mildly.

"I've just given you a personal shield, dear Corlis," he said. "If you ever feel you are in a dangerous situation, just remember that you can create your own sacred space around you by imaginin' that I am ringin' this bell in a circle to trace your aura."

And instead of feeling foolish or cynical, Corlis glanced around her front parlor, filled with gratitude for the clear shafts of daylight slanting through the floor-to-ceiling windows. A strange humility seized her, and she gave thanks for the extraordinary, lanky young man with the golden eyes who neatly packed his odd assortment of space-clearing implements back into his briefcase.

"And now, Ms. WJAZ," Dylan Fouché announced cheerfully, "you may buy me lunch. An expensive one. At Antoine's."

In the days that followed Dylan Fouché's "psychic cleansing" of Corlis's apartment on Julia Street, a gradual sense of serenity enveloped her home environment. With it came the conviction that she could now forget about the strange visions she'd been having and simply get on with her normal existence as a feet-on-the-ground reporter.

High on her list of priorities was to follow up on something King's assistant, Chris Calvert, had mentioned to her recently. She wanted to find out if Grover Jeffries was using strategic campaign contributions "donated" to members of the New Orleans City Council to help smooth the way toward downgrading the zoning of the 600 block in the historic district along Canal Street. Such freewheeling largesse was also bound to help Jeffries's cause with the politically appointed City Planning Commission, a body that would be required to give its permission to demolish the Greek Revival structures in order to make way for the proposed hotel.

King Duvallon was obviously doing research along the same lines.

"Hey, Ace . . . how ya doin'?" he asked a few days later over the telephone. It was five-thirty and Corlis had returned to her office cubicle after broadcasting a story about the metropolitan water district's plans for new pumping stations. "You looked real nice on TV tonight."

"You watched?" she asked, pleased.

"Sure did," he replied. "Now listen, sugar . . . want to go to a masquerade ball with me on Saturday? It'll be a real New Orleans experience," he added invitingly.

Surprised and secretly delighted, she smiled into the phone receiver. "A costume ball? Do they still have those things?" Then she frowned. How would it look to be seen at a social function with a date who also figured in the ongoing public controversy she was covering for WJAZ?

"Don't worry. . . . It's absolutely, *positively* business," he said, as if reading her mind. "It provides a chance for us both to do a little sleuthin'—you for your cause, me for mine."

"How's that?"

"Grover Jeffries's wife is giving a fancy-dress extravaganza at their mansion to benefit the symphony association. It'd give us a golden opportunity to nose around a bit."

"Can we wear masks the whole time so no one will know who we are, or that we're there together?"

"That's part of my plan," he assured her. "In fact, you're my ticket *in*. Grover and Bonita Jeffries love publicity. I'm sure WJAZ is on the invitation list. Get yourself assigned to cover the party, and I'll go as part of your crew."

"What—specifically—are you looking for?" she asked warily.

"The same thing I expect you are." He sounded amused. "Information about how Grover intends to get the Landmark Commission, the Plannin' Commission, and the city council to see things *his* way and vote to change the historic zonin' and okay demolition of the Selwyn buildings. I understand he has a home office. . . ."

"And you want to rifle through his files to see who he's giving campaign contributions to, right?"

"Well, it wouldn't be exactly breakin' and enterin'. Not like that time at *Ms. UCLA*—"

"Pretty close to it, Professor."

"Who knows what we might pick up on if we just have a little look-see?" King suggested, ignoring her previous remark. "You're exactly the person I want to have with me while I poke around. Besides, it might help you too. Advance the story, and all that. Are you game?"

"Why not," she drawled. "What shall we go disguised as?"

"The four musketeers," he replied promptly.

"Four? Are we double-dating?"

"Kinda," King said, laughing. "You gotta get Virgil and Manny invited, too. They'll provide me the best cover. And y'know how much that Bonita Jeffries dearly loves to be interviewed. It'll be a piece of cake."

Chapter Sixteen

April 4

On Saturday the two-man camera crew, along with King and Corlis, eased themselves, their television equipment, and their bulky costumes out of the WJAZ news van. As they donned black satin face masks, they caught sight of Grover and Bonita Jeffries's imposing mansion, lit up as gaudily as a birthday cake created for the King of Carnival.

The quartet of masked duelists advanced up the drive, capes and swords swinging in unison. Up ahead, lights glowed in every window, beckoning the guests to make their way along the brick path to the open front door.

Standing in stark splendor at the top of a circular drive that branched off stately St. Charles Avenue, the Jeffries's house was a concrete monument to unadorned postmodern design. Massive plate-glass windows looked out in every direction across wide cement verandas distinguished by stark, pencil-thin cypress trees planted in what looked like oil drums painted gunmetal gray.

"It looks like Saddam Hussein's bunker!" Corlis marveled.

King burst out laughing behind his plastered-on mustache and goatee. "It doesn't much look as if it belongs in New Orleans, that's for sure."

"Nice lawn," Virgil offered hopefully, nodding in the direction of a half acre of manicured turf that was dotted with flowering magnolia trees and artfully sculptured hedges. Musical strains from a dance band hired for the occasion drifted toward them as they mounted the front stairs and entered the impressive foyer paneled in silver-tone brushed metal.

Bonita Jeffries was the first to greet the arriving contingents. Attired as a plantation belle with chestnut ringlets cascading behind each ear, she gaily tossed her head, framed by a large broad-rimmed picture hat trimmed with dusty-pink ribbons, Scarlett O'Hara style. Both she and her husband—who was posing as a Texas Ranger—had elected not to wear masks while society photographers from the *Times-Picayune* and *Arts This Week* scurried about.

"Keep your camera under your cape, Virgil. . . . And the rest of us just nod and walk past 'em—*fast!*" King advised, sotto voce, as they approached their hosts.

Fortunately a boisterous troupe of harlequins clad in black-and-white-domino costumes was entering the house just ahead, and the crew passed unnoticed. They entered an enormous living room that looked more like a hotel lobby than a private home, and quietly fanned out in search of Grover Jeffries's office.

Corlis had taken only a few steps when a butler, dressed in the gold-braided livery of the French king Louis XVI, approached with a tray filled with champagne flutes.

"Thank you so much," she said, accepting a glass from the servant's gloved hand. On impulse, she cast him a coquettish glance from behind her mask. Then, in an approximation of a southern drawl she asked, "Do you 'spose you could direct me to someplace *very* quiet? I have to make a very important call later to check on my baby. It's the first time we've left her with anyone, and I'm *so* nervous!"

"Why certainly, ma'am," he replied, eyeing her male attire with some surprise. "You just take that metal staircase up to the second floor. There's a nice quiet spot on the landin' where you'll find a phone."

Corlis glanced at a huge flight of stairs that looked as if it would lead to an aircraft factory.

"Oh . . . well, I have a problem," she said hastily. "I wanted to conference call with my husband who's in Texas on business, y'know? He wants to be on the phone with the housekeeper at the same time, so we can both make *sure* everything's all right. Wouldn't it be better if I used Mr. Jeffries's office or somethin'?"

The waiter looked doubtful, so Corlis continued brightly, "And also, Harry said he's probably gonna fax me somethin' to give to Mr. Jeffries tonight. Some big deal, cookin'," she said with a wink. Then she leaned forward and added in a confidential whisper, "My husband does all sorts of business with Mr. Jeffries, y'know, and Harry wants to surprise 'im with the good news when the papers are signed. I don't think Grover'd mind if I went into his lil' ol' home office, do you? It'll only take a few minutes."

"Sure, ma'am. I 'spect that'd be all right. Go up the stairs, down the hall on your right, and it's right there, first door on your left."

Corlis squeezed the man's satin sleeve and said, "You are such a darlin'. *Thank you!*"

Pul-eeze! I'm starting to sound like a genuine magnolia!

Corlis quickly gave the high sign to her confederates to follow her at a discreet distance and soon made her way through the milling crowd, disappearing up the stairs. After an appropriate interval her three companions followed suit.

"Rock 'n' roll!" King said when the group reassembled in Grover Jeffries's study.

Virgil shut the heavy door behind his companions. "Wow! These digs are something else, aren't they?"

Corlis followed his gaze around the elegantly appointed library and state-of-the-art electronic office. On one wall a bank of television sets was framed by the same gray-slate paneling that adorned all four sides of the spacious study. A vast, matching chrome-and-slate desk stood on polished concrete flooring in front of large picture windows overlooking a sloping lawn. The horizontal work surface served as a platform for a twenty-one-inch monitor, keyboard, and other streamlined equipment that appeared to qualify Grover Jeffries as a member of the computer literati. Shining black enamel filing cabinets were built into an entire wall on the far side of the room.

"Mama Roux!" echoed King on a long breath. "Guess the first thing to do," he declared, flipping the ON switch on Grover's home computer, "is to access Grover's main directory on this thing."

"Okay," Corlis agreed with trepidation, "but this sure *feels* like breaking and entering. And I told a couple of incredible whoppers to get us *in* this place, so we can't stay long."

"Why, sugar," King said with a sly smile, "you're really gettin' into doin' things southern style!"

Ignoring him, she turned to address her television crew. "Manny, Virgil . . . while we're here, just give me close-ups of that bank of TVs . . . stuff around the room—in case anyone walks in on us. It'll look as if we're just shooting background shots."

"Gotcha," Virgil said, hoisting his camera onto his shoulder. "But first, I've got to take off this stupid mask. It itches somethin' crazy, and I can't see anything through my viewfinder." Taking the cameraman's lead, the others tossed their masks onto Grover's expansive desk.

"Jackpot!" King said suddenly under his breath, scrolling down the computer screen. "Just have a look at this little ol' file that was stored under 'Lafayette Marchand'!"

They all crowded around the computer screen.

"Sweet Jesus, Duvallon, you're somethin' else," Virgil said admiringly, pointing to the glowing screen. "You preservation guys *are* guerrillas."

"Just lookee here," King announced gleefully. The screen displayed a memo entitled "Del Mar Hotel Development Proposal—First Draft," authored by Grover Jeffries's public relations specialist, Lafayette Marchand. "I'll figure out how to print out a copy while you look for it in the file cabinet. . . . Maybe a copy's in there, too. We gotta get this."

"*You* get it," Corlis said worriedly. "We can video the hard copy, but WJAZ can't actually pinch it. Those are the rules, remember, Mr. Guerrilla?"

"Whatever," King muttered, looking around the room for a printer.

Virgil continued recording video around the office, with Manny following behind, tied to his partner by the umbilical cord connected to his sound equipment.

King spoke up suddenly. "Double jackpot!" He held up several sheets of paper that had been in Jeffries's out box on top of his desk. "Grover already printed out the same memo! I can't believe it was right in front of us! And *this* version's got notes in the margins. . . ."

Corlis and King studied the memo closely.

"Oh m'God!" she murmured. "I can't believe it's right here in black and white."

Manny and Virgil crossed to the desk and stood beside Corlis and King. Four pairs of eyes stared at the memo that Corlis now held in her hand. In the left margin was written in bold penmanship, "INSERT HERE OUR OWNERSHIP OF THE BUILDINGS." Further down on the page was another notation: "TELL DEL MAR WE HAVE LOCK ON P.C. RE ZONING CHANGE."

"What's P.C.?" she asked. "Some sort of computer?"

"No," King said grimly. "P.C. is the Plannin' Commission. They have to okay the zonin' change and approve the demolition order before it can go on to the full city council."

At the bottom of the memo, a third handwritten comment read, "DIRECT ACCOUNTANT TO MAKE CC'S TO FRIENDLY CITY COUNCIL MEMBERS—NOW!"

"CC's?" Corlis echoed. "Copies?"

"CC's in this town, sugar, can mean only one thing," King explained with a cynical laugh. "Campaign contributions. It sure looks as if Grover is directin' his money man to grease the palms of various members of the city council to see things *his* way on the order to demolish."

"And did you see *this*?" Corlis said excitedly. "This memo more than implies that Grover himself owns the Selwyn buildings now!" Corlis looked over at King. "How can we prove that? Wouldn't there be a deed on file somewhere downtown? And how can we *prove* 'CC' means campaign contributions?"

"Well, first we need a copy of this with Grover's notes all over it," King asserted, hurriedly scanning the memo's second page.

"And after you photocopy it and we get out of here, Virgil can get it—nice and clear—on videotape for WJAZ!" she said excitedly, nodding at her cameraman, who continued to shoot close-ups of objects around the office.

Just then a raucous burst of laughter from down the hallway brought the foursome up short.

"Did any of you see a copier?" King asked, taking the memo from Corlis.

"*Yes!*" She pointed across the office. However, before anyone could move, the door to the office opened, and in walked a black-caped figure wearing white tie and tails. The man's face was obscured by a white porcelain mask that covered only half of his face, immediately suggesting that the reveler was masquerading as the Phantom of the Opera.

"Well, well . . . look who's here. King Duvallon." The masked man took in Corlis and her fellow TV crew members. "Aren't y'all enjoyin' the party?" inquired the intruder. "What're you doin' in *here*, may I ask?"

With a sinking heart Corlis realized she'd recognize Jack Ebert's voice anywhere.

"We were getting some cutaways for a video profile I'm doing on the charitable activities of Mr. and Mrs. Jeffries," she declared swiftly and with as much aplomb as she could muster.

If only they'd kept on their masks!

Virgil spoke up.

"And I was just about to check in with the assignment desk at WJAZ to let 'em know how long we'd be here," he lied, shifting his heavy camera off his shoulder and nodding in the direction of the telephone on the desk.

Corlis didn't dare look at King. "What're *you* doing in here?" she demanded suddenly.

Jack advanced further inside the slate-paneled study. His gaze swept the room and rested on the desk. Corlis blessed the fates that King had dropped the memo approximately where they'd found it in Grover's out box.

"I'm merely a guest," Jack declared evenly. "I thought I'd have a look around this palace." His eyes narrowed as he addressed King. "Do the Jeffries know *you're* here?"

King ignored the question and instead asked Corlis, "Ready for that drink, Ace?"

"Are you servin' as Corlis's production assistant these days, Duvallon?" Jack persisted.

"Naw . . . just interested in how you folks do your stuff, so I asked my pal Virgil, here, if I could tag along." Jack's expression made no secret of his skepticism. King turned to Corlis. "I say we all get a drink," he repeated. He snatched his and the other remaining black face masks off the desk. "See ya, Ebert."

Without further farewells, Corlis, King, and the two television technicians filed out of Grover's office and walked in silence down the hallway that led to the staircase. When they arrived at the large front salon, filled with noisy partygoers clad in elaborate fancy dress, Corlis muttered, "Jeez Louise, talk about your unwanted intruders."

"More to the point," King said tersely, donning his face mask, as did his companions, "we didn't get a copy of that smokin' gun memo. But it sure goes a long way to prove that Grover's definitely up to his usual tricks, tryin' to use his money to influence folks."

"But we still don't have the hard evidence," Corlis reminded him. "And we nearly got *caught* red-handed," she added under her breath, wondering how Andy Zamora would feel if his star reporter got hauled away to jail for breaking and entering, handcuffed to Grover Jeffries's archenemy.

Dangerous. This was getting very dangerous on about ten levels, she thought worriedly.

Virgil appeared to be reading her mind.

"Let's do the interview with the Jeffrieses and then get outta here," he said gruffly. He turned to King and said, "Do us a favor buddy . . . and get lost."

King disappeared into the crowd of masked revelers. The remaining musketeers soon found themselves back inside Grover's inner sanctum, a suitably quiet spot in which to ask Mr. and Mrs. Jeffries about their worthy goals for the symphony organization that Bonita Jeffries chaired.

During the interview Lafayette Marchand, who was dashingly attired as a red devil, stood to one side and looked on approvingly as his clients settled into two handsomely upholstered chairs and began to speak enthusiastically about their generous support of the arts in the New Orleans community.

At the conclusion of the interview, Virgil asked, "Okay if I photograph some of the pictures on the wall and stuff like that? I'll use 'em later for cutaways with the story, okay, Mr. Marchand?" he inquired, his eye glued to his camera's lens piece.

"Fine . . . fine," the PR consultant agreed.

The incriminating memo with Jeffries's handwritten directives to virtually pay off key public officials was no longer in sight on the desk, and now that the interview was at an end, she couldn't get a good view of Grover Jeffries's in and out boxes without drawing attention to herself. However, she was relieved when the cameraman took close-ups of Grover's chrome-accented slate desk. That way she at least had footage over which she—as the TV correspondent—could narrate, at some point in the future, an account of having *seen* the damning document with her own eyes in Jeffries's office—even if she didn't have physical possession of a copy.

"We do so appreciate your coverin' this event," gushed Bonita as the crew packed up their gear. The hostess eyed Corlis closely. "Doesn't that mustache *itch*, dear?" Then she added quickly, "Of course, we really appreciate y'all in the media comin' in costume, too!"

"Actually, it does. Quite a bit. Is it all right with you, Mrs. Jeffries," Corlis asked politely, "if the crew tapes some party atmosphere out there on the dance floor?"

"Why, I'd be mighty pleased if you *would*!" Bonita responded with enthusiasm.

"More fun than doin' a story about those bleedin' heart malcontents at the university, eh, Corlis?" Grover said pointedly.

"While we're on that subject, Mr. Jeffries," Corlis replied, "I'd like to get your views on the growing controversy about your future plans for the Canal Street project that's on your drawing boards." She looked over at Marchand expectantly. "We've been hearing a lot of intriguing rumors about a twenty-eight-story hotel you want to build there. How do you plan to corral the necessary votes to get the Planning Commission to down-zone a declared historic district so you can demolish the existing structures?"

"Have you *seen* those buildings?" Grover demanded. "They're about the ugliest things in all of New Orleans! I'd be doin' this town a favor to get rid of 'em!"

"I've seen *behind* the metal screen, Mr. Jeffries," she said quietly. "There are eleven perfectly preserved Greek Revival facades that apparently go back to the first half of the nineteenth century."

Grover's benign expression hardened, but before the veteran developer could reply, Jeffries's public relations mouthpiece smoothly intervened.

"I'd be most happy to supply you with plenty of solid background material on the major economic benefits that the city will derive from our plans for that entire area," Marchand assured her. Then he added, "I'm sure that when the time is right, we can arrange an on-camera interview about that, don't you think, Grover?"

Jeffries eyed Corlis skeptically.

"Give her the new press kit," he said grudgingly. "If she'll promise to *read* it, maybe we can talk sometime later."

"It's my *job* to ask questions, Mr. Jeffries," Corlis said with a level gaze.

"Yeah, right," Grover grunted.

Corlis quickly exited Grover's office. Once outside, she scanned the crowded dance floor for a glimpse of a tall, dark-haired man wearing a sword and sporting a wide-brimmed hat trimmed with feathers.

"Need a little somethin' to drink to settle your nerves?" a voice said behind her.

She whirled around in time to catch King, his face concealed once again by his black mask. He bowed from the waist and made a sweeping flourish with his feathered hat. Laughing, she offered a mock bow in return. Just then Jack Ebert threaded his way through the undulating throng of dancers.

"King, dance with me!" she demanded. "Quickly! Jack's coming this way. I don't want to have to deal with that creep twice in one night."

Instantly King took her in his arms. The pair was oblivious to the odd picture they made dressed as two musketeers in tunics and capes, swaying to the rhythms of a homogenized rendition of Dr. John's howling "Goin' Back to New Orleans."

"To do this to Dr. John is sacrilege," King noted, inclining his head in the direction of the stodgy band and some dancers of advanced years making fools of themselves in public. Meanwhile, Corlis was conscious both of Jack's hovering presence and King's warm embrace as he whirled her around the dance floor.

"Why won't Jack Ebert just get lost?" she complained. King

followed her gaze. The menacing Phantom of the Opera was leaning against one wall and staring directly at them. "I swear, that man should get the Lounge Lizard award," she groused. "All he ever does is lurk about." She glanced defiantly over King's shoulder and locked stares with her fellow journalist, who eventually had the grace to look in another direction.

"What do you think Jack was doin' in Grover Jeffries's study?" King wondered aloud as he skillfully avoided a collision with another couple dressed as Miss Piggy and Kermit the Frog.

"Mr. Poison Pen? I don't know." Then she had a curious thought. "Maybe he's after the same information we are?"

"Possibly," King replied as he maneuvered between a gyrating twosome attired in identical chartreuse-and-pink clown costumes. "Didn't you tell me he was writin' about architecture now for *Arts This Week*?"

"That's right," Corlis confirmed, startled. Then she shrugged. "I suppose he could be doing some decent investigative reporting for a change, instead of just his usual slicing and dicing."

"I seriously doubt it," King scoffed. "Jack invariably looks for the easy way in all things. He probably saw us go in there . . . and wherever *you* are, sugar, there's usually a good story close by." He glanced over his shoulder and smiled. "He's gone now. Shall we find Virgil and Manny and hit the road?"

Within minutes, the foursome made their exit down the front steps of the mansion just as a silver-haired, well-built figure dressed entirely in red accosted them at the circular drive. Lafayette Marchand was waiting for the valet parking attendants to deliver his car.

"Hello, again," Marchand called out. Corlis sensed that Grover Jeffries's media adviser had been closely observing one of her three companions. "Is that you, King?" he asked sharply. "I wasn't dead sure, because of that wig . . . not to mention the mask. Good to see you," he said, walking toward them. "May I say that you all look quite spectacular as seventeenth-century French noblemen."

"You seem to know your history," King replied coolly.

"With a name like Lafayette, I was rather forced into it," Marchand responded pleasantly. The older man paused, then added, "I didn't see you here before, King, but I take it from the looks of your coordinated costumes that y'all came here together." Corlis glanced quickly at the other musketeers, but nobody said anything. "Well," Marchand continued, "I'm actually glad for this unexpected opportunity to speak with you, son. I hope you'll take this as it's intended."

"As *what's* intended?" King asked sharply.

Surprisingly, Corlis thought, Lafayette Marchand's attitude held no hint of threat or condescension. In fact, the older man's blue eyes had an almost benevolent aspect to them as he addressed King.

"I have some concerns about your position as an associate professor at the university, should you involve yourself in any further public campaigns against Jeffries Industries."

"Now, why would *you* have those kinds of concerns, Laf, unless you were part of the pressure that's being exerted on the dean to deny me tenure and get me thrown out?"

Corlis placed a restraining hand just above one of King's lacy cuffs. Had his job at the university actually been threatened? She felt a flash of anger at the notion and forced herself to inhale slowly.

King Duvallon can fight his own battles, dearie.

Oddly, Lafayette Marchand shifted his attention just then to Corlis and her television crew, as if he wished to gain their support. Then he glanced back at King. "You have a perfect right to your opinions, of course, King," he said, "and you have a perfect right to act on your conscience—especially when I'm sure that your intent is to protect historic buildings. I merely speak on a personal basis." His face grew grave, and he laid his hand lightly on King's shoulder. "Remember, now, I know how hard you've worked for that Ph.D., son." King's icy stare slid from Marchand's face to the man's hand that had remained resting on his shoulder. However, Marchand didn't seem to notice and continued speaking. "There's no need to sabotage your future at the university. Grover Jeffries *hears* you," he emphasized. "And once you've gotten tenure, he cannot hurt you as seriously."

"You mean *you* can't hurt me as seriously, don't you, Laf?" King asked evenly. "Because everybody knows you're Jeffries's mouthpiece. The hired flak that's supposed to make a highway robber look like a civic hero at every opportunity." He regarded his godfather with more curiosity than malice. "On a *personal* basis, Lafayette," he drawled sarcastically, "I actually don't know how you can stomach it, workin' for a guy like him. But then, we all make choices in life, don't we?" He turned toward Corlis and the two crewmen. "Are we outta here, or what?"

And without further conversation, the four musketeers turned their backs on Lafayette Marchand and strolled down the drive toward St. Charles Avenue. As King walked beside her, Corlis sensed he was struggling with feelings both of anger and melancholy, but he remained silent. It must be hard, she thought, for him to accept what Marchand did for a living these days.

Once inside the news van, however, King's customary good humor returned. He asked her if she'd seen anything else interesting when she went back into Grover's office to shoot the interview.

"Actually, yes," she said with a thoughtful expression. "It was really weird, though."

"What was?"

"Grover took a few moments to clean off his desk just prior to my interviewing him."

"So?"

"Virgil was busy shooting 'B' roll while Grover fiddled with a pen and fussed around with papers on his desk, and so on . . . you know, close-ups we can use to cut away to when we edit the interview. Well, anyway," Corlis continued, "Grover initialed a one-page something-or-other and slipped it into his out box. It was a single sheet with columns and words typed on it."

"So? You said he was cleaning off his desk, right?" King said, shrugging.

She heaved a sigh of resignation. "Anyway, whatever that one-pager was, it had a headline at the top that I could just barely read upside down. It said: 'Writing Assignments.' "

"Maybe after we all left the office the first time tonight, Lafayette Marchand presented Grover with his monthly bill?" King suggested. "He was right there in Grover's office when you did the interview, correct?"

"Oh . . ." Corlis replied, crestfallen. "That's probably it. I'll bet that Marchand doubles as a ghostwriter for the guy, as well as handling his regular PR. Grover's always giving keynote speeches at the Petroleum Club and places like that."

In the middle of this exchange, Virgil suddenly floored the accelerator in order to speed through a yellow light. Corlis grabbed hold of King's arm.

"Sorry," she murmured.

Making no reply, he put his arm around her shoulders and gave her a soft squeeze. His reassuring embrace made Corlis irrationally yearn to snuggle against his chest and tuck the top of her head under his chin.

Ignore it, lady! There's too much at stake this time around!

King drew her closer against his chest, and she felt his body heat raising her own temperature several degrees. As she stared into his eyes, only inches away from hers, she was forced to swallow hard and close her lids. Then, slowly, she gave him a warning shake of her head.

"How 'bout we rattle some folks at the Hummingbird Grill and go get a late-night breakfast?" she heard him ask.

"Dressed like *this*?" Virgil protested, looking into his rearview mirror and pointing to his elegantly coiffed wig and the lacy jabot at his throat.

"Great idea!" Manny chimed in. "Virgil and I missed dinner."

"Okay, okay," grumbled Virgil. "Let's give those late-night characters in Corlis's neighborhood a thrill."

Corlis heaved another sigh. The sooner she put a Formica tabletop between herself and King Duvallon's handsome presence. . . . Even better, it was less than a block from the all-night restaurant to her front door on Julia Street, behind which she'd be safe from the odd, tingling sensations that were percolating in her solar plexus.

"The Hummingbird it is," she quickly agreed.

Man, oh, man, she thought, she'd gone from having visions of long-lost relatives to suffering serious palpitations over somebody she'd wanted to throw in *jail* a decade or so ago.

Within minutes Virgil parked the van outside the restaurant in the Warehouse District. Inured from years of Mardi Gras excess, few of the late-night denizens in the Hummingbird bothered to note the entrance of the four musketeers. Before they devoured their breakfast, however, Corlis ducked into the ladies' room, removed her wig and mustache, and stuffed both inside her voluminous leather shoulder bag.

King laughed when she sat down, pointing to her upper lip. "You looked pretty cute with all that hair . . . but a lot better, now."

When their food arrived, King, Corlis, and her crew set about their enthusiastic consumption of waffles saturated with thick, sweet cane syrup, plus multiple cups of coffee. Corlis resolutely snatched the bill away from the men to establish that the meal was a purely business affair, but she hadn't the strength to protest when King insisted on walking her around the corner to her front door. Manny, Virgil, and the WJAZ news van headed down St. Charles Avenue past one of the streetcars that King would eventually take back to the edge of the French Quarter.

It was long after midnight, and Julia Street was deserted. The silent row of brick facades thrust both sidewalk and street into shadow. On the opposite side of the road, old-fashioned globed streetlamps stood like a line of night watchmen, casting circles of mellow light over the sidewalk. Side by side, King and Corlis strolled silently down the hushed block. Suddenly she was brought up short by the clip-clop sound of horses' hooves.

Oh no! Corlis thought, she couldn't be—

Please, don't let it happen again. Not now. Not in front of King!

Chapter Seventeen

April 5

An open carriage with battery-powered headlights turned the corner at Church Street, heading toward a livery stable. At the reins was a tourist guide with a boom box blaring full blast on the seat next to him. Vastly relieved, Corlis gave silent thanks that she was still tethered to her own century.

"Got your key, Ace?" King asked, leaning a cloaked arm against the carved white molding that framed the entrance to her building.

"The damn thing's in here somewhere," she muttered as she rooted at the bottom of her purse. At almost the same moment she found her key ring she felt King slide his hand up her arm.

"Well, sugar," he murmured, his mouth only inches away from hers, "that was quite a party tonight, huh?" To both her joy and dismay, he slowly and deliberately bent down and brushed his lips against hers with a come-hither invitation that she'd have to be unconscious to ignore. After a few long, delicious seconds, he backed off a bit and scrutinized her closely.

"I guess this is good night," she murmured. For another long moment, she was virtually incapable of breaking from his steady gaze.

Then, in an act of pure instinct, she released her grip on her key ring and allowed it to fall to the bottom of her purse. She withdrew her right hand from the depths of her shoulder bag and felt the leather pouch slide down her arm and land with a soft plop near her feet. As if someone had switched her to automatic pilot, she put both arms around King's shoulders, closing the short space between their lips, and held on to steady herself. She tilted her head back and sought to inhale *his* breath—as if the man's very life force could keep her grounded.

When she thought about it afterward, Corlis couldn't recall who had made the next move, but their second kiss was electrifying, terrifying, and foreshadowed a potential for intimacy that was shocking in the extreme. She opened her mouth the merest fraction and nearly gasped when she felt his tongue's feathery touch, redolent with the honeyed taste of cane syrup. Like his breath, the tip of his tongue felt hot against hers . . . hot as the flames that had licked sugarcane fields in some other life she had once briefly glimpsed.

Then another heady fragrance piqued her senses: King's aftershave. It was a sophisticated blend of tangy lemon verbena, overlaid with the unmistakably masculine scent of a man who had spent a long, sultry evening in a heavy velvet costume. She was faintly conscious that she had begun to lean into him, so that now their bodies were pressed against each other with nothing separating their torsos except for a few layers of fabric. Their kiss became an exploration, a first, tentative probing around the edges of their secret selves.

She felt bereft when King finally pulled away from her. He hesitated, as if waiting for her signal that she would welcome him further. "My, my . . ." he murmured, "the lady from California certainly likes to be kissed."

"And the gentleman from New Orleans?" she whispered.

"The gentleman from New Orleans," he mumbled, brushing his lips against hers again with galvanizing sweetness, "very much likes . . . kissing the lady from California . . . after midnight . . . on Julia Street." She felt him smile briefly against her lips before he began to nibble seductively along her jawline to her earlobe.

"Midnight on Julia Street . . ." she echoed. "It's so beautiful. I've never been outside *on* Julia Street this late . . . kissing. . . ."

"Glad to hear it . . ." he said with a mock growl, and kissed her some more. Finally he leaned back a second time to gaze at her. "You know, darlin', we are literally takin' our lives in our hands to be standin' in a doorway in the Warehouse District at this late hour . . . *so?*" His questioning glance clearly seemed to say, *It's your decision, my dear Scarlett.*

This pause in their avalanche of kisses provided Corlis with a sane moment in which to come to her senses.

"What time is it really?" she asked, peering at King's wrist-watch. "Two A.M.? Oh, boy. I think we'd better—" she floundered, embarrassed now.

King straightened to his full height. "We'd better . . . what?" he asked, the faintest hint of coolness edging his voice.

"We'd . . . I mean I . . . well, *I* should probably . . ."

"Probably go inside," he finished her sentence. "And I'd better hop that streetcar I hear trundlin' down St. Charles. Got hold of that door key again?"

Corlis grabbed her purse off the sidewalk, plunged her hand into its recesses, and in an instant located the key. She swiftly inserted it into the lock and opened her front door. Then she turned to King and bit her lip.

"We can't, you know . . . ah . . ." she began helplessly. "I mean, you're a news source, and I'm a reporter covering a story that *involves* you. So, I hope you can understand that, even though I . . . responded to . . . ah, I *can't* . . . or rather, I don't think that we should . . ."

King stared intently into her eyes and seemed to come to an unhappy conclusion. "I've been down this road a few times before, sugar pie," he reminded her with a smile, just short of being curt.

"Look, King—"

"Don't worry 'bout tonight," he interrupted, as the streetcar squealed to a halt. "You're a gorgeous woman, Corlis McCullough. Who wouldn't want to kiss you senseless?"

Gorgeous? Wow . . .

"King?" she said softly, trying hard not to put a hand on his arm.

"Look . . . sometimes people get their signals crossed. These things happen. Gotta go." He turned and began to sprint toward the waiting streetcar that was nearly empty of passengers. "The main thing is," he shouted over the shoulder of his velvet cape as he leapt aboard, "we're beginnin' to get the goods on you-know-who. See ya, Ace!"

No! Corlis wanted to shout to the dashing cavalier. *Come back here!*

But she didn't.

By the next morning Corlis awoke determined to put out of her mind what had happened between King and her on Julia Street in the wee hours of the morning, and to forge ahead on the information she'd gleaned from the memos in Grover Jeffries's home office. To do anything else would be personal and professional suicide. As long as she was on this current assignment—if she ignored King's kiss, then *he'd* ignore it. Of that she was certain. It was the written Code of Southern Gentlemen. And besides, the negative repercussions, if they *didn't* put aside personal feelings, could be as profoundly dangerous for him as they were for her. They would both be flirting with disaster, bigtime, if they didn't abide by these rules.

By midmorning she had settled down in her living room to read the Sunday papers, sipping a cup of steaming, chicory-laced coffee. Scanning the arts section of the *Times-Picayune*, an advertisement suddenly caught her attention. It announced a list of performers participating in the celebrated Sunday afternoon jazz concerts at Café LaCroix. She would go. It was time that she got down to business and advanced her story in a new direction.

Just before two o'clock in the afternoon, Corlis walked through the beaded curtain that marked the entrance to Café LaCroix, a small club off Decatur near Governor Nichols Street in the heart of the French Quarter. Even with bright April sunshine pouring down on the street outside, the small, intimate interior was cast into dim shadow. Generations of smoke hung suspended in the air and clung to walls painted black to absorb the fumes.

Corlis spotted Althea LaCroix standing next to a battered upright piano on a small stage at the front of the room. The woman was conferring with a man whose round features resembled her own, as did those of another portly young man standing nearby. The LaCroix Brothers and Sister—all six of them—were part of a renowned musical family in New Orleans.

Althea looked up as she heard Corlis approach, and after an initial pause, grinned with a look of recognition.

"You're Corlis McCullough!" she exclaimed. "Now you're workin' for WJAZ, am I right? You did that *ah-mazin'* story about my friend Daphne's wedding."

"Guilty as charged," Corlis said with a wary laugh. "And you played an ah-mazing number of Bach sonatas while we were waiting all that time in the church."

"You comin' to the session here this afternoon just to see if I can actually play anything else?" she joked.

"I hear you play great jazz, " Corlis said, nodding.

"Well . . . welcome!"

"I'd love to hear all of you play," Corlis amended diplomatically. "I also have an idea about a story for WJAZ, and I'd love to ask you a couple of questions before you get too busy to talk."

"Yeah?" Althea said, sounding intrigued. "Hey, Rufus," she called, "get the lady a cup of coffee, and your sister one, too, okay?" To Corlis she added, "Rufus is next to the youngest, so I boss him around a lot, don't I, baby?"

Rufus nodded with an air of mock resignation and headed for a small room behind the bar to their right. Althea's other brother, Eldon, nodded politely and resumed making notations on a piece of music he'd propped against the piano.

The two women sat down, and Corlis withdrew her reporter's notebook from her shoulder bag. She quickly explained the general background to the controversy concerning the demolition of the buildings on Canal Street in favor of a high-rise hotel.

"Since you're friends with King and Daphne, I expect you already know about some of this," she finished.

"I just know that King is real fierce about protectin' these old buildin's he loves," Althea said with an affectionate laugh. "He saved this one from the wrecker's ball, sure enough."

"He did?" Corlis asked, glancing around the room with renewed interest. She added carefully, "Well, I was just wondering if your family had any associations with the Selwyn buildings . . . way back, say a hundred years ago?" A recollection of a furious Althea Fouché shouting at Julien LaCroix as he stormed down the stairs of Martine's town house flashed before Corlis's eyes.

"You mean those ugly ones with the woven metal front over on Canal Street?" Althea asked, puzzled. "Well . . . our family bought *this* building a few years back, thanks to King's efforts, actually." Just then Rufus appeared with two cups of steaming café au lait. "Hey, you ever hear Daddy talk 'bout anyone in the family ownin' buildin's over on Canal . . . way back when?"

"Naw . . . don't think so," Rufus replied, eyeing Corlis curiously.

"By any chance, are you LaCroixs related to a family named Fouché?"

"As in Dylan Fouché?" Rufus replied.

Corlis nodded, her heart quickening.

Rufus looked at his sister. "Didn't Cousin Keith say we're all connected somehow? I think Dylan's a distant cousin, too— though those Fouchés are big-time Catholics. Not exactly the line of business we LaCroixs are in," he said, grinning widely.

"Keith LaCroix's our *first* cousin, on Daddy's side," Althea explained.

Rufus spoke up. "I get kinda antsy when Keith starts in on all that family relations stuff." Then his eyes narrowed. "What you wanna know all this for, sugar? Not doin' any big exposé, are you?"

"No," Corlis hastened to assure him. "I'm just looking for descendants of the people who built the Selwyn buildings back around 1840. Grover Jeffries wants to tear them down and build a twenty-eight-story high-rise. King Duvallon and the preservationists oppose the plan. I'm trying to track down the history of the buildings so our viewers can decide if they're worth saving or not."

"And you think *black folks* owned those?" Rufus scoffed. "You gotta be crazy! The land's probably worth millions now. It's smack in the middle of downtown! No black people own nothin' on Canal Street *today*! Ain't none of us owned that kind of real estate way back *then*, either. Don't you Yankees realize that we was slaves before the Civil War, sugar pie?" he added caustically.

"I'm not a Yankee. . . . I'm from California," she said stiffly.

"And Free People of Color *did* put up some of the money and land to build them. I've already found records from the late 1830s to prove that." She turned to Althea. "As a matter of fact, a free woman named Martine Fouché might have been the principal owner of the original property. There's a possibility she developed it in a partnership with a white man named Julien LaCroix," she disclosed. "And Martine's mother's name was Althea, which is fairly unusual, right?" Althea nodded, her expression kindling with interest. "That's why I came to talk to you about all this," Corlis explained. "Is there any way you could introduce me to . . . Keith, is it? To see if there's some sort of a blood connection that can be proved between the plantation-owning LaCroixs and the African-American LaCroixs and Fouchés?"

"Maybe," Althea said thoughtfully. "As Rufus told you, Keith's our first cousin, and he's a fiend for all this family history stuff, " she added. "He's a little older than me. He's an architect and has an office in the Warehouse District."

"You're kidding? *I* live in the Warehouse District," Corlis exclaimed.

"Our cousin Keith knows King pretty well, as a matter of fact, 'cause his architecture firm specializes in rehabin' old buildin's, and King specializes in . . . well, he specializes in helpin' people get approved for mortgages."

"So, Keith, King, and Dylan Fouché all know each other and are involved in historic preservation and restoration together?" The interrelationships were beginning to make sense now, Corlis thought, as well as King's offstage role of mortgage angel in the city's Live in a Landmark program.

"Haven't you figured it out yet, Corlis?" Althea laughed. "In New Orleans, families go back forever. Everybody knows *everybody*, and most folks round here are related, one way or another."

"Though lots of folks don't like admittin' it, these days," Rufus added sourly.

"Can I ask you another thing?" Corlis inquired, suddenly feeling uncomfortable. "Do either of you . . . or maybe Keith . . . know for sure if your branch of the LaCroixs were . . . ah . . .

associated with white plantation owners a hundred or so years ago?"

Eldon LaCroix looked up from his music, and the three siblings burst out laughing.

" 'Associated'!" Rufus echoed. "That's a mighty polite way to put it!"

"*Look* at us!" Althea exclaimed, pointing two fingers at her brothers. "Café au laits!" she said, and all three LaCroixs succumbed to another round of laughter. "Used to be the lighter you were, the better you were, 'cause it proved you were kin to fancy white folks. Nowadays, with Black Pride and everything, the LaCroixs aren't black *enough* to suit some people!" Corlis stared at her hosts, unsure what to say next. Althea touched Corlis's hand. "Way, way back, the white LaCroixs owned Reverie plantation, upriver. It's open to the public now . . . like a big ol' museum. If you ever go there, you'll see a bunch of photographs taken round the time of the Civil War that show some of our great-great-granddaddies workin' the cane fields."

"Oh . . . wow . . . that's *great*," Corlis enthused, picturing Virgil getting the shots she'd need for the three-part series she was planning. Then she sobered. "How do you know for certain you're related?"

" 'Bout the time you're talkin' about, and earlier, too, those white LaCroix planter gentlemen had their way with some young, pretty African slaves and—" She pointed to her brothers and herself. "Granddaddy told me that's how we all ended up with the LaCroix name a long time ago. We've got the light skin to prove it—but we're still *black*, right baby?" she nodded to Rufus and Eldon. "The white LaCroixs all died out."

"Could you take me to meet Keith . . . say, later today or tomorrow?" Corlis persisted. "Do you think he'd know what ancestor of yours was the *link* between the white LaCroixs and the black Fouchés?"

"Hey . . . girl, you're real pushy 'bout this stuff, aren't you?" Rufus said.

"I'm on a deadline," Corlis said apologetically. "There's a move to get those buildings torn down really quickly. I'd like to get the facts out about their history before it's too late."

"Are you working for King on this?" Althea asked with a knowing smile.

"I'm an independent journalist," Corlis said tersely. "Some of our interests coincide on these issues . . . and some might be different. I'm just trying to get the facts straight."

"Those Selwyn buildings are real ugly," Rufus commented. "And a new high-rise would sure give lots of needy folks round here some mighty good jobs."

"There are competing ideas about this," Corlis agreed carefully. "The other side says that renovating and restoring the old buildings provide just as many jobs. You can certainly make an argument both ways." Of Althea, she asked, "Would you introduce me to your cousin?"

"Sure," Althea shrugged. "That'll be real easy. He usually shows up here on Sundays."

However, it wasn't until the following Thursday that Corlis and Althea sat down for a formal meeting with architect Keith LaCroix. Engrossed in listening to his cousins' music, he suggested that the two women drop by his office on Girod Street, just a few blocks from Corlis's apartment.

In the full light of day in Keith's architectural office, Corlis was struck by the similarity of the cousins' features. Keith LaCroix was also light-skinned, and like Althea, his facial traits suggested his mixed heritage.

"We've also got some Tchoupitoulas Indian thrown in, too," he said with a laugh, pointing to a Mardi Gras poster on his wall that pictured a swarthy man dancing in the street attired in a bright yellow-feathered headdress and elaborately sequined costume. "That's Bernard LaCroix," he explained. "Swamp Indian on his mother's side, he claims. As they say, New Orleans isn't just a meltin' pot, it's a great big batch of gumbo!"

Corlis explained her mission: to track down some descendants of the original free blacks who'd constructed the block of threatened Greek Revival buildings on Canal Street. "Besides the white partners—Paul Tulane, William Avery, and Jacob Levy Florence—the names that keep popping up on documents relating to the Selwyn buildings are LaCroix and Fouché and . . ."

"Well, sugar . . . you're lookin' at their direct kin," Keith declared, referring to himself and his cousin Althea.

"No way!" Althea exclaimed, staring at Keith and then at Corlis, looking pleased. "Really?"

"Just ask Professor Barry Jefferson at the university. He's got all the family charts to prove it." He elaborated for Corlis's benefit. "He teaches history of the South . . . black history . . . that sort of thing. He wrote a college text on the Free People of Color in New Orleans." He swiveled his office chair, pulled a volume off the shelf, and handed it to Corlis, opened to a page with a bookmark and a genealogy chart. Then he cuffed his cousin Althea gently on the chin. "Don'cha know, girl, that your baby brother, Julien, is named for an octoroon who was the black Creole grandson of a mulatto woman named Althea Fouché?" he explained, pointing to the chart.

"Run that one by me again, will you?" Althea said, shaking her head.

"The original *black* child your youngest brother was named after was Julien LaCroix, the son of a *white* man—Julien LaCroix—an early owner of Reverie plantation."

"Bin-go . . ." Corlis said on a low breath, staring at the family tree.

"Look here how Professor Jefferson traced it back for years and years . . ." he said, running his finger down the page. "The names Julien, Etienne, Martine, and Althea are peppered all through the black Fouchés and LaCroixs, here . . . see?"

"Julien's seventeen," Althea explained for Corlis's benefit. "He plays slide trombone."

Keith LaCroix turned to gaze at Corlis with renewed interest. "And you think Althea Fouché's daughter Martine owned the land the Selwyn buildings are on?"

"There's an old deed and a plot map that says she did indeed take title to the land in 1838. And I'm pretty sure that a white man named Julien LaCroix was involved, too, as a result of having a . . . personal sort of relationship with Martine," she said, slightly breathless. "I also believe some other Free People of Color and white investors were involved in the building project as well. I'm still digging. . . ."

Not to mention having been whisked back as latter-day eye-witness myself!

Corlis yearned to reveal what she'd "seen" of Julien LaCroix and Martine Fouché's unusual partnership in commerce, as well as romance. Instead, she returned her attention to Keith LaCroix's genealogy records.

"Well, Professor Jefferson's chart proves that black Fouchés are definitely related to our branch of the black LaCroixs, as well as to Etienne and Julien LaCroix—the white father and son who owned Reverie plantation in the 1830s."

Althea suddenly squared her shoulders and demanded of Corlis, "And you tell me this Grover Jeffries character wants to demolish these historical buildings—once owned by black folks durin' slavery times?"

"That's what I hear," Corlis said with a sly smile. "Want me to give you two a really interesting tour of the six hundred block of Canal Street?"

WJAZ's cafeteria was deserted, except for Virgil and Manny, who sat slumped in one corner, recovering from four days of grueling work. Corlis poked her head through the door.

"Now, *that's* what I call a great crash," she said cheerfully, the adrenaline still pumping a good five minutes after she'd left the news set. "A three-part series that actually *said* something! How'd you like that shot I used of Dylan Fouché and his eighty-year-old mother standing in front of the Saddlery restaurant?"

"Hey, baby," Virgil groused, "you're gettin' the reputation for bein' the *Queen* of Crash!"

"And didn't you love the sound bite of Mr. Levy saying he had no idea that Jewish families had been in business on Canal Street so far back?"

"I never shot so much stuff so fast in my life, and that's the honest truth!" Virgil declared, shaking his head.

"We musta done interviews with every damn descendant of every damn bricklayer that ever worked on those buildings!" Manny said. "Man, oh, man, Corlis—half this town can claim that *somebody* had *somethin'* to do with that place. They'll probably turn it into a holy shrine, now you've got done with it."

"I don't think Grover Jeffries wants the Selwyn buildings

turned into any shrine," declared a voice from the door to the cafeteria. Corlis whirled in place and came nose to nose with her boss, Andy Zamora. He tapped her on the shoulder and pointed down the hallway. "The very man himself is on the phone in my office, along with Lafayette Marchand—who's a lawyer, as well as a PR guy, in case you didn't know," he warned. "Come along with me, McCullough, and you'd better have gotten every single fact right on *this* one, m'girl."

Corlis grimaced and obediently followed Zamora into his small office. Seated at another extension was Marvin Glimp, the station's attorney who had been called in at the eleventh hour to read her scripts for the three-part series whose final episode aired earlier that evening. A small, neat man in a Brooks Brothers shirt and bow tie, he looked nervous.

"Now, Mr. Jeffries, if what you claim is true," Glimp was saying soothingly into the phone's receiver, "I'm sure Ms. McCullough won't object to making a correction." He paused, listening. "*Certainly,* on the air."

"I'll do *what*?" Corlis whispered hoarsely. "Let him prove *one* thing that's inaccurate in those reports!"

Glimp looked up and pushed the button to activate the speakerphone.

"Why, here she is, right now. I'll let her explain her relationship with Mr. Duvallon herself." Glimp pantomimed putting a gun to his head and pulling the trigger.

"Grover . . . why don't you let me speak to Ms. McCullough first," another voice intervened. "Corlis? Lafayette Marchand, here. How are you tonight?"

"Fine, Mr. Marchand," she said, but her heart was racing. "What can I do for you?"

"You can damn well retract every flippin' lie you put in that report of yours, young lady!" Grover interrupted belligerently.

"Now, hold on, Grover," Marchand cut in. "Let me just try to get a few things sorted out here, will you? Corlis?" he said, his velvety tone of voice alarming her more than Jeffries's bluster. "I was just sayin' that I'm sure you can clear up for us why you and King Duvallon were havin' what looked to outsiders like myself as an . . . intimate dinner à deux at Galatoire's that night when I was dining with Jack Ebert."

Corlis's heart shifted into overdrive. She had been scrupulous with Marv Glimp to show documentation for every single statement she'd made in all three pieces, but even so . . . Marchand had *seen* her with King at Galatoire's being fussed over by his "private waiter" Cezanne, who probably hinted at romance to all his other patrons. And even a whiff of romance meant that Grover Jeffries could make a legitimate claim of bias on her part in favor of King's point of view about the controversial hotel project.

Even though her dinner at Galatoire's had taken place before she and King had kissed so passionately in front of her door, *had* her increasing fondness for the man influenced even one line in her script?

No! Every single thing I said is supported by the facts!

"Corlis?" Marchand said sharply. "Are you there?"

"I'm just listening," she said with as much aplomb as she could muster.

"Well . . . let me ask you this," Marchand continued. "You and King and your television crew were all dressed alike at the Jeffries's costume ball, so I assume you were . . . ah . . . keepin' company with King that night as well. *Do* you have any special relationship with King Duvallon that would interfere with your objectivity on this series that you've been doin'—sayin' such damagin' things as that Mr. Jeffries engages in undue influence through questionable campaign contributions?" His soft, insistent tone of voice was more threatening than any loud legal posturing. "And do you have *proof* to back up your insinuation tonight—despite your prudent use of the word 'allegedly'— that Mr. Jeffries has given anyone money in relation to the Canal Street project currently before the Plannin' Commission? Any proof whatsoever?"

Corlis thought longingly of the printed memo from Lafayette Marchand to Jeffries, along with Grover's explicit handwritten comments that he would be contacting his accountant to dispense campaign contributions to certain members of the city government. She'd bet Aunt Marge's dental bridge that such shenanigans were common practices for Jeffries Industries. But—*proof?* No, she had no concrete proof.

Another thought suddenly struck her. Had Grover or

Lafayette suspected she might have spotted the damning memo in the out box on Jeffries's desk during her interview of his wife and him the night of the ball? Maybe Marchand was merely trying to find out for *sure*, as part of his efforts at damage control? Perhaps this speakerphone duel was just a cat-and-mouse game.

"I stand by every single thing in my story," Corlis said quietly.

Regardless of King Duvallon, she'd done her due diligence on this series and hadn't been in contact with King while she'd established the solid link between the present-day LaCroixs and Fouchés and their forebears.

Yes, in her journalist's judgment she believed that King Duvallon raised legitimate reasons why these buildings should be saved from the wrecker's ball, and she had said nothing in her series about Grover Jeffries and his past actions that wasn't true. If Grover hadn't crossed the palms of certain city council members with silver yet, he certainly intended to, and probably had done so on previous crucial votes. And besides, in this week's TV series, she didn't say he *had* given city politicians money to get them to vote his way on the Canal Street project—just that his *critics* had reason to believe he had. She'd win in a court of law.

Corlis looked at Marvin Glimp and Andy Zamora, who stared back at her with worried expressions. Would they support her? Would they have deep enough pockets should Grover Jeffries decide to file a suit for libel or defamation just to scare off WJAZ?

"You haven't answered his question!" Grover's voice boomed into Zamora's office. "Are you gettin' it on with King Duvallon, Miz McCullough? Just how unbiased can you *be* if you're spreadin' your le—"

The line went dead. Corlis stared, dumbfounded at her employer and his lawyer, who peered back at her, equally nonplussed. Within twenty seconds the phone rang again, startling them all. Andy Zamora picked it up.

"Yeah? We wondered what happened. Okay, Mr. Marchand . . . thank you. . . . I'll do that. We'll be in touch."

"They had some problem with their speakerphone," Andy explained.

"The hell they did!" Corlis said, her heart returning to its normal rhythm. "Marchand cut Jeffries off before *he* could defame *me* in front of three witnesses. Those guys are bluffing, Andy. They won't sue us because they know we've got the goods."

"You haven't shown me any bona fide list of campaign contributors," Glimp hastened to point out. "And before you mention *that* aspect of the story in any follow-up reports, I'd have to see one—in black and white."

"Right," Corlis agreed immediately.

Now, how in the world was she going to get her hands on something like that?

"And another thing," Zamora said, wagging his finger. "The only time I want to hear of or see you in the company of Duvallon is when it's strictly business. You're advancing the story—nothing else. Got that, McCullough?"

"Got it."

"And as far as I'm concerned, having an intimate dinner at Galatoire's with a source and appearing to be . . . close . . . was an error in journalistic judgment. You're on probation."

"Double got it."

"Good. Now go take Virgil and Manny out to dinner. I hear you work those poor guys to death." Zamora began to unroll his shirtsleeves and straighten his tie. "And if you keep the tab under sixty dollars, you can charge it on your expense account. Good job tonight. Now get outta here, will you?"

Chastened, and also relieved to still have her employer's support, Corlis retraced her steps to the lunchroom and announced to her crew she was taking them to Miss Pearl's Saddlery to celebrate. It was cheap enough, and she was curious to see what the former stable and livery supply shop looked like.

"Boy, this is a surprise," Virgil volunteered. "We thought we all were gettin' canned again."

"You guys go on ahead," she directed, ignoring his quip. "I'll meet you at the restaurant in twenty minutes. I have to make one quick call."

An odd fluttering in her chest accompanied her dialing

King's home number. It seemed sensible to tell him, as dispassionately as she could, about her recent conversation with her boss concerning her three-part series on the preservation controversy. The phone rang, unanswered. Eventually King's voice mail picked up.

"Have a decent day," King's voice concluded wryly as always.

That's not so easy these days, Mr. Preservation!

Corlis wondered if members of King's family, or his colleagues working on projects at his home office, ever picked up his messages for him.

"Ah . . . this is a message for King Duvallon," she said self-consciously when she finally heard the signal to record her message. "Corlis McCullough, here. Need to confirm some facts on the story I'm doing about the buildings. Call WJAZ and they'll track me down on my pager. Thanks."

Better to deal with this problem on the phone, she thought resolutely. And besides, she didn't trust herself to be alone with King anymore, especially when she had to tell him there could be no more dinners at Galatoire's—or kisses on Julia Street.

Corlis parked a half block from Miss Pearl's Saddlery, the restaurant situated on the ground floor at the corner of the Selwyn buildings on Canal Street. For a moment she sat silently in her car. Grover Jeffries meant business. He'd bring her down if he could, and he had a lawyer-cum-slick PR consultant on his payroll to help him do it.

It was at times like these that Corlis yearned to be just a nine-to-five assistant to a local dentist, or a travel agent with a nice house, two kids, and a husband to come home to. Once again she felt a familiar loneliness settle over her. She began to tap her fingernails on her steering wheel, mulling over what Andy Zamora and his lawyer had said. Maybe there was no need to make a dramatic announcement to King that they'd have to keep their distance, she thought ruefully. After all, he hadn't called her following any of the three broadcasts this week, had he? There'd been no bouquet of flowers or box of chocolates to mark the final program tonight, had there? And she'd certainly been too busy editing those miles of videotape all week to call *him.*

Cool your jets, Ace. . . . You've been reading too much into everything, as usual.

Their kisses outside her house on Julia Street probably didn't mean that much to him, she considered with regret. Better just to leave it at that.

Virgil and Manny were waiting for her at the restaurant entrance.

"Sorry, sugar. No go tonight," Virgil announced. "We just got paged by the assignment desk. Bailey got wind 'bout ten minutes ago that some country-western star I never heard of is arrivin' at the airport in a half hour, and we've gotta go grab a shot of him gettin' off the plane. Nothin' fancy, but we gotta do it."

"How 'bout a rain check, boss?" Manny suggested hopefully, " 'specially since Zamora's pickin' up the tab. We gotta encourage this free stuff at WJAZ!"

"Catch you later . . . like maybe next week." Corlis heaved a sigh and shook her head with resignation. She hadn't eaten anything decent in more than eight hours. Even though she didn't feel much like celebrating the broadcast of their miniseries alone, she waved her crew good-bye and walked inside Miss Pearl's Saddlery.

It wasn't difficult for her to imagine the place as it must have looked in the early 1800s when it was actually a livery stable and shop where all manner of horse paraphernalia had been sold. A waiter dressed in a leather blacksmith's apron led her to a wooden booth that resembled a horse stall. He handed her a menu decorated with sketches of bridles and other equine equipment. Corlis glanced over it with little interest, wondering absently how long it might take a person her age to train as a dental assistant. Her morose speculations were interrupted by the depressingly cheerful waiter who returned to take her order for a bowl of shrimp étouffée.

Settling back into the booth, she considered her surroundings. The entire restaurant retained the aura of the livery stable the place had been more than a hundred years ago. As part of the decor, antique saddles were suspended on invisible fish line from the ceilings, along with leather harnesses and oxen yokes that had been nailed on the wall space above each of the wooden booths.

Idly Córlis reached up and seized a leather rein from one of the bridles, sliding her thumb over the smooth, saddle-soaped patina. The aroma of leather polish and cowhide grew even stronger as she pulled the slender strap toward her. An earthy odor of horse sweat floated up from the rough side of the leather.

Gradually the sounds of clinking glasses and boisterous laughter from the adjacent bar faded, and in their place, the steady clip-clop of horses' hooves falling on brick flooring assaulted her ears. The other diners in the room seemed to vanish slowly, as if into the mists of *Brigadoon*, and she inexplicably found herself outside, on Common Street, around the corner from Canal, surveying the entrance to the very same structure that had mysteriously altered in the blink of an eyelash.

For indeed, according to a freshly painted sign overhead, Miss Pearl's Saddlery, "Home of Fine Louisiana Cuisine," had unaccountably transformed itself into Bates's Saddlery—an establishment, so said the sign, that sold all manner of "Horse Tack, Animal Feed, and Wagons by the Day." The livery stable also boarded horses and provided "Carriages to Gentlemen of Means" who didn't maintain their own stables in the city.

And standing in the doorway was a flush-faced Corlis Bell McCullough, who appeared mad as a water moccasin, and twice as ready to bite someone!

Chapter Eighteen

May 21, 1842

"They're common *thieves*, those two!" Corlis Bell McCullough muttered, catching sight of her husband inside the livery stable's gloomy interior. In addition to the insufferable heat, the heavy atmosphere smelled pungently of animal feed, leather saddles, horse tack, and manure.

Randall was standing halfway up a ladder, supervising several Negro laborers who balanced precariously on scaffolding twenty-five feet above the newly installed brick flooring. The workers were plastering the last area of ceiling space inside the row of buildings that had been bankrolled by Julien LaCroix, André Duvallon, and a consortium of free black tailors and white merchants on land owned by Martine Fouché. Meanwhile David Bates, the new lessee of the saddlery, was proudly leading draft animals into spacious wooden stalls whose floors were lightly dusted with straw.

Corlis wrinkled her nose at the mixture of odors that assaulted her nostrils. Angrily she surveyed the stable's interior, hoping to confront that scoundrel Ian Jeffries at the same time she gave Randall McCullough a piece of her mind.

She swore by all that was holy that she would *not* be the wife of an out-and-out swindler whose partner was a trickster of the same stripe!

"Why, Mrs. McCullough, what can I do for you?" inquired Mr. Bates genially. "Come to see your husband put the finishing touches on the place, eh?"

Corlis cast her eye heavenward. Randall appeared absorbed

in a lengthy discussion with the men on the scaffold and seemed unlikely to break free any time soon. Well, there was no point in creating a public scene, she thought grimly, though the Lord knew that might be the only way to shame Randall into undoing his latest bit of chicanery.

"I'd be most obliged if you'd tell him I was here and that I have something *important* to discuss with him, Mr. Bates."

Bates glanced curiously at her flushed face but merely nodded. "I surely will, ma'am."

"Would you be so good as to ask him to return to home immediately."

"Yes ma'am," Bates said respectfully.

Corlis stalked past the stable owner and onto Common Street, heading in the direction of Julia Street, seething with fury.

Randall McCullough had promised his wife that he would retrieve her sapphire necklace and earrings from the pawnbroker on Girod Street just as soon as he received the last payment for his services from the building consortium. What a shock it had been—not ten minutes earlier—to be standing a few doors away, in Chez Annette's, having a hem measured for the first new dress she'd purchased in more than a year, and to see a perfect stranger waltz into the dress shop wearing the very jewelry her husband had promised *on a Bible* he would soon return to her!

The question was, had he lied to her and sold the jewelry, out and out, to finance Jeffries & McCullough while the project was still being constructed? Or had he gifted some fancy woman whose charms he had purchased at the brothel that he and Ian were known to frequent on Girod Street?

Either way, she was in a murderous rage. As she advanced along the *banquette*, she nursed her anger by recounting the many instances in which her husband and his partner had behaved like cads.

But if the gossips were correct, they were no better than the almighty Julien LaCroix, whose recent peccadilloes were the talk of the town. Annette Fouché had let it be known that the young heir to Reverie plantation was living openly, when in town, with her first cousin, the celebrated quadroon Martine Fouché, and that Julien considered Martine a full partner in the

Canal Street enterprise. The scandalous pair had moved into elegant new quarters above Annette's dress shop and adjacent to the commercial enterprise run by two tailors, also Free People of Color, in the same block as Bates's Saddlery. Annette even announced, proud as you please, that Martine was expecting a child.

Poor Adelaide LaCroix, Julien's wife, Corlis sympathized, eyeing the new signage attached to the warehouse's brick facade. The paint that was barely dry announced the location of the newly constructed warehouse of Lacroix & Company, Exporters of Cotton & Sugarcane.

Corlis paused by an open wooden door leading into the warehouse itself, where hogsheads of sweetly scented sugarcane were piled nearly to the ceiling. Angry voices could be heard inside.

"Jeffries, you are the worst sort of blackguard!" said a very familiar voice. "I was warned to steer clear of you, and I only wish I'd heeded those who attested to your treachery."

"Such plather is neither here nor there, André," Ian Jeffries said mildly. "The point is, you don't really have much choice, do you? Either you pledge me the credit for my next project, here and now, or I let Julien and your fancy friends know the truth about your . . . peculiar friendship with the late, lamented Henri Girard, and the pains you, Girard, and Etienne LaCroix took to cover it all up!"

"And if I reveal to Julien how you hounded poor Henri to take his own life in a base attempt to get your *own* hands on this land?" André Duvallon retorted.

Corlis stood in the shadows just outside the office. Despite André's challenging words, she detected a slight tremulousness in his voice.

"Henri is dead and buried," Ian Jeffries said bluntly. "Even the priest saw nothing amiss at his funeral. Who'd believe you weren't just trying to cover up your own unnatural, disgusting behavior . . . loving *men*! Not a person in the entire French Quarter would want you as their banker if they knew that you and Henri Girard were damnable *sodomites*! And what would they say if they knew that the pillar of Creole society, Etienne LaCroix, covered your abomination by allowing Henri to pose as Martine Fouché's patron while he himself had been enjoying her charms for years?"

"How *dare* you sully Henri's memory and denigrate the feelings we had for each other," André shouted. "And how dare you attempt this extortion!"

"Call it what you will," Ian retorted. "Julien is due back here at any minute. I suggest you write me a bank draft for five thousand dollars before he arrives, as I have requested. I'll call for it later this afternoon."

"I have had enough of your threats!" André exploded. "I will not do it. Furthermore, I demand satisfaction."

"A duel?" Ian Jeffries taunted his prey. "How French." His voice grew cold and even more menacing. "I have no patience with such nonsense. Either you put in writing a guarantee of five thousand dollars, on account in your bank made out to Ian Jeffries, Builder, or I shall tell Julien that his trusted financier was the go-between for his adored black whore—who had long lain with LaCroix's own *father*—and neither of you ever confessed to it."

"Why, you—" André began.

Ian chuckled. "Let's see . . ." he mused. "Unbeknownst to Julien, his lover Martine's child, Lisette, is his own half *sister*. Therefore, Lisette could *also* be the aunt to Julien's new bastard . . . only Julien doesn't know it! Have I got it right? Family relationships among you French and Negroes can be *so* complicated."

Corlis heard herself gasp at the revelation of such incestuous behavior. André, too, appeared blindsided by the viciousness of Ian Jeffries's attack.

"Surely, man, you will not be thanked for acting the town crier of such intelligence . . ." André said, sounding shaken.

"Ah . . . the scandal of it all should keep you Creoles chattering across your courtyards in the *carré de la ville* for months!" Ian retorted with a harsh laugh.

"Jeffries, have you no decency at *all*?" André exclaimed in a voice tinged with despair. "You already tried this vicious blackmail, before Julien returned from his honeymoon," he added accusingly. "Did you think Etienne, Henri, and I would simply accede to your demands? Your foul behavior is precisely why you Yankees are so hated here. To you, money is God."

"It is merely business," Jeffries said, sounding mildly offended.

"Well, whether you acknowledge it or not," André said with a renewed show of emotion, "you and Randall McCullough have blood on your hands! Henri's blood."

A deadly silence fell between the two men. As for Corlis, the memory of a horrifying sight swam before her eyes. Ugly black-and-blue bruises had encircled poor Henri Girard's neck when she had applied the powder puff to his taut skin, already stiffening with rigor mortis. Randall had convinced her that Henri had killed himself because he knew he would die of an excruciatingly painful liver disease.

"Unless you use your skills with powder and cosmetics, Corlis," Randall had insisted, "the wretched man will be refused a proper Christian burial in sacred ground by those damnable Catholics."

Now she knew the truth. Her husband and his partner had obviously been threatening to expose the homosexual relationship between Henri and André as a means of gaining that choice parcel of land. The partners had also threatened to reveal to one and all that the patriarch of Reverie plantation, Etienne LaCroix, had enjoyed a long, secret liaison with the enigmatic Martine Fouché—and had a daughter by her. It now appeared that Henri Girard had committed suicide by hanging from a beam in the old warehouse to avoid such public disclosure. However, before he took his own life, he had most likely persuaded his partner, Etienne, to join him in signing over land on Canal Street that would provide for the future of Martine and Etienne's secret child, Lisette—thereby *also* thwarting an attempted extortion of the parcel by the aggressive newcomers to New Orleans.

Corlis leaned heavily against the warehouse wall and thought back to the oddly insistent behavior of her husband and his partner after Henri's death. Ian and Randall obviously didn't dare reveal the role they had played in hounding the poor man until suicide seemed his only alternative. Therefore, the two conspirators had concocted, for Corlis's benefit, *another* reason Henri had committed suicide while she—fool that she was—entertained girlish, romantic notions about the dashing André Duvallon!

It was all too much. Corlis blushed at having fantasized that André felt anything stronger for her than polite friendship. His attentions, she wagered, were merely calculated to discover what dastardly trick Randall McCullough and Ian Jeffries were likely to play next!

Martine . . . Adelaide . . . even Corlis herself—the women in this passion play—had merely served as pawns for the grander pageant of men's lust and driving ambition. And all for this land on Canal Street.

She fought a growing sense of panic. With trembling fingers, she raised her hand to massage her forehead.

Nothing in this blighted city was what it had seemed. She had been lied to and manipulated by her husband, just as surely as had poor André Duvallon. And despite the shattering of the fragile dream that André might have harbored some genuine affection toward her, she pitied him and the stark, sad countenance of Henri Girard, cold in his coffin on the Rue Royale. Etienne LaCroix must have been so angry and shaken by what André had surely revealed to him that it brought on the fit of apoplexy. Unfortunately for the LaCroixs, the patriarch's malady had silenced any chance Etienne might have had to bring his enormous power to bear against such American upstarts as her husband and his unscrupulous partner.

Corlis thought again of her lost necklace. The man she had married eight years before was as unscrupulous as Ian Jeffries, but he was *also* a coward. Randall McCullough could be handled, if *only* she played her cards correctly.

Just then André appeared at the office door. Before Corlis could slip outside, he caught sight of her huddled against the wall. Even in the warehouse's dim light, she could see the color drain from his face.

"You!" he growled accusingly. "Be gone, damn you!" he hissed, and stormed past her and into Common Street.

Corlis dashed outside into the sweltering sunlight, lifting her skirts above her ankle boots in an effort to speed to André's side.

"No! Wait! Please, wait!" she cried. She made a grab for his arm, but he shook free of her and stalked on. "André, you *must* believe me! I knew none of this. . . . I—"

André's carriage was waiting outside Bates's Saddlery. Corlis ran to the vehicle's opposite side as he hopped aboard and yanked furiously on the reins. Somehow she managed to climb up onto the seat beside him, just as the vehicle careened around the corner and headed for the Lower Garden District, where Corlis knew André, his sister, and her husband lived in a graceful pillared house on Orange Street.

Surprisingly, André neither slowed the horses nor attempted to eject Corlis from the speeding carriage. Instead, he continued to snap his reins smartly against his horse's rump as the light, two-wheeled carriage sped forward. Corlis found herself grasping his arm and staring up into his frozen countenance.

"Please . . . *please*, André," she begged. "There *must* be a way to put an end to this treachery. I'll do anything I can to help you stop Ian and Randall. They've stolen from me as well! We shall go to the authorities! Perhaps your fellow bankers would—Slow *down*! You'll kill us both!"

However, André Duvallon barely heard the frantic woman at his side. What did it matter if he lived or died, or if his bank failed? he thought with a crushing sense of futility. His life had ceased the night he had discovered Henri dangling from a rope. The ghastly sight told the hideous tale: Henri Girard had leapt off an office chair to escape the cruelty of those grasping, avaricious American devils! He had gone for help, only to return and find Henri's body cut down and taken to the Rue Royale.

And now André finally understood why the dearest man in all the world had abandoned him to this living hell.

At Miss Pearl's Saddlery, a jazz quintet blared from the small cabaret that adjoined the restaurant. As the band swung into a raucous number, Corlis sat bolt upright in her booth and gazed at the leather rein she was still holding. Her heart pounding, she winced at the sound of laughter and applause that had roused her from—*what*?

"Hey there, Corlis!" a voice inquired sharply. "What's goin' on? Are you asleep or somethin'? Where are Virgil and Manny? I thought WJAZ was treatin' y'all to dinner?"

"King!" she said, barely above a whisper. "What are *you* doing here?" She blinked several times, attempting to clear the cobwebs from her brain, and gazed at him across the wooden booth.

"I picked up the message that you'd called," he said, looking at her speculatively. "I called you back at the station and they said you, Manny, and Virgil had come here to celebrate the broadcast tonight." He glanced around the restaurant. "Where are the guys?"

"We were *supposed* to be celebrating, courtesy of Andy Zamora," she replied with a shaky laugh. "Before we could even sit down, our assignment editor dispatched them to the airport on some cockamamy story that didn't need a reporter. I was . . . ah . . . just sitting here, waiting for my dinner."

"You looked like you were hypnotized by that horse rein," he said. "It took me a while to get your attention," he said with a worried frown. "You sure you weren't in outer space again?"

"What're you doing here?" she asked, ignoring his question.

"Thought I'd come tell you in person how good I thought your series was," King said, regarding her closely. "I watched all three nights."

"Oh . . . thanks," she replied weakly.

While King hailed the waiter to place an order of his own, Corlis stared overhead at the bridle and its dangling reins in an attempt to regain her bearings. Why in blazes had this very space been transformed into a genuine livery stable and then suddenly transformed back again? She reached for her glass of iced tea and took a deep draught.

It had happened *again* . . . only this time she was frightened down to the toes of her sling-back pumps! What was poor André Duvallon going to do? she wondered distractedly, peering across the table at King. And furthermore, was this man who had just taken a seat across from her truly a direct descendant? How was that possible?

Whoa, there, Corlis! Better disregard whatever happened when you had a whiff of that bridle rein. Concentrate on the present—pronto!

She was acutely aware that she was sitting, à deux, on a Friday night, in one of the most popular watering spots in New Orleans, with the very man Grover Jeffries and Lafayette Marchand claimed was exerting undue influence on her journalistic judgment. She glanced nervously around the restaurant. This was precisely the kind of situation that could cause major trouble for them both, yet somehow all she could think of was how relieved she was to see King again.

"King . . . you and I haven't spoken in a few days, but—"

"I know," he interrupted. "I've been upriver since Tuesday." He gazed forthrightly into her eyes and added somberly, "A dear family friend passed away suddenly, and I've been tryin' to help her son get her affairs in order before the funeral tomorrow."

So *that* was why there had been such a long silence, Corlis thought, feeling ridiculously giddy. She gazed at his sorrowful features and felt instantly ashamed.

"Oh, King . . . I'm *so* sorry," she replied softly. "Was it someone you were close to?"

King's expression softened. "Do you remember the day I walked you through the Good Times Shoppin' Plaza and I told you about our cook, Emelie?"

Corlis nodded, recalling how King had paused in the midst of their tour and angrily smashed the side of his fist against the concrete wall.

"Oh, no . . . *not* the woman you called your black mother?" she cried. She impulsively seized his hand and encased it with both of hers. "Oh, King . . . how really sad. Had she been ill?"

"I don't think that Emelie ever adjusted to bein' displaced from that ol' Creole cottage on Tchoupitoulas Street," King said slowly. "Last year her memory began to fail, and then she simply lost the will to go on. Her son said that she'd just sit on his porch in an ol' rockin' chair . . . tears streamin' down her face most of the time."

King's voice suddenly cracked, and Corlis felt her own throat close. From everything she had surmised about the lack of closeness between King and his parents, Emelie's death was obviously a bitter loss to him.

"Will your family attend the funeral?" she asked, unsure for what else to say.

"My aunt Bethany would, but she's down with a bad spring cold, and my grandmother Kingsbury . . . well, she's as fragile as Emelie was. . . ." He glanced at their joined hands and gave hers a soft squeeze. Then his blue eyes caught hers. "Would you consider comin' to the funeral with me, sugar?" he asked softly. "We can drive across the lake to Covington and stay tonight at an ol' cabin on some land my family still owns. It's only about ten miles from there to the Dumas place. I guarantee . . . it'll be real Louisiana. . . ."

For an instant she heard the smooth, intimidating voice of Lafayette Marchand in her ears. She pushed the thought from her mind and continued to hold King's hand between her own. Then she reached up and grazed the fingers of her right hand along King's jawline.

"Sure, sugar . . ." she said in a lightly teasing tone of voice that belied her emotion. "I'd be honored to be among Emelie's mourners."

King waited in the blue Jaguar on Julia Street while Corlis ran up the stairs to her apartment. She filled Cagney Cat's water dish to its brim, poured a pile of dry kibble into his dish, and did her best to ignore his reproachful stare as she swiftly packed a small overnight bag.

The drive along the twenty-four-mile concrete causeway that stretched across a dark and silent Lake Pontchartrain passed swiftly while King recounted numerous tales about Emelie's role in the Duvallon household. Corlis listened attentively. Yet, a small voice in the back of her mind continued to fret about the nature of Grover Jeffries's threats and her boss's recent edict not to fraternize with King unless the interchange was strictly business—an injunction that she was obviously ignoring.

And then there was the dilemma she and King faced concerning the state of *their* relationship, though what *that* actually was she could not explain, even to herself. There could be no doubt that the Hero of New Orleans felt *something* toward her. As for Corlis, she'd known for some time now that she was . . . well . . . *crazy* about the man sitting to her left in the driver's seat.

Aunt Marge would have a cow if she knew I was zipping along in King's Jag, heading for his cabin in the bayou!

"He's a source, with a capital *S*!" Corlis could just hear the veteran journalist scold. "There are no exceptions to this rule while the business with Grover Jeffries and the fate of the Selwyn buildings remains unresolved."

It's a conflict of interest, Ms. McCullough . . . and it could get you fired!

Oh, for Pete's sake! she complained silently as she peered through the dark at the exotic moonlit landscape whizzing by. As far as her TV minidoc was concerned, she'd reported the facts of the controversy as she saw them and wouldn't change a word of what she'd broadcast, *regardless* of her feelings for Kingsbury Duvallon! And if she was lucky, no one would even know that she'd attended the last rites of King's family retainer in this remote, moss-draped Louisiana outback. Emelie's funeral had virtually nothing to do with the Selwyn controversy, and surely Andy Zamora, King's buddy, would understand if she offered a dear friend her moral support in the wake of Emelie's sudden death. Besides—

"You okay, sugar?" King asked, reaching across the luxurious leather seat to touch Corlis's left arm.

"W-Wha—?" she stammered, turning to study his handsome profile as he drove in the semidarkness.

"You've been so quiet. I'm sorry to have gone on so about Emelie. It's just—"

"Oh no, King!" she hastened to assure him. "I love hearing all your stories about what it was like growing up as you did . . . and about what Emelie meant to you. I'm only sorry I never met her. She sounds like an absolute dear."

"Emelie Dumas was certainly that," he agreed soberly, pointing to a roadside sign that announced they'd reached their destination.

The community of Covington, on the other side of the lake, was silent, too, when King's car made a right turn down a narrow tarmac road. Corlis gazed in awe at the large houses set back from the road. Many of these residences, King explained, were constructed in a spacious style, commonly seen in the West Indies, that featured white pillars, wide verandas, and tall windows, shuttered for the night.

"Somehow," Corlis commented, "I never expected to see so many pine trees."

"They provide an odd counterpoint to the tropical feel of the place, don't you think?"

"If it weren't so muggy," she agreed, peering to her right, "I'd think I was in the High Sierras!"

King wheeled his sleek blue car off the paved road and down a smooth dirt track for several yards.

"The main house on our last property upriver burned to the ground durin' World War Two," he related as they drove past two hulking brick chimneys whose outlines stood starkly against the night sky. "Unfortunately, the Kingsburys were completely out of cash when that happened, and the place was never rebuilt. I use the old slave cabins when I come out to Bayou Lacombe to go fishin'."

"How many acres have you still got?" Corlis asked, fascinated and slightly spooked by the sight of the ghostly remains of the Kingsbury family's lost glory.

"Oh . . . only about twenty-two acres now," he said, shrugging as he pulled the car in front of one of two small log cabins set fifty yards from a swampy pond. "My folks inherited fifteen acres and what's left of the main house. Daphne and I got the rest and an old slave cabin each. Used to be about four hundred acres in all. My grandparents sold almost everything in the fifties to a developer who then sold big chunks to rich white folks wantin' to flee New Orleans's crime and poverty. You know the old story," he continued. "The developer made a fortune, and the Kingsburys paid their inheritance taxes."

"Very *Gone with the Wind.*"

"Very," King agreed with a grim smile.

Through the windshield Corlis gazed at the two wooden structures that both featured slanting shingle roofs flanked by tall pine trees.

"You know, this place could be smack in the heart of Yosemite National Park!" she said.

"Maybe those trees and the cabins could," King said with a smile as he turned off the ignition, "but have a look at Bayou Lacombe."

"It's awfully dark out here," she said doubtfully, peering through the gloom. "I get a sense that there's water nearby. . . ."

"There's a *lot* of water round here, sugar pie," he repeated. "Stick with me."

Corlis shut the car door and heard rustling in the tall grass nearby. "There aren't any *alligators* around here, are there?" she asked in a hushed voice.

"Oh . . . just a few," King replied in an offhand manner, "but don't worry . . . they're busy chasin' the water moccasins."

"Snakes!" she shuddered. "You're joking, right?" she asked, ignoring his proffered hand and instead swiftly making for the elevated wooden porch. She was thankful that King immediately appeared by her side to turn the front doorknob, allowing a speedy entrance into the one-bedroom abode.

Once inside, Corlis gazed around the cozy cabin's updated interior. Two sturdy dark-brown leather club chairs faced a stone fireplace nearly large enough for a man to stand in. Glass-and-brass hurricane oil lamps stood on the rustic wooden coffee table, as well as on the surface of a round calico-skirted table surrounded by four straight-backed chairs.

"Wow . . ." she breathed appreciatively. "This place looks like Ralph Lauren slept here!"

"Is that good, or is that bad?" King asked with mock solemnity.

"In my book, it's very good and *very* tasteful. Who did your decorating?"

"Yours truly."

"Double wow."

Surveying the well-appointed cabin, Corlis felt another pang of conscience about having accepted King's invitation to spend the night at Bayou Lacombe so they'd be on time for the funeral early the next morning. From the quilt-covered double bedstead in the next room, to the bottle of wine King pulled from a canvas satchel he'd retrieved from his car, the situation right *now* smacked neither of business—nor of a mission of mercy for a friend in need.

"Dibs on the sofa!" she said, laughing nervously as she tossed her overnight bag onto a forest-green couch sporting lavishly plump down pillows and a burgundy-colored lap robe made of plush bouclé. At least she could make it plain that their sleeping arrangements would be separate. "I'm a foot shorter than you, so you deserve to sleep in the bed." King gazed at her from across the room. He smiled but didn't respond. "After the week we've both had," she added lamely, "I'm bushed, aren't you?"

King nodded as he slowly walked across the cabin in her direction. "Actually . . . so I am."

And with that he leaned down and kissed her lightly on her forehead. Then he put a hand in the middle of her lower back and propelled her into the bedroom.

"However . . . the lady gets the bed."

"But, King—"

He walked into the adjacent bathroom, closed the door, and began brushing his teeth. He reappeared shortly and said, "Just give a holler if any alligators come knockin' at your window, okay, Ace?" Then he quietly shut the door behind him, leaving her safely to her own devices.

Corlis couldn't help but burst out laughing. "I'll holler, all right! Thanks." Then she remembered that she had told him nothing about the menacing phone call to WJAZ made earlier that evening by Grover Jeffries and Lafayette Marchand. She started for the door but thought better of it. Best to leave things just as they were. She'd fill him in on all that unpleasantness on their way to the funeral, she thought, reaching for her toothbrush tucked inside her cosmetics kit.

And after tomorrow, she resolved, *just as Zamora decrees— there can be no more private contact between King and me until the fate of the Selwyn buildings is decided.*

Chapter Nineteen

April 18

"Coffee?" inquired a deep voice.

Corlis raised her head from beneath her pillow and peered up at King with sleep-dazed eyes.

"Huh?" she asked, rolling onto her back. She carefully tucked the bedsheet and quilt under her arms for modesty's sake. Then she propped herself against the wooden headboard. "How was the couch?" she asked sheepishly.

"Fine. Careful, sugar . . ." he cautioned with an amused smile, "it's scaldin' hot."

"How long have you been up?" she asked, brushing her hair from her face before accepting his proffered mug of very black coffee. King was dressed in navy-blue suit pants and white dress shirt but had not yet donned his tie and jacket. His dark-brown hair was wet and slicked back, giving him the appearance of a hip, freshly laundered model right out of *GQ*.

"A while . . ." he replied. "This should give you a kick-start—pure caffeine, no sugar, no milk. We're due at the church in half an hour."

She glanced at a handsome brass alarm clock on the bedside table.

"I *never* sleep this late!" she protested. She glanced out the window doubtfully, catching sight only of pine boughs pierced with golden shafts of light. "Especially when there're alligators and water moccasins lurking about."

"They're havin' their morning snooze at the bottom of the swamp," he teased. Then he reminded her gently, "Look, you worked hard last week. Don't you ever take time off to cool your jets, Ace?"

"Hmmmm," was all Corlis murmured as she took a sip of the deliciously robust coffee. Alligators or not—she knew why she had slept in peaceful bliss: It had been comforting merely to know that King was in the next room.

Easy, now, McCullough! Just picture lawyer Glimp and get a move on!

Within twenty minutes she had showered, dressed, and headed out the door. During the short drive to the church, there seemed no right moment on this sun-splashed Saturday to bring up the stern edict laid down by her boss. And before she knew it, King was easing the Jaguar to a halt between a rusted pickup truck and a dented sedan. In the center of the field stood a white clapboard church sorely in need of a fresh coat of paint. A long hearse was parked at the foot of the wooden stairs, poised to transport the casket to a cemetery. From inside the small church, Corlis could hear sonorous organ music.

At the top of the stairs, King cradled her elbow and guided her inside the cool confines of the building. An enormous black man in his late forties, neatly attired in a dark suit, white shirt, and tie, waved in greeting. Nodding in their direction, he excused himself from a cluster of mourners and strode to their side.

"Did my brother James tell you you'll be number three pall bearer, walkin' between him and me?" the man inquired.

King nodded and swiftly introduced Corlis to Emelie's second son, Tyrone. She was acutely aware that she and King were the only white people in the entire church. "We have seats saved for you, up front," Tyrone explained with a friendly smile. "King, you sit on the aisle, so's you can get out again when we take Mama to the cemetery after the service, all right?"

"Sure thing, Tyrone," King assured him.

A stocky, gray-haired figure in his late sixties suddenly materialized by their side.

"Well . . . well . . . King Duvallon," the man said with an unpleasant edge of irony. "Observin' how we black folks bury our dead?"

"My condolences about Emelie," King replied, as if the man had greeted him cordially.

"Tyrone says she was doin' mighty poorly for a long while . . . so I guess you could call it a blessin', " he said with a slight shrug of his padded shoulders. "Won't you introduce me to your friend?" he added, casting a cool, appraising glance at Corlis.

"Meet Corlis McCullough," King said, tight-lipped now. "Corlis, this is the Honorable Mr. Edgar Dumas, Emelie's brother-in-law, and the next president of the New Orleans City Council."

Corlis was perfectly aware of the identity of Edgar Dumas and wished only that she could disappear through a trapdoor in the cypress-planked floor. According to WJAZ's assignment editor, last election Dumas was rumored to have received handsome campaign contributions from the checkbook of none other than Grover Jeffries. Would she *never* learn a crucial truth about this city?

In New Orleans everyone's related, stupid!

For a brief moment Edgar Dumas's eyes widened with recognition, then narrowed as he scrutinized King's companion. "Why, what an *unexpected* pleasure," he said softly, "to meet such a pretty lady in person. I thought your three-part TV series on the Selwyn buildings this week just fascinatin', Miz McCullough."

"Thank you," Corlis murmured. Why hadn't King warned her Edgar Dumas might be here? she demanded silently. Perhaps he had been too upset yesterday by the news of Emelie's sudden demise to think clearly—just as she hadn't been thinking too clearly herself! Automatically she extended her right hand to the councilman, and reluctantly he shook it. "Good to see you, *in person,* Councilman," she countered with deliberate emphasis, "though I'm sorry it's under such sad circumstances."

"Sure looks like you had some mighty good sources on that documentary," Dumas declared with a glance at King.

"Well . . ." she replied slowly while her mind spun in several directions at once, "I just hope the television pieces shed some new light on the subject."

"Oh . . . they did, indeed," Dumas replied. "It was certainly interestin' to be enlightened about what's 'sposed to be black folks' history—by a white woman," he said coolly, "and a Yankee to boot." Dumas was smiling like a water moccasin, coiled and ready to strike.

"I'm a westerner, Mr. Dumas," she corrected him more sharply than she intended, "with ancestors who lived in New Orleans once upon a time. I hope you can agree that the LaCroixs and the Fouchés on my TV series told the viewers their *own* story."

"Folks have always claimed their granddaddies were somethin' more than they probably were," he replied peevishly.

Corlis met Edgar Dumas's gaze unwaveringly. "As a matter of fact," she countered evenly, "your sister-in-law, Emelie, is also part of the tale I'm trying to unravel. I'm interested in looking into the ways in which the lives of ordinary people like her are profoundly affected by political and economic decisions to demolish historic buildings." She deliberately arched an eyebrow. "I understand that Mrs. Dumas was unwillingly displaced from her home when you voted with the majority on the city council to tear down her block to make way for the bankrupt Good Times Shopping Plaza."

"She was recompensed and signed a waiver. Everything was perfectly legal," Dumas snapped, "so, I suggest you get your facts straight, Miz McCullough!"

"She was a seventy-eight-year-old woman, Mr. Dumas. My sources tell me she was pressured and coerced to sign," she stated flatly, "and losing that little Creole cottage she'd lived in all her life literally broke her heart."

"She made a perfectly fine home with her son," Dumas retorted with some heat.

Corlis smiled sweetly into the snake's eyes, daring him to strike again. "All the same, it must have been a stressful change for her at her advanced age—since she wanted to hold on to her house . . . wanted to *die* in it, I'm told she said. Isn't it true that she suffered from acute heart congestion?"

Dumas's bullying, belligerent attitude turned into one of mild alarm. After all, the man knew the dangers of bad publicity. He glared at King and countered swiftly, "Now, Miz McCullough, surely you don't accuse me of causin' the death of my own sister-in-law."

"I'm not accusing anyone of anything," Corlis replied dispassionately. "I'm merely attending Mrs. Dumas's funeral as a means of trying to see all sides to this complicated story."

Wheels within wheels . . .

"Is that so?" Dumas replied skeptically.

"Absolutely," Corlis said as another idea for a television piece began to take root in her mind. "I'm interested in exploring how a city balances its need for progress—and the necessity of having a firm economic base and high employment—with its desire to preserve the unique history of a venerable old city like New Orleans." Edgar Dumas pursed his lips and nodded half-hearted agreement. "I've been fascinated to learn how the city's history involves families—black *and* white—with all their entanglements going back generations. And then, of course, there are the hundreds of beautiful old buildings, along with musical and culinary culture, that attract millions of *crucial* tourist dollars into this city, am I right?"

"I've always supported the tourist industry," Dumas asserted, flustered. "I was one of the first to support those gamblin' boats to tie up—"

"Well, then," Corlis hastened to add, "don't you agree that historic properties like Emelie's little house, as well as the Selwyn buildings that Grover Jeffries wants to tear down—not to mention those darling paddle-wheel steamers *you've* championed that the tourists love so much—comprise the many-sided issues that WJAZ wants to lay before the public? That's certainly a big part of why *I'm* here today," she finished, a little breathless.

And in a very real way it was, Corlis thought, relieved, at least, to be able publicly and privately to justify her presence.

"I see . . ." Dumas said, although Corlis knew he still wasn't completely convinced.

"Perhaps you'd let me come interview you one day soon as to *your* thoughts on this issue of balancing the need of new construction in New Orleans with preserving historic buildings?"

"Call my office next week," Edgar Dumas said, his eyes suddenly alight at the notion of airtime devoted to broadcasting his point of view. "We'll see what we can do."

King nodded curtly to the councilman and ushered her to a

seat next to Sherilee Dumas, one of Emelie's middle-aged daughters.

"How did you know that Edgar Dumas voted for the Good Times Shopping Plaza?" King asked under his breath as he handed her into the pew. "That happened two years before you moved here."

"I'm a reporter, remember?" she whispered back. "I did some checking recently on the breakdown of the city council votes on that fight."

"I guess that shouldn't really surprise me," King said, his low voice laced with admiration. "Edgar was rumored to be on the take from Grover Jeffries for quite a while."

"I heard that, too."

"Well, you sure stopped that blowhard right in his tracks."

But Corlis wasn't as sanguine about her interchange with Edgar Dumas.

No matter how you sliced it, it was sheer bad luck to run into one of Grover Jeffries's principal functionaries in city government while Kingsbury Duvallon was her obvious escort. Furthermore, she didn't need Aunt Marge to remind her that sleeping at King's cabin and being served coffee in bed *could* cloud her journalistic judgment!

King and Corlis settled back against the wooden pew and gazed toward the altar where the open casket stood at the front of the church. Corlis glimpsed the gray crown and brown brow of a woman's head resting on a plump ivory pillow. An enormous wreath of red roses, emblazoned by a wide white ribbon on which BELOVED MOTHER was written in flowing black script, hung from a three-legged stand nearby. Unbidden, Corlis's thoughts flew back to Henri Girard's casket and the black-bordered card that proclaimed his death in 1837.

Death is death, whatever the century, she thought.

Just then Sherilee Dumas handed Corlis a tissue from the small packet of Kleenex she held clutched in her hand. "Here," she whispered with a watery smile. "You King's new girlfriend?"

"No . . . no!" Corlis whispered emphatically. "Just a friend," she added primly.

"Mama sure did have a soft spot in her heart for that boy," she smiled, nodding in the direction of Corlis's companion.

Organ music swelled and filled the church, marking the beginning of the funeral service for Emelie Dumas, which was like nothing Corlis's Scots-Presbyterian upbringing could have possibly prepared her for. The organist kicked off the first hymn with a rollicking beat, prompting the choir, along with the congregation, to burst into ecstatic singing and clapping. When the minister launched into his eulogy, the mourners celebrated Emelie Dumas's memory with hearty "Amen's!"—some people even leaping to their feet and shouting "Say it, brother!" to punctuate the perspiring reverend's enthusiastic praise.

Next a heavy-set middle-aged soloist mournfully sang "Precious Lord" in a rich, heart-tugging contralto that brought tears to Corlis's eyes. She glanced in King's direction at the precise moment he turned to gaze at her, his own eyes moist.

Afterward Tyrone and James Dumas stepped forward to Emelie's casket and gently closed the top. In response, sobs rose in an accelerating crescendo from members of the congregation, including Sherilee, who cried brokenly into her wad of Kleenex. King and his fellow pallbearers rose from their seats and carried the coffin down the aisle and out the door. Corlis felt her throat tighten at the sight as King passed by her pew, shouldering Emelie's casket. Then she noticed that Edgar Dumas was not among the chosen six pallbearers.

The interment, at a cemetery less than a mile away, took place near a bank of palmetto trees that grew within a few feet of the grave site. Instinctively Corlis reached for King's hand as Emelie's coffin was slowly lowered into the ground. The pressure of his grasp increased as Tyrone, James, and several other members of Emelie's immediate family began to shovel dirt on top of the casket. She glanced at King and saw that he was fighting a wave of emotion, so she held on to his hand even more tightly, willing him to seek strength from her. The last in a line of Emelie's four children thrust the shovel toward the only white male standing among the group of mourners.

"Here, King," Tyrone said in a low voice. "Mama'd want you to see her through this, too."

In response to Tyrone's heartfelt invitation, tears began to stream unashamedly down King's cheeks. He seized the shovel and scattered earth along the wooden coffin.

I called her my black mother.

Corlis's heart ached for King's loss, and for the love given him so freely by a woman whom Corlis had never met . . . a woman King's parents had not deigned to honor with their presence here today, despite Emelie's long years of service to the Kingsbury-Duvallon household.

"May our sister Emelie rest in peace," intoned the pastor, and Corlis joined with the others murmuring, "Amen."

The mourners then dispersed to their various cars, forming a caravan that rolled down a long dirt road to James Dumas's clapboard family home. The old house stood surrounded by rusting wrecks and a weed-strewn yard adjacent to a stand of wild reeds edging a finger of water that eventually flowed into Bayou Lacombe. Set out on long tables near the sagging front porch were steaming pots of red beans and rice, simmering gumbo, and piles of crawfish.

Apparently Councilman Edgar Dumas's busy schedule precluded his sharing this bountiful feast. After King and Corlis had eaten their fill, King ducked his head and whispered in her ear.

"Ready to go, sugar?"

"Back to New Orleans?"

"Well," he replied, nodding farewell to various members of Emelie's family as he guided her toward his car, "we could certainly head right back . . . but, actually, I was thinking of something else."

All *she* could think about was that Andy Zamora might cancel her probation and simply fire her if Edgar Dumas raised a protest that a WJAZ reporter, assigned to cover the controversial Grover Jeffries's building proposal, had accompanied the project's most visible opponent to the funeral of the Duvallon family cook. How could Corlis possibly convince Zamora—or herself, for that matter—that her relationship with King wasn't personal?

"For one day, at least, let's just forget our troubles, Ace, and go fishin'."

Every ounce of good sense told her to go straight back to town. Nevertheless, she found herself helpless to ignore the unguarded expression in King's blue eyes silently petitioning her to stay with him while he took some private time to mourn Emelie's death.

"Okay," she said softly. Then she added, half-seriously, "Just keep me away from the alligators . . . promise?"

"Piece of cake," he said with a smile filled with sadness and gratitude.

Neither the soft purr of a small outboard motor attached to the narrow pirogue nor the sight of moss-laden trees rising from the bayou's waters could serve as an effective distraction from the jumbled thoughts careering through Corlis's brain.

I shouldn't be here.

Don't I have the right to a personal life?

What would Aunt Marge say?

I feel so sad for King.

Glimp and Zamora will kill me!

I love fishing with this man. . . .

A look of tranquillity had settled on King's features while he repeatedly cast his line into the pellucid waters of Bayou Lacombe. It had been a deliciously mild April day. With great relish, King had described the flora and fauna as they floated past odd-angled cypress trees rising like specters out of the river.

During the peaceful afternoon they'd spent meandering along tributaries that King had fished since his childhood—and in deference to his recent loss of his beloved Emelie—Corlis had refrained from bringing up the subject of Jeffries and Marchand's ominous phone call to WJAZ the night that her TV series had aired.

Let the man have a little relaxation and serenity.

As the sun began to slant through the ghostly trees, King nosed the boat into the quiet, weed-choked cove near the log cabin. Gingerly, Corlis rose from her perch in the boat's bow and cautiously stepped onto the embankment. Together they pulled the pirogue ashore and emptied it of its fishing equipment and a few catfish they'd caught that afternoon. King stowed their fishing gear in a shed nearby while Corlis returned to the cabin to pack her few pieces of clothing into her duffel bag. Then she walked to the sink to rinse out the coffee cups they'd used that morning.

She heard the outside door open, and soon the small cabin was filled with the muted strains of The Radiators pulsating from a CD player in the main room. The rock 'n' roll group was a favorite band of New Orleanians, recorded live at the legendary Tipitina's.

Without warning, she felt two warm arms envelop her. King's broad chest pressed against her back. She shivered slightly as his lips brushed against her right ear.

"It's Saturday. Let's forget work and politics and all that other stuff. Stay here with me tonight," he said in a low voice, and in those words, Corlis heard the heartbreak, longing, and loss that King had not been able to express while they floated in the misty bayou all afternoon. "Don't go. I need to be with you, sweetheart."

The words he whispered were simple, direct, honest, and totally disarmed every one of Corlis's defenses—and *all* of her good intentions. Her hands remained frozen on the kitchen taps as water continued to flow into the sink.

"Oh, King," she said helplessly as she stared at the faucet's stream disappearing down the drain.

"What, baby?" he said, stooping once more to nuzzle his lips against her neck.

Corlis felt a rush of affection so intense that it was all she could do to keep from throwing her arms around King and kissing *him* senseless. However, though every cell in her body said "yes!", every professional fiber in her brain was on full red alert.

With her back still pressed against his chest she pleaded, "Wait a sec." She looked over her shoulder but did not meet his gaze. "I—I need to ask you something." The corners of their lips were only inches apart, and the caress of his warm breath was having its usual unsettling effect on her racing pulse. "Are we talking slumber party here, or what?"

"No party games, Ace," King said, his voice suddenly raw with emotion. He reached around her waist to shut off the cascading water. He gently turned her around by the shoulders to face him. "From all the evidence . . . what's been goin' on lately between the lady from California and the gentleman from New Orleans is the real deal for sure, baby." As The Radiators's beat throbbed seductively in the background, King nodded in the direction of the small bedroom. "From the moment I kissed you, I've fantasized about you . . . and fantasized about gettin' you under that quilt in there that my great-great-grandmother made." He paused and flashed her a lopsided grin. "Naw . . . that's a lie. I started fantasizin' when I saw you in that wrinkled UCLA sweatshirt the day after my sister's weddin', when I dropped by to tell you about the job at WJAZ."

"I'm actually disappointed you didn't want to jump on my bones when I had magenta hair and was editing *Ms. UCLA*," she replied with a deadpan expression.

"You felt it, *too*, that morning last December, didn't you?"

She wondered if her heart had stopped beating, which might account for the light-headed feeling clogging her thought processes. "But what about the buildings?" she said earnestly. "You're a news source and I'm a repor—"

"Please don't change the subject, sugar," he interrupted, his eyes boring into hers. "I'm askin' you to tell me how you felt that day I came by your house."

Corlis lowered her eyes and replied good-naturedly, "Okay, okay! I do admit to feeling . . . drawn to you that day. But I merely ascribed it to a lack of sleep, or perhaps those great legs of yours and your ratty tennis shoes."

"You can be sure, darlin', that *you're* the absolute winner in the Great Legs Sweepstakes—but you're still avoidin' my question."

Without warning, he ducked his head and seized her in a kiss so electrifying, it hummed with energy powerful enough to trip circuit breakers. Corlis felt every ounce of willpower draining from her, as if an entire relay grid had shut down. The menace of Grover Jeffries's and Lafayette Marchand's threats—implied or otherwise—faded into the charged atmosphere that virtually crackled with excruciating sexual tension. Gone, too, was the memory of Andy Zamora's probationary warning and lawyer Glimp's disapproving grimaces. Even Margery McCullough's professional code of journalist ethics that Corlis had learned at her great-aunt's knee faded into oblivion.

The only thing she was conscious of was that King Duvallon held her in his arms in a log cabin overlooking a moss-shrouded tributary of Bayou Lacombe—and she *wanted* him.

King pulled back from their embrace and stared at her with unnerving intensity.

"Don't stop kissing me," she whispered, "or my batteries will go dead."

"Believe me, I won't let that happen," King replied, drawing her near him until they were nose to nose. "And I haven't forgotten that the lady from California likes being kissed very ... very ... much." To confirm this fact, he pressed his lips against hers again for an exploration of tongue and mouth while he slid both his palms down her back until they came to rest on her derriere. "Then you'll stay?"

"Unfair tactics ..." she sighed, powerless to stem the surge of high voltage that continued to course through her veins. "I love it when you do that."

He began kissing her on her nose, her eyes, and at the base of her throat as he leaned her against the edge of the kitchen sink. Corlis sensed every sinew and bone and corpuscle between them was in tune, yet King slowly pulled away from her, a troubled expression clouding his eyes.

"Look, darlin'," he said as he gently cupped her chin in his hand, "if you think we should wait till after all this is over with ..."

Wait? she thought, unable to mask her disappointment. Should they wait? At that moment, an avalanche of desire engulfed her, making her dizzy.

Then, as if Corlis were some person she hardly recognized, she reached up and placed her palms on either side of King's face and leaned forward. She kissed him slowly, provocatively, and with a determination that could leave no doubt as to her decision to spend this evening on the banks of Bayou Lacombe.

McCullough! a warning voice echoed in her head.

Oh, be quiet for once, will you?

King sought out the tender spot he'd discovered at the base of her throat and began a tantalizing, torturous journey toward her mouth, nuzzling and nibbling at her earlobe en route.

"Oh, baby," he murmured. "Now, *look* what you've gone and done ..." The angle of his hips left no doubt as to his rising passion. King's lips seized the nub of her earlobe and tugged sensuously. "May I take you to bed, darlin'? We're way overdue."

"Oh yes . . ." she moaned in a fog of desire. "Yes, *please!*"

Hand in hand, they walked into the bedroom. The last rays of afternoon sunshine had given way to dusk as he paused beside the bedside table. He reached for a book of matches that lay between the brass clock and a hurricane lamp. He lifted the lamp's glass and lit the wick that extended into the metal base below. Within seconds a soft, golden glow illuminated the room.

Next to the lamp King had also placed a bottle of wine. Carefully he poured a ruby stream of merlot into two pieces of stemware and handed one to her.

"To lovers, past and present," he declared softly.

King didn't know about Julien and Martine . . . or André and Henri. . . .

In the flickering lamplight a shock of dark hair fell across his forehead, turning his blue eyes nearly to indigo. Corlis's thoughts drifted to the inviting bedroom in Martine Fouché's elegant cottage on Rampart Street . . . the mellow candlelight dancing on the walls . . . Julien pouring champagne into fluted glasses. She felt herself flushing—all over. Her lowered glance rested on King's shirtfront, where curling black chest hairs peeped through his open collar.

Good Lord, this is a sexy man!

"To lovers . . . then and now . . ." she echoed his toast, and took a sip of her wine.

A silence fell between them, except for the slinky rendition of The Radiators's "Solid Ground" coming from the living room.

Was she standing on solid ground or quicksand? she thought with sudden apprehension. She took a second sip of her wine to the accompaniment of the music's riveting backbeat, thinking that it was the kind of melody that a person could easily get into a lot of trouble listening to. . . . It was music to make love by. But was she about to commit her proverbial act of self-sabotage, or—

At that moment King relieved Corlis of her wineglass and returned it to the table, along with his own. He began kissing her again, blotting out all rational thought. The throbbing music enveloped them in a cocoon of sound that forged a veritable link between their bodies that felt wonderfully familiar and highly charged.

It seemed the most natural thing in the world for Corlis to lean even closer to King and brace herself against his chest, as if he were one of the sturdy, moss-draped trees sheltering their cabin outside. The mesmerizing scent of his verbena aftershave filled her head, its lemony tang imprinting itself permanently upon her senses.

Solid ground . . . why do I feel so . . .

Languidly Corlis watched King reach toward the bed's wooden headboard and give the quilt a tug. He gently bent down and kissed her hard, signaling loud and clear that beneath the surface of this self-contained, highly intelligent and disciplined former marine boiled a cauldron of emotional intensity that was certainly a match for her own. After several long minutes Corlis again pulled away from his embrace, her eyes widening with pleasure and a soupçon of mischief.

"Ah, Professor . . ." she said with a throaty laugh, "there's one thing needed before we can proceed."

His eyes locked onto hers like a heat-seeking missile. "Could you be referrin' to condoms?" he inquired with a rakish grin. She nodded affirmatively, feeling both shy and shameless all at once. King dug into his pants pocket and pulled out a small square cellophane-wrapped object that he placed on the bedside table. "I have to confess . . ." he said, turning toward her once more, "I planned ahead, hopin' somethin' like this might happen sometime soon."

"Well, hussy that I am," she admitted sheepishly, "I'm glad you did."

"Great minds think alike, Ace."

Strong hands that had, in his youth, pounded nails to renovate a tumbled-down fishing cabin on Bayou Lacombe began to tug gently at the waist of her cotton shirt, pulling it free of her jeans. Corlis remained absolutely still, reveling in the sensation of the soft fabric sliding along her torso. King eased the material away from her body and leaned back. For a moment he merely gazed at her, his dark blue eyes roaming over her slender form, a satisfied smile playing about his lips.

"What a very pretty lady you are," he said, unfastening her jeans and then gently unzipping them. "But then, I already guessed that."

"Well . . . let's see how pretty *you* are, Mr. Preservation," she said, playfully unbuttoning his khaki shirt.

The rest of their garments began to fall on the floor, as if she and King were in a contest to see how quickly they could cast them off. King won, taking Corlis into his arms and gently laying her against the quilt and the bed's plump white pillows.

"Ohhhh . . ." she luxuriated against the bed linen, "this is sinfully delicious."

"No, sugar," King replied, easing her last scrap of underwear down her naked legs. "*You're* the one who's sinfully delicious." He moved closer and drew her into his arms again.

They lay quietly for a moment, adjusting to the newness of their bodies pressing against each other. Then King shifted his weight to lean on one elbow. He gently began to trace his forefinger from the base of Corlis's neck down, down, between her bare breasts, to her waist.

"Oh . . . boy . . ." she said on a long breath.

King's hand continued its serpentine route toward a sweet softness between her thighs, producing sensations that made her feel both brazen and bashful. Back and forth King's fingers strayed in some wild, erotic rhythm that seemed part of the sensuous musical beat pouring from the next room.

Could they put their love on solid ground?

King's touch was relentless. It was as if he were pulling from her notes and cadences contained in the song that floated in the humid air. The rhythms they created together forged an expanding link between them that grew so intense, she felt she would either start to sob or scream.

Corlis reached for one of King's hands and pressed it against her heart. "Feel that?" she demanded.

"Oh yes," he whispered. "Mine, too."

Every movement between them was synchronous, each embrace a complex harmony as balanced and fulsome as the music wafting from the living room. Finally, when neither could bear their separateness another instant, King reached for the small packet he'd placed earlier on the bedside table. Corlis sat up and smiled a woman's smile.

"Here," she said softly, taking it from his hand and easily tearing the cellophane. "Let *me* do this. . . ."

Then she was beneath him, her back sinking into the tufted quilt. He hovered above her, teasing her, refusing just yet to give her what they both knew she yearned for.

All she knew was that she wanted to kiss this man, caress his back, touch him—and be touched. She lightly ran her fingertips along the crease between his leg and torso and was immediately rewarded by a soft moan of satisfaction. There was no predicting the outcome of her actions this night, but she carried on blindly, flying on faith, bestowing feathery kisses under his ear and along his jawline, until she reached his lips once again—in response to which he promptly seized her wrists and pinned them on either side of the pillow. To her delight, he announced his pleasurably wicked intentions while covering her with more kisses.

"Despite my legendary bad behavior," she murmured with a provocative smile, "you are *so* good to me. . . ."

"Bein' good to you," he replied, nuzzling the side of her pelvis, "is just being good to myself."

"Oh, yes . . ." she murmured. "Good. Very . . . good . . ."

Heat shimmered in her soul like the burning cane fields at an October Roulaison. She ached for him to enter her and wondered briefly if her bones had turned to liquid molasses, like the sugar boiling in metal cauldrons at Reverie plantation so long ago.

"King, please . . . I *want* you," she cried out with an abandon both shocking and utterly foreign to her. "I want you to—"

His drugging kisses bathed her stomach, her breasts, the hollow at the base of her neck. "I know, darlin' . . ." he murmured. "I want you just as much—"

He entered her swiftly with the instinct of someone certain that he was being welcomed home. When she lifted her hips off the quilted coverlet to meet his seeking embrace, he pressed her even closer to him, finding her, filling her, telling her wordlessly now that their dancing and the music would soon come to a longed-for conclusion. The harmonies of touch and taste invented this night were for the two of them alone, striking chords that resonated deep and true. Theirs was a union full of passion and loss, reconciliation—and burgeoning trust.

In the most primal way, this act for them was both an acknowledgment of Emelie's passing and an urgent, eager reaffirmation that the beat of life does, indeed, go on. Neither could speak of this heartbreak and happiness, but could only cling to the other, as wild creatures cling when a force so elemental fuses them like lava pouring into the sea.

There was silence now, except for the rustle of a night wind outside the old log cabin, blowing gently against surrounding pine branches adrift in cascading moss. Across the silken waters of Bayou Lacombe, a series of ripples fluttering in concentric circles hinted at life teeming just below the surface—unheard, unseen, fecund in the murky depths. Now their song was a soundless melody that spoke to wounded hearts and lingered long after the tiny waves had been reduced to invisible tremors.

Corlis and King drifted off to sleep beneath the stitchery wrought by a long-deceased Kingsbury ancestor.

Chapter Twenty

Corlis awoke first. She sat up and stared out the window at the mist rising in thin ribbons off the water. As she glanced around the shadowed bedroom, a litany of doubts began to assault her.

In the bathroom she'd seen a vial of coral nail polish residing in the medicine cabinet when she'd searched for toothpaste in the wee hours of the morning. How many women had Kingsbury Duvallon brought to this cozy little love nest? she wondered ruefully. Had she in fact behaved like a naive idiot last night? Had King actually experienced the same overwhelming desire for her that she had for him, or was he merely a red-blooded male in need—especially last night—of consolation for Cindy Lou's betrayal, as well as for the deeply felt loss of Emelie?

Worse yet, she fretted silently as she gazed at King's sleeping form, had she done something genuinely self-destructive by going to bed with a professional source? Had she just done something that would result not only in shooting herself in the foot—again—but in her getting trounced emotionally?

"Mornin' sugar," King said sleepily.

Startled from her gloomy reverie, Corlis leaned over and kissed him lightly on his forehead. Then she said abruptly, "King? We have to talk. I have to tell you something."

King opened both eyes. "You hated baitin' your own hook?"

Corlis laughed in spite of her lagging spirits. "No, nothing like that."

"Don't tell me some ghostly visitors turned up in this ol'

cabin last night?" he said, half-seriously, half in jest. She gave him an odd look but shook her head. "Well . . ." he said, pulling himself up to lean on one elbow, "my mind's not workin' well enough yet for any more guesses. Shoot."

"I *loved* the fishing, loved the scenery, and I don't mind baiting my own hook one bit. And," she added, feeling suddenly shy, "I certainly loved . . . making love with you."

"Why, thank you, darlin'," King replied, seizing her hand from the bedcover and raising it to his lips for a kiss. "I feel the same way." He gazed at her steadily. "So . . . what do you want to talk about?"

"It's . . . something else. Something that I should have told you yesterday, before we even came out here."

"Ah . . ." was all he said. He sat up in bed and indicated she should lean on the large square pillows he placed against the headboard for both of them. The resulting silence grew louder as Corlis searched for an unemotional way to pose her current dilemma.

"Yesterday, at Emelie's funeral . . . when Edgar Dumas—"

"Look, Corlis," he volunteered with a slight grimace, "I feel terrible 'bout that. I should have realized Edgar was likely to turn up there. He and Emelie weren't close, especially after his vote in favor of the Good Times Shoppin' Plaza and the underhanded way he got her to sign the demolition papers, but I should have considered that he might come to her funeral. I just wasn't thinkin' clearly."

"Oh . . . it's not only that," she replied, wondering if King's fuzzy-headedness extended to his decision to bring her here with wine and condoms at the ready.

Pushing that depressing possibility from her mind, Corlis spent the next minutes bringing King up to date on everything that had transpired in Andy Zamora's office following the final broadcast of her three-part minidoc about the Selwyn buildings. She included her boss's edict that she was on probation and forbidden to see the advocate for historic preservation on any personal basis whatsoever as long as she continued to be assigned to the controversy between Jeffries Industries and the preservationist community.

"So, you see . . ." she concluded, lowering her eyes to study the bed quilt, "I absolutely knew what the stakes were—and I chose to come out here with you anyway. Any resulting trouble from what happened yesterday with Edgar Dumas is *my* responsibility, not yours. And, therefore, much as I regret it, we . . . we can't see each other anymore like this—*remotely* like this— until this whole thing comes to some conclusion."

King remained silent for a moment. Then he said quietly, "Gotcha."

"Thanks."

She swung her legs to the side of the bed just as King said, "But . . . I sure have trouble imaginin' goin' back to the way it was for us before last night."

She turned to look at him over her shoulder. "Me, too."

He reached out and brushed the back of his fingers against her cheek. "And I sure am happy you stayed over. Especially if it has to be the last time we'll be alone together for a while." He playfully put his arm under the covers and placed a proprietary hand on the side of her naked thigh.

Corlis inhaled deeply, shifted on the bed to face him, and reached under the quilt to still his hand.

"And another thing . . ." she said, swallowing. "To me . . . what's happened between us is very *serious*! As far as I'm concerned, this isn't a little fling, you know . . . not for me, at least." She peered at him solemnly. "Are you *sure* you're up for this sort of 'real deal,' as you call it? I mean, *really* up for it?"

"Oh . . . I'm up for it all right," he said, his dark-blue eyes boring into hers as he seized her hand and pressed it against his groin.

Corlis's gaze clouded, and she was suddenly assailed by another avalanche of doubts.

"Let's . . . be . . . straight with each other, okay?" she said. "Goodness knows, there was—and is right *now*—more than enough lust floating around this cabin to send us both into outer space. However, that's not what I'm talking about—"

"Neither am I," King cut her short. "You said this is serious," he repeated, "and I want you to have no doubts as to exactly *how* serious it is for me, too. I wouldn't have risked what we're riskin'—" He paused abruptly and then amended, "Asked *you* to risk what you're riskin' if I . . . could've helped what I felt last night."

An enormous sense of relief flooded through her.

"Me, too," she murmured.

He pulled her hard against his chest. Roughly seeking her lips, he kissed her long and thoroughly. Then he guided her hand once again to his midsection. "Oh, baby . . ." he groaned. "Look, darlin' . . . you've done it again. . . ."

"King . . . I . . ."

He gazed at her quizzically. Then he smiled. "Why, Corlis McCullough, I do believe you're nervous as the proverbial cat on a hot tin roof!"

"I am. Sort of," she admitted.

"Does the notion of makin' love in the clear light of day make you nervous—or do *I* make you nervous?"

"Both," she confessed.

"Ah . . ." he said quietly, "then you'd better tell me why."

"Well . . ." Corlis began, averting her eyes, "in addition to feeling worried about my job . . . about doing the right thing as a journalist, I—" She stopped short, shook her head in frustration, and said, "Oh . . . I can't really explain it!"

"Yes, you can," King insisted soberly. "Just say it. Tell the truth in real time, Corlis."

" 'Tell the truth in real time.' What a great phrase."

"It's what Emelie used to say to me when I was a boy. It helped get me out of all sorts of jams."

She raised her eyes and looked around the beautifully appointed log bedroom.

"Well . . . the truth . . . in real time . . . is that I began wondering this morning if . . . if this cabin is the place where you bring . . . women you hope to . . . seduce."

There! Now that's a first, she thought. She'd told a man she cared for the truth about the way she was feeling in *real time*.

"And you're wonderin' if you're just another notch on my thirty-five-year-old belt?" he asked. Corlis glanced down at her hands resting in her lap and nodded with embarrassment.

"I saw a bottle of nail polish in your medicine cabinet," she mumbled.

"Oh. I understand. Well . . ." he said, staring at the foot of the bed, "in the last four years, I have been here, on occasion, with . . . one other woman. Cindy Lou. It was a 'serious' relationship—as you put it earlier," he continued. "Or at least *I* thought it was. But I wasn't ready, then, to make a commitment. A commitment to marriage." He gestured toward the log wall nearby and smiled sardonically. "I just wasn't sure we were right together for the long haul. She barely tolerated this place, hated fishin', and loved the New Orleans Country Club scene."

"A genuine magnolia, huh?"

King nodded. He reached over and tousled her hair. "Unlike you, Ace, she *did* despise baitin' her own hook."

"And my problem has always been allowing anyone else to *help* me bait my hook." Corlis confessed, laughing. She cocked her head and asked, "How 'bout we put our cards on the table, Professor?"

"Absolutely," he agreed with an emphatic nod. "Cards on the table."

Wondering at her own courage, she began, "Although I am compelled to reveal that I find you a sinfully attractive man, King Duvallon—"

"Why, *thank* you, Miz McCullough," he replied gallantly. "I'm duly flattered."

"I've also had my share of rebound relationships," she disclosed doggedly. "I absolutely *hated* them, so . . . I was wondering if you aren't possibly reacting to—"

"This is definitely not *that*," he interrupted, a hint of irritation tingeing his words. "With Cindy, we had all that family stuff in common, and she supports historic preservation and so on, but on some level, as I look back on it, I think she thought that little toe dance she did with Jack Ebert in the cloak room at Antoine's would make me jealous . . . get me to finally propose to her. It was a *classic* magnolia maneuver. Instead, as you and everybody else in town witnessed, she got caught by my sister, with her panties down, and our relationship came to a screechin' halt. It was pretty embarrassin' for everybody involved," he said grimly.

"Especially since I put a lot of it on TV," Corlis reminded him ruefully.

King shrugged and continued, "So . . . after that happened, I decided to let some time pass . . . to kinda let it all settle in my mind, you know?" He regarded her levelly. "So, to answer your original question, I haven't brought anyone else out here . . . till now."

King leaned forward and began kissing her again. Corlis sensed it was also a cover to avoid elaborating on the degree to which Cindy's betrayal with Jack Ebert had humiliated him.

"Oh, King . . . what a saga," she whispered against his collarbone. "For everyone." And she knew that she would have done anything to spare him that kind of pain. Now, however, her empathy was mingled with a tremendous resurgence of sexual excitement.

She leaned toward him and initiated an eye-opening exploration on her own, skimming the tips of her fingers along the contours of his chest, paying homage to muscles she'd yearned to touch for months. Then she reached up and cupped his face between her hands. "My guess is that you were lonely, and a little sad, *long* before Miss Cindy Lou appeared on your radar screen," she whispered. "But I'm here now," she added simply, "and I am so sorry for the losses you've had."

At first King didn't answer but continued to hold her gaze, and his eyes grew moist. "Thank you," was all he said. He studied her for a moment. Then he murmured, "Such a powerhouse of a person . . . yet, you have an incredible sweetness about you."

No one had *ever* called her sweet. It sounded rather nice the way King said it.

"Well . . . Professor," she proposed with a throaty laugh, slyly slipping her hands beneath the covers, "since this has to be our last time together for a long while . . . let me show you just how sweet I can be. . . ."

On Julia Street, Cagney Cat was forced to wait for his morning meal. It was nearly 10 A.M. by the time King and Corlis came off the Lake Pontchartrain causeway and headed down Interstate 10.

"Do you mind if I just check in at my family's house?" he proposed. "My parents are spendin' the weekend on somebody's boat down on the Gulf, and I promised Aunt Bethany I'd fill her in about Emelie's funeral and say hello to my grandmother. It'll only take a minute; then I'll drop you on Julia Street and go on down the block. I'm supposed to meet with Chris and a few others at the Preservation Resource Center around noon."

"Sounds like a plan," Corlis said, nodding. Despite her best resolutions to quickly go their separate ways this Sunday morning, she was overwhelmingly curious to see King's childhood home.

When they reached Orange Street in the Lower Garden District, King drew up in front of a tropical jungle that nearly obscured a faded blue two-story residence. Turning off the ignition, he said, "How 'bout I call you later today, to let you know if there've been any new developments? Afterward, we can talk sexy."

"King!" she protested, "I'm *serious*! We can only talk if it's about business! We just can't get involved in anything personal from now on. Promise?"

He reached across the car seat and caressed her left earlobe.

"Nothin' personal, huh? That's a tough order, but . . . I'll do my best."

Corlis peered doubtfully through the windshield at the overgrown vegetation surrounding the Kingsbury-Duvallon residence. She stared at the house whose four white Corinthian columns anchored the venerable wooden structure and its twin verandas on the ground floor and second story.

King suddenly said, "They didn't have the time to go to Em's funeral, but by God, they'd never turn down a last-minute invitation to hang out on a labor lawyer's yacht."

Corlis reached across the car and took his hand. "It really bothers you, doesn't it, that you were the only one from your family to have gone upriver," she said quietly.

"It really bothers me that my *mother and father* didn't show," he replied bitterly. "The woman worked for us for thirty years!" He shook his head resignedly. "Well . . . such is life. Let's go in," he added with a renewed sense of purpose. "I'd like to show you the house, and besides," he said with a teasing smile, "don't you want to see where I caught sight of the ghost?"

In actual fact Corlis wasn't keen to be reminded about her own string of eerie experiences. However, King's invitation to peek inside the magnificent old residence was too tempting to refuse.

"Well, I do admit, darlin'," she said in her best magnolia accent, "that I *am* a bit curious to see the last remainin' Kingsbury-Duvallon family manse." More seriously, she added, "But after that, I've *got* to get on home. Poor old Cagney—"

"Ah . . . Cagney," King echoed. "We certainly can't let that boy starve." He ruffled her hair. "If you come inside the house, I promise I'll behave, though really, after this mornin', that's asking a lot of a poor southern boy like me."

"King! Stop that!" she said sternly, and broke into laughter. "Well, at least *try* to stop that." She gently touched his cheek. "This is going to be hard for me, too, you know."

With a bittersweet sense that their short, sensual idyll was drawing to a close, they left King's car and walked, hands clasped, down the brick path that led along the side of the graceful old house. In Corlis's view, the structure's faded blue exterior walls, the peeling white trim and the odd broken shutter merely gave the grand old dwelling a romantic, melancholy appearance. As they continued down the uneven moss-covered path, King pointed out various architectural features on the two-story facade that was both elegant and decadent, a testament to past glories and present decay.

He led the way around the side of the house, heading for the back door. Inside the kitchen King's aunt, Bethany Kingsbury, stood at a large, old-fashioned white-enameled stove, clad in an apron and wielding a large spatula. Her gray hair was pulled back in a tidy bun, but for a few stray wisps grazing the nape of her slender neck.

"Oh, King, darlin'!" she exclaimed delightedly. "I'm so happy you're back!"

"Mornin', sweetheart," King said. "How's the cold?"

Bethany brought a lace hanky out of her apron and waved it cheerfully, "A bit better, sugar . . . but don't kiss me and thanks for askin'. Now, you *must* tell me everything about poor, dear Emelie's funeral. I was so sorry I was feelin' so under the weather—" She stopped short when she saw Corlis step beyond the screen door. "Why, hello!" She deposited the last piece of French toast onto a platter and wiped her hands on her apron.

"You're that newswoman on WJAZ, aren't you, dear?" She scanned Corlis's face. "Why, you're just as pretty as you are on TV. *Prettier,* in fact."

King swiftly accomplished the introductions.

"Got any *pain perdu* to spare there, Aunt Bethany? We're starvin'."

"Of course, darlin'. You two just sit right down at the kitchen table while I take this breakfast tray up to your grandmother." She leaned toward Corlis and disclosed, "My poor mother has difficulty feedin' herself nowadays, you know? I won't be too long. Now, y'all enjoy every bite, y'hear?"

"What a lovely woman," Corlis commented, taking a bite of crisply fried bread that Bethany had slathered with powdered sugar and cane syrup.

"Believe me, she, my grandmother, and my sister, Daphne, are the only members of my family that I'd subject you to," he declared.

"Well, consider yourself lucky that I'm an out-of-towner," she retorted. "Except for my aunt Marge, of course, there's *nobody* else in the McCullough clan I'd subject *you* to."

"You have the makin's of a first-rate southerner, my dear."

When they had finished their breakfast, King led the way down a shadowed corridor toward the front of the house. En route, he described the curious features of his family residence.

"The foyer is typical for a place of this vintage," he explained, opening a door on his right, "but this curving staircase is rather grand for the size of the house."

"It's absolutely magnificent!" Corlis exclaimed, craning to get a better view of a line of family portraits marching up the wall to the second floor.

"And here's the double parlor," he said, escorting her into the living room.

"Why double?"

"See the two fireplaces? Very European. A throwback to pre-Revolutionary France."

"I think my place on Julia Street had one of these double parlors," she said eagerly, "but they put up a wall to make the bedroom when they turned it into apartments."

Corlis gazed around the room, her attention caught by two

elegant marble fireplaces with a raft of family photographs on each mantel.

"Wow . . ." she said on a low breath. "No wonder you knew what costumes we should wear to the Jeffrieses' ball. Looks like *everybody* in your family likes to play dress-up!" she added, staring at a raft of broad-shouldered, handsome young men in their prime dressed as courtiers in doublets and silken hose.

King chuckled, pointing to a silver-framed color photo, now anemic with age.

"That's Mardi Gras, 1962," he explained. "That's my mother, Antoinette, as queen."

"Boy, is she good-looking. . . ."

"'Prettiest debutante of the sea-son,' as my grandmother would be quick to tell you."

"And who's that gorgeous guy next to her?"

"Let's see . . ." King said, taking a close look. "Avery Labonniere was king that year . . . and—"

"No . . . not the king . . . *that* guy!" she insisted, pointing to a tall, exceedingly handsome figure standing to the right of the carnival king.

"Believe it or not, that's Lafayette Marchand," King said with a slight grimace. "He was a duke in my mother's court when he was in Tulane Law School."

"You're joking," Corlis said. "He's a good-looking man now, but where I come from, looks like *that* can make you a movie star. Wow . . . Lafayette Marchand."

"Here's Aunt Bethany when *she* was queen two years before my mother," King said, pointing to another photo in a matching silver frame showing a striking young woman with black hair.

"What a knockout *she* was," Corlis exclaimed. "Gee . . . your mother and your aunt knew Lafayette Marchand way back then. Were they upset when you fired him as your godfather?" she asked curiously.

"Well, when it came to Lafayette, Bethany had the good sense to figure out that appearances weren't everything. My mother and I try not to discuss it."

"Did your aunt Bethany never marry?" Corlis asked.

"No, she never did. She takes care of my grandmother. Always has."

King continued to gaze pensively at the photos on the mantel.

"So?" Corlis asked after a few seconds. "Where did this supposed ghost make himself known?"

"What?" he said absently. "Oh, the ghost." He pointed across the room to a stately rosewood cabinet whose open doors revealed a wide selection of liquor bottles. "Right over there. See the mirror on the wall next to the armoire?" He took her by the hand and walked toward the massive piece of furniture. "I was standin' alone, right here, seriously reflectin' on what libation I felt like makin' myself that day prior to a Sunday family dinner, when this . . . presence . . . this *somethin'* seemed to appear and glide past the lookin' glass, turnin' into a kind of vapor trail as it wafted into the foyer. It was mighty strange, I can tell you."

"You think it could have been André Duvallon?"

"Who?" King asked, puzzled.

"The banker my aunt Marge told us was mentioned in Corlis Bell McCullough's diary," Corlis prompted.

"Oh, right," he agreed, nodding. "I never knew the name of whoever supposedly shot himself in this room, or even that there *was* an André Duvallon in the bankin' business. My grandmother just mentioned one time that *somebody*, way back when, reportedly died in this house by his own hand."

"Too bad nobody knows which unhappy relative it might have been," Corlis commented.

"Frankly, I would've thought it was an André Kingsbury, not an André Duvallon," King mused. "My mother's family built and has owned this house since the 1830s, and as far as I ever heard, the Kingsbury-Duvallons in *my* line were only joined together when my parents got married."

"Oh," Corlis responded, disappointed. Had she incorrectly surmised that poor, distraught André was heading his horse and buggy home to Orange Street when Corlis's namesake had hopped aboard his carriage?

"Listen, sugar," King broke in, rousing her from her reverie, "let me just run upstairs and say a quick hello to my grandmother. She's pretty frail, or I'd introduce you. Then I'll take you back to Julia Street. I'll just be a few minutes."

"Fine . . ." Corlis murmured, hardly aware of his departure as her attention was drawn to the armoire that doubled as a drinks cabinet.

Nearby, a beautiful blue-and-white Spode bowl filled with fragrant potpourri stood on a curve-legged table under the gilt mirror where King said he'd thought he'd once seen a ghost. As she approached the beautiful inlaid cabinet to inspect its brass hardware more closely, an aromatic whiff of dried flowers floated up from the porcelain container of crushed petals, giving off a melancholy perfume of ashes of roses, solemn and funereal, and evocative of tragedies past.

Corlis braced her hands on the table's highly polished surface to steady herself against the unsettling effects of its potent aroma.

Get away from that smell! Just walk over to that window and breathe some fresh air!

However, all she could do was hold on to the edges of the table for dear life because, much to her dismay, a vision began to form—the Kingsbury-Duvallon double parlor in an earlier day, lit by gaslight, and filled with additional furniture as massive as the rosewood armoire. Her swift intake of breath intensified the pungent, evocative scent of potpourri that, despite her best mental efforts to stay grounded in her own century, began to transport her to a time in which poor André Duvallon paced to and fro between the matching pair of fireplaces, appearing dangerously distraught.

"Oh . . . no . . ." Corlis whispered, as she fought off a frightening blackness that was fast engulfing her. "Not now! Not *here!*"

Corlis Bell McCullough stood off to one side, watching André Duvallon stride over to a magnificent wooden cabinet and pour himself a large tumbler of absinthe. With an unsteady hand, André lifted the glass filled with the potent spirits to his lips. Tears drenched his cheeks. He drank deeply of the milky-green liquid, then set the glass upon the table next to the rosewood armoire. Immediately, he refilled it.

"André . . ." Corlis pleaded worriedly, "Really . . . I wonder if you should—"

But he waved his free hand at her in dismissal and began to

pace the parlor once again, his finely polished boot soles slapping against the cypress floor's wide planks.

"It's over. . . . It's finished. There's nothing further to be done."

"But surely, André, you could go to the authorities about these . . . these threats, and—"

"Authorities!" André scoffed. "Will they care if your husband and his partner ruin my good name, or Etienne and Julien LaCroix's? The local officials have been so corrupted by you Americans and your damnable money, they'll merely turn a blind eye." He paused in the middle of the room and raised one hand to his forehead, as if to ward off a throbbing headache. "I am seriously overextended financially, Corlis, with notes coming due on money I have advanced your husband and Ian Jeffries to keep them quiet."

"Oh, dear Lord . . ." Corlis murmured.

"And Julien LaCroix is now so besotted with Martine and the idea of becoming a father to the poor little bastard they have created together, that he cannot see what is right in front of his face!"

"Lisette . . . ? He has not realized that the little girl is—?" Corlis could not bring herself to finish her scandalous sentence.

"Yes. Lisette," André confirmed in a low, defeated voice. "Julien's half sister, Lisette. His unborn *child's* half sister, Lisette. His own *father's* child—Lisette!" he cried, his handsome features grotesquely distorted by burgeoning anguish. He slammed his fist against the chimneypiece, rattling a blue-and-white Spode bowl filled with aromatic potpourri. "Damnable *le plaçage!*" he shouted, impotent with rage. "White men's lust for these women has forged alliances far more sordid than anything Henri and I were party to." André's cheeks were ashen now.

"Please . . . for your own sake, you must remain calm," Corlis pleaded, but André was oblivious to her entreaties.

"My family's good name, the financial stability of my bank . . . this very house, which I persuaded my unsuspecting brother-in-law to pledge as collateral to save my bank from insolvency—all will be lost!"

"Who?" she asked, confused.

"My sister . . . Margaret's husband, George Kingsbury!" he railed. "He has pledged *this house* to help me keep afloat!"

Corlis had not met this branch of André's family with whom the bachelor made his home, and she wondered if they were aware of how desperate the man had become.

"No, André!" Corlis cried with sudden resolution. " 'Tis not as dire as you think. Ian and Randall are bullies! They have vulnerabilities as well. I know that I could probably—"

He bestowed on her a look of pity. "If I cannot fathom a way to stop their calumny, surely you, a mere woman, cannot either."

Corlis was reeling with the shock of it all. She could no longer avoid the plain fact that she had mortgaged her own future and *her* good name to her husband who was an out-and-out swindler. She seized André's hand and held on to it, willing him to pay her heed. He had been kind to her, even if his interests had never been romantic. In fact, she realized with a start, André Duvallon could be said to be the only person she had come to know in New Orleans who even approached the status of being a friend.

"Listen to me, André!" she begged. "My father is a banker in Pittsburgh. I know it doesn't hold out much hope, but let me inform my husband of the penalties he faces for practicing such blatant extortion. And believe me," she assured him, "Randall and Ian's own finances are precarious, to say the least. That's probably why Ian Jeffries is so desperate to get you to pay him the five thousand dollars he demanded this afternoon." She attempted to smile encouragingly. "If Randall and Ian know that *I* am aware of their skullduggery—"

"No!" André exclaimed fiercely. "You musn't let on that you know any of this."

"Why ever not?" Corlis demanded. " 'Tis outrageous that they think they can succeed in intimidating—"

"I do believe, my dear Corlis," André said ominously, "that Ian Jeffries would not hesitate an instant to do you—or your husband, for that matter—bodily harm." His shoulders sagged. "I have never been certain that Henri's suicide wasn't a staged affair and that Ian Jeffries may have made it *appear* as if Henri hung himself." He raised his head, his expression haggard. "No.

Go, please. Your presence and your fruitless offers of help only add to my burdens. Just go."

Corlis stared at the beaten man with an overwhelming feeling of dread.

"Promise me you won't do anything rash," she pleaded. "Promise me we can speak again tomorrow and I shall give you a report . . . from behind the lines, so to speak."

She was certain now that she must plan her own escape from New Orleans. She had a premonition that her only chance to sort out her life was to get as far away from this place as possible. She would pawn her last gemstone bracelet, if she had to, she thought, her mind racing. It was a bauble she had utterly forgotten about until just this instant. She had sewn it into the hem of her traveling suit the night she eloped with Randall. Fortunately her husband didn't know of its existence.

Corlis laid a hand on André's finely tailored sleeve. "At an earlier time, you were kind to me when I was feeling terribly distraught myself," she said. "I consider you a friend, André. Please say I may call on you tomorrow?"

"As you wish," he replied wearily. "I shall ask one of my servants to drive you home. Forgive me for not seeing you to the door."

Without further conversation André left the parlor. His footsteps echoed down the hallway, leaving Corlis no recourse but to let herself out of his elegant front door. While waiting for André's carriage to appear, she stood on the veranda, gazing through a thicket of lush greenery toward the wrought-iron garden gate. Her mind whirled with events that had unfolded in stunning and rapid succession.

Preoccupied with her churning thoughts, Corlis was unaware that André soon reentered the parlor following a brief conversation with his groomsman. He immediately sat down at a small desk positioned against a wall to the right of the front fireplace. Taking quill pen in hand, he swiftly scratched an explanatory missive addressed to Julien LaCroix. In it he revealed the relationship of Julien's father to Martine Fouché and Lisette, as well as Jeffries's and McCullough's blackmail and extortion plots. He paused for a long moment, then commenced to write again.

And so, dear Julien, I ask your forgiveness for not acting sooner to protect both your interests and those of my beloved Henri. Use this foul information I give you concerning those two scoundrels as a battering ram against the American scum. Tell Ian Jeffries and Randall McCullough that you intend to show this letter to every banker in New Orleans, if you have to, to turn the blackguards' shameful game against them and shut them up forever. As for me, I will no longer have to endure the infamy sure to be heaped upon me by my own class.

I am deeply sorry, however, that in revealing the truth to you of this damnable situation, I must also disclose the unholy links that connect you and Martine Fouché.

I have long believed that white men's lust for an enslaved people will wreak havoc on generations that succeed our own. To live a lie, to live in the shadows, as plaçage demands, may I say from sad experience, is to live a kind of slow death. In honor of Henri's memory, I ask that you tell those two swine that if they do not leave New Orleans immediately, you will reveal to the weekly journals the story of how these wretched Americans extorted us, causing, also, your father's attack of apoplexy and virtually hounding to death two men who strove to live honorably, despite the unusual affection by which Henri and I felt ourselves possessed.

Let God be our judge, and not the likes of those avaricious rogues with our blood on their hands. Let Him decide which of us has committed the greatest sins.

Yours in truth,
André Duvallon

André addressed the front of the letter to *Julien LaCroix, Reverie Plantation*. He secured it with molten sealing wax into which he pressed the flat surface of his gold signet ring. Next he summoned a servant, who swiftly put the missive into the custody of the waiting carriage driver, with instructions to continue upriver after seeing Mrs. McCullough safely back to Julia Street.

Corlis had remained on the veranda, wondering why it was taking so long for André's groomsman to bring the carriage around. Suddenly the loud, unmistakable crack from a discharging pistol rent the air.

She whirled in place, ran to the front door, and rattled the brass knob. It was locked. Just at that moment she heard the sound of horses' hooves coming along the side of the house.

"Oh, God! No!" she cried over her shoulder as the driver brought the carriage to a halt. "Come here! Quickly! It's Mr. Duvallon!" she screamed at the bewildered servant. She began to pound on the front door with her fists. "Let me in!" she shouted. "Oh, André . . . please, *please* let me in!"

The groomsman leapt down from André's carriage and, in three strides, reached the veranda. "Massa André tol' me not to disturb him no mo'—"

"André!" she shrieked, continuing to hammer on the door with all her might.

She sprinted the length of the wooden porch, cupped her hands over her eyes, and peered into the front parlor through the glass window. There, on the floor near the armoire, lay the handsome young banker, a ragged bullet hole laying waste to the side of his silken dark head. Next to the body was an overturned glass of absinthe, its peculiar chartreuse color dissolving into the crimson pool of blood spreading across the floor.

A few feet away on the plush Persian carpet in front of the fireplace lay a blue-and-white Spode bowl that had been swept from its perch on the mantelpiece. Miraculously, the bowl was unbroken. The flower petals it had contained were strewn everywhere—almost as if André Duvallon were already in his grave.

Corlis did not recall the carriage ride back to Julia Street, nor wearily trudging up the stairs past the nursemaid, who was taking the McCullough children out for their daily walk along the riverfront. Numbly she closed her bedroom door and sank down, fully clothed, on the wide bed that she'd shared with Randall McCullough these last eight years.

Dry-eyed, she stared at the ceiling, mesmerized by the intricacies of the sculptured plaster moldings that fanned out in a wheeled design from the chandelier. She was faintly aware that someone nearby was wailing, the sounds growing louder and more desperate in her ear, until she realized, with a start, that the shrill, keening cries were coming from her own lips by way of some despairing black hole piercing her heart. She shoved her fist to her mouth, scraping her knuckles, willing herself not to think about the way in which André's head had been—

No . . . *no!* she cried silently. Everything would be all right if she simply focused her attention on the unbroken blue-and-white porcelain bowl that lay upon the floor. . . . She should think only of that lovely piece of Spode that had been overflowing with fragrant potpourri. . . .

And then she remembered the scattered petals, fallen like pastel snowflakes in all directions, their melancholy scent filling her with horror and regret, until she thought she would truly suffocate. All she could see was a crimson tide of blood washing over the polished cypress floor, engulfing the dried rose petals in a scarlet sea. And she was grateful that there was no one present in the flat on Julia Street to hear her mournful cries.

Only the walls.

Chapter Twenty-one

❧❧❧

April 19

Corlis was startled to feel arms embracing her and a deep voice demanding, "Sweetheart! What's the matter?"

In response, she pressed her moist cheek against the comforting surface of a zippered jacket. The fabric served as a convenient sponge for tears that were coursing down her cheeks for reasons that seemed unfathomable to her at the moment.

"Corlis . . . darlin'!" the voice persisted. "Why are you cryin'? What's happened?"

She opened her eyes and found herself standing next to a table where the familiar blue-and-white Spode bowl sat, heaped with dried flowers.

"Oh, glory . . ." she whispered, fighting off a vision of André Duvallon lying in front of the rosewood armoire that stood not five feet from where King now held her in his arms. Then suddenly that memory triggered another recollection: the terrible sense of sadness she'd experienced when King's friend, Dylan Fouché, had entered her bedroom on Julia Street with a burning sage smudge stick and tinkling bell in hand . . . the very same room where her ancestress may well have mourned, alone, the tragic death of a man who had abruptly taken his own life with a pistol shot to the head.

"Corlis, what on earth happened in the space of ten minutes to bring you to tears?" King questioned softly.

"Is that how long you were gone upstairs?" she said, barely above a whisper.

" 'Bout that," he confirmed. He grasped her gently by both

shoulders. "C'mon, now, sugar. What gives? Do we have ourselves a serious case of buyer's remorse?"

"I saw your ghost just now . . ." she disclosed slowly. "You may think I'm crazy, but I saw André Duvallon right here, in your living room. And he *did* shoot himself over near that armoire. If I'm not entirely out of my mind, I think he was the brother-in-law of some earlier Kingsbury relative of the Duvallons."

"Well . . . well," King said, putting a protective arm around her shoulders and guiding her toward a small settee covered in moss-green silk. "Aren't you the clever reporter to find out all that information from the phantom of the parlor," he teased gently. "So the Kingsburys and Duvallons have gotten into each other's hair *twice,* in two different generations. How New Orleans."

"Oh, God . . . who knows if a George Kingsbury was really married to André Duvallon's sister, Margaret, in the eighteen-forties?" She shook her head despondently. "This stuff's getting pretty heavy, King."

"What stuff—exactly—are you talkin' about?" he asked intently.

"The . . . ghosts . . . visions . . . trips back in time . . . whatever they are," she said weakly.

"Here . . . sit down, sugar," he urged. "Can I get you a glass of water?"

"No, nothing," Corlis said, declining to take a seat. "Let's leave, okay? I . . . I'd rather not stay . . . in this room," she finished weakly.

King took her by the hand and led her down the hallway toward the back of the house. "I can now vouch for the sayin' 'you look as if you've seen a ghost.' By the way," he asked gently, "how often do you encounter these otherworldly characters?"

Corlis halted midway to the kitchen door.

"Promise me you don't think I'm a complete loon?"

King gave her shoulders another squeeze. "Look, Ace . . . I'm the one who first *saw* this guy in my front parlor, remember? I don't exactly advertise that fact to people on the street, but who am I to say you've lost your grip?" He guided her into the kitchen, saying, "I want you to sit here and tell me all about it."

However, before she could elaborate further, a short, stocky figure suddenly appeared at the screen door in the pantry.

"Well, well," declared the balding man who appeared to be in his mid-fifties. "Took the Jag to the funeral, did you?" The man gave Corlis the once-over as he advanced further into the kitchen. "That must've impressed everybody. Did you give our regards to the Dumas family?"

"I did." King nodded brusquely as a woman with perfectly coiffed hair and a brittle smile also stepped into the kitchen. "I thought you and Dad were on Patrick Ryan's yacht this weekend?"

"We were," King's mother said shortly, "but your father wanted to come home early to watch some baseball game." The couple exchanged steely-eyed looks. Obviously there had been words on the journey home from the Gulf.

"Mother . . . Dad . . . meet Corlis McCullough," King said. "Corlis, this is my mother, Antoinette, and my father, Waylon." To his parents he said, "We just came by to check on Bethany and Grandmother Kingsbury. Gotta run. I'm just going to drop Corlis off at . . . her office."

"So *you're* Corlis McCullough?" Antoinette exclaimed. "From WJAZ, now, am I right?"

Still feeling shaky from her recent ordeal, all Corlis could do was nod.

"You're the TV gal that did the story about the weddin'," Waylon said accusingly. "And aren't you also the lady, all the way from California, helpin' King, here, stir up that bad publicity about the Selwyn buildings over on Canal Street?"

"I live in New Orleans now," Corlis replied, wondering how best she and King could make a rapid exit without seeming impolite.

Antoinette took a step closer to Corlis and said with an expression of solicitude that set Corlis's teeth on edge, "You were the one who did that real nice segment recently about the symphony's annual luncheon, didn't you?" She turned to Waylon, "There were some lovely shots of our floral centerpieces she showed on TV, Waylon," she reminded her husband sharply.

Then she smiled ingratiatingly at Corlis. "That was real sweet of you to give Flowers by Duvallon such a big boost."

Corlis nodded politely at both Mr. and Mrs. Duvallon. "I'm glad you were pleased," she managed lamely.

Just then King's grandmother appeared in the kitchen doorway on her walker, flanked by Aunt Bethany. Antoinette frowned and said, "It's not time for mother's lunch yet, Bethany."

"She heard your voices and wanted to come down to be with everybody," Aunt Bethany said timidly. She nodded in friendly fashion at Corlis and added, "She also wanted to meet King's friend, didn't you, Mother? She likes to watch you on TV."

"How do you do, Mrs. Kingsbury?" Corlis offered warmly.

"Very pretty," the frail old lady said, nodding solemnly. "Very, very pretty."

King's mother plastered another smile on her face and directed Bethany, "You'll have to organize Mother's dinner tonight. The drive home just wore me out. I think I'll lie down, and then I have my bridge club later."

"Well, we're off," King interjected quickly. He deposited a quick kiss on the cheek of his grandmother and aunt. Then he nodded in the direction of his parents and swiftly guided Corlis out the kitchen's back door.

They walked in silence to his car. Finally Corlis said, "King . . . can I ask you a question? Your mother and father *saw* the WWEZ-TV piece about Daphne's wedding, right?"

"They sure did," King replied, putting his key in the ignition and starting the Jaguar.

"Then why was your mother so civil to me, and why did she compliment me on the symphony luncheon story—which, by the way, was a totally worthless exercise in puff!"

King wheeled the car down St. Charles Avenue, heading for the Warehouse District. "Number one," he said, staring stonily through the windshield, "when it comes to Flowers by Duvallon, Mother loves publicity. Number two, in Louisiana, a person might kill you, but they'll be *real* polite doin' it. And number three, it's not a magnolia's style to tell you what she *really* thinks."

"Wow," Corlis said on a long breath. After a pause she added, "Your father seemed a little . . ."

"Testy? Abrupt? Rude?" King inquired with undisguised sarcasm. He thrust out his chin and spoke in a voice that was a close echo of Waylon Duvallon's, " 'How much you makin' now, boy? How 'bout payin' me back for bein' your daddy all these years?' "

"I caught the dig about the Jaguar."

"My daddy doesn't approve of the way I spend and donate the money I've earned," King said in an exaggerated drawl. "Says I owe him an early retirement."

"He talks to *you* that way? And what about your mother?"

"She's mainly interested in findin' out if I've been granted tenure yet." King flashed Corlis an ironic smile. "The son of one of her cousins is also up for the same slot. You remember him—Jonathan Poole."

"*Not* the guy named to Grover Jeffries's so-called Chair of Historic Preservation?" she gasped.

"The very one."

"A relative?" she confirmed philosophically.

"In N'awlings, darlin'? What else?"

She reached across the Jaguar's plush leather seat and patted his hand resting on the steering wheel. "They'd be crazy not to give you full tenure and a corner office!"

"Thank you, sugar," he replied quietly. "Believe me, I appreciate the vote of confidence in a town where the opposition to savin' historic buildings usually comes from my parents' best friends and business associates." Then he appeared to regain his even disposition and said with a grin, "Hey! Look at it this way: If I loose my teachin' job over fightin' for the Selwyn buildings, then I can give more time to the Preservation Resource Center—"

"Not to mention becoming a billionaire with your investments," she teased.

"That depends on the crazy market," he nodded judiciously. "And guess what else? I'd just be down the block from *you*!" His lighthearted tone reassured Corlis he'd at least partially recovered his morale. "Maybe I can stand under your window after midnight, and you can tell me more about André, the friendly ghost?"

"He wasn't so friendly. He was depressed, big-time," she replied soberly. Then, as dispassionately as she could, Corlis related the numerous instances in the last few months where her sense of smell had transported her to pre–Civil War New Orleans. Once again, she choked up when she described André Duvallon's suicide.

"It's all right, sweetheart," King said soothingly as he reached for her hand. "It must've been a real frightenin' experience for you today. Tell me why you think André Duvallon took his own life."

To her relief none of King's questions was facetious or skeptical, and he listened intently to her answers. "You know," she mused as King turned his car into Julia Street, "André Duvallon clearly hated the Americans that were pouring into New Orleans in the eighteen thirties and forties."

"The enmity between the two cultures is well documented," King agreed. "Why would a man with André's background feel any differently toward money-grubbin' Yankees? His despair about being extorted apparently drove him to end his life."

"I can't *believe* we're talking so casually about my seeing some apparition *off himself* in your front parlor! Tell the truth, now. You don't think I've got a screw loose or am coming unglued, do you?"

"No more than I am," he responded ruefully. King parked the Jaguar in front of Corlis's front door and turned off the ignition. Then he tilted his head back, lowered his lids, and regarded her speculatively. "And even if you are, it doesn't change *one* thing."

"And that is?" she asked warily.

"You may be wacky, but you're still a great kisser."

"King!" Corlis protested. "Be serious."

"Would you consider lettin' this source kiss you one last time before you turn into a pumpkin?"

"King . . . no! We made a deal, remember, and we'd better start getting used to it. Besides, I don't trust either of us to exercise restraint in the kissing department."

He arched an eyebrow and gripped the steering wheel with both hands.

"Okay . . . a deal's a deal, but you'll pay later, Ace. Big-time."

"Fine by me," she said, her spirits lightening a notch. She turned and held his gaze, yearning to touch him again. "However," she added regretfully, "given the heat that the Selwyn buildings fight is bound to generate from here out, I don't think you and I should be talking about ghosts—or anything else that isn't strictly to do with the story."

"You sure are a stickler for followin' rules, sugar," King replied mildly. He got out of the car, came around to her side, opened the passenger door, and helped her retrieve her overnight case.

She dug for her key in her shoulder bag as they walked toward her front door.

"Let *me* do that," he said, taking the door key from her hand.

Corlis laughed self-consciously. The front door ajar, they turned to face each other again.

"I can't wait for this to be over," she said, fighting a wave of melancholy.

"Me, too," he replied softly. King seized her hand and pressed it to his lips in a gesture as courtly as any André Duvallon had ever employed. Then he flashed her his killer grin. "You know what?" he demanded. "We're goin' to *win*!"

Feeling as if she were about to burst into tears, Corlis answered with an earnest plea, "We've got to get something straight. Much as I applaud what you're trying to do, as a *reporter*, I just can't be a partisan in your cause, King. I just *can't*."

"You went to the costume party with me," he reminded her. "You were as excited as I was to find Grover's incriminating memo."

"But I went there with a different agenda than you did," she protested. "My role as a journalist is to tell the story concerning the threat to those buildings *as it unfolds*, without my trying to influence the outcome. I'm sleuthing for facts for the benefit of the television viewers, not the preservationists. You guys will *use* the information you uncover to try to change public policy, which is *your* job!" she explained. "My job is different. The *public* owns the airwaves and grants people like Andy Zamora a license to use them for profit. In return, the public is owed honest information. My sole task is to gather and disseminate information about what's happening in the community, so the viewing public can make up its *own* mind about political issues that are important to it."

"Why, Miz Reporter," King grinned. "You're just as much of an idealist as I am. I bet your aunt Marge taught you that speech."

Corlis reached up and smoothed away a shock of dark-brown hair from his forehead. "She did," she said soberly. "So, what about it, King?" she asked with a level look. "Can you understand what I'm saying here, about our *separate* roles?"

"I'll try," he responded, his gaze troubled. "I guess I have to keep remindin' myself that we really *do* have different jobs."

"That's right," she nodded, "and thanks for recognizing that." She hesitated a moment, and added, "Good luck."

"Do the rules stipulate it's okay to wish me that?" he asked in a slightly mocking tone.

She pushed her front door open wide and tossed her bags onto the foyer's floor. She hesitated a moment, then turned to face him.

"Oh, *screw* the rules!" she exclaimed, kissing him hard on the mouth. She dashed inside the door and quickly shut it behind her so she wouldn't be tempted to ask him in. She shouted through the thick wooden panels, "That's the last kiss you get from me until this damned Selwyn story is *old* news!"

During the next weeks Corlis and King both kept true to their pledge. They met and spoke only in public while the proposal for demolishing the Selwyn buildings made its way successfully through hearings before the Landmark and City Planning Commissions. Nor did they communicate when Edgar Dumas assumed the presidency of the New Orleans City Council and put the matter of demolition and the Del Mar hotel project on the upcoming council agenda for further debate.

They didn't even exchange phone calls after Corlis's boss handed her a copy of *Arts This Week* in which Jack Ebert hinted at a "cozy—some say personal—relationship between the leader of the opposition to the construction of the Del Mar Hotel and a high-profile TV reporter covering the story." Ebert reiterated King's brush with the law when a student in California and raised the issue of the associate professor's moral fitness for being granted tenure at the university, come June.

"*Jeez,* this is outrageous!" Corlis exclaimed to Zamora.

"I assume Ebert based part of his piece on seeing you with King at Galatoire's and at the costume party, correct?" Zamora pressed.

"I imagine so," Corlis replied, staring across her boss's wide desk while trying to avoid the piercing stare from his lawyer, Marvin Glimp.

Read out of context, Jack's magazine story was devastatingly damaging to King personally. The piece also went so far as to cast the preservationists as part of the "lunatic fringe element" of the environmental movement. The story could be lethal to *her* if her name was revealed publicly as the reporter in question. Jack also must know, she thought darkly, that he was treading close to the line in the defamation department.

"And am I correct that you and King are not seeing each other in any other context than reporter and source?" Zamora asked, obviously for Glimp's benefit.

"I haven't seen King alone or talked to him privately in just under a month," Corlis replied. However, her conscience prompted a further disclosure. "You both should know, though, that in mid-April, I attended the funeral of Edgar Dumas's sister-in-law. Emelie Dumas had been the Kingsbury-Duvallon's cook for thirty years. King provided the entrée. I seized the chance to judge the impact on one elderly woman whose entire way of life was uprooted by the Good Times Shopping Plaza project."

Her recitation was the truth—if not the *whole* truth, she considered with a twinge of guilt. Corlis hesitated for a moment and made the decision not to reveal that she and King had stayed together at the old Kingsbury fishing cabin. Certainly not that they'd slept together while there.

It's my private life, and it's not affecting how I cover the story, especially since King and I are now giving each other a wide berth.

And oh how hard that separation was turning out to be, she thought bleakly.

"Did Edgar Dumas see you at that black woman's funeral?" Glimp demanded, his harsh words forcing Corlis's attention back to the two men. Marvin turned to address Zamora. "Edgar's bound to know that his sister-in-law was the Duvallon's family cook, and you know how touchy—"

"Yes, he knew the connection," Corlis interrupted, turning to face the agitated lawyer. "That day I asked Dumas if he would be willing to do an interview with me. I told him I'd like to hear his views regarding the difficulty for elected officials to balance the need for new construction projects, which help the city's economy, with the desire to preserve the unique history of New Orleans, where tourism is the number one industry."

"I'll just bet Edgar'd *love* to pontificate on that subject!" Zamora said with a cynical laugh.

"I already put the interview on tape and stored it in our vault," she replied. "I'm saving it for when you give me the okay to do another piece—after the city council votes whether to demolish the Selywn buildings."

"Good," Zamora said shortly.

Marvin Glimp chimed in, "Even so, McCullough . . . just remember, you're still skating on thin ice around here."

Aren't I just? Corlis answered silently, thinking of Jack Ebert's twisted use of the facts.

"Just tell the story as it happens, you got that?" her boss admonished her gruffly. "No fancy stuff, and avoid any more junkets with Duvallon, no matter what! You can be in the same public place, at the same time—if it has to do directly with this story—but you can't be seen *going* anywhere together. You got that?" he repeated.

"Got it," Corlis replied stiffly. She turned to leave.

"And by the way," Zamora added in an offhand manner. "Good job getting Dumas to go on camera. That footage'll save our ass when we need some balance after the showdown at city hall next week, right?"

Corlis gave both men the thumbs-up sign and hurried out of Zamora's office before Marvin Glimp or her boss could hand out any more directives that would further tie her hands.

She immediately made for the employees' lot and soon was steering her Lexus down Canal Street toward the river for a meeting called by Althea LaCroix. She passed the Selwyn buildings and turned left into the French Quarter, parking as close as possible to the library that housed the Historic New Orleans Collection.

"Hey, Corlis!" Althea hailed her as she headed up the granite steps of the elegantly restored beaux arts building. "Whatcha know? Thanks for comin' here today."

"Thanks for asking me," she replied as the pair trudged up the marble staircase and entered the beautifully appointed reading room on the second floor. "Are Keith LaCroix and Dylan coming, too?"

"The Gang of Three?" Althea said, laughing. "You betcha! We've actually gotten several black history professors, African-American business folks, and owners of historic properties around town to join together to fight Jeffries's petition to demolish the Selwyn buildings. Keith and King see it as sort of our very own Rainbow Coalition to preserve this landmark. How's this for a battle cry? 'Long live Free People of Color and their nineteenth-century entrepreneurial spirit!' " she joked.

"Have you already approached the Preservation Resource Center?" Corlis asked, ignoring her mention of King's name. "Will they support you guys?"

"Oh yeah!" Althea enthused. "As a matter of fact, King Duvallon's gonna meet with us today, too. He's a great buddy of the librarian, who's been a huge help trackin' down the buildin's history."

King was coming to this meeting? Corlis felt her heart lurch with forbidden anticipation. She lectured herself severely to calm down.

"Hmmmm," she replied noncommittally.

"It was King's idea to ask *you* to come," Althea added. "He thought you might be interested in our next project."

"You mean, to do another story for WJAZ?" she asked warily.

"Well, maybe. But first of all, we want to do a TV *commercial*!" Althea announced proudly. "You know, a public service announcement to the community. Somethin' catchy that touts the black history aspect in the fight to preserve the Selwyn buildin's, that tells folks this is *their* history that Grover Jeffries and the Del Mar people want to demolish!" Althea pointed across the reading room where King stood next to the reference desk, deep in conversation with the librarian. "King figured you and your cameraman, Virgil, would know just how to pull off makin' this commercial."

"Oh, Althea . . ." Corlis began, her heart sinking, "WJAZ can't take sides in this. We're not supposed to show any favoritism—"

Just then they both turned at the sound of someone's footsteps taking the stairs behind them, two at a time.

"Hey, baby, where y'at?" Virgil said, patting Althea smartly on her derriere. Corlis's stalwart crew member was minus his camera, which startled her. "Hi, boss," he added, more subdued.

When Althea strode on ahead, Corlis took Virgil aside and whispered, "We can't help them produce a TV commercial, Virgil. We're supposed to be neutral, remember?"

"What's wrong with givin' a little friendly advice in my off hours to my black brothers and sisters?" he asked, his brown eyes widening innocently. "And besides, I'm not gonna be the shooter on the deal. . . ."

"Well, *that's* a relief. Zamora and his legal beagle called me on the carpet, saying I was *already* being too sympathetic to the preservationists on this story."

"To me," Virgil said softly, "this is more than just another story. I didn't even *know* some black folks were free before the Civil War. And I sure as hell didn't know blacks *owned* most of those buildin's way back then and ran their own businesses on Canal Street!" He cuffed her gently on the chin. "This is *history*, girl, so if I steer Althea in the right direction for this TV idea she's got, go sue me."

"I won't sue you," Corlis whispered back. "I just don't want Zamora to *fire* you!"

"I'll be cool," Virgil grinned. "Very cool. C'mon, boss lady," he urged, "if you and I don't join them over there, people'll be talkin' 'bout *us* instead of you and King!"

"What?" she protested.

"Even when you two are walkin' on opposite sides of the street, the temperature rises," he teased her. "You're not foolin' nobody, sugar."

Corlis leveled a disgusted look at him but didn't reply.

During the meeting held in a small conference room off the main reading room, Corlis did her utmost to keep her attention focused on everyone in the group except King. She nodded politely at architect Keith LaCroix and historian Barry Jefferson. However, she couldn't fight off a big hug from Dylan Fouché.

"No more weird stuff goin' on when you go into your bedroom?" he whispered in her ear.

"Nope," she replied, ignoring the curious glances from the others. Someday she might tell him about seeing André Duvallon in King's living room, but certainly not *now.* As the meeting progressed she studiously made notes in her reporter's notebook, never offering an opinion or even asking a question.

"So," Althea said, "a reliable source has given me the name of a freelance team who can shoot our 'Save the Selwyn' spot." She looked over at King. "Now it's up to you to find us the money to pay these guys that Vir—" She interrupted herself, then continued, ". . . pay these camera crew guys I heard about. Any ideas?"

King glanced briefly at Corlis and replied, "Mr. and Mrs. Mallory and a few other folks have said they'd match what I'm willin' to put up to help pay for this thing—though they haven't told me yet how much. Mrs. Mallory is related to Paul Tulane on her mama's side. As you all know, Tulane was a successful merchant, before the university was founded, and one of the original white partners in the buildin' project," he explained further.

Mallory . . . Mallory. As in Cindy Lou Mallory? *Ms. Magnolia, wrecker of weddings? Her parents?*

My, my, Corlis thought ruefully, Miss Cindy and her mama must be willing to do virtually anything to try to win back the affections of the dashing—and discreetly wealthy—Kingsbury Duvallon. But why in the world would Mr. Integrity accept money from the Mallorys? Couldn't he get anyone else to match his contributions besides *them*?

Well, sugar, this is N'awlings!

Before Corlis could recover from this bit of intelligence, Althea was asking her a question. "Would you and your TV crew be interested in doin' a story that follows black LaCroixs and Fouchés touring Reverie plantation, tryin' to find their roots?" she asked with a sly smile.

"Why, Ms. LaCroix," Corlis said, forcing a reciprocating smile while she put everything else out of her mind except doing her job, "I'm sure my boss would consider that legitimate news. WJAZ would *love* to tag along. Tomorrow?"

"They open at ten A.M.," Althea replied.

Corlis then gathered up her belongings and said good-bye to the group, offering only a curt nod in the direction of the Hero of New Orleans—a veritable powerhouse, apparently, when it came to raising funds for a cause he believed in.

Corlis spent the next morning supervising Virgil and Manny while they followed Althea and Julien LaCroix and Dylan Fouché, with video and sound recorders, around the magnificent Reverie plantation's grand manor house.

It had been a distinctly unnerving experience to wander about a place she'd already "seen" in one of her strange visions. In the slave quarters at the back of the property, sepia-colored photographs of African-American women in long calico skirts and men in work clothes bore startling resemblances to the profiles of the visitors who possessed the same last names as the early white owners.

"When was photography invented, anyway?" Althea wondered aloud.

"The caption here says this was taken in 1843," Corlis murmured. "I think I read somewhere that daguerreotypes were invented in the late 1830s."

"White Fouchés owned the neighboring plantation back then," Dylan explained, pointing to entries in a family Bible that lay on a table in one of the sparsely furnished cabins. "The original Althea Fouché was probably a mulatto fathered by the white owner and a slave woman on that plantation. Eventually Althea's daughter, Martine, a quadroon, caught the eye of Julien LaCroix. Any children they had together would have been octoroons and probably would have taken the name LaCroix."

But ah . . . let us not forget Julien's father, Etienne, Corlis mused silently. If only she could verify that, through a twist of fate, Martine had had sexual relationships with both father and son. How had poor Julien taken the news of André's suicide?

Had he ever received the letter his banker wrote to him, detailing the unholy link the LaCroix men had forged with the beautiful Free Woman of Color? Was Julien and Martine's mixed-blood baby perhaps the progenitor of the musical LaCroix family?

And what of her own ancestors, the McCulloughs? pondered Corlis. What ultimately happened to Corlis Bell McCullough and her ne'er-do-well mate, the builder named Randall? Had they and Ian Jeffries actually been run out of New Orleans on a rail?

"Can you all finish shooting this last bit without me?" she abruptly asked her crew. "I want to check on something in the main house, okay? Meet you out front in twenty minutes."

Virgil shot her a startled look and shrugged. "Sure, boss lady," he replied accommodatingly. "But make it half an hour."

"Will do."

Corlis dashed across the wide lawn to reenter the front door just as the final tour of the day departed out the back steps. She was certain that no one saw her slip past the red velvet rope, enter the small room off the front foyer, and quietly close the door. Earlier she'd spied a crystal decanter filled with absinthe standing on a leather-topped desk. Hesitating only a moment, she sat down and gazed apprehensively at the bottle of chartreuse-colored spirits. The guide had said it was a less potent mixture than in the old days, made of green dye, crushed eucalyptus leaves, and anise, whose combined odors closely approximated the lethal liquor brewed in the nineteenth century.

Corlis involuntarily shuddered. The sight of the decanter recalled the vision of André Duvallon lying in green absinthe and dark-red blood.

I must find out what happened to Corlis after André's suicide. Just one more time . . .

Corlis stared at the crystal decanter, took a deep breath, and removed the stopper. Could she actually *bring about* one of these sojourns back in time, she wondered, as butterflies began to flutter in her stomach.

She bent over the container, closed her eyes, and inhaled deeply. Immediately her nostrils began to sting from the concoction's pungent aroma. How could she possibly give her television viewers an accurate background of the Selwyn buildings if she didn't know the resolution of the story, or whether the visions she'd experienced depicted historical truth?

I have to know what happened to these people. . . . I have to know. . . . I have to know. . . .

By her second whiff of the enervating drink, Corlis was conscious only of the mixture's asphyxiating odor of menthol and licorice—a smell so strong, it took her breath away.

Chapter Twenty-two

May 22, 1842

"I *have* to know!" Adelaide cried, pointing a trembling finger at a letter lying open on the desk. "Is it true? Did you deliberately choose your *father's* own concubine as your mistress?"

Outside the study window, the wide veranda was deserted, as were the cane fields that stretched beyond the oak grove where lacy moss hung motionless in the quiescent May air.

"Good God, Adelaide . . . you've been drinking that damnable absinthe again," Julien said accusingly. His wife reeked of alcohol, and the mere sight of her turned his stomach.

She looked as if she'd slept in the white cotton gown she was wearing. Her pudgy ringlets were unkempt, frizzing unbecomingly around her mottled cheeks. Dark pouches swelled prominently beneath her haggard eyes, and her nose was mottled with tiny broken blood vessels.

Julien had carried his own portmanteau up to the slope-roofed house, while Albert secured the plantation's steam packet down at the dock. From a second-story window, Adelaide had spotted the boat and was waiting for him on the veranda. She'd followed him into his study, haranguing him at every step. Now he took a seat at his desk, and his gaze settled on the letter that she had opened, breaking its wax seal.

"Well?" she demanded harshly. "At least have the decency to tell the truth! Answer me! Did you deliberately pick your father's slut as your *placée* to publicly humiliate me?"

"I haven't been in this house two minutes, and you begin to fling your invented insults in my face." He grabbed the missive from his wife's hand and placed it on the desktop, where a silver tray holding a crystal decanter three-quarters full of pale green absinthe stood beside two matching cut-crystal tumblers. "And how dare you open a letter from my banker, addressed to *me*!" he added angrily.

"I! *Inventing* insults, you say?" Adelaide burst out. "You have been gone from this house for weeks!"

He turned, intending to bolt from the room, but Adelaide's next words immobilized him.

"Your mother lies dead upstairs from yellow fever, and you—"

"What?" Julien exclaimed, shocked.

"Dead," she repeated succinctly. "Three days ago she fell ill from the fever. All the slaves ran away when they heard it was yellow jack, and therefore, I had no way to get word to you at your precious warehouse. And now your father is about to breathe his last. Not a servant remains in this house, and yet you chastise me for opening the *post*!" she screamed shrilly. "You are an *imbecile*, Julien LaCroix. All lies in wreckage around you, and all you can think—"

Julien's eyes were riveted on the first paragraph of André Duvallon's letter. He waved a distracted hand, as if to ward off a pesky fly. Then he began to read again from the top of the page, his lips parted in horrified surprise. André's sordid account of his relationship with the late Henri Girard was only a precursor to the scandalous revelation that Julien's father had, in fact, been Martine's "patron" all those years, and Lisette, his own half sister!

"Julien!" Adelaide broke in sharply. "Look at me! Do you deny that Martine Fouché is the strumpet your father kept on Rampart Street—whom *you* have now gotten *with child*?"

Julien looked up and, with a murderous glare, spat out, "Get out of this room! Go! Leave me in peace, you damnable jade!"

"I, a jade?" Adelaide gasped. "You left *us*! You LaCroixs always leave your white women. Your great-grandfather regularly sated his lust with slave women at the Fouchés's, upriver. It seems to be a family tradition."

"You speak like a common guttersnipe," Julien exclaimed doggedly. "You know nothing of these matters."

"Oh, you think not?" Adelaide retorted. "I learned at my mother's *knee* to turn a blind eye to the outrages that are visited on wives by their husbands! And now André reveals that your father betrayed your mother with your beloved Martine. In case you haven't sorted it all out, your own progeny by that harlot will be a half sister to the child, Lisette—as are *you*, my fine cocksman! This is the kind of *family* that your ambition and lechery have spawned!"

She looked at Julien with an expression of abhorrence so intense, he thought she would surely shoot him, had she a pistol in her possession. Shaking his head as if to wake from a living nightmare, Julien turned away from Adelaide and peered at André's letter.

"It cannot be true . . ." he murmured. "André sounds as if he intends to—"

"Ah, but it *is* true, if Martine Fouché is actually your *placée*," Adelaide said. "You and your father have unwittingly plowed the same field, monsieur. By now, I assure you Etienne has come to that conclusion, even if you did not—fool that you are."

A terrible silence descended in the room, unbroken but for the ticking of the grandfather clock that stood in the adjacent hallway.

"But I loved her," Julien whispered brokenly as he finished reading the letter. "I truly—" He raised his eyes from André's frantic scrawl and stared at his wife, unseeing. "Martine never told me. . . ." he murmured wonderingly. "All this time, while we were partners during the construction of those buildings . . . she *never told me*!"

"What a pity Etienne couldn't call you out for cuckolding him," Adelaide laughed with bitter irony. "But then, in his rage over the threats to expose LaCroix, Duvallon, and Girard's dirty little secrets, his brain's blood vessels burst," she taunted, "and rendered him a mute! And of course, neither of you thought to ask your mother or me what *we* had heard whispered about, did you?"

With a lightning sweep of his hand, Julien brushed the entire silver tray off his desk. In one blinding act of fury, the absinthe sprayed a pale emerald shower onto his wife's disheveled white dimity dress from neck to hem, staining her long gown the color of rotting limes. The two tumblers shattered in a flurry of glass shards, but the heavy crystal decanter rolled, intact, across the sisal carpet to the other side of the study.

"And now you know the whole, squalid story," Julien exclaimed harshly, "and you rejoice in my anguish, do you not? You absolutely *revel* that Martine never revealed that Lisette is my father's child."

"All the pieces didn't fall into place until I read André's letter," Adelaide said in a dull monotone, all her passion spent. "I didn't know for certain that your father had sired a child by some black whore, and I didn't know, until we returned from France, that the whore was Martine Fouché."

"I always suspected that André Duvallon and Henri Girard were . . . unnaturally fond of each other," Julien murmured, "but I found them both decent chaps. But I never thought Henri served as the shill for my father's lust for . . . Martine," he concluded softly.

"Or your father . . . as a shill for Henri's lust for another *man*! It worked out so conveniently for everyone," Adelaide said spitefully.

In an explosion of fury, Julien pounded his fist against the desk and glared at his wife.

"Oh, do *spare* me your hypocritical rantings!" he shouted. He surveyed Adelaide's rumpled state with a look of pure loathing. "You've spent your entire life hiding behind your own *unnatural* appetites—for food and spirits and, I would wager, for foul manipulations by your own hand—for *I* certainly have never succeeded in stimulating any pleasure in you," he added caustically.

He was gratified to hear her shocked gasp at his crude accusations. Adelaide's pale cheeks, as devoid of color as her mother-in-law's decomposing corpse upstairs, began to stain with streaks of red. After all that had happened between them, he mused absently, there would not, *could* not be any reconciliation after this day. He might as well speak his mind and be done with it!

"Let this whole diseased family be damned to hell!" Julien exclaimed.

Adelaide met her husband's tormented gaze. "Oh, don't look

so injured, Julien," she declared coolly. "The villain in this piece is, and always has been, your father. He's been wild with fever these last days and behaved contemptibly to me, even though I was the only one left to nurse him. He is *finally* dying, too, thank God, if he isn't already dead. No matter."

She stooped to pick up the unbroken crystal decanter, still a quarter full of absinthe. Then she faced her husband and declared softly, "One last thing. If I don't succumb to the fever, in the future I shall make my home with my brother, Lafayette, in New Orleans. Eventually he will marry, of course, but he is kind and will shelter me for the rest of my days as a result of what has happened here," she added with a satisfied air. "Etienne LaCroix is now your problem. I leave the disgusting creature in your care."

"My God, Adelaide, have you no—?"

However, his sentence remained unfinished as he watched his wife turn away and advance unsteadily toward the study door. She held the neck of the crystal decanter between the fingers of her plump right hand, and in the ensuing silence, the liquor's opalescent green contents made a faint sloshing sound as she made her exit.

"Good-bye, Julien," she said pleasantly over her shoulder. "Yellow jack has killed half your slaves, and the healthy ones, you'll have to hunt down. But," she added, turning toward him briefly with a mocking smile, "Reverie is finally yours. Perhaps you, the Fouché woman, and your father's bastard—along with the new babe that the dressmakers in the town whisper is nigh to term—will *all* make their home here. How delightful for you," she added with biting sarcasm. "In any case, *au revoir*. I shall go to my brother in New Orleans on horseback."

Julien sat stock-still, listening to the sound of Adelaide's receding steps. He had no notion of how long it was before he again heard her heavy footfall on the stairs and watched her through the open study door make her departure across the front threshold. In her pudgy hand she clasped a carpeted satchel. In a daze, Julien stood and observed through the window the sway of her frothy skirts as she waddled across the veranda and down the path in the direction of the stables. His wife's enormous derriere bloomed beneath her stiff, corseted waist. The sight of her retreat disgusted him almost as much as the contents of André's letter lying on his leather-topped desk.

Eventually Julien summoned the energy to climb the grand, curving staircase. The fetid stench filling the air announced that the LaCroix patriarch and his wife were no more. Within an hour Julien had donned gloves and a silk handkerchief to cover his nose and mouth, and dug his parents' graves. In a shallow trench he buried his mother and father in the bedsheets in which they had died. By late afternoon he made his way through the eerily deserted cane fields to the riverbank. His boyhood friend, Albert, was nowhere to be seen. Alone, he fired up the small steam packet *Reverie*.

Numb with fatigue and shock, he guided the boat downriver at a slow, steady speed, careful to stay at enough distance from the shore to avoid sand bars, and close enough to keep out of the treacherous currents that could swamp the craft in an instant.

Martine hadn't told him . . . hadn't told him . . . a sorrowful voice repeated in his head.

From the moment Corlis Bell McCullough returned from André's house on Orange Street, she had not donned a corset or, for that matter, left her rooms on Julia Street. Nor had Randall returned home. By late afternoon she had sent Hetty out with her two sons to play at the house of a neighbor child. Somehow the sound of their piping voices made her want to scream.

Corlis opened the bedroom door and, like a sleepwalker, wandered slowly down the hallway toward the parlor. An unseasonable May rain had been falling in sheets for several hours, but now watery sunlight pierced the thunderheads outside the sitting-room windows and glistened on the wrought-iron gallery that hung over the street.

What in the world had been happening since André had shot himself? she wondered. Who had learned of his death by now? Would Randall be arrested if André had left a suicide note somewhere that revealed the whole sordid business? Or perhaps the secret of Ian Jeffries's financial hooliganism would simply die with the young banker, and she alone would know of the calumny committed by her husband and his partner. André's ominous prediction echoed in her ears.

Ian Jeffries would not hesitate to do you or your husband bodily harm.

She *must* find out what was going on! At the very least she should venture over to Girod Street and pawn her last gemstone bracelet for her flight from New Orleans.

Corlis quickly donned a wide-collared hunter-green jacket and skirt trimmed with black braid. She must appear as if everything were normal, she cautioned herself. She selected a small black bowler hat, with feathers to match, and pulled on black crocheted gloves. Lastly she seized a lacy black parasol from the umbrella stand near the door and squared her shoulders.

No one must know what I've been privy to.

It could mean her own personal safety.

The *banquette* outside glistened from the recent rain. However, Julia Street had remained a channel of alluvial mud. Several times en route she was forced to press her back against buildings to avoid being showered in muck from a passing carriage.

At Girod Street the pawnbroker leered at her over the counter.

"I'd pay for more than what this bauble's worth if you've a mind for a different exchange," he said suggestively, fingering her wrist as well as the bracelet in question.

"Sir," she replied stiffly, "I will take this gem to your competitor across the road if you do not quote me a fair price for it."

Grudgingly he offered half the bracelet's value, but she grabbed the gold coins he offered. At least the money was enough to cover an escape from this swamp for herself and the children.

It was close to dusk when Corlis neared the structures that her husband and Ian Jeffries had erected. She eyed the stately row of columns stretching down the entire block and considered the irony that their classic Greek design had come from the minds of such lowly creatures as Randall McCullough and his partner.

Her apprehension turned to a grinding foreboding when she went around to Common Street and cautiously peered into the saddlery. Mr. Bates sat at his desk, unmindful of her presence in the doorway. Adjacent to Bates's office, she could hear horses pawing the straw in their stalls, but she saw no sign of anyone but the stable boys.

She retraced her steps to Canal Street and stopped a moment to gaze into the shop window of the dressmaker, Annette Fouché. Out of the corner of her eye she caught sight of Julien LaCroix, at a dead run, approaching the front entrance to the town house of Martine Fouché.

"Mr. LaCroix!" she hailed his harried figure. She plastered a smile on her face. "Excuse me, Mr. LaCroix. . . . May I have a word with you for a moment?"

But Julien apparently hadn't heard her call to him, for he had already disappeared through the front door. Corlis followed in his wake, drawn as if by someone reeling in a fish on Bayou Lacombe. She stared, her mouth slightly ajar, as the heir to Reverie plantation dashed through the large foyer, down a hallway, and took the stairway to Martine's small gas-lit reception hall, two steps at a time. Corlis had just reached a round table where visitors left their calling cards when Julien, on the landing above, began to pound on Martine Fouché's door.

"Martine!" he shouted. "Let me in! Martine, I demand that you open this door at once!"

In an instant the door did open, but only a crack.

"Hush!" a voice hissed. "Martine's just fallen asleep!"

"It is five o'clock in the afternoon!" Julien retorted. "I demand—"

"She's had the baby," the voice said accusingly. "As I predicted, the minute you left to go upriver—"

Dumbfounded, Corlis gazed up the stairwell at Julien, who applied his shoulder to the door and forced it open.

"Well . . . what was it?" he asked in a trembling voice that revealed his agitation. "Boy or girl?"

"A boy. We've named him Julien . . . after you," Althea Fouché announced reproachfully.

"Sweet Jesus!" Julien exploded in bitterness and despair.

"Julien . . . I—I . . . thought you'd be pleased," interposed a voice from farther inside the Fouché apartments.

In the flickering gaslight Corlis could barely make out the shadow of Althea Fouché, who stood blocking Julien's entry into the flat. Behind her, an open door framed a large ornately carved canopied plantation bed in the chamber beyond. In the parlor, on a bloodred silk chaise longue, a figure lay supine, poised against an enormous mound of lacy pillows.

"Pleased?" Julien echoed. "*Pleased?*" he repeated, his voice rising in a wave of angry accusation. He strode into the foyer and slammed the door behind him. Corlis heard a muffled voice say, "Would you two have played me for a fool until the bitter end?"

By this time Corlis had advanced up the stairs to the top of the landing. She could distinctly hear the argument that was raging behind the closed door.

"Julien LaCroix!" Althea cried. "Stop this at once!"

Next Corlis heard the sound of an object being flung against an interior wall.

"Damn you both!" Julien shouted.

"I simply cannot permit this!" Althea declared loudly. "Control yourself. It's outrageous that you should barge in like this . . . especially *now*!"

"I suppose you expect me to leave my calling card, like Etienne or Henri once did?" retorted Julien, furious at the women's betrayal. "I am the *father* of this infant, Althea, and I demand to hear the truth from Martine's own lips!"

"Julien . . ." protested the feeble voice of Martine Fouché. "You are no gentleman to be behaving this way. You must go at once. We will talk of these complicated matters when I have regained my strength. I promise you," she beseeched. "Return in two days' time and I shall—"

"You shall *what*?" Julien shouted. "Erase all that has happened? Mend what cannot be mended? You two have *lied* and *cheated* and *deceived* us all! You were in league with Jeffries and McCullough all along, weren't you?"

"*Never!*" Althea exclaimed.

"Well, believe me, those two blackguards will be run out of New Orleans forever, if I don't kill them first!" Julien shouted. "And your daughter, Lisette, will never forgive you, Martine, when she learns of your treachery!"

Corlis suppressed a small gasp when she heard Julien rage against Randall and Ian. She glanced over her shoulder, debating if she should make a hasty retreat down the stairs and escape undetected. Yet, she was driven to speak to Julien about André. To ask him—

"Lisette will understand that what was done was done for her security, *and* the future of my new grandson!" Althea declared stoutly. "Don't think we weren't aware that it was *your* ambition, as well as that of McCullough and Jeffries, to wrest this land from Martine. And all the while you protested your love for her."

"I did love her! I *do* love you, Martine," Julien cried, anguished. "As God is my witness, I saw *past* the differences in our races, but you never *disclosed* to me—"

"All you really wanted was the deed," Althea interrupted. "My daughter may nót be bold enough to say it, but I shall. You behaved like a cad, Julien LaCroix!"

"Julien?" Martine said softly. "Be just. I truly care for you. But my mother and I were being threatened at every turn. What could you expect us to do, under the circumstances?"

"To be true to our love," he replied sorrowfully. "Speak truth to me. That is what I expected of you."

"And did *you* always speak the truth to Martine, monsieur?" Althea demanded.

Corlis was startled when the door at the top of the stairs was yanked open and Julien appeared at the threshold.

"Julien," Martine called beseechingly. "I am your mistress, with no legal claim to you *or* your affections. . . ."

"We had long gone past being merely patron and mistress, Martine," he said in a voice laced with despair. "At some point in this sorry affair, you should have told me of your prior relationship with my father. Who knows better than his son what he . . . was like? I would have understood. Now I cannot."

"So you are judge *and* jury!" Althea spat. "The tale is always about *you*, isn't it Julien LaCroix? The white man's drama!"

Shocked to hear such disgust openly expressed by a woman—and a black one at that—to a white man, Corlis retreated into a corner shrouded in deep shadow.

"I cannot answer for what I might do," Julien said stiffly, "if I remain here a moment longer!"

"Then *go!*" ordered Althea, who stood by the door.

Julien strode out of the apartment and down the staircase. He seemed oblivious to Corlis's presence, less than five feet away. Nor did Althea glance in her direction, but flung shut the door after their visitor with a resounding bang. Corlis remained frozen on the landing only an instant, but by this time Julien had reached the foyer.

"Mr. LaCroix!" she called in a loud whisper. "Mr. LaCroix . . . please wait!"

Julien whirled around in the corridor with a startled look written on his distraught features. "What in heaven—?" he began. Then he scowled, his black mustache drawing into a tight straight line above his upper lip.

"Please, just spare me a moment," Corlis pleaded, rushing toward him. "I was with André when he—"

She fell silent, emotion constricting her throat. She gazed up at his pain-filled countenance as her own eyes misted over, and wondered at the misery they'd all suffered in this infernal swamp.

"*You* were with André?" he asked, incredulous. "He showed you his letter to me?"

"Letter? There was a letter? He must have written it while I was waiting on the veranda," she murmured. "Before he—"

"Before he *what?*" Julien demanded.

Corlis stared at him, stricken. "You don't know what happened? André's letter didn't tell you what he was planning to do?"

"No," Julien replied, his eyes full of dread. "What did he do?"

"André's dead. He shot himself. In the temple."

"Oh, God! No!" Julien said, bringing a hand to his ashen face as if to ward off a blow.

"But his *driver* knew he'd killed himself! Wasn't he the one who delivered the letter to you?"

"He delivered it to Reverie when I wasn't there. My wife received it. We've had the fever up there. Perhaps he merely handed it to a servant near the gate and left without calling at the house. André's missive did not state directly that he planned to take his own life, but I was worried. . . . I wondered—"

"It was so . . . dreadful," Corlis said, barely above a whisper. "He had asked me to leave his house," she disclosed honestly. "I told him that I had only just learned of Ian Jeffries's extortion, but I had no idea that he would . . . that André would do . . . what he did." She choked as tears began to stream down her face.

"Your husband was Jeffries's partner," Julien said, unmoved by her show of emotion, "and I'll wager he was in the thick of it."

"He may very well have been. He's a weak man," Corlis agreed sadly. "I dare say he didn't put up much protest against Jeffries's scheme to extort money and influence, but I really don't think Randall was anything but an accomplice. At least that is what André led me to believe. André warned me that Ian Jeffries, if pushed, wouldn't hesitate to do Randall and me bodily harm." She looked at Julien beseechingly. "That's why I had to warn you! Please be careful. There's been too much—"

"Did you actually see . . . André kill himself?"

"No," she said slowly, dropping her hands from her face. "But I heard the shot and ran to him immediately afterward." She tilted her head in order to meet Julien's troubled gaze. His face was very pale and glistening with perspiration. His cheeks were sunken. What a lot they had both endured, she thought. She lightly touched his arm as if to steady herself. "I . . . I rather impulsively jumped into André's carriage on Canal Street, after overhearing André and Ian's dispute at the saddlery. I *had* to try to see if there wasn't some way to put a stop to what Ian Jeffries was doing. André was distraught . . . and nothing I said offered him hope." She shook her head. "I should have *realized* how despairing he was! If I'd had any *idea* . . ."

"None of us can predict what others will do," Julien said in a low voice, and Corlis knew that he was also referring to the behavior of Martine Fouché.

"When André asked me to leave his house," Corlis continued her story, "I waited for his driver on the veranda. Oh, Mr. LaCroix . . . it was . . . so ghastly!"

Julien's demeanor shifted, and he put a sympathetic arm around her shoulders, as if he had also endured some hideous brush with death. She rested her head on his chest and heard the beating of his heart through his black frock coat, a heart that had been sorely wounded, no doubt, to learn that his own *father* had also had a long liaison with the woman Julien obviously loved—despite his fury.

"Ian Jeffries *does* have blood on his hands," Julien murmured. "André said it in his letter, and I believe it to be true."

"Your father's partner . . . Monsieur Girard . . . was found hanging from a rope," Corlis whispered into his chest. "And now André Duvallon with a bullet in his head. Two men driven to suicide . . ." she said, her throat starting to choke again. "Oh, God! How could things have come to such a state?" Then Corlis took a step back and studied this man whose arms had just sheltered her. Beads of sweat dotted his brow. "Mr. LaCroix, are you all right? You're very pale, you know, and I wonder if you—"

Julien withdrew a handkerchief from his coat pocket and mopped his forehead. "Actually, I regret to say that I . . . don't feel very well . . ." He wiped his brow a second time. "I don't wish to alarm you, but yellow fever has struck at Reverie."

"Oh, dear God!" Corlis exclaimed. "You poor man! But you should be in bed yourself if you feel unwell! Quickly . . . we must get you to a—"

"I don't wish to expose you any more than I already have," he said weakly, putting a hand against the brick entranceway to steady himself.

"You can't endanger me," Corlis said firmly. "I've already had it—on a steamboat on my way to this damnable place."

"I buried my mother and father this morning," Julien said tiredly. "I tried to protect myself, but—"

"Come . . . let me take you somewhere."

"Reverie . . ." he murmured. "I must get back to Reverie. . . . I must . . ."

"I shall take you to my house on Julia Street until you're recovered," she determined firmly. She led him outside to the *banquette* and leaned him against one of the building's pillars for support. "Can you stand up for just a moment longer?" she asked. "I shall get Mr. Bates to bring your carriage around, and he can take us to my house and fetch a doctor right away."

"Send for Lafayette Marchand," Julien said hoarsely, pressing his soaking handkerchief to his lips. "I must make my will. Please! Bates will know where he lives. He makes his home on the Rue Dauphine, in the *carré de la ville.*"

"Just stay where you are and I will summon Mr. Bates. I'll just be a moment. Courage, Monsieur LaCroix," she urged.

However, when Corlis returned to the saddlery, Mr. Bates would only agree to bring the carriage to the front of Canal Street.

"Yellow jack!" he exclaimed. "Why, Mrs. McCullough, you're risking your life!"

"I'm not. I've had it myself, and if it weren't for the brave souls who nursed me, I'd be dead, and so would my son!"

"Suit yourself," Bates said doubtfully.

Corlis ran back to the entrance to Martine's apartment, where Julien appeared near collapse. After a quarter of an hour, the livery owner finally arrived in the LaCroix carriage and stopped some yards from the front door. Bates glanced furtively at the Fouché residence as if miasmic vapors were pouring out the doorway where Julien stood, leaning weakly against the pillar. The stableman jumped down from the vehicle and immediately strode off in the opposite direction, calling over his shoulder, "I'll be gettin' back to the saddlery, now."

"Well, at least send for Lafayette Marchand, on the Rue Dauphine, and tell him to attend Mr. LaCroix at Julia Street!" Corlis shouted after the retreating figure, incensed.

"Yes . . . yes," Bates agreed hurriedly. By this time he had reached the corner, where he quickly turned heel and fled.

Corlis eyed the sleek pair of steeds harnessed to Julien's handsome conveyance and rushed to the stricken man's side. "Come, now. . . . Let me help you into your carriage, and then I'll do my best to drive these beasts."

Julien seemed oblivious to the world around him as she half led, half dragged him to the door to his coach. Several passersby eyed them oddly, but Corlis didn't dare request their assistance. Once she'd settled him inside the cab, she climbed up to the driver's seat, grasped the two sets of reins between her fingers, and called out in a show of bravado, "Giddyap!"

In ten minutes she was congratulating herself as she managed to turn the vehicle into mud-slicked Julia Street. Just then, however, another carriage careened around the corner, raising a sheet of water and narrowly avoiding a head-on collision. One of Julien's horses shied to the left while the other rose up on its hind legs, frantically pawing the air. Without warning, the reins were jerked out of Corlis's white-knuckled grip, pitching her forward. Her right shoulder smashed into the terrified horse's rump, catapulting her in a swirl of skirts and petticoats straight into the mire.

Corlis's last conscious thought was that the rolling carriage wheel, not two feet from her head, would surely crush her skull.

Chapter Twenty-three

May 14

Corlis lay slumped over the leather-topped desk, her head cradled in her arms, her shoulder bag and voice pager at her elbow. The small study at Reverie plantation was plunged into shadows cast by the declining afternoon sun.

"Corlis? *Corlis!* Hey, girl . . . whadcha doing in here?" Althea demanded. "We've been lookin' all over for you! They're 'bout to close this place, and you'da been shut up with the ghosts!"

Corlis gazed confusedly at Althea and Dylan, and then looked at the crystal decanter and its stopper. Disoriented, she peered around the book-lined study and attempted to get her bearings. The tour guide, earlier that morning, had explained that this room had been used by a long line of LaCroix plantation owners, including Julien LaCroix, "who, unfortunately, had no legitimate heirs and had bequeathed Reverie in 1842 to a distant cousin from Baton Rouge."

"You all right?" Althea persisted.

"Of course," Corlis said weakly. The truth was, she had a fierce headache. She began to root around in her shoulder bag for a candy bar, which she finally located under her bulging address book.

"Grabbin' a little shut-eye in here, were you?" Dylan suggested, eyeing her curiously. "I must say, they sure work you like dogs at that station. Virgil and Manny took the videotapes back with them and said they'd meet you at WJAZ after supper to screen what y'all shot of us today." Dylan cocked his head and demanded, "Where you been all this time, girl?"

"You wouldn't believe me if I told you," Corlis replied, thinking to herself that even Dylan might have difficulty accepting that she could now, apparently, flip back to the 1840s at will by inhaling scents common to both the nineteenth and twentieth centuries!

"I'd believe you, whatever you'd say," Dylan replied, watching intently as Corlis rose to her feet and immediately grabbed the edge of the desk for support. "Try me."

"Maybe later," she replied shortly while waiting for the brief spate of dizziness to abate. Then she glanced at her watch. It was just after five o'clock. "We'd better get out of here or we *will* get locked up!"

Althea looked down at her own watch. "Yowser! I'm due at a production meeting at seven. We shoot the 'Save Our Selwyn' public service spot tomorrow, you know," she said proudly. "It's gonna alert people that Jeffries and those Del Mar hotel folks want to bulldoze *our* history! It'll air a day or so before the city council has the first reading of the ordinance to tear 'em all down and build the hotel."

"You raised enough money to bankroll the spot *in toto*?" Corlis asked, gathering her belongings.

"Yeah. Believe it or not, Cindy Lou Mallory, her mother, and King Duvallon came through, big-time, and hit on some of their uptown friends yesterday for the rest of the dough. The good ol' preservation guerrillas are gonna be on TV!" she chortled gleefully.

So, thought Corlis, her spirits flagging, King and Miss Cindy Lou had proved to be an effective fund-raising team. Exactly when had he gotten back in touch with his former girlfriend? she wondered. Before or *after* Emelie Dumas's funeral?

Merde! Double merde!

"Way to go, Althea!" Dylan exclaimed as the trio left the plantation house and started walking toward the public parking lot past an enormous oak tree, dripping with moss. Corlis eyed the rope swing that hung, motionless, from a high branch and felt a slight shudder. However, her companions passed by, oblivious of its presence.

Althea glanced in Corlis's direction. "Is WJAZ gonna cover the story of a grassroots group like ours, gettin' together to save a bunch of buildin's that black people once owned?" she demanded.

"Pitch, pitch, pitch!" Corlis intoned good-naturedly, side-stepping Althea's loaded question.

"Well, *are* you?" she insisted.

"If I can get a crew assigned at that hour," she said evasively. Then she gently cuffed Althea on the shoulder. Even though the pair had become friends during the course of the last few weeks, Corlis knew that the same sort of personal-professional boundary issues she had with King were at work in this situation as well. "Look, Althea," she added earnestly, "I really hope WJAZ can be there tomorrow. It'd work nicely with the footage we shot of you two today—but it's up to my boss." She tossed her car keys to Althea. "You know something?" she said, "I guess I *am* pooped. You want to drive?"

"Lordy, lordy . . . *me* behind the wheel of a Lexus!" Althea exclaimed. She shot Dylan a gleeful look. "You just never know what's gonna happen when you hang out with white folks, do you?"

"Nope," he agreed, eyeing Corlis speculatively. "You're right 'bout that, Althea. You never know."

Corlis ignored her ringing phone and, for the third time, allowed her voice mail to pick up while she moodily stabbed a fork into a cardboard container of two-day-old Szechuan noodles.

Cagney Cat lazed on top of her desk. His eyes were mere slits, and he cast a disdainful look at the telephone as the last ring faded into silence. Then he closed them again and heaved a sigh.

"My sentiments exactly," Corlis said.

She stared at her glowing computer screen and swiftly scanned the half-completed narration she was writing for a voice track due to be recorded at WJAZ in an hour's time. Earlier that morning, pleading a crammed schedule, she'd persuaded the assignment editor to send Virgil and Manny on their own to grab sound and video of the preservationists making their public service announcement on Canal Street. A call to the

Preservation Resource Center confirmed that Cindy Lou Mallory's family, along with Kingsbury Duvallon, were indeed the principal source of funds underwriting the public service announcement—civic-minded citizens that they were, Corlis thought cynically. Of course, it never hurt to remind one's neighbors in New Orleans that one's ancestor was the celebrated Paul Tulane!

Get off it, McCullough! You're not accusing Althea or Dylan of self-aggrandizement, and they're also in this public service spot!

No, Corlis thought crossly, she didn't object so much to the Mallorys *giving* the donation to make the TV spot, as to King's *asking* them—of all people—to help fund it! After what Cindy Lou Mallory had done to his sister Daphne—and to *him*, for pity's sake—why would King want to have anything to do with the devious, two-timing magnolia?

She gazed down at her notebook, one of nearly a dozen she'd filled with facts concerning the Selwyn buildings controversy. Then she looked over the stacks of file folders crammed with her research, and suddenly thought of the diary belonging to the original Corlis Bell McCullough. She'd completely forgotten that Aunt Marge had never sent it by FedEx, as promised. Her aunt was probably so absorbed in the process of writing her memoirs that she'd never gotten around to photocopying the old volume.

Acting on impulse, Corlis reached for the phone, prepared to ask that Aunt Marge send the McCullough diary to New Orleans, posthaste. Just then her intercom buzzed. Irritated by the interruption, Corlis padded in her stocking feet into her parlor, where she pushed the TALK button on the wall next to the door.

"Yes?" she barked.

"Want to let me in?" a familiar voice demanded.

"No . . . I don't!" Corlis answered, and then chastised herself for sounding petulant.

"C'mon, Corlis . . . buzz me through. I want to talk to you."

"Look, King . . . I don't think that's such a good idea. Right this minute, you're in the red-hot center of the campaign to save the buildings, and I'm a journalist covering the story. I think, for both our sakes, we should keep our distance."

"That's a load of crap!" he exclaimed, his irritation crackling through the intercom. "That's not the reason you won't talk to me."

"Maybe to *you* it's crap," she snapped, "but not to *me*."

"Why, Miz Reporter," King said. "Where's your fabled journalistic honesty? You sent Manny and Virgil to do your work for you today, didn't you? You couldn't be sufferin' from just a tiny bit of unfounded jealousy, could you—and *that's* why you won't let me darken your door?"

Corlis felt herself go rigid with indignation. How *dare* he trivialize the personal and professional issues that confronted them! Typical southerner! Typical *male*!

"You think this is just about jealousy, huh?" she countered, steeling herself to sound cool and collected when she was anything but. "You think this just concerns how devastatingly attractive you are to all the women who flit across your radar screen—*especially* if they're willing to write a check to your favorite cause?" She put her lips a millimeter away from the speaker box. "No one pays *your* way, huh, Mr. Preservation? Well, maybe—unless you decide it's for a good enough cause! And now I'm sorry to buzz off, but I've got a four o'clock deadline. See ya."

She released the TALK button and congratulated herself for coming up with such a great exit line.

Then why, she wondered, did she feel so damned miserable?

King, Dylan, and Althea hovered in a corner of the antiseptic concrete-and-chrome foyer that stood adjacent to the New Orleans City Council chambers.

"Sweet Jesus, what I wouldn't do to have a copy of that memo you saw in Grover Jeffries's office the night of his costume party!" Dylan exclaimed.

"Amen," Althea said fervently.

King made no comment and beckoned toward the double doors leading to the council chambers.

The hall was packed. Many people in the audience sported large buttons that read SOS—SAVE OUR SELWYNS!

Althea and Dylan began handing out the brochures while Cindy Lou distributed handmade protest signs to people sitting down front. As the group made their way through the hall, a number of television crews, including Corlis's, began recording their actions, along with shots of Grover Jeffries, Lafayette Marchand, and a gaggle of gray-suited lawyers representing the interests of the Del Mar Corporation. These gentlemen sat huddled in the back row, conferring in agitated whispers.

A few minutes later, Edgar Dumas, the recently elevated president of the city council, along with his elected colleagues, took their places on a raised dais. Dumas gaveled the meeting to order and began calling a series of city planning officials and Landmark Commission members to the podium to deliver their reports.

For forty-five minutes, the civil servants and appointed officials droned on. The council members rarely questioned those testifying about the more controversial aspects of the proposed building project. Instead, they chatted quietly among themselves or took the opportunity to catch up on their reading.

As the last witness took his seat, Councilman Roscoe Bordeleon leaned toward his microphone and made a proposal in a sleepy, low-pitched voice.

"President Dumas? Before we finish tonight and take our first vote on the proposals in front of us, I'd like y'all to hear from Professor Barry Jefferson 'bout some of the history connected with these buildin's that this body seems hell-bent on demolishin'."

Althea leaned toward King and whispered triumphantly, "Roscoe's my mother's second cousin, once removed. He promised me he'd at least smooth the way for Professor Jefferson to address the council."

"Way to go, Althea!" King said, smiling gratefully. "I'm on the agenda, too . . ." he added with a worried glance at the clock on the wall.

Edgar Dumas cast an annoyed look at his fellow council member. "I think we have more than enough information about this particular city block—especially if you folks all watch *television*," he added sarcastically, glancing in the direction of the battery of TV crews positioned below the dais. The audience responded with a mixture of snickers and cheers.

"Well . . ." drawled Althea's distant cousin into his mike, "*I* sure didn't know that forty-five percent of all black folks here before the Civil War were Free People of Color and owned buildin's, did *you*, Edgar?"

"Who says?" Edgar challenged. "That's got to be wrong, Roscoe. There was nothin' but slaves in Louisiana back then."

Roscoe waved the color pamphlet over his head. "Why don't you read Professor Jefferson's brochure? It says here that the source for that statistic comes from our own city archives. There's also a book," he continued, squinting at the fine print in a footnote. "You'd better get a copy of *Creole New Orleans: Race and Americanization* by Hirsch and Logdon . . . outta Baton Rouge, it says here. Barry Jefferson's a highly respected professor of African-American history, Edgar. He wrote a college textbook on this stuff, so he should know what he's talkin' 'bout, don't you think? I move that we invite the good professor to speak to us for just a few minutes, so we get our facts straight!"

The atmosphere in the auditorium was suddenly charged with excitement. The lobbyists and civil servants had ceased talking quietly among themselves, and everyone in the audience was hanging on Roscoe Bordeleon's every word.

"I don't think—" Edgar Dumas began.

"Maybe all of us *weren't* descendants of slaves!" Bordeleon said languidly. "Maybe a few of us have a *different* heritage that we don't know much about." For the second time Bordeleon waved the brochure over his head. "I know of not *one* black-owned buildin' on Canal Street today, and yet lots of folks on this council seem determined to demolish the block where Professor Jefferson and the preservation folks say black people once built and occupied a whole *set* of beautiful buildin's!" he declared, pointing to the easel. "I say we invite Professor Jefferson to talk to us, Edgar," he challenged, his lethargic manner suddenly becoming surprisingly passionate. "I say we slow down before we all vote to wreck a place that Free People of Color put up a hundred and sixty years ago. If not, we're *crazy*, man!"

Corlis noticed that the reporter from the *Times-Picayune* was making furious notes, as were other representatives of the print and electronic media. At some point in these proceedings, Jack

Ebert had slipped in, unnoticed, and was also writing in his notebook. She glanced over her shoulder and could see Grover Jeffries whispering into Lafayette Marchand's ear.

"We're outta time, today." Edgar Dumas announced, clearly also out of patience. A low rumble rolled through the contingent of preservationists who began to shift in their seats and to raise their cardboard placards. "I'll do this much, Councilman," Dumas temporized, pointing his gavel in the direction of the city clerk. "I order Professor Jefferson's brochure to be submitted to the record. It's time that the clerk read the ordinance and we vote."

"Point of order! Point of order!" a loud voice rang out. Kingsbury Duvallon leapt out of his seat, waving a sheaf of papers over his head.

"I would ask that you sit down, sir!" thundered the council president, banging his gavel.

"Point of order, before you take the vote!" King shouted. "I have information here that speaks directly to the highly irregular way in which this project comes before the city council."

"Sit *down*, sir!" Edgar bellowed. "Or I'll have you ejected!"

Ignoring this directive, King strode over to the microphone reserved for the public to address the lawmakers.

"Is *everyone* in this chamber aware of who the brand-new owner of the Selwyn properties is?" King barked into the mike. He waved the set of documents and declared, "A few months ago, the eleven buildin's on Canal Street were secretly purchased by an entity called B and G, Limited, an out-of-state holdin' company, registered in Delaware."

"It makes no difference to this proceedin' who the Selwyn family may have chosen to sell their property to," Edgar Dumas interrupted furiously.

"Makes no difference?" King echoed caustically. "Not if B and G, Limited, stands for Bonita and Grover . . . *Jeffries!*"

"I'm warnin' you, Mr. Duvallon . . ." Edgar Dumas growled.

"This purchase was never made public, even though I would suspect that many of you council members knew full well about it. Yet y'all failed to disclose to the *public* that Grover Jeffries secretly owns the land and he's bribin' officials to let him tear down the historic structures on it to build whatever he wants."

"Security!" barked the council president.

"And I also have proof," King declared, overriding Dumas's admonition, "in the form of articles of incorporation on file in the Louisiana State Capitol, that Grover Jeffries is the silent and principal shareholder of the magazine *Arts This Week*, and that he hired Jack Ebert—standin' right over there with the media—specifically to write a series of deliberately damagin' articles to smear not only *my* character—"

"Mr. Duvallon, *sit down!*" Dumas bellowed.

"—but the character of anyone else in the historic preservation movement or the media in New Orleans who dared voice opposition to—or *even question*—this Del Mar hotel buildin' boondoggle!" King continued as if the city council president hadn't interrupted.

Startled private exchanges ricocheted around the hearing room, swelling the hall with a cacophony of sound. Corlis, who stood not four feet from Ebert, stared, slack-jawed and dumbfounded at the notion that Jack had been *hired* by Grover Jeffries to craft damaging articles about King. Meanwhile, the arts critic's features registered an astonishing succession of emotions: shock, alarm, and finally pure, unadulterated fury.

Edgar Dumas pounded his gavel for order, to little avail. "Mr. Duvallon, you're out of order! *Take your seat!*"

Despite Lafayette Marchand's herculean efforts to keep Grover Jeffries in *his* seat, the developer sprang to his feet and sprinted down the aisle toward King at the podium.

"I submit to the members of the city council," King shouted above the burgeoning melee, pointing at Jeffries like an avenging prophet, "a copy of an invoice that Jack Ebert presented to Grover Jeffries for services rendered at *Arts This Week*. Ebert's a hack for hire who'd write *any* lie—for a price. And I submit," he continued to thunder, "that *this* man, Grover Jeffries, has used undue influence in the form of *illegal* campaign financin' to city officials!"

Whoa there, Mr. Preservation! Corlis thought, pleading silently with King.

Surely he didn't have *that* smoking gun memo in his possession. She could vouch that he'd *seen* a piece of paper on which

Jeffries ordered behind-the-scenes campaign contributions, but he didn't have a hard copy.

No documents, no story! Journalism 101.

King had gone too far, Corlis thought, anxiety invading her every pore. Meanwhile Jeffries stood outside of the ring of humanity that had formed protectively around King. The portly developer was impotent with rage. Members of the city council, however, had a clear view of both the crusading preservationist and the incensed developer. In various stages of surprise and agitation, the five men and two women elected to represent the city of New Orleans gaped at the furious combatants.

By this time Grover Jeffries's complexion had turned a livid shade of puce. He savagely elbowed his way through the group near the podium and shoved King to one side. Then he grabbed possession of the microphone.

"You'd damn well better have *proof* of what you're sayin', Mr. Duvallon!" Jeffries shouted above the fracas. " 'Cause I'm gonna sue your ass from here to Natchez, and so is the Del Mar Corporation! Yes, I own the Selwyn buildin's, fair and legal, and if I want to keep that information *private*, that is my right! And yes, I participate in the political process, just like you and your preservation creeps. But y'all have gone too far this time, young man! You are interferin' with free enterprise—and every other goddamn thing Americans stand for in this country. And if you don't shut up, I'm gonna—"

Lafayette Marchand finally managed to catch up with his volatile client. He made a grab for Grover's arm and bodily pushed the furious developer away from the podium, back up the aisle, and out of the hearing-room door. All the while Edgar Dumas continued to pound his gavel until, finally, there was some semblance of order.

"Security!" he exclaimed, pointing his finger at King, who remained standing at the public microphone. "Arrest Mr. Duvallon and remove him from this chamber for disturbin' the peace!"

Chapter Twenty-four

May 19

Two uniformed guards of generous girth elbowed their way toward King through the crowds that clogged the city council chambers. Without hesitation, they roughly yanked his arms behind his back and clapped handcuffs around his wrists. While the officers hustled their prisoner up the aisle and through the doors that Jeffries and Marchand had just exited, Roscoe Bordeleon leaned toward his microphone for the second time and, in his distinctive, gravel-voiced fashion, suggested calmly, "I move we table this discussion until staff can review the pertinent information that's been presented here today . . . and can report back to us as a body."

One of the two female council members quickly seconded the proposal. From her colleagues' expressions, all appeared profoundly relieved to have found a way to put an end to the turbulent meeting. The majority on the board swiftly concurred with the motion to table, and then the council voted to adjourn. The mass of reporters headed for the exits, rudely jostling one another in a rush to meet their evening deadlines.

Corlis, however, could only stare as King was hustled out the door. Next to her, Virgil and Manny quickly stowed their gear and prepared to race back to WJAZ with the tumultuous footage for the evening news. As she turned to follow in their wake, she felt a viselike grip take hold of her arm. Jack Ebert was glaring at her with a look of pure hatred.

"You stole my invoice that night, didn't you, bitch? That's how you and King knew I was workin' for Jeffries!"

Corlis reacted with shock, her mind racing to make sense of what he was saying. Invoice? What invoice?

"Jack, what are you talking about? I didn't steal any invoice. I've never even been *in* the offices of *Arts This Week*!"

"You and King were both right there, in Grover's office the night of the ball," he growled. He tightened the grip on her arm. "I'm warning you! You *still* don't understand how this town works—"

"Well, I know how *I* work!" she interrupted. She yanked her arm away. "I *didn't* steal any invoice, and I *don't* hand over information to sources—even ones I *like*—or to competing journalists, for that matter, though I suspect no one, even in New Orleans, will consider *you* a member of our fraternity anymore, you pimp. Now, get lost, will you?"

And before Jack Ebert could say another word, she strode up the aisle without looking back. She did, however, wonder how King Duvallon had obtained the incriminating invoice that proved Jack had been in Grover Jeffries's employ all this time.

It was nearly eight o'clock before Corlis finished editing her expanded piece for the ten o'clock news and pulled her Lexus out of the parking lot at WJAZ. She was mentally and emotionally exhausted and fully intended to head directly home. Why, then, she wondered, was she now on the ramp that led to Interstate 10?

Because Central Lockup was off I-10, that's why, she answered herself silently. She had to talk to King. It was for the story.

It's not just the story, you nit!

Well, it was for the story *as well as* for personal reasons, she reassured herself. Something in her solar plexus had gone haywire when those cops hauled King off in handcuffs—a situation she realized, suddenly, that she simply could not tolerate as long as she had the means to do something about it.

Fifteen minutes later she pulled her car in front of the jail. The street was deserted, except for a battered pickup truck and a fire-engine-red Mustang convertible that looked as if it might belong to a convicted drug lord. Corlis locked her own vehicle and headed for the glass doors.

As she walked through the front entrance, she began rooting around in her shoulder bag for her trusty wad of WJAZ cash. Her head down in concentration, she heard King's deep, distinctive voice before she saw him standing near the bail bond window.

"Let me take you to dinner. It's the least I can do for comin' all this way to rescue me."

Startled, Corlis halted, a broad smile beginning to unleash itself across her face when suddenly she became conscious that a second voice had begun to speak.

"Why King, darlin', I'd *love* to! Can we go to Galatoire's?" Cindy Lou Mallory begged with a coquettish smile.

Tonight the maid of honor of the short-circuited Duvallon-Ebert nuptials wore a stunning imperial-blue jacket and matching skirt that showed plenty of leg. It was the perfect outfit for a woman who assumed she'd be taken to dinner because of her good deeds.

For the second time in her entire life, Corlis literally wanted to scratch a woman's eyes out. Instead, she swiftly reversed direction and headed for the exit.

"Corlis!"

Oddly, King's exclamation had the force of a command. Corlis stopped midstep and reluctantly turned around. Blood pounded in her temples; it seemed her heart would leap out of her chest.

Talk about déjà vu all over again!

She stared at the sight of King and Cindy Lou standing side by side and felt as if she were the victim of an emotional hijacking. In two strides, King was by her side.

"What are *you* doing here?" he demanded.

"I . . . ah . . . I . . ."

Corlis held up her left hand in the stance of a school crossing guard forbidding a pedestrian to step off the curb. She shifted her gaze to the perfectly made-up countenance of Cindy Lou Mallory. She was bearing down on them with a determined look in her eye. Corlis turned to face King.

"Well?" King pressed. Then his face softened and he added, "It's nice to see you in person again, Ace. I was plannin' to watch you on the late news tonight from my cell."

"I—I just wanted to talk to you about what happened at today's city council hearing . . . and I had a few . . . questions to ask about the revelations concerning Jack Ebert. But I see now's obviously not a good time," she finished pointedly.

Why in the world would King offer to take this woman out to dinner? she fumed. *Why would he even* speak *to Cindy Lou Mallory again?*

Rather than voice this question, however, she thrust out her hand in Cindy Lou's direction. "Let me introduce myself. I'm Corlis McCullough. WJAZ."

"Oh . . . everybody in New Orleans knows who *you* are," Cindy Lou retorted archly. "And anyway, how could *I* forget?"

So much for that supposed Louisiana politesse that King had once described as being the hallmark of a magnolia in the Bayou State!

Cindy was gazing at King with a forgiving smile. "It's *so* sweet of you, darlin', to offer to take me to dinner," she purred. "I accept." She smiled with a dismissive air in Corlis's direction. "'Bye, now. Nice meetin' you." The Mardi Gras Queen of 1991 tucked her well-manicured hand through King's arm and said, "Shall we get you out of this horrible ol' place, sugar? Daddy said he'd talk to Judge Bouchet in the mornin'."

"You hungry, McCullough?" King inquired abruptly.

Corlis was starving.

"Thanks, but I have a dinner date."

She turned on her heel and marched on ahead of the happy couple. She was already nosing her car out of her parking place by the time King gallantly opened the driver's door of the fire-engine-red, seduce-me Mustang.

Double merde! Corlis cursed under her breath.

King shifted in his chair outside the dean's office and glanced at his watch. He'd been a free man since nine-thirty that morning, and as of this moment, he'd been waiting forty-five minutes beyond the time he'd been requested to appear before an interdisciplinary committee of the university's architecture and history departments.

"Mr. Duvallon?" said a neatly dressed woman who stuck her

head through the door and was smiling nervously. "Please come in. The committee's waiting for you."

Dean Avery Labonniere, along with his colleagues, sat in a small sterile conference room that had been designed some five years earlier by a flunky in the employ of Grover Jeffries. A woman whom King didn't recognize—attired in a female version of a pinstripe suit—sat perched in an uncomfortable chrome-and-Naugahyde chair positioned against the wall.

A lawyer, he surmised. Present so that she could make this all nice and legal.

"How y'all doing?" King asked pleasantly, wondering if they could really toss him out of his department two months before he was due to be granted tenure.

The missing person in the room was Grover Jeffries, of course. Grover and his henchman, Lafayette Marchand. Their names were never mentioned, but everyone present knew what this meeting was all about.

The dean cleared his throat. "I am sorry to have to say this, Mr. Duvallon, but this committee has determined that you have behaved in a manner that brings dishonor to this institution and the alumni who support it."

"For actin' on my conscience as an architectural historian to try to save the Selwyn buildings?" King inquired evenly.

"Your conscience is not at issue in this situation," Tallon replied sharply. "You've been arrested twice and had your name in every newspaper and magazine in this state. You've publicly accused one of this university's staunchest supporters of—"

"Ah . . . Mr. Jeffries is upset with me," he intervened affably. "But what about my rights of free speech and assembly?" he asked, casting a faint smile in the direction of the lady lawyer.

"The issue here is what's in the best interest of this institution," Dean Labonniere countered, tight-lipped. "I must have your word that you will not in the future do anything that will heap ridicule on your colleagues in this department, or the university in general."

King heaved a silent sigh of relief. As with Judge Bouchet's earlier pronouncements from the bench that morning, he was being let off again with only another warning. Well, he would allow them to have their pound of flesh today, he thought, lowering his eyes in a false show of respect. He knew the drill. He would simply appear sufficiently chastened so as to allow himself the time he needed to nail that son of a bitch Grover Jeffries! After that, whatever happened to him regarding tenure at the university was up for grabs.

Smiling faintly, King said, "Of *course* I don't want to embarrass anybody. And certainly, I agree never to do anything that compromises the School of Architecture's commitment to savin' worthy historic structures, or the university's solemn pledge to uphold that ideal."

The committee members exchanged confused looks. Dean Labonniere glanced at his watch.

"Well . . . ah . . . that's good to hear, son," the dean replied. "I shall hold you to your word." He gazed at his fellow committee members, who nodded their agreement. "I think that about winds up our business here today. And please, King, do give my regards to your sweet mama. I shall never forget serving with Lafayette Marchand in her court that year!" He smiled broadly at the other two male professors. "I do declare that Antoinette Kingsbury was the prettiest Mardi Gras queen New Orleans has—or will ever see."

King shook hands with his superiors and hurried out of the conference room.

He would have to move fast if he was to stop the demolition of the Selwyn buildings *and* gain tenure as a professor at this goddamned incestuous university, he thought grimly.

The phone next to Corlis's bed rang in the darkness. However, it was the motion of Cagney Cat's twenty-three pounds leaping off the mattress that roused her to full consciousness. She made a grab for the receiver, her heart pounding. Had something happened to Aunt Marge?

"Sorry to disturb you, Ace," King's voice said gruffly. "Don't worry. . . . This is purely a business call."

Corlis sat up in bed, uncertain whether to be relieved that King was following the rules she had set down, or upset that he sounded so cool and detached. She hadn't seen or even heard about what he was doing in more than a week.

"What's up?" she asked cautiously.

"We've just gotten word that the good Mr. Jeffries is plannin' a little demolition derby about three this mornin'. I thought WJAZ might be interested in coverin' it."

"How do you know this?" Corlis demanded.

"Can't reveal my sources," King shot back, "but trust me, Ace. There'll be lots of dramatic pictures of big ol' bulldozers doin' their thing."

"And what do *you* plan to do?"

"Some friends of mine and I plan to lie down and catch a little shut-eye . . . at various spots around the six hundred block of Canal Street."

Corlis leapt out of bed and began to shed her nightclothes as she stood, holding the receiver to her ear. "I'm on my way! I'll get a hold of Manny and Virgil—"

"Already did that," King interrupted.

"You did *what*?" Corlis countered indignantly.

"This is war," King declared in a chilly tone of voice.

"Yeah . . . but Virgil, Manny, and I are the war *correspondents*—we're not the combatants, and you can't order us to the front unless *I* say so!" By this time she was really steamed and was glaring at the telephone. "Don't you get it, Mr. Preservation? WJAZ is not your private PR department. You and I have different *functions*!"

"Yeah. . . . Well, get that good-lookin' derriere of yours in gear, and start functionin' as a reporter! Gotta go."

And with that the line went dead.

Corlis called Virgil on his cell phone and directed him to meet her on Common Street behind the Selwyn buildings to avoid being seen by anyone on Canal Street. She wanted the trio to remain inconspicuous until they were geared up and ready to go.

At ten minutes to three on this early May morning, the neighborhood of three- and four-story buildings was silent, except for the Saddlery restaurant, where patrons at the all-night bar were still whooping it up. Corlis gazed up and down the street and began to wonder if King had been pulling a practical joke.

Without warning, Chris Calvert, King's teaching assistant,

sprinted around the corner and dashed through the entrance to the restaurant, looking for all the world like Paul Revere shouting, "The British are coming! The British are coming!"

"This is it!" Corlis shouted. "Let's move it! Start rolling tape *now*!"

They entered the restaurant in time to capture the last of Calvert's announcement made to some very familiar faces that were clustered around the bar.

"They've just about finished unloadin' the heavy equipment," Calvert declared, panting for breath. "I think it's time we get goin'!"

King leapt up onto the bar and surveyed the group of some thirty preservation stalwarts, plus Cindy Lou Mallory, who wore a pair of crisply pressed blue jeans, a white silk blouse, and a stunning squash-blossom turquoise Navajo necklace. Everything about her soigné appearance shouted "par-tee!"

"All right, everybody!" King bellowed. "Settle down!" He flashed a smile of recognition at Corlis. "Y'all have your stations and assignments?"

"Yes!" they shouted.

"Then let's move on *out*! Go! Go! *GO!*"

Like a well-trained battalion—with King serving as their marine drill sergeant—men and women of various ages filed briskly out of the restaurant.

"Stick with Duvallon," Corlis shouted hoarsely amidst the hubbub. "I'm guessing he's going to lie down in front of the bulldozers at the main entrance of the building."

"Right!" Virgil shouted back. "Just follow me."

Canal Street had been transformed into a stage for a modern enactment of a medieval passion play. Large work lights were positioned near generators that had been parked opposite the aluminum facade obscuring the Greek Revival structures. A gigantic crane with a wrecker's ball was poised near the front entrance. The metal monster was flanked by two enormous yellow bulldozers, fifty feet distant on either side.

With amazing precision, King's preservation guerrillas fanned out in front of the demolition equipment. The silent protesters stood with their backs to the woven metal screen and squinted into the blinding work lights. Corlis noted that Cindy

Lou picked a spot five or six volunteers away from where King was standing directly under the twenty-foot-high metal letter *S*.

A sleek black late-model Lincoln Town Car pulled up near one of the bulldozers, and a barrel-chested man got out of the backseat. The expression on Grover Jeffries's face revealed his surprise—and wrath—at the sight of King Duvallon and his band of protesters.

"You'd better clear off, Duvallon," Grover shouted furiously, " 'cause I own these buildin's and my men have orders to pull 'em down—*now!* "

"This is an illegal action," King yelled, his own rage barely contained. "These buildin's are in a landmarked historic district! The city council has not voted yet—"

"Fuck the city council!" Jeffries said. "They're just a bunch of pussies. Payin' the fines they're gonna assess me for pullin' these eyesores down is just the cost of doin' business, boy! This is *my* property, and I can do whatever I damn well *want* with it, so clear out, or y'all are gonna get run over—and I sure as hell ain't payin' your hospital bills, I can tell you that! You were *warned!*" He waved his right arm over his head to signal the bulldozer crews should begin moving toward the buildings.

The sound of the behemoths' engines revving up was deafening. Several other news vans drew up behind Grover's car and their camera crews tumbled out, scrambling for position. Virgil, Manny, and Corlis had already taken places between the bulldozer on the right and the crane with its heavy wrecking ball suspended from an enormous chain.

Grover Jeffries glared at the assorted members of the media and waved a piece of paper clutched in his hands. He seemed on the verge of an apoplectic fit.

"I *own* these goddamn derelicts!" he cried. "This is my *deed*! I'm doin' the public a service, pullin' 'em down and not costin' the taxpayers money while pussy preservationists like *him*"— he jabbed a trembling finger at King Duvallon—"delay and maneuver and use the law to twist the meanin' of the goddamn Constitution that's supposed to *protect* private property!"

However, the cameras were ignoring the furious developer and focusing instead on the line of protesters who stood defiantly in the glaring lights with their backs pressed symbolically against the aluminum-shrouded wall. Corlis knew instinctively that Grover Jeffries had no idea what a bonanza he was handing his adversaries. It was going to be page one in the *Times-Picayune* and the top of the newscast at WJAZ and everywhere else, including, possibly, *Today* on national television.

"Do it!" Grover screamed at his work crew. "*Do it*, goddamn it! Take 'em down!" Jeffries signaled emphatically to the bulldozer operator on the right. "Take out the front door and that big ol' *S first!*"

The engines shifted from idle gears into a roaring wall of sound. Black diesel smoke billowed out, jettisoning choking fumes toward Jeffries, the television crews, and Corlis and her colleagues. The bulldozer nearest her began to inch forward, crossing in front of the wrecking ball, creeping closer and closer to the spot where King had taken up his protective post.

Twenty feet distant, the second bulldozer did likewise, inching toward a stunned-looking Cindy Lou Mallory. The closer the bulldozer approached, the more horrified Cindy Lou's pretty features became.

Corlis tapped Virgil on the shoulder and shouted, "Get the redhead! Get the redhead!" Just at that moment Cindy Lou looked desperately to the right and left at her stationary colleagues. She bolted like a startled gazelle, running past the lumbering bulldozer and disappearing in the darkness beyond the perimeter of lights. With great aplomb Chris Calvert moved over five feet and immediately took Cindy Lou's place. The others adjusted themselves in similar fashion. She wasn't even missed.

Meanwhile, King was still standing under the *S* like a defender of the Alamo as a bulldozer bore down on his part of the line.

In an adrenaline rush Corlis screamed at Virgil over the roar of the mammoth engines, "From now on, stick with Duvallon, *no matter what!*"

She stared at the unfolding drama as if she were viewing a film, one frame at a time. The enormous piece of equipment drew closer . . . and closer . . . yet King didn't flinch. Closer and closer, until the gigantic scoop was only three feet away. The man showed no sign of blinking first.

"Preservation chicken . . ." Corlis muttered to no one in particular.

And still the bulldozer advanced.

Corlis suddenly couldn't watch any longer. She turned her head, unable to witness what she feared would happen next.

Then suddenly she heard one engine conk out.

The bulldozer nearest King had shut down.

Astonished, Corlis turned just in time to watch the other heavy equipment operator lean forward and turn the ignition key, silencing his roaring beast.

Grover Jeffries glared first at one of his employees, then at the other. Finally the engine of the giant crane also went silent. The crane operator pointed to the wrecking ball and said, "We're not pullin' anything down tonight, Mr. Jeffries." He gestured in the direction of Corlis and her crew. "I do that, somebody gets hurt, and the city'll pull my license and cancel it—forever. I'll be out of business. Sorry, sir, but this is a no-go."

Grover Jeffries remained silent, then slowly shook his fist at King before turning abruptly on his heel. He stormed to the side of his waiting vehicle and yanked open the back door of the luxury car. Within seconds his driver sped away from the curb, the taillights receding until the red pinpoints disappeared down a darkened side street.

King was the first to start clapping and yipping like a coyote on a moonlit night. Soon Chris Calvert and the rest of the protesters joined in until they were transformed into a rollicking mass of cheering humanity—with King in the center, accepting everyone's hearty congratulations.

Everyone, of course, except Corlis McCullough and Cindy Lou Mallory. Miss Mallory was nowhere to be seen. Corlis, on the other hand, calmly walked around the corner and then sprinted toward her car in hopes of beating her television crew back to WJAZ.

"Can you magnify the close-up of Grover's desk?" Corlis asked of Sam Lombardo, the tape editor.

"Yeah . . . gimme a sec," Sam replied, tapping console keys in the darkened editing bay. The editing room was tiny. To relieve the closeness in the small room, Corlis opened the sliding glass doors behind them, allowing air in from the office corridor.

She looked at her watch. She'd been up for almost twenty-four hours straight. Early in the day she and Lombardo had put together "Demolition Derby," as the story of the early morning fracas on Canal Street had been slugged on the show rundown for the morning and noon news broadcasts. She'd done additional interviews with city officials during the day concerning the implications of Jeffries's patently illegal action to demolish the Selwyn buildings without a permit, then repackaged a longer version of the story that had run on last evening's news magazine program. Now Corlis was intent on reviewing videotape Virgil had shot inside Grover's office on the night of the Jeffries's masked ball.

"Woof!" Corlis declared excitedly. "That's it! See the letterhead with 'Writing Assignments' written beneath it? That's the invoice that Jack Ebert slipped into Grover's box *after* our crew left Jeffries's home office but *before* we came back to shoot the interview with Mr. and Mrs. Demolition about their wonderful charity work," she elaborated. "Virgil just happened to catch the invoice when he did a pan shot of the desk. Fabulous!" she clapped excitedly. "Can you freeze-frame it, magnify, and download a hard copy for me so I can read the fine print?"

"No problem," Sam replied with a matter-of-fact shrug.

How in the world had King gotten access to a copy of this invoice before the city council meeting that day? she wondered.

Just then Virgil ambled by.

"Havin' fun?" he asked dryly as he walked past their door.

She nodded obliquely to the cameraman but kept her eyes on Sam's video screen. "Now . . . back the tape up . . . to the stuff we shot earlier, *before* we got the shot of the invoice," Corlis instructed the tape editor. Then she looked up. "Hey, Virgil," she called down the corridor, "what are the chances you might have inadvertently gotten a close-up of the memo from Lafayette Marchand we found in Grover's in box the first time we went into the office on the night of the Jeffries's costume ball?"

"I dunno . . ." Virgil replied, his hand on the doorknob at the end of the hallway.

Corlis turned back to the editor. "Do you remember seeing

such a thing when you edited the interview with Jeffries awhile back?"

"I edit ten stories a day," replied the taciturn Lombardo. Corlis could tell he was tired and wanted to go home.

"Just make one more pass at fifty-forty-two, okay?" she said, staring closely at the digital tape counter. Virgil retraced his steps and stood in the hall behind them. The trio watched silently as footage flew by on one of the small TV screens. "Aha!" Corlis said triumphantly. She pointed to a piece of paper on top of the in box on Grover Jeffries's desk. "Magnify, please."

Into sharper focus came the first page of the memo with the handwritten comment, "DIRECT ACCOUNTANT TO MAKE CC'S TO FRIENDLY CITY COUNCIL MEMBERS—NOW!"

"Bingo . . ." Corlis said softly.

Sam sat up in his chair and whistled. "Wow . . . there's your proof that Grover was using campaign contributions to persuade certain council members to see things his way on the hotel project."

"Well, it goes quite a distance in that direction," Corlis agreed, smiling faintly. "Sam, would you print me a hard copy of this one, too?" She turned to Virgil and said, "Zamora and the creep lawyer'll *have* to let us go on air with this stuff, don't you think?"

"I dunno," Virgil allowed. " 'Cause that lawyer, Marvin Glimp, *is* a creep." Without further comment, he headed down the hall toward the WJAZ lunchroom.

"It is my advice, Andy, that you do *not* go on the air with this," Marvin Glimp declared, pointing to the photocopy of Jeffries's memo taken from the videotape.

"Why the hell not?" Corlis demanded, looking to Andy Zamora for support.

"Because there are no names of city officials he's supposedly gonna give the illegal money to, that's why!" Glimp declared. "All you've got is just the proposal on Jeffries's part that *some* council members were *possibly* going to be offered money. We have no way of knowing if Mr. Jeffries's accountant *gave* any of them money. He could have considered it, but it is unfair to the elected officials to create smoke when we do not know, for certain, if there was actually a fire."

"Andy!" Corlis exclaimed, unable to disguise her mounting frustration at the direction the meeting had been taking for the last five minutes. "Jeez Louise . . . it's *right there* on our own videotape!"

"I don't know. . . ." Zamora said, shaking his head. "You had a solid story yesterday about Grover's sneak attack on those buildin's, and the preservationists who prevented it. I say, why buy trouble when we're on a roll? Let's sit tight, try to get some additional proof to make this accusation a lot more solid."

"But, Andy," Corlis protested, "you *know* this back-channel stuff is the way Grover Jeffries operates. He *obviously* told his accountant to spread some money or promises of future goodies around *somewhere*. What if the city council takes a vote before we can prove *which* members are on the take?" she demanded.

"That's my point," Zamora snapped. "We've gotta prove *which* elected officials got dirty money, Corlis, before we can go with it. That's final."

"And I must remind you, Ms. McCullough," Glimp added officiously, "that you are to continue to stay at arm's length from King Duvallon, do you understand?"

"Perfectly," she replied, forcing a polite smile.

But outside, in the corridor that led past the editing bay, Corlis could barely contain her irritation.

"Hey, boss lady, why so glum?" Virgil asked.

"They won't let me use the stills from the tape yet. I have to get outside corroboration as to *which* council members have their hands stretched out before I can even *hint* on the air at what Grover's up to!" She gestured with the photocopies she held in her hand. "Alluding to the possibility that elected officials have gotten paid off would probably flush some whistle-blower out of the woodwork who *could* corroborate, but Glimp just put up a blockade."

"Yeah . . . well, why wouldn't he?" Virgil drawled. "His sister is a receptionist at Lafayette Marchand's PR joint."

Corlis's jaw dropped. "I swear to God, Virgil. You know everything in this town! Do you think Andy Zamora knows this?"

"I don't 'spect so, 'cause she just quit the place where *my* sister works to go work for Marchand." He shrugged, mildly apologetic.

"This town is driving me *crazy!*"

Virgil patted her on the shoulder and added, "I wouldn't tell Zamora 'bout that yet. He'll confront Glimp, and then Glimp'll try to fry your oysters some *other* way. Save that kind of ammunition for when you really need it," he counseled. "But watch your back with Glimp."

"Always," she replied grimly. Virgil was a really smart cookie, Corlis considered gratefully.

Manny walked through the door.

"Our assignment editor just told me that city council's called an emergency session," he said. "Tomorrow morning, nine o'clock. Be there, or be square."

"They're going to ram through the demolition," Corlis predicted, shaking her head in disgust. "I smell a railroad job, and Kingsbury Duvallon and his preservation guerrillas are about to get flattened on the tracks."

"You never know 'bout stuff like that round here," Virgil replied philosophically.

"I've been around just long enough to take an educated guess," she replied morosely. "Adios, guys. See you at city council tomorrow, eight-thirty sharp."

Chapter Twenty-five

May 28

The assignment editor hung up the phone and shouted across the newsroom, "Hey, McCullough! Zamora wants to see you before you take off for the city council meeting! In his office . . . on the double."

"Damn it!" Corlis muttered. "You guys go on over to city hall and set up," she said to Virgil and Manny. "I'll be there, soon as I can."

Her heart sank when she spotted Marvin Glimp standing beside Andy Zamora's desk. Both were staring at the front page of the *Times-Picayune*, where a headline in the lower left corner of the front page read: RUMORED MEMO LINKS DEVELOPER TO SECRET CAMPAIGN CONTRIBUTIONS.

"Read the paper this morning, Corlis?" Andy asked, expressionless.

She gazed at the headline and slowly shook her head. "Didn't have time."

"Did you leak this to the *Picayune*?" Glimp asked bluntly. " 'Cause if you did, young lady, you have committed a very serious offense and—"

"I didn't leak it," Corlis cut in. "Any number of people on Grover Jeffries's end could have access to that memo. I don't know who leaked it, but *I* didn't." She stared squarely into her boss's solemn gaze. "Do you believe me, Andy?"

Her employer remained silent. Marvin Glimp, however, did not.

"We can't risk the liability, Andy," Glimp declared. "If she's lying, every asset you've got would have to be channeled into defendin' a suit filed by Grover Jeffries, who'll claim the station's accusin' him of illegal campaign contributions. It could effectively put you and WJAZ out of business."

"I don't *lie!*" Corlis retorted with heat. "And I don't leak information! And furthermore, Mr. Glimp, if you get me fired over this, I swear to you, I will find the best damn lawyer in America who will sue *your* ass for defamation and wrongful termination from here to Baton Rouge!" she threatened, taking a leaf out of Grover Jeffries's own book of intimidation.

Glimp appeared taken aback by the force of her words. "Look . . ." he temporized, "I'm just advisin' my client, Mr. Zamora. My job is to give *other* people ulcers, not get them myself."

"Well, let me ask you *this*, Mr. Glimp," she said, her eyes narrowing. "Have you advised your client, Mr. Zamora, here, that your *sister's* working for Lafayette Marchand, and maybe *that's* why you want us to go easy on the Marchand-Jeffries crowd?"

Zamora's surprised expression told Corlis she'd scored a bull's-eye.

Glimp looked nervously at Zamora. "She's a receptionist, for god's sake, Andy. It hardly seemed relevant."

"Well, it *is*," Zamora retorted.

Corlis turned to face her employer. "What about it, Andy? Do you believe me when I tell you that I did not leak that memo?"

Zamora hesitated and seemed to be turning something over in his mind. "Yes. I believe you."

"Then, do I still have my job?" she demanded. "Am I still assigned to this story?"

Zamora inhaled deeply and opened his top desk drawer. He extracted a fresh roll of Tums and popped one into his mouth.

"You're still on the story, McCullough. And you're still on probation."

By the time Corlis arrived at city hall, the council chambers were deserted, except for Manny and Virgil and a few other news crews who were packing up their gear.

"Where *is* everyone?" Corlis inquired, gazing at the empty rows of seats. "What happened?"

"Edgar Dumas opened the meetin' and immediately announced that the matter of the Selwyn buildin's required further extensive study and tabled the sucker again."

"You're kidding," Corlis replied, shaking her head. "Do you think that leaked memo to the *Picayune* this morning has got certain members of the council running scared?"

"I think you could say that," Virgil replied, smiling slyly and rolling his eyes toward his hairless eyebrows. "Some of 'em *must've* accepted money from Jeffries at one time or another, if not recently."

"So, now what happens?" she demanded. "I can't believe Grover Jeffries will just roll over on the Del Mar hotel project because of a newspaper story that only hinted there *might* be an incriminating memo."

"Oh no . . ." Virgil agreed. "The council's merely adjourned. Probably to allow time for Jeffries to dig up some dirt about King Duvallon and the preservationist folks."

Corlis blanched at the thought of the kind of "dirt" Jeffries and henchmen like Lafayette Marchand were most likely to try to dig up. She suddenly flashed on the sight of city council president Edgar Dumas ordering King Duvallon handcuffed. If Dumas accepted money from Grover Jeffries, he'd do almost anything to publicly discredit King. And since Dumas figured she and King were working hand-in-glove in the fight to save the Selwyn buildings, he wouldn't hesitate to go after her as well.

Virgil waved his hand around the empty hall. "What happened here today is likely just an intermission, you know what I'm sayin', sugar? If King and his preservationist pals are interested in savin' those buildin's, they'd better come up with some really good stuff that'll tug at the heartstrings of this town between now and the next city council meetin'. It's the only way."

Corlis looked at Virgil sharply. "You got any particular suggestions along those lines?" she asked. She had come to understand that Virgil Johnson had never quite been the kind of disinterested fellow he presented to the world.

"Did you ever get around to readin' Professor Barry Jefferson's brochure he was passin' out at the last meetin'?"

"Skimmed it," Corlis replied impatiently. "I already know the background."

"Well, girl, I suggest you read it *very* carefully," he advised, handing her a copy. "I sure hope *King* has."

Corlis glanced at the cover and opened the pamphlet to its fullest extension. Positioned in the center of the page were two oval engravings depicting the head and shoulders of well-dressed African Americans with bushy sideburns and top hats. They were attired in black business suits with starched white collars and neckcloths. In a box below, Corlis scanned a description of the lives of "two Free Men of Color whose success as tailors in the employ of white men-of-fashion in the late 1830s resulted in their joining forces with merchant Paul Tulane, Free Woman of Color Martine Fouché, the French Creole grande dame Marie Lavaudais, sugar and cotton exporter Julien LaCroix, and saddlery owner David Bates in a consortium to construct a commercial-residential block of buildings on Canal Street."

"So?" Corlis said. "I know all this."

"For a smart woman, you are sometimes real dopey, boss lady," Virgil said with an exasperated expression, pointing at the pictorial rendering of one of the tailors. "Now, what does it say right there, under their portraits, will you please tell me?" he demanded gruffly.

" 'J. Colvis, Tailor' . . . and 'Joseph Dumas, Tailor,' " she repeated. Then her mouth formed a little O. Eyes wide, she stared at Virgil and grinned. "Dumas! Dumas!" she exclaimed. "As in city council president Edgar *Dumas*!" She threw her arms around the video operator. "Virgil, you are a blooming *genius*! It sure might give Edgar pause if he knew he was voting to tear down a piece of *his own family's* history."

"Well, you gotta somehow prove Edgar's a direct descendant of this tailor guy, but . . . ain't New Orleans a grand place?" he said, grinning widely. "It's the only city in America where there's a real good chance that everybody—black or white—is related to *everybody else*!"

By this time, however, Corlis was already sprinting through the auditorium toward the double doors at the top of the aisle, praying that her cell phone battery hadn't died.

* * *

"Aunt Marge, you've just *got* to FedEx the diary!" Corlis pleaded over the telephone. "I can't wait for you to go photocopy it. I need it *now*! It could be an important starting place for tracking down specific information about Joseph Dumas, and it might give me some clues for finding out if the city council president is a direct descendant. There's a slew of Dumases in the telephone book, so I've got to narrow it down. I've got to have absolute *proof.* And besides, I have no idea when the council will meet again to decide the fate of the buildings, once and for all. They could order demolition on a moment's notice. I *need* that diary."

"Now, Corlis, calm down," her aunt admonished. "This is primary source evidence. I'm not about to let it out of my hands without a copy, and that's final! I'll see what I can do about getting this reproduced tomorrow and send it along immediately."

Corlis recognized her aunt's implacable tone of voice and took a new approach. "Well . . . can you tell me if you remember coming across the name Joseph Dumas in the diary?" she implored. "Any little lead, at this point, would be helpful."

"Dumas . . . Dumas . . ." Aunt Marge muttered into the phone receiver, and Corlis could picture the old lady squinting through her spectacles as she thumbed the diary's brittle, yellowed pages. "My stars, but this is spidery script! Wait one moment, dear. . . . I'll have to get the magnifying glass. I'm having a little trouble with my eyes lately. They're just not as sharp as they once were."

"Oh . . . look," Corlis conceded gently, "it's too hard for you to do it this way. Just do the best you can to get a copy to me right away, will you, darling?"

"If I can get a ride to the copying place, I'll try to get it done this afternoon, dear." There was a pause. "And how's that nice young man I talked to that time? Mr. Duvallon?"

"He's a source," Corlis replied neutrally. "So we don't socialize these days."

"Ah . . . yes . . . well, then," Aunt Marge conceded, "the next time you run into him on the story, please do send my regards. I liked his voice."

"I will tell him that you send your best," Corlis promised, wondering to herself when *that* would ever be.

By noon the next day she also had reason to wonder when—or if—she would ever receive a copy of the McCullough diary. The FedEx delivery never arrived, and the latest message on her voice mail was alarming.

"Now, I don't want you to worry, dear," a fragile-sounding Marge McCullough said, "but I had a minor fall when I was going through those heavy doors at the copy shop. The good news is, the doctor said I've only bruised my hip and my right shoulder and arm. The paramedics were so nice. . . . One of them said he'd drive me home from the emergency room when he goes off duty. I didn't want you to wonder why you hadn't received the diary. I'm so sorry to have disappointed you."

Corlis closed her eyes and inhaled deeply. This had long been the kind of call she had dreaded receiving from California. "Poor baby," she murmured into the receiver.

"And don't worry about the McCullough diary," Aunt Marge's message continued. "Those dear people at the copy shop made sure it was put in my bag when the ambulance came. I'll be home soon. I'm sure I'll be able to work my e-mail with my left hand, and I'll write you a note, just so you know I'm fine, so don't spend money calling California. Love you, dear."

Aunt Marge was something else, Corlis thought admiringly. What an old warhorse she was. Disregarding her aunt's directive, she quickly dialed Marge's number and was dismayed when the voice mail picked up. Corlis left a message of love and sympathy and hung up.

Well, so much for getting the diary to New Orleans any time soon, she fretted, gazing around her home office. Nevertheless, she *had* to find out more about that tailor, Joseph Dumas—and fast! Furthermore, what had happened to her namesake, Corlis Bell McCullough, when she was tossed from the carriage, right in front of the door downstairs? Had her two young sons, Warren and Webster McCullough, lost their mother? Had Julien LaCroix died from yellow fever? And what had happened to Martine Fouché?

Just then Cagney Cat startled Corlis by hoisting his furry bulk from floor to desk. He settled comfortably near the phone and stared at her with a beady gaze. An idea . . . a bizarre, off-the-wall idea that she would never repeat to another living soul—but one—sprang to mind. She quickly looked up Dylan Fouché's telephone number at his real estate office and dialed.

"I need your help," she said briskly, and proceeded to detail her last odd excursion into the nineteenth century, which had been launched from Julien's former study when they'd video-taped at Reverie plantation.

"I thought you looked pretty wigged-out that day," he drawled, "especially when you let that terror behind the wheel, Althea, drive your Lexus back to New Orleans."

"Believe me, the modern version of absinthe is still pretty lethal stuff, even when you just inhale it."

"And so you think that the fumes from the decanter of ab-sinthe whisked you back to those days in New Orleans, before the Civil War?" Dylan asked thoughtfully.

"*And* the incense at Saint Louis Cathedral, *and* the lilies in my apartment, *and* the pralines at the old warehouse," she added impatiently. "What I want to know, Dylan, is how in hell can I get back to the tailor shop of Joseph Dumas—or the deathbed of Julien LaCroix, for that matter? Do I have to start sniffing a spool of tailor's thread or a vial of carbolic acid?" she demanded.

"What a good idea!"

"Give me a break!" Corlis retorted. "I was kidding! But can you put me into a trance or something? Ask me to recall the past?"

"I don't think it would be reliable at this point," Dylan mused. "You're too anxious about figuring it all out. Whatever you came up with could be merely a product of your own projection . . . your own wish to come up with an answer—even one in-vented by your subconscious mind."

"Well, what do you suggest?" Corlis asked, feeling foolish for even hinting at the possibility of conducting genuine re-search into the past in such an unorthodox fashion.

"Sit tight," Dylan announced suddenly. He appeared to have settled something in his own mind. "I'll be right over. And after you hang up from this call, unplug your phone and don't answer the door until I get there!"

* * *

The shades were drawn in Corlis's back bedroom, making her enormous four-poster plantation bed appear to loom even larger than it was. In the sepulchral light, its luxurious yellow brocade hangings cascaded from the canopy, much like a stage curtain.

Dylan placed a briefcase on the bedspread and opened the metal catches. Inside were a number of unusual items, including a feather, a box of matches, a thick ivory candle about six inches high, and a brown glass vial.

"Carbolic acid?" Corlis asked dryly.

"Close," Dylan chuckled. He withdrew the silver bell he had used during his space-clearing session, and a soft linen cloth. "Why don't you recline on that chaise longue over there?"

She did exactly as Dylan had instructed and lay down. She eyed the brown glass vial. "How's *that* going to flip me into Dumas's tailor shop?"

"It probably won't," Dylan responded calmly, dripping a bit of the liquid from the bottle onto the piece of clean linen. "I think we should stick with the types of circumstances that have sent you backward in time on previous occasions."

"And you think reclining on a chaise like Blanche DuBois in *Streetcar Named Desire* will help?" Corlis teased.

"Did you know that Desire is the name of a *street* in New Orleans, and it had a streetcar on it in Tennessee Williams's day?"

"Do tell?" Corlis replied with a smile. "Actually, about twenty people told me that the first week after I moved here." Then she said quietly, "You know ... I'm actually kind of scared. Maybe I'm asking questions I don't want to know the answers to."

"It'll be all right," Dylan assured her, patting her shoulder. "I'll be right here with you. I won't let anything bad happen." Dylan closed his eyes and inhaled deeply. Corlis guessed that the former Catholic seminarian was saying a prayer, and closed her eyes as well. "Now," Dylan instructed, "just start takin' deep, calmin' breaths. That's right ... in and out ... in ... and out. Empty your mind of all extraneous thoughts while I light this candle and place it beside you so you can gaze at its flame. Just breathe in ... and out ... that's good. Now open your eyes and focus them on the flickerin' flame and breathe evenly ...

deeply. Good. Now close your eyes again and cleanse your body and mind of everythin' but the sound of your breathin'. That's right. Inhale . . . exhale. . . ."

Dylan's hypnotic, melodious voice had a tranquilizing effect, and before long Corlis began to feel wonderfully relaxed as she concentrated solely on the sound and sensation of her own breath. She smelled a strange, pungent odor, but she kept her eyes closed, as she knew Dylan would ask her to do if she opened them to identify the medicinal scent.

It was an oddly familiar aroma, she thought idly, an odor that spoke of the sickroom and fainting spells. She inhaled deeply. An acridness bloomed all around her, as if to rouse her from her state of stupor, rather than put her into a trance.

The smell grew stronger still—biting, astringent, and quite unpleasant. Then her eyes began to water, and Corlis was forced to swim to the surface of complete consciousness when all she longed to do was sleep . . . and sleep. . . .

"Mrs. McCullough! Oh, dear God, sir. . . . She won't wake up! *Mrs. McCullough!*"

Corlis Bell McCullough was able to identify the high-pitched squawk of Hetty, her children's nanny, but for the life of her, she was unable to open her eyes so that she might insist that the hysterical woman lower her voice.

"Out of the way, girl!" barked a gruff voice. "I'm a doctor. These smelling salts should do the trick!"

Corlis heard the cacophony of voices shouting on all sides, but her eyelids remained heavy as two lead weights. A horse's whinny told her she was out of doors, and several unpleasant odors she was inhaling—over and above the piercingly sharp fragrance placed beneath her nostrils—confirmed that she was lying in a muddy street dotted with horse manure.

Julia Street!

Now she remembered! Julien LaCroix's team of horses had shied and thrown her from her precarious perch on the driver's box.

Oh, dear God! What had happened to that poor man who had been nearly delirious with yellow fever?

Corlis fluttered open her eyelids and found herself staring

into the wrinkled countenance of a man with grizzled sideburns growing from beneath his ears to the tip of his chin.

"Dr. Rayburn, at your service, ma'am," he announced, his breath laced with the smell of the port or claret he'd consumed at his last meal. "How's your head feeling, my dear? You've had a nasty thump, I'm afraid, when you pitched yourself out of the carriage."

"I did not pitch myself out, sir," Corlis countered archly. "Those wild beasts bolted, and the reins shot right out of my hands." She struggled to sit up but sank back, moaning slightly. "Ooooh . . . I've quite a headache."

"I'm not surprised," replied Dr. Rayburn. "We've taken your companion upstairs to your apartments—"

"How is he?" she interrupted anxiously.

"Not good," the doctor pronounced shortly. Dr. Rayburn leaned forward and whispered into Corlis's ear, "And I did not mention to your neighbors the malady that I suspect he's suffering from. However, I suppose I should tell *you*, since by necessity, you're hosting him in your home at present."

"I know what his malady is," she replied in a low voice, glancing up at the handful of curious bystanders who had gathered around. She smiled at one of the men. "Please, sir . . ." she said with energy that depleted her just as quickly as she had summoned it, "would you be so kind as to help the doctor to get me upstairs? I believe I can walk, if I may lean on both of you."

Fortunately Corlis had not broken any bones, but was merely bruised on her right side, and she continued to suffer a headache for the rest of the afternoon. Julien had been placed in the four-poster bed in her upstairs bedchamber and lay prone, like a corpse, with his eyes shut and beads of perspiration dotting his brow.

After Dr. Rayburn departed, she dutifully sponged Julien's forehead, wondering if the man would last the night. She had instructed her sons and their nanny to take refuge with a nearby neighbor.

As for her husband, Corlis couldn't have cared less what happened to the rogue. Randall had obviously spent the last night or two in the stews of Girod Street. Let him remain there! A note on her front door downstairs advised him as much.

A soft knock on the bedroom door roused her from her gloomy thoughts. A handsome, dark-haired young man poked his head into the shuttered bedchamber.

"Lafayette Marchand here," he announced softly. "I let myself in. Mr. Bates said it was an emergency." He glanced at Julien's still form. "Julien?" He looked questioningly at Corlis.

"I'm Corlis McCullough. I found your brother-in-law on Canal Street . . . taken ill."

"With what?" Marchand asked, suspicion clouding his chiseled features.

"The doctor and I both believe it's yellow fever."

"Good Lord!"

"Marchand?" said a weak voice. "Is that you?"

Julien struggled to sit up, only managing to balance himself on his elbows.

"Yes."

"I must have you write a codicil to my will. I must . . ."

"Sh-h, there now," Corlis said soothingly, easing Julien back onto the pillows. "I will get pen and paper and will write exactly as you tell me, then your brother-in-law can co-sign."

"Thank you," sighed Julien.

Marchand eased his lanky body into the sickroom but stood with his back against the wall, a few feet from the door. "Is my sister, Adelaide, all right out at Reverie?"

"I have no idea," Julien murmured. "She set out to find you. . . ."

"I've been . . . out of touch," Marchand said, and there was no need for him to explain that he'd been attending the competitions at Metairie Race Course outside New Orleans proper. "My butler sent word to me after Bates called at Dauphine Street, and I came directly here. Is Adelaide ill, too?" he asked again with a look of alarm.

"In her mind . . . and soul . . ." Julien whispered. "We have wounded each other greatly, when that was not our . . . intent." Corlis pulled up a chair beside the bed and sat with pen and paper, ready to receive Julien's labored dictation. "This is my last will and testament . . . before . . . these witnesses," he said, breathing with difficulty. With the economy of a dying man, Julien bequeathed Reverie plantation to his only surviving white male cousin, Edouard Picot, of Baton Rouge, "allowing my wife a lifetime tenancy at Reverie, perhaps in the *garçon-niere*, and a yearly allowance of eight hundred reals, should she survive me."

Corlis called a halt to Julien's strained efforts in order to sponge the perspiration that was pouring from his brow. Then she brought a glass of water to his parched lips. Marchand remained a silent witness to the unfolding drama.

"Drink just a little," she urged. "It will help you speak."

"Yes . . . thank you," Julien replied weakly. Then he appeared to summon every ounce of his draining energy. "I grant my share of the Canal Street holdings to my infant son, Julien LaCroix, a Free Person of Color . . . on the condition that his mother will also leave him her share of said buildings, upon her death, and that during her lifetime, she will rely upon the wise counsel of Joseph Dumas, the tailor, who is a full partner with Paul Tulane and the rest of our consortium."

Corlis heard Lafayette Marchand's swift intake of breath.

"You choose a Free Man of Color to guide your affairs, rather than your *lawyer*?"

"Joseph Dumas is a fine man," Julien whispered hoarsely, "as is his son, whom I should hope would one day make a match with Martine's Lisette." Unbidden, Corlis noted this request in the will, for she knew that Free People of Color, by order of the Code Noir, were permitted to marry only other free blacks.

"This is not *done*," Marchand muttered. "These family holdings should remain with the LaCroixs and be administered through proper channels by trustees."

"My son, Julien . . . my half sister, Lisette . . . and Martine *are* LaCroixs, you imbecile," Julien replied with astonishing verve.

Julien sank into the mound of pillows and fell into a paroxysm of coughing. Corlis quickly brought the glass of water to his lips, and in a few moments, visibly weakened by this attack, Julien attempted to continue.

"The warehouse, as well as profits from the sale . . . of the remaining cane and cotton therein . . . shall be administered solely by Martine Fouché . . . who is a capable woman of business," he declared in a rasping voice while Corlis frantically scribbled his directives. He glanced across the bedchamber at his brother-in-law, who remained with his back plastered against the wall. "To my wife's brother, Lafayette Marchand, I bequeath all my horses and carriages."

Lafayette's eyes widened with astonishment, but he did not interrupt.

"My brother-in-law has always been . . . a fine appreciator of equines and . . . of quality flesh."

Corlis stared at the lawyer, recalling the bright eyes and expectant feminine smiles ringing the dance floor on the night of the sugarcane festival. Was this debonair bachelor to take his place among yet another generation of gentlemen who married among their class, only to have their pleasure in one of the cottages dotting Rampart Street?

Corlis Bell McCullough slowly shook her head. The convoluted ways of these Frenchies were too dark and mysterious for *her* simple soul, she thought, shifting her gaze to Julien's sunken cheeks, whose hollows hinted at the cadaver he would soon become.

"Is there anything else you desire me to write, Julien?" Corlis inquired softly.

"Yes . . ." Julien said hoarsely. "Anyone who mounts a challenge to this will shall, as a consequence, receive one picayune. And please write this: 'Martine . . . despite everything . . . I loved you without prejudice . . . or reservation. . . .'"

Another fit of coughing erupted from deep in his chest. Exhausted, he stretched out his trembling right hand toward Corlis, his clawlike gesture signaling that he wished to sign the makeshift document. That accomplished, he sank back against the perspiration-soaked bed linen.

"Sign!" he croaked. "Both . . . of . . . you. Now!"

Corlis hastily scratched her signature and rose from Julien's bedside. When she crossed the room to stand next to Lafayette Marchand, she sincerely doubted that he would serve as the necessary second witness.

However, she was mistaken.

"My sister has been properly provided for," he murmured. "I will sign."

By the time Corlis and Lafayette Marchand looked up from

Julien's will, the waxen countenance of the short-lived owner of Reverie plantation told them both that the last written testament they all had just signed would immediately come into full force.

For Julien LaCroix, age thirty-one, was dead. '

Chapter Twenty-six

May 29

Corlis's nose twitched.

Something was burning.

Off to one side, she heard the faintest sound of a tinkling bell. The pungent odor grew stronger and stronger, until she forced open her eyes. Then she sat bolt upright on the chaise longue in her shadowed bedroom. Dylan Fouché was leaning over her, a silver bell held in one hand and a smoldering white feather in the other.

"Welcome back," he said with a worried expression.

"What are you *doing*?" she demanded, batting away Dylan's hand from beside her face.

"Well, I could hardly use smellin' salts to bring you round, now could I?" Dylan replied peevishly, "since it was smellin' salts that put you in the trance in the *first* place! I used these." He rang the little silver bell in one hand and fanned the white chicken feather back and forth with the other in order to extinguish the small flame that continued to consume it. "I'm not exactly an expert in this particular aspect of psychic phenomena," he confessed with a studied show of modesty, "but I remembered readin' somewhere that a burnt feather was a handy alternative for women needin' to be revived after sufferin' the vapors."

"Well . . . it worked," Corlis replied ruefully, swinging her feet from chaise longue to floor.

"It sure took a while," Dylan said, frowning. "You had me worried there when you didn't come out of it at first."

"Boy, have I got a doozy of a headache." She recalled the vision of Julien LaCroix, lying still and cold, on a bed very much like the one looming on the other side of the room. "Whatever trance you just induced turned out to be a big-time woo-woo experience," she added. She cocked her head in Dylan's direction. "Well . . . I suppose you're waiting for me to treat you to a very nice dinner?"

"I was thinkin' you'd never ask," Dylan replied with a grin. "But first . . . what *happened*? Did you learn any more about the saga of Joseph Dumas?"

"Not about *him* specifically," Corlis replied, discouraged.

"Enough to link his family to the city council president's?"

"Edgar Dumas?" she asked. "No. I did learn, though, that Joseph Dumas had a son who worked with him in the tailoring business and whom Julien hoped would one day marry Lisette, the daughter of *your* ancestor, Martine Fouché."

"Well, at least we know that Joseph Dumas had someone to carry on his family line, but too bad you couldn't make a direct connection to Edgar closer than that," Dylan said. "We'll have to show a stronger link than merely the name Dumas to get ol' Edgar to wax nostalgic and vote against demolition, 'cause then he'd have to give up whatever might be comin' his way from Grover Jeffries's coffers."

"Right," Corlis agreed, and added, "I *can* confirm that poor Julien LaCroix died of yellow fever. At least that's what I *saw*. There might be an official way of nailing down a fact like that through parish death records or wills filed with the state or something." She allowed Dylan to take her arm while she rose unsteadily from the chaise longue. "I'll fill you in on the rest at dinner, if you'll swear to absolute secrecy, Mr. Wizard."

Dylan struck a tragic pose.

"Cross my heart and hope to die." Then he grimaced. "Cancel that. Under the circumstances, I think a simple 'I promise to keep my mouth shut' will suffice."

"McCullough!" a voice boomed over WJAZ's intercom, penetrating every nook and cranny of the television station, including the ladies' room. "You're wanted in Zamora's office. On the double!"

"Oh boy," Corlis sighed, applying a swipe of color to her lips. "What *now*?"

She smacked her lips together and peered into the mirror at her freshly made-up face. Then she glanced at her watch. It was quarter to eleven. Chances were excellent that Zamora's unexpected summons meant that her nice working lunch with Althea LaCroix at the Acme Oyster House in the French Quarter would be history.

In the hallway outside the rest rooms, Corlis and Marvin Glimp nearly collided as they both headed for the station owner's corner office.

"An emergency city council session on the Selwyn buildings has just been called," Glimp announced anxiously as he scurried down the corridor. "Andy and I want to be sure you understand the ground rules before you take off for city hall."

"How about just employing fairness and accuracy?" Corlis inquired testily.

Glimp shot her a *watch it, young lady* look over his shoulder as they entered Zamora's office.

The station owner slid the last tiny disk from his roll of Tums and put it under his tongue, balling up the shredded wrapper. "The meetin' is called for four this afternoon," Zamora told her. "I want you to interview both sides of the controversy for the early news today. Ask them for reactions—win or lose. *Both* sides, got that?"

Corlis nodded.

"Then, after the vote, pick up reactions from people on the street: from the descendants of the original builders, from some of the union construction guys who'd ultimately work for the Del Mar hotel folks—whatever you can get, so we can do a full wraparound on the late news."

Her boss's suggestions were standard operating procedure, even for a rookie television journalist.

"And?" she asked, waiting for the other shoe to drop.

"Lafayette Marchand's already called the station this mornin'," Zamora announced grimly, handing her a written record of a call marked "urgent" from Grover Jeffries's public relations henchman. "I talked to him briefly. He asked specifically to speak to you. Wants you to call him right away."

Corlis felt that familiar anxiety-ridden fluttering in the pit of her gut. Marchand's call couldn't be good news. The fix was in about the city council vote on demolition, and Lafayette Marchand wanted to be given the first opportunity to sock it to her on camera.

"Mind if I get King Duvallon and Althea LaCroix's reactions on tape first?" she inquired, trying to sound casual. "I'd feel more comfortable if we had some of the players in the can before the city council meeting starts. Afterward it'll be a mad scramble to find everybody before our show deadline."

Marvin Glimp studied her narrowly. "Just be sure you give Grover Jeffries's side equal time—to the nanosecond! Since I'm a bettin' man, and I'm bettin' all twenty-eight stories of that new hotel's gonna be towerin' over the French Quarter some day *very* soon." He shrugged apologetically in Zamora's direction. "And if that happens, Andy . . . I just want WJAZ to still be broadcastin'."

"I'd be sorry to see those Greek Revivals come down," Zamora admitted with resignation, "but I think you're probably right, Marvin."

"So, you think it's a done deal?" Corlis asked sharply.

Both men exchanged glances.

"That's an inelegant way of phrasin' it," Zamora said with a sour laugh, "but that's my guess."

"Whatever," Corlis replied, feebly attempting to mask a mounting sense of desolation. "Equal time for everybody concerned—to the nanosecond," she added for Glimp's benefit.

It seemed certain now that King's beloved buildings were about to become rubble and dust, she thought bitterly. And even though she could practically hear Aunt Marge's voice warning her not to take sides on this issue, she felt as if she might start to weep. In fact, she *would* burst out crying if she didn't get out of her boss's office pronto. She turned toward the door.

"Good luck," Zamora said quietly.

"See y'all later," she drawled, wishing she could erase from her mind the sight of Kingsbury Duvallon—courageous, implacable, unmoveable King—braving the onslaught of Grover Jeffries's giant bulldozers.

What would the man *do* if he lost this fight?

* * *

By 11 A.M., Corlis swung by the deserted Café LaCroix and picked up Althea. Surprisingly, her friend directed her to drive down St. Charles Avenue toward the Kingsbury-Duvallon house on Orange Street.

"What?" Corlis protested, dismayed at the notion of encountering King's parents.

"I want you to do your interview with us *there*," Althea insisted stubbornly, "in front of a beautiful historic buildin' *white* folks saved! King would agree."

"I really don't think that's such a great idea."

"We've used the garden as a background for video stuff several times," Althea replied, unmoved. "When King's parents are at work, we've zipped in and zipped out, with Antoinette and Waylon none the wiser. The place looks real New Orleans, ya know?"

"But it's *me* doing the interviewing, remember?" Corlis fretted as they drove by a stand of moss-draped oaks flanking the thoroughfare. "King's parents might not like the idea very much, considering the piece I did about their daughter's wedding."

"It'll be fine," Althea assured her, gazing through the windshield. "This is an emergency. I left a message on voice mail about the city council meetin' at King's house, the PRC, and at his office at the university. Chris Calvert's been tryin' to track him down, too. He said he'd alert King about our interview with you at the same time. He'll show up."

"Okay," Corlis replied resignedly as the car drew closer to the Kingsbury-Duvallon residence. "You and King are the costars of this little show, so have it your way." She quickly dialed Virgil on his cell phone and directed Manny and him to meet her on Orange Street.

"Should be nice and relaxin'," Virgil replied, " 'specially since we just finished shootin' this cockamamie story they got us doin' this mornin' about a lady with thirty-nine black cats who lives next door to a cemetery. See you in ten minutes," he said, signing off.

Corlis pulled up to the curb in front of the Kingsbury-Duvallon family home, parked, and locked her car. The sooner she got this interview over with, the better. She felt butterflies in her stomach at the mere thought of seeing King again. She glanced once more at her watch, remembering suddenly that she still hadn't returned Lafayette Marchand's urgent call. Too bad she couldn't catch his client, Grover Jeffries, on camera, passing out the thank-you checks to certain members of the city council before they took the vote! she thought darkly.

Much to Althea and Corlis's surprise, however, they discovered when they rang the front doorbell that King's mother was still at home—and King wasn't there.

"I don't rightly know *what* to tell you," Antoinette exclaimed, a worried frown creasing her alabaster forehead. "Everybody's been tryin' to get hold of him today, but no one's heard from or seen King since yesterday!" She stood at her door, framed by the carved wooden moldings and fanlight that arched over the threshold of the venerable old house. Mrs. Duvallon wore a smartly tailored St. John knit suit and sleek kid pumps, looking as if she might have a luncheon at Galatoire's on her agenda this afternoon.

"Since yesterday?" Corlis echoed, her pulse quickening. "Do you have any reason to think there's cause for concern?"

"Well, with all the controversy brewin' at city council, and those awful public protests . . . that boy has ruffled a few feathers in the town, I can tell you *that*!" she said in her soft, steel magnolia accent.

"Do you think you should call the police?" Althea asked anxiously. "Report King's gone missin', Mrs. Duvallon?"

"The police have put King in jail so often this year, I don't know what good it would do to call *them*," Mrs. Duvallon declared. Then she heaved a sigh and added, "In actual fact, I said the exact same thing this mornin' to my husband, Waylon, but he thinks it's premature to file a missin' person report, and I—"

King's aunt, Bethany Kingsbury, appeared at the door. Her normally tidy gray hair fell in disarray about her shoulders, and her face was etched with worry. "Missing person report? Oh, goodness! Why would you think—"

"That's just the problem I'm tryin' to tell these ladies about," Antoinette cried. "When Waylon went out to the curb this mornin' to get his newspaper, he found a bunch of King's preservation literature and his briefcase lyin' on the sidewalk, right in front of the house. We had no idea he'd been by here. After we tried all his numbers, we called his next-door neighbor on Dauphine Street who's got a key to his place, you know? And when he looked in his room, his bed hadn't been slept in last night. I *told* Waylon that the police should at least know about the briefcase and that he hadn't been at his house all night, but then Waylon said that when King was datin' Cindy Lou, there were plenty of nights when he probably didn't—"

Just then the WJAZ news van pulled up in front of the house. Antoinette stared accusingly at Corlis. "Why are the TV people comin' here?" she demanded to know.

Looking like a scared rabbit, Bethany spoke up quickly. "I told Althea, here, it'd be all right if they just used a corner of the garden to—"

"You did *what*!" Antoinette screeched.

"*We've* been trying to reach King all mornin', too, Mrs. Duvallon!" Althea intervened swiftly. "We were supposed to tape an interview here, prior to the city council meetin' this afternoon."

"I never gave my permission to do that," Antoinette declared heatedly. "A TV interview about the controversy? That's *all* we need at this point." She glared over their heads at the sight of Virgil and Manny assembling their camera equipment on a small dolly near the news van.

For his part, Virgil was oblivious to the tension-filled drama taking place on the front porch. The cameraman waved and shouted, "Good mornin' ma'am!" Then he waved his cell phone in one hand and directed his next words to Corlis. "Hey, boss! Lafayette Marchand's on the phone for you. The station forwarded his call to us in the van. He sounds mighty agitated."

Corlis watched, surprised, as streaks of scarlet suddenly flooded Antoinette Duvallon's cheeks. In contrast, her sister, Bethany Kingsbury, seemed to blanch.

"Lafayette . . . ?" King's aunt repeated faintly.

"Lafayette's callin' here?" Antoinette murmured with astonishment. "Ever since King and he had that fallin' out, he never calls anymore. . . ."

"I'm supposed to do an interview with him, too—or with Grover Jeffries—sometime today," Corlis explained, dreading to take Marchand's call. "We're just trying to cover the building controversy fairly, Mrs. Duvallon. We're giving both sides a chance to air their views. . . ."

Antoinette nodded absently, as if mesmerized by the sight of the enormous black man making his way, cell phone in hand, past the iron gate and up the path to her front door.

"Nice to see you again, Mrs. Duvallon," Virgil said politely.

"Hello, Mr. Johnson," Antoinette said curtly.

"Good mornin', Miss Kingsbury."

Bethany nodded warmly, but her features were pinched and careworn.

Then, as if Antoinette had suddenly been reminded of her manners, she said, "You were very nice doin' all those pretty close-ups of our flowers at the symphony luncheon this spring. I appreciate that . . . very much."

All eyes were now on Corlis as she put the phone to her ear.

"McCullough, here," Corlis announced in a businesslike voice while taking a few steps beyond the group at the Duvallon front door.

"Lafayette Marchand. I'm callin' regardin'—"

"You were on my list to call back, Mr. Marchand," Corlis replied hurriedly. "Sorry for the delay. I was hoping you could arrange an interview—"

"This call is about . . . King."

"King?" she echoed, surprised. "What *about* King?"

Both Antoinette and Bethany were staring intently at Corlis while she spoke into Virgil's cell phone.

"Look, could you meet me at Commander's Palace at twelve?" he asked, referring to one of New Orleans's most renowned eateries located in the heart of the residential Garden District, only minutes away from the Kingsbury-Duvallon home.

"I really don't think this is a day for a lunch date, Mr. Marchand," Corlis said pointedly. "As you well know, the city council is meeting late this afternoon and I had hoped that either you or Mr. Jeffries would be willing to talk to me on camera about—"

"That's *not* why I'm callin'," Marchand intervened

brusquely. "And I'm not invitin' you to lunch." He sounded increasingly grim. "To put it as clearly as I can, Ms. McCullough, I am strongly suggestin' that you meet me in front of the restaurant as close to twelve as you can make it."

Before Corlis could reply, the phone line clicked. Marchand had hung up on her.

"What did he say about King?" Antoinette demanded. "What did that man say about my *son*?"

Nonplussed, Corlis exchanged confused glances with Althea and Virgil.

"Lafayette Marchand wants me to meet him in front of Commander's Palace for purposes unknown," she disclosed reluctantly. "It's a pretty weird request," she added for Virgil's benefit, "but my instinct says we should go there, okay? Maybe we can grab an interview with him in case Jeffries won't talk to us on camera after the city council vote." She turned to King's mother and aunt and added gently, "I don't know what all this is about, but I will call you right away if I learn anything about King's whereabouts . . . all right?"

"Thank you," Antoinette said faintly.

"That'd be mighty sweet of you," Bethany said.

"And would it be all right with you if I did a quick interview with Althea here in the garden? It shouldn't take more than ten or fifteen minutes, and I may not have a chance to do it later in the day. I'll shoot it over there," she added, pointing to a thicket of palmetto trees in the side yard. "The TV viewers won't even know where we are . . . just that we're somewhere pretty."

Antoinette glanced nervously over her shoulder. "Well, my husband's gone on down to our shop, so I suppose it'd be all right."

Bethany reached out and touched Corlis's forearm. "You *will* call us if Lafayette knows anything about King, won't you? Laf's an old family friend, and even though he and King have been mighty rude to each other 'bout this Selwyn buildin' business, I'm sure he'd want to help us . . . find Antoinette's son."

The chances of Lafayette Marchand caring a damn about King's welfare at this stage of the game were zero to none, she thought bitterly.

Following the brief interview of Althea LaCroix in the garden, Corlis and her television crew headed in two vehicles toward Commander's Palace. Meanwhile, Althea called United Cab to take her back to the Preservation Resource Center.

"What's your cell phone number?" Althea asked Corlis as she got into the taxi. "I'll call you if I hear anything from our end." The black woman shook her head. "We've gotta *find* him, Corlis. We'll be a totally lost cause at that council meetin' if we don't."

"I know," Corlis agreed, her voice tight.

"I'm puttin' all the guerrillas on the case, soon as I get back downtown," Althea vowed, "and I'm callin' my second cousin, Councilman Bordeleon. This is serious. See you later at city hall."

On Washington Avenue, a crowd of hungry patrons lined up outside Commander's Palace, a blue-and-white Victorian situated directly opposite the historic Lafayette Cemetery Number 1.

"How fitting to be meeting Lafayette Marchand *here*," Corlis noted sarcastically when she caught up with Virgil and Manny, who were parking the news van a few spaces away from her Lexus beside a large, imposing wrought-iron fence.

The trio found Marchand standing in the shadow of one of the wooden pillars of the restaurant that supported the gallery and its jaunty blue-and-white-striped awning. As usual, he was impeccably attired, this time in a southern classic: a blue-and-white seersucker suit with a white shirt made of fine Egyptian cotton. Even Marchand's perfectly knotted silk tie sported regimental stripes of sapphire and ivory, as if he had intended to serve as a visual complement to Commander's color scheme.

"Let's head on over to the cemetery," he announced without preamble. He started to cross the street in the direction of the picturesque wrought-iron gates marking the entrance to a graveyard notable for its aboveground tombs.

"You want us to interview you in the *cemetery*?" Corlis exclaimed as she and her TV crew scampered across the street in Marchand's wake. Was this man such an egotist that he wanted the ornate ironwork arching overhead that spelled out

LAFAYETTE CEMETERY NO. 1 to serve as background for his comments concerning the inevitable demise of the Selwyn buildings?

Some people in this town are just too weird!

Marchand didn't halt his forward progress to reply. Instead, he pushed open a waist-high iron gate and hurriedly ushered them through.

"Oh m'God," Corlis said under her breath to Virgil as a phalanx of marble crypts loomed ahead. "Places like this give me the creeps."

"Me, too," Virgil whispered back, and Manny nodded.

In front of them stretched an asphalt path that was deeply fissured by cracks and potholes. On each side was a line of trees, followed by row upon row of miniature marble structures that looked like a community of stone dollhouses. Sepulchers were distinguished by crosses, rotund stone cherubs, winged angels, and graceful urns—elaborate carvings that struck odd notes of individuality among the hundreds of tombs that had been inhabited by deceased citizens of New Orleans since 1833.

Ahead of the television crew, Marchand continued at a brisk pace. After a few minutes he did an abrupt about-face. Corlis saw that his blue eyes expressed the same kind of sorrow as the doleful cherub gazing mournfully down at their oddly assorted group.

"May I speak with you alone for a minute?" he asked Corlis.

She glanced at Manny and Virgil, who appeared as surprised as she was by Marchand's sudden request. She hesitated and then replied, "Okay. Guys, wait here. We'll be right back." To Marchand she suggested, "How about over there? On the other side of that big mausoleum?"

The well-dressed public relations man strode across the grass another fifty feet and waited for Corlis to join him behind a solid marble obelisk guarding the entrance to a large crypt dedicated to the Moreau family.

Without preface Lafayette Marchand said, "I need you to help me locate King Duvallon. And when you find him, you must promise me you'll have your crew record it all on videotape."

Corlis gazed at Marchand, dumbfounded by his bizarre request. "I think you'd better explain," she said finally. "Why have you brought us to a cemetery, Mr. Marchand?"

"We don't have much time," he said agitatedly, no longer the smooth-talking spin doctor with whom Corlis was accustomed to dealing. "I've asked you to help me locate Professor Duvallon because . . . Kingsbury is my son. Mine and Antoinette Duvallon's."

Corlis took a step toward the stone tomb and held on to it for support.

"Oh . . . my . . . God . . ." Corlis said on a long breath.

She envisioned King, tall and slender, with the kind of patrician good looks, natural grace, and aristocratic manners that had never really jibed with Waylon Duvallon's short, stocky physique and gruff nature. Her gaze drifted from Lafayette's sleekly trimmed silver-streaked hair to his crisp seersucker suit and elegant brown loafers. King Duvallon certainly possessed the man's physical characteristics.

"Mardi Gras, 1962," Corlis murmured. "I saw the picture on Antoinette's mantelpiece in the house on Orange Street."

"That picture is a snapshot of my entire life," said Marchand somberly.

She did some fast calculations. Lafayette Marchand and King's mother were contemporaries. They'd grown up in the same social circles in the late fifties and early sixties. Corlis pulled from her memory the details of the photographic portrait of the 1962 Mardi Gras court starring a girlish Antoinette Kingsbury, with Avery Labonniere as King of Carnival and Lafayette Marchand serving as "duke." The picture had been given pride of place in the front parlor filled with one-hundred-fifty-year-old treasured family heirlooms.

"Well . . . it'll take more than a snapshot to explain what's going on here," Corlis declared. "But, obviously, all that'll have to wait. Will you just answer me one thing, Mr. Marchand? Why have you told *me*, of all people, about this?" she demanded. "Why now? And why do you think I can find King any better than you can?"

"It's obvious that you care for my son," Marchand replied tersely. "And you're the best investigative reporter in town.

I'm . . . desperate. I've tried all morning to find him by myself. You and your crew provide my greatest chance—at this late date—for finding him alive."

"But why did you drag us all the way into a *graveyard* to tell us this?" she demanded.

"Because King's locked up in one of these tombs."

Chapter Twenty-seven

June 1

The noonday sun beat down with increasing intensity on Lafayette Cemetery Number 1. "Who did this to King?" Corlis demanded, simultaneously furious and fearful.

"I'll give you a full explanation, but first let's begin to search."

Her thoughts were racing in various directions, but underlying every possible scenario was a terrible sense of foreboding. Whoever had risked a kidnapping charge was probably capable of a lot worse things.

Like fitting an adversary with a pair of cement shoes!

"Okay, let's get started," she agreed shortly, "but I've got to tell my crew what's going on and let them decide for themselves if they want to get involved with this."

"Fair enough," Marchand replied, "but I'd rather King be given the choice of acknowledging me publicly as his father."

"Okay. That part's between us . . . off the record," she nodded.

Marchand followed behind her as she strode back to Manny and Virgil, who still waited on the other side of the central path. Immediately she explained that King Duvallon had been kidnapped.

The crew looked astonished as Marchand elaborated.

"Jack Ebert let it slip this mornin' that Grover'd told him to tail King last night. He picked him up outside his parents' house," Marchand disclosed. "Accordin' to Jack, he and one of the hearse drivers from the Ebert-Petrella funeral homes brought King to some cemetery and locked him up in a tomb till after the council voted Grover's way today."

"Jack Ebert? The mortician's son?" Virgil interjected gruffly. "Jesus, Marchand! You gotta know there's no love lost between *those* two."

"Jack knows the city graveyards like the back of his hand," Marchand said. "Jack claims Grover told him to find a tomb that has a steel grate or marble filigree, so King can get plenty of fresh air till the city council meetin' is over. Trouble is, Ebert took off and I couldn't find him after our telephone conversation. There are cemeteries like this all over greater New Orleans," he disclosed with a sweeping gesture that encompassed the vast grounds. "This is the third one I've been to this mornin'."

"And you trust his archenemy to pick a nice ol' comfy tomb for the guy?" Manny spoke up angrily. "What if the jerk deliberately chose *wrong?*"

"Believe me, at this point, I don't trust any of that bunch on any level, whatsocver. That's why I got in touch with you all."

"God knows what some of these mausoleums are like on the inside," Corlis exclaimed with a shudder. "Something could have happened and King's hurt! Doesn't that idiot Jeffries know that kidnapping—even for a *day*—is a federal offense?"

"I'm sure he knows," Marchand said tiredly. "He just figures he can get away with it. No harm, no foul. Jack warned me to keep my mouth shut, if I didn't want to be accused of bein' an accessory after the fact and if I wanted to receive the hundred thousand dollars he knows Grover owes me on account."

"And *you* said?" Corlis asked caustically.

"I hung up the phone and started tryin' to get hold of you, Miz McCullough."

"Why me?"

"I'd seen the way you and King were together when you were dinin' at Galatoire's, and then I heard through the grapevine that you'd attended Emelie Dumas's funeral with him." Corlis glanced at Manny and Virgil and felt herself flushing. "I knew instinctively that King must have some strong feelin's for you if he'd taken you there," he continued, "and you for him as well. So I hoped you'd be willin' to try to help me find him and then put pressure on Grover to stop manipulatin' members of the plannin' commission and the city council about this demolition business. Sooner or later, all this arm-twistin' is gonna earn him, and anyone who works with him, an indictment."

"What do you think I *am*?" Corlis asked indignantly. "Your damage control officer? You want me to do the rescuing *for* you, is that it? Keep your fingerprints off such an embarrassing incident, so you can stay out of jail and still collect those fees?"

"I can understand why it may look that way to you," Marchand replied, shifting his gaze from Corlis to her TV crew, who stood in a circle within the grassy area separating several crypts. "But we're wastin' time with all of this! My first priority is to make sure King is all right, and I don't want any of us to get hurt. Public exposure is the *only* weapon that can do Grover real harm—and he knows it."

"Well, then . . ." Corlis said, somewhat mollified, "what do you suggest we do next?" She looked over Marchand's shoulder. "There must be five hundred aboveground tombs in this place" she calculated worriedly. "It could take forever to find him, and if the ventilation isn't good, or if he's unconscious and can't answer our calls . . ." Her voice trailed off.

"We've got a couple of hours before the city council meetin' is due to begin. Let's fan out systematically and go house to house, so to speak," Marchand urged.

"But what if Jack or the chauffeur were ordered to stand guard?" Manny asked apprehensively.

"Ebert said Grover told them not to hang around, in case someone spotted them. He and his buddy wore ski masks and blindfolded King so he wouldn't know who did it. Jack's 'sposed to unlock the tomb after midnight . . . once the city council has taken its vote, and while it's too dark for King to see."

"And so, no harm done," Corlis said bitterly, "except that the one thing King truly cares about—preserving those buildings for posterity—would be a lost cause, correct?"

"Accordin' to Jack, that's the plan," Lafayette Marchand replied grimly.

"Well, you're right, we're wasting time standing here," she cried.

"Let's get started," Virgil said.

Lafayette stepped behind a nearby crypt and retrieved a

crowbar he'd stowed there earlier. "When one of us finds him, we may need this to spring him free." He dug into his pockets and handed each of them a whistle. "Blow this if you hit pay dirt, and the rest of us will come runnin', agreed?"

Without further conversation the foursome began roving through the vast cemetery in search of a captive encased somewhere on the grounds in an ovenlike marble tomb. Their ensuing hunt proved to be slow, sweltering, unnerving work. They'd began at the center, moving outward in four directions, down row upon row, searching only those structures with open grates or filigrees incorporated into their designs.

After nearly forty-five minutes, Corlis reached the end of a lane that stood at the farthest point from the cemetery's gated entrance. She prayed that Jack Ebert had followed instructions and picked a tomb open to the air to guarantee King's survival. A goodly distance from her fellow searchers, she could only faintly hear the others shouting King's name.

She approached the corner of a tomb whose slate roof had caved in and began to work her way down the next path, now pausing at crypts large enough to house a tall man like King. At the doors and gates she called into dusky, sepulchral depths and was greeted by unearthly silence.

After ten more minutes Corlis was perspiring heavily and fighting rising panic.

She approached the entrance to a large, nineteenth-century crypt with the name MILLING engraved on all four marble sides. Her spirits quickened at the sight of an elaborately filigreed wrought-iron gate secured with a modern padlock and chain.

"King?" she shouted. "King . . . are you there? King!"

Inside, a shadowy figure suddenly rose like a specter from on top of a sarcophagus at the far end of the Milling family mausoleum. Corlis gave a little scream of surprise.

"Corlis?" a voice echoed.

It was King's voice!

"Oh my God!" she cried. "It's *you*!" She pressed herself against the gate.

"Sweet Jesus, Ace . . . you are somethin' else!"

"Are you all *right*? I got so scared when I saw this body rise up—"

"Just catchin' forty winks, you might say," he replied with a shaky laugh. He reached through the gate to touch her shoulder. "I'm not dreamin', am I? This place can do that to you, y'know. It's really *you*?" In the dim light behind him, four marble-sided coffins were neatly stacked, two to a side. A fifth at the far end of the tomb had provided him with a bed.

"It's me, all right," she acknowledged. "Oh, King . . . I was so afraid that—"

As their fingers hooked through the grillwork, they sought each other's lips but managed only the barest contact through the rusty iron bars.

"Boy, am I one happy fella to see *your* sweet face!" King exclaimed. "How'd you know to come here?"

Corlis leaned away from the gate and rolled her eyes heavenward. "It's a long story. I'll fill you in later, but first we've got to get you out."

"Last week you weren't even takin' my calls."

Corlis gazed at his haggard face peering through the bars and felt like weeping. "I am *so* glad to *see* you," she whispered, near tears. "All that nonsense about Cindy Lou and the Mallorys making a donation to help your cause . . . I was jealous and acted like an ass. The Mallorys have a perfectly legitimate stake in wanting to help save those buildings."

"The lady from California is apologizin' again?" King declared through the iron gate. "My, my, sugar. You haven't been out in too much sun, have you?"

"I mean it," Corlis said doggedly. "It was a cheap shot on my part."

"Well, thanks for sayin' you're sorry."

Corlis drew closer once again and said with a shaky laugh, "Look, now that we've got *that* settled . . . we've got to get you to the city council meeting." She put the orange plastic whistle to her lips and blew hard. Then she clasped King's fingers again "Oh, baby . . . thank God you're all right!"

Suddenly a hand appeared from thin air and seized her forearm in a deathlike grip. In an instant another batted the whistle out of her grasp. From behind her she felt a palm clamp itself over her mouth, and the next thing she knew, she was being yanked back against her assailant's chest.

"Goddamn you, Jack!" King shouted from behind the locked gate. "I figured it was your shitty little ferret's face behind that ski mask. If you hurt her, I swear I'll—"

Corlis didn't hear the conclusion of King's threats, for within seconds Jack had dragged her into the narrow space between two tombs. She screamed and fought against him frantically.

"Shut up, you bitch!"

"Let me go!" Corlis shouted, her words muffled by Jack's hand pressed across her mouth.

"Oh, you'll go, all right," Jack snarled. "You're gonna keep your mouth shut till you pack up and get out of this town. Good thing I came back to check on ol' King in there. Otherwise I might not have had such a wonderful opportunity to teach you a lesson, *Miz* McCullough."

A cold rage began to take possession of her. Without warning she slammed her left elbow into Jack's narrow chest. She heard him grunt and felt his hand loosen on her face.

"You are *such* a slime ball!" she screamed.

She twisted her body with all her strength and brought up her right knee in a swift, sharp, well-aimed blow to his groin.

"Ahhhh . . . ohhhh!" he moaned, doubling over.

Jack fell and rolled into a fetal ball on the grass. Corlis darted around the pitched-roof vault on her right and began to search frantically for the bright orange plastic whistle he had thrown into the turf near the Milling tomb.

In a panic King called, "Sweet Jesus, Corlis! Are you all right?"

"Yes!" she shouted triumphantly as she spotted a brilliant flash of color in a tufted hillock near the wrought-iron gate behind which King stood, helpless.

"Run!" King yelled. "Get the hell out of here!"

Corlis ignored his command and instead made a grab for the whistle and blew as hard as she could. Within seconds whistle blasts answered her call from the other side of the cemetery. "Over here!" she screamed, waving her arms frantically and not caring whether Jack heard her. "I found King! Over *here*! Watch out for Jack Ebert!"

Her foot suddenly encountered something hard. Glancing down, she caught sight of a small stone angel that had fallen off the corner of the adjacent tomb's caved-in roof and lay half-buried in the grass.

Next to it lay one of its wings that had been sheared off. Corlis reached down and seized the heavy piece of marble. Suddenly she experienced a piercing memory of Dylan Fouché ringing his little bell in an arc over her head the day he performed the space clearing on Julia Street. "This will keep you surrounded in sacred space," he'd said by way of benediction. "It is here for you whenever you need protection." She cast a distracted glance at King and began to creep toward the spot where she had left Jack writhing on the ground.

"Corlis, *don't!*" King hissed, but Corlis ignored his plea, concentrating instead on imagining a bell jar of protective white light encircling her as she cautiously moved forward.

By this time Ebert had risen to his knees. His pale, slender hands splayed protectively across his groin. Out of the corner of her eye, she was startled to see Virgil's camera lens nosing its way around the edge of an adjacent tomb, following her every move.

How long had he been videotaping this macabre scene? she wondered, her spirits rising. Then she saw Manny, his headset clamped on his ears, holding a boom mike on an extender pole.

"We were just a couple of rows from here when we heard your whistle," Manny grinned. "Marchand's way over on the Washington Avenue side."

"You guys are fantastic," she said, keeping her eye on her cornered prey and clasping the broken piece of angel's wing in her right hand like a pitcher on the mound. Then she yelled at Jack, "Get up!" Ebert slowly, painfully rose to his feet. "We'll just let Virgil, here, take some pretty pictures of you unlocking the Milling tomb," Corlis said, "so we'll have them to show to your employer, Mr. Jeffries, to remind him that ordering someone's kidnapping is a federal offense."

From behind his camera Virgil announced triumphantly, "Hey, boss lady! I got great shots of Jack tryin' to wrestle you to the ground and you givin' him a chop to his privates."

Corlis gave him the thumbs-up sign with her free hand. "Just a little maneuver I learned in L.A. doing a story about women's self-defense," she replied grimly, taking a menacing step toward Jack with her marble weapon still in hand.

"Way to go," Virgil said loudly from behind his camera.

"Would you two have just kept tape rolling, even if I hadn't been able to deck the guy?" she asked, never taking her eyes off Jack. "Or would you have rescued me?"

"Naw . . . you're a tough cookie," Manny called from his position near the corner of the tomb. "We *knew* you'd deck 'im!"

"Thanks a bunch," she muttered, and both men laughed.

However, Jack Ebert wasn't laughing. He was staring at her, glassy-eyed. He attempted to shift his weight slightly and cried, "Ohhhh . . ."

Corlis took a step closer and wagged a finger at him. "Now, if you'll just be a good boy and do exactly as I say," she declared to King's abductor, "I'll *consider* not broadcasting this on the ten o'clock news. However, if I *do* put this bit on the air, I'll just do a voice track at this point so no one can hear me say, 'Get over here, you *rodent*, and show me the keys!' "

Jack remained hunched over in obvious pain. "They're . . . in my pocket," he said, wincing. "The whole idea for this was Grover's, y' know."

"But you just *loved* writing that garbage about King and me, didn't you, you hack," Corlis snapped. "Take the damn keys out of your pocket and unlock the gate."

While Virgil kept his video camera rolling, Jack gingerly extracted a set of keys from his pants pocket and shuffled toward the wrought-iron gate. Behind the rusted filigree, King stared stonily at his adversary but remained silent. With trembling fingers Jack finally got the key in the lock and opened it.

"Just get *out* of here before your prisoner flattens you!" Corlis growled at Jack. "And if you tip off Grover Jeffries about what's just happened here, we'll first show this videotape to the cops, and then, when you watch WJAZ news tonight, you and your boss will think the story I did about your wedding was a love letter. Now, beat it!"

Jack flushed scarlet to the tips of his ratlike ears. "How do I know you *won't* just turn me in to the cops?" he asked truculently.

Before she could answer, King intervened. "You don't. But

you'd better just be grateful that I've got bigger fish to fry." He shot Jack a murderous look.

Corlis added, "And, in case you're tempted, later, to get creative, remember somethin', Jackie boy . . . we've got everything documented on videotape."

While Virgil recorded the man's departure, Ebert turned and slowly limped in the direction of a small, open gate, sandwiched in the middle of the wall running along a side street. The camera operator swiveled in place just as King ducked under the tomb's low threshold and stepped onto the grass. He stood to his full height and inhaled a deep, cleansing breath. Then, recorded by Virgil for all to see, King pulled Corlis toward him and enfolded her in his arms.

"What is it with you, Ace?" King murmured into her hair. "You always seem to be bailin' me out of jail." His arms tightened, and she felt all the coursing adrenaline gradually subside.

"Thank God you're all right," she whispered brokenly into his chest.

"I'm fine," he reassured her soothingly, stroking her hair. Then he held her gently away and stared down at her. "Are *you* okay?"

She smiled ruefully. "Barely," she replied. Now that the danger was over, she was beginning to tremble.

King kept a steadying arm around her shoulders while he reached over and shook the hands of the television crew. "Hey . . . Virgil . . . Manny!" he exclaimed. "You guys are unbelievable!"

Still peering through his viewfinder, Virgil countered with undisguised admiration, "Yeah . . . well, maybe . . . but *this* lady, here, was nothin' but balls-to-the-walls."

Just at that moment a breathless Lafayette Marchand rounded the corner of the Milling tomb in a dead run. For a while, King and his godfather took each other's measure. King broke the silence first.

"Will someone explain to me what in hell *he's* doing here?" He turned to address Marchand directly. "You do know, don't you, Laf," he declared, his eyes narrowing, "that this little caper could earn your boss Jeffries a criminal indictment?"

"Well, now . . . wouldn't that . . . be nice?" Lafayette replied, attempting to catch his breath.

"You could get nailed, too, if you're an accessory," King added, his temper barely under control.

"I wasn't," he said shortly. Then he pointed a well-manicured finger in the direction of Corlis and her crew. "What I've revealed about Kingsbury Duvallon's . . . detention . . . is off the record . . . and not for attribution. I have given WJAZ-TV this information only as deep background *until* I lift the embargo regardin' today's events. You have my word I will do so before the final vote is taken this afternoon on the demolition of the Selwyn buildin's."

"Wait a minute," Corlis snapped. "What if Jeffries gets Edgar Dumas to postpone the vote again today when he sees King walk in?"

"You and I will have to negotiate."

"Well, then, will *you* agree that I can broadcast what we have on tape concerning Jeffries's illegal activities within a week—or before a final vote is taken, whichever comes first?" she demanded.

"I will agree to your usin' this material in such a way that the Selwyn buildin's will be saved from demolition but that my privacy is maintained. How's that?"

"*His* job is to save the buildings," she reminded Marchand sharply, indicating King, who was watching their discussion like a spectator at a Ping-Pong match. "*My* job is to keep the public informed about issues that affect their lives and pocketbooks."

"You're gonna have to trust that I'm keepin' both matters clearly in mind," Marchand countered tersely.

Before Corlis could reply further to Marchand's skilled horse trading, King shouted, "*Trust?* Why in the world would you even *consider* trustin' a guy like this? Will *somebody* please tell me what's goin' on here?"

"Okay," Corlis said abruptly to Marchand, ignoring King for the moment. "If this business isn't settled at city council today, I'll negotiate with you in the public's best interest as to how much of what we shot today we put on the air."

"And the *personal* side of this story is strictly confidential, agreed?" Marchand pressed. He held Corlis's gaze. He had indicated that he was willing to put his personal fate in her hands—*if* she would risk putting her professional future in his.

"Yes," she said slowly. "I'll agree to that, too."

"Corlis," King exclaimed. "What in hell is this all about? And why is Virgil *still* shootin' videotape?"

"Because he never stops rolling tape until I tell him to," she explained succinctly. "It's a pact we made when we first started working together."

Lafayette Marchand addressed Virgil. "Will you make me a copy of that tape in your news van right now—for my records?"

Virgil, still rolling, looked to Corlis for confirmation. After a long pause, she asked Marchand, "You'll use it to arm wrestle Jeffries, correct?"

"Smart lady."

"Strictly speaking, I shouldn't, but okay—if you swear it's for nonbroadcast purposes."

"Agreed."

She turned to Virgil and asked, "And we've recorded the entire story, *including* this visual record of our agreement with Mr. Marchand, correct?"

"Yep."

"Then make him a dub of what you got today."

"Corlis," King exclaimed again. "Are you *crazy*?"

"It may look that way, but no . . ." she answered with a sympathetic smile. To her cameraman she said, "You can stop tape now."

Virgil flicked a switch on his camcorder, lowered the heavy piece of equipment from his shoulder, and set it to rest on the grass. Manny pulled his earphones from his head and allowed them to dangle around his neck.

"Well, then," Lafayette said with an ironic smile. "It's nearly three-thirty. Let's see about dubbin' that tape, gentlemen. Then I say we all hustle down to city hall. This should be a very interestin' meetin'."

And with that the nattily attired media expert strode off with Virgil and Manny toward the wrought-iron archway to the cemetery that bore his name, while King stared after him, dumbfounded.

"We'd better get going, too," Corlis said.

"And you'd better tell me what in hell is goin' on here, Ace,"

King said in a low voice etched with anger and fatigue as they, too, began to walk toward the cemetery gates.

Corlis shook her head regretfully. "I can't do that," she replied with an apologetic smile. "Not until after the vote is taken by the city council and I'm officially off the story."

"Oh, come on, Corlis," King exploded. "I've just spent seventeen hours locked up in a graveyard! One of my liberators turns out to be Grover Jeffries's main lieutenant . . . and *you're* gonna hold to some silly rules of television reportin'? Give me a break!" he said, disgusted. "There's a little bit more at stake here than Journalism 101."

Twenty feet from the entrance gates, Corlis halted dead in her tracks and turned slowly to face King. "What's at stake here, Kingsbury Duvallon, is not *just* the buildings, as precious as they may be," she retorted, stung. "You are not in possession of all the facts. You're making judgments based on half the evidence. There's *a lot* at stake that you know nothing about."

"Then *tell* me what I need to know," he exclaimed, exasperated.

Corlis shook her head, discouraged. She knew they were both exhausted and their tempers were at the breaking point. Clearly she and King had different agendas this day: King wanted to save irreplaceable Greek Revival buildings from being demolished, while her professional obligations were to the public.

"Look, King," she said earnestly. "My mandate is to diligently seek out the facts, protect my sources—and that means *all* my sources," she added as an aside, "and to cover the story fairly, regardless of what ultimately happens to the structures on Canal Street. I know that doesn't seem enough by your standards, but that's what I'm paid to do."

King's response to this statement was stony silence. Corlis touched his arm, *willing* him to understand things from her point of view, but he merely stared over her head across the cemetery.

"I realize," she said sharply, her exasperation getting the best of her, "that to *you*, all this might seem a quaint notion in this era of tabloid news, but there it is. Fairness, objectivity, and *protecting sources* represent everything Aunt Marge and I have always believed in in the news business. It's my *credo*, don't you understand? Just like saving historic buildings from the wrecker's ball is *yours*."

She waited for him to reply. Nothing.

"King," she said softly, reaching for his hand, "I would be lying if I told you that I wasn't rooting for your side. I hope you *win*. Having said that, however, I can't be *part* of that, and I can't betray my sources. I can't use what I know to tilt the balance in your favor . . . just as I would never pass on the information I gained from you to the other side, even if I happened to think a new high-rise on Canal would be good for the city's economy—which I don't."

"But this isn't just a little skirmish," King said finally, breaking his silence. "This is *war*. You know it, and *I* know it. This calls for extraordinary measures, just as Grover Jeffries employed extraordinary measures to keep me away from the crucial city council meetin'."

Corlis held his hand more tightly. "I completely understand how you feel! It's just that *I* can't be the one to tell you what I've learned from Lafayette Marchand," she exclaimed, feeling miserable. "Not until it's over. You're a source. *Marchand* is now a source. You two can talk to each other if you like, but *I* have to respect *everybody's* confidentiality. Otherwise I'm just a fact-twisting PR pimp . . . an information opportunist—and the kind of journalist you and I both despise."

"By the time this little shindig is over, none of this hair-splittin' will matter. It'll be too late," King retorted, abruptly releasing his hand from her grasp. "Those 1840 buildin's will be a pile of rubble. Let your overactive reporter's conscience chew on *that* for a while."

Exasperated, Corlis cried, "Look, King. You have a choice. Either allow me to play by my rules, as I've allowed you to play by yours, or . . . or . . . you can *walk* to the goddamned city council meeting!" To her mortification, she was close to tears. She turned her head and wiped her sleeve across her eyes. King took a step closer and put a hand on each of her shoulders.

"That goon, Grover Jeffries, had me kidnapped and locked in the cemetery so he could run roughshod over everyone else," he reminded her urgently. "I *need to know* what kind of lion's den I'm about to walk into at city hall—and *you* have that information."

"I'm so sorry . . ." she whispered, "but I can't tell you why Lafayette Marchand asked me to meet him in the cemetery *until* all of this is over. Then, if Marchand agrees to release me from our agreement, I'll tell you absolutely everything. Please understand," she pleaded.

And I'm certainly not the one to reveal that he's your father.

King's mouth drew into a straight line. "As far as I'm concerned, my fallin' out with Lafayette—way back when—is all blood under the bridge. What I need to know from you has to do with Jeffries's current schemes and why Marchand has pulled this latest stunt, involvin' you."

"Don't you *get* it?" Corlis shouted, finally at the end of her tether. "All this has nothing to do with me, or how I feel about you. I *love you*, damn it! I was terrified something awful might have happened to you today. But, right now, I *cannot* tell you everything. I can't and I won't!"

King's look hardened. He dropped his hands from her shoulders. "Well, then, as far as I'm concerned . . . if you're usin' Lafayette Marchand as one of your trusted sources to nail this story and beat your competition," he said sarcastically, "you've either got terrible judgment or you've gone over to the enemy, McCullough."

Corlis declared hotly, "Good God, you see everything as black-and-white!"

"The same might be said of you and your god-almighty reporters' rules," King retorted.

The pair stared silently at each other for a long moment.

"I am really sorry . . ." she repeated forlornly, "but I can't be the one to help you."

King shrugged. "Then I think I'll just hitch a ride with Virgil and Manny over to city hall. Maybe they hold to journalistic standards a poor mortal like me can hope to comprehend. See ya, sugar."

Stunned by this response, Corlis watched King stalk through the cemetery gates. He hailed her camera crew and sauntered across Washington Avenue.

"King!" she shouted across oncoming traffic.

He turned around near the van and said, "Yes?"

"I told your mother and your aunt I'd let them know you were okay." Her voice was tight with unshed tears. "They're worried sick about you. Will you call them?"

King nodded brusquely and climbed into the van, leaving Corlis to wonder if Virgil and Manny would remain loyal to her and WJAZ or sell out to their own gender.

What do you think? This is N'awlings, darlin'!

It was the same old story with her. What difference did it all make? she wondered, fighting a flood of tears. Her camera crew would probably think her highfalutin notions of journalistic integrity were pompous and dumb—given the stakes on the other side of this controversy. As King had said, if the preservationists didn't win today, those beautiful historic buildings would be reduced to rubble and dust—lost forever. And King would blame *her*.

But if she or Virgil or Manny played partisan, something equally important would be demolished, she argued silently as she unlocked her car door. Citizens had the right to assume that media organizations will be true to the public trust and have no special ax to grind when it comes to reporting the news. She'd always held a core conviction that America's very *democracy* depended on informed voters and unbiased reporting, and that—

Yada, yada, yada. Jeez Louise, but you sure do sound like some kind of journalistic dinosaur. Just get yourself to that city council meeting, lady, and do your job!

Chapter Twenty-eight

June 1

Corlis stood by her car and gazed at the postmodern building that housed the New Orleans City Council chambers, along with other government offices at city hall. She dreaded going inside. The sultry afternoon sun beat down on her shoulders, and the hot pavement penetrated the soles of her sling-back pumps. The only incentive for her to enter the building was the promise of igloolike air-conditioning.

Reluctantly she mounted a short flight of stairs to the lobby. As far as she could tell, King was about to receive a thorough thumping from Grover Jeffries's legal goon squad, and she didn't think she could stomach witnessing the carnage that was bound to result. Even worse, the Hero of New Orleans already blamed her for aiding and abetting the enemy. Once he actually lost the battle, it would likely be impossible for the two of them to sort out what had gone wrong between them.

And when he finds out that Lafayette Marchand is his father . . .

Corlis was still angry with King for his bullheadedness, but her heart ached for him at the thought that, on top of losing the Selwyn buildings, he was about to learn of painful family secrets hidden from him for so long.

Suppressing a sigh, she entered city hall's frigid foyer. She couldn't afford to wrestle with any of this now, she reminded herself. She had a story to cover. Once inside the echoing marble entranceway, however, she turned left and headed straight for the ladies' room.

* * *

"Would someone please point out Mr. Kingsbury Duvallon?"

The faintly imperious old lady asked the question of a pha-lanx of media people pouring down the aisle into the crowded auditorium. She spoke in a strong, firm voice that belied her fragile appearance—heightened by the fact that her left arm was in a sling.

A large, broad-shouldered African American with a head as shiny as a chocolate malt ball paused and said kindly, "He's right over there, ma'am. Can I take you to 'im?"

She nodded brusquely. Despite the sultry temperatures outside city hall, the grandmotherly figure was wearing a vintage navy-blue gabardine suit with a nipped-in waist, velvet collar and cuffs, and a matching velvet turban reminiscent of the fashion that famed gossip columnist Hedda Hopper made popular in the forties. She accepted the young man's proffered arm as they made their way through the milling throngs in the direction of the city council chamber's first row of seats.

From beyond the open exit doors came the incongruous sounds of musicians tuning their instruments in the hallway. Inside the hall a platoon of people handed out signs that read SOS! SAVE OUR SELWYNS!

Meanwhile, Kingsbury Duvallon, his coalition of architects, lawyers, preservationists, historians, and supporters of the city's Live in a Landmark program had staked out their turf close to the dais at the front.

At the back of the large chamber, a distracted Grover Jeffries was surrounded by several somber gentlemen wearing nearly identical lightweight gray worsted suits. This group was confer-ring with the head of the security detail assigned to the hearing room. The officer's beleaguered expression indicated that the situation had clearly gotten out of hand.

To be sure, the city council chamber was so jammed that the turban-clad woman and her escort had considerable diffi-culty threading their way down one of the aisles and reaching their final destination. The pair passed by the speaker's podium beside which stood two easels. The first held a black-and-white rendering of the 600 block of Canal Street as it looked in 1842. It showed the classic architectural features of the Greek Revival structures—long hidden by the ugly aluminum screen erected in the sixties. The second easel held enlarged copies of nineteenth-century etchings showing the faces of black businessmen labeled "J. Colvis and Joseph Dumas."

The old lady paused and stared at the engraved images of the two tailors. "Ah . . . so *that's* what they looked liked. Absolutely *fascinating.*"

The black man gently guided his charge a few more feet until they arrived at the first row of seats.

"King?" he said, tapping Duvallon on the shoulder.

"Yeah? Oh, hi Virgil," King responded with a decidedly pre-occupied air as he handed out protest signs to his supporters nearby.

"You have a visitor."

King turned and took in the eccentric-looking woman whom he had never before seen in his life.

"I'm Margery McCullough," she announced without pre-amble. "I'm a *retired* reporter," she continued with studied em-phasis. "I understand from my niece that something I have in my possession might be of use in your fight to save the historic buildings I've heard so much about."

"Really, ma'am?" King said, intrigued. He glanced briefly at the elderly woman's royal-blue velvet turban. "That sure would be welcome news."

"I've just flown in from California to deliver the McCullough diary to Corlis, in person. I called her television station when I arrived at the airport here, and they told me she was due to be at city hall at four. Do you know where she is?"

"I expect she'll be here momentarily."

Margery reached inside her voluminous shoulder bag, not unlike the one her niece carried everywhere, and withdrew from its roomy depths a tattered brown leather-bound volume. "I've used these slips of paper to mark the salient passages. I'm sure my niece wouldn't mind my showing you what I found," she said, a gleam of mischief in her eye.

"I'm not so sure about that, ma'am," King replied with a wry smile.

"Well . . . since my niece isn't here yet, I'll take responsibility for putting this precious primary source in your custody, young man," she declared grandly, handing it to him. "And now, may I please sit down? I'm rather tired from my journey."

"Of course," King replied instantly. "Chris!" he addressed his teaching assistant, "would you please offer Ms. McCullough, here, your seat?"

"Sure," Calvert said, moving two seats over as he cast a curious glance at the oddly attired visitor.

King immediately sat down beside Corlis's aunt Marge. Without pausing, the pair bent over the McCullough diary.

"Now . . . I think this might be useful," she volunteered, pointing to the page on the right. "And perhaps this passage . . . and certainly *this* passage, don't you think?"

King scanned the paragraphs in question, occasionally asking for clarification when he encountered difficulty deciphering the spidery script.

"This is unbelievable," he said under his breath. He leaned back in his seat and addressed a handsome African American wearing a three-piece business suit and sitting in the row of seats behind them. "Professor Jefferson, you've gotta *see* this!" he exclaimed, handing him the McCullough diary. Then King glanced over at his unexpected benefactress. "Does Corlis know you were coming to New Orleans?"

"No," Aunt Marge declared primly. "I disobeyed doctor's orders and went straight from the hospital to the Los Angeles airport."

"And your arm?" he asked with concern.

"Only strained. I can still type with one hand."

"Does Corlis know you've hurt yourself?"

"She knows I've had a fall and that I didn't break any bones. I feel remarkably well, considering."

"Well, then," King said, chuckling, "since you tell me that you've retired from the journalism trade . . . would you consider holding one of our SOS signs with your good hand?"

"Why, I'd be delighted," Aunt Marge replied gaily. "First time I've hoisted one of these things in my life." She smiled conspiratorially. "I'm writing my memoirs, you know. It's such a joy to finally be able to state my *opinion* about things. I've spent a *lifetime* being purely objective."

* * *

Corlis stared into the cracked mirror in the city hall ladies' room and couldn't help wondering if King would press kidnapping charges against Jack Ebert and Grover Jeffries. Even if he did, she considered morosely, that wouldn't happen in time to save the Selwyn buildings from the wrecker's ball once the city council had taken the vote. Preventing their demolition was *all* King really cared about. As he said, he was fighting a war, and as far as he was concerned, the usual rules of engagement didn't apply.

That was always where it ended, wasn't it? she reflected, pulling from the deep recesses of her shoulder bag her hairbrush and lipstick. When you got down to it, the men she had known always thought a crisis was only about *them*!

No wonder the magnolias down here resort to underhanded methods to try to even the odds!

But somehow, Corlis had to admit to herself, that wasn't the whole story here. There was a piece of the dilemma between King and her that she wasn't owning up to.

You're always so ready to take offense. So ready to be hurt.

She pulled her brush through her brunette mane with swift, agitated yanks as she gazed moodily at her reflection in the mirror and wondered in her heart of hearts if this unhappy conflict with King was simply about . . . fear. Maybe she put hurdles higher than they really had to be?

Wasn't that what her Beverly Hills shrink had said after she broke up with Jay? Was she merely afraid that if she *did* commit to her feelings without equivocation, there was always the chance she could get emotionally trampled on? Like she had with her warring mom and dad? Like she had with Jay Kerlin?

Kingsbury Duvallon does not remotely resemble Jay Kerlin. Try again, Corlis. Something else is bothering you, dearie.

Slowly Corlis began to apply a new coat of lipstick. The fact was King had been born into a milieu of family and southern tradition where women—uppity, outspoken women—were shunned. The truth was Corlis was nothing if not uppity, and always would be. Yes . . . Cindy Lou Mallory could betray King, big-time, yet, as Corlis had witnessed, ties of family and history around here would never be broken. Those connections were sunk deep into the swampy Louisiana soil.

The magnolia factor would triumph in the end.

Face it, McCullough ... a magnolia you ain't! It probably would never work between you and King.

That's why King had left her standing alone by the curb in front of Commander's Palace today. That was probably at the core of their contretemps at UCLA twelve years ago. And despite all the heavy breathing between them, King had come to recognize that truth, and now she must, too.

Corlis swiftly stowed her makeup kit and hairbrush in her shoulder bag and walked purposefully out of the ladies' room to face the music. She would get through this, she told herself, by doing what she'd always done: giving her all to the story she was there to cover for her viewers. *That* never changed.

When she entered the packed auditorium, she stared straight ahead and made for the section down front that had been roped off for the working press.

"Hey, whacha know, boss lady?" Virgil hailed her. "Isn't this somethin' else?" he commented, nodding at the full house.

"Amazing," Corlis replied curtly.

"Have you talked to King since you got here?"

"No," she said more sharply than she intended.

Virgil cocked an eyebrow and said no more.

Corlis inhaled deeply. "Okay. So. You guys ready to rock 'n' roll here today?"

"Yep," Manny replied, exchanging looks with Virgil.

Corlis glanced at Virgil. Had he leaked to King information Marchand had revealed to the three of them, she wondered? She instinctively knew that Virgil Johnson greatly respected Kingsbury Duvallon and now felt fiercely invested in his own black heritage, as represented by the Selwyn buildings. Who was she to judge the man? she thought.

"Thanks for setting everything up," she said by way of a peace offering. "Sorry I was late and ... sorry I snapped at you."

"No problem," Virgil said, and grinned.

"Why are you smiling?" she asked suspiciously.

However, just then a door opened and a few council members strolled in. The clock on the wall said it was five minutes past four. The meeting was late getting started. Corlis gazed around the hall, now chock-a-block with a churning, noisy mass of picket-toting protesters. Sprinkled around the hearing room were gaggles of downtown businesspeople, lobbyists, council staff, and curious onlookers, as well as a squadron of grim-faced lawyers and technical advisers who represented Grover Jeffries and the Del Mar Corporation.

And sure enough, even Cindy Lou Mallory and her mother had taken seats in the second row. Out of the corner of her eye, Corlis caught a brief glimpse of King's tall, dark-haired figure, but she quickly looked away.

Eyes front! Keep your concentration, McCullough!

The remaining members of the city council finally began drifting toward the dais. One by one they took their places behind their name plaques. She saw Lafayette Marchand rush through the double doors into the chamber as city council president Edgar Dumas loudly banged his gavel.

"This meetin' will come to order!" Dumas shouted above the noise. He glanced around the packed chamber with a frown. "The clerk will please commence the final readin' of the proposed ordinance and use permits we have before us," he announced as the television cameras began to whir. "Then we will allow time for public comment in the order in which everybody signed up."

The room was silent as the clerk recited the legal language granting an ordinance that would allow for the "upgrading of the six hundred block of Canal Street." Then she read the accompanying proposals for demolishing the existing "derelict buildings" and various use permits that would allow "developer Grover Jeffries and the Del Mar Corporation to erect a twenty-eight-story high-rise."

As the clerk wound up her recitation, Corlis's attention drifted once again to the first row of spectators seated around Kingsbury Duvallon. Suddenly her jaw went slack, and she stared in amazement. Sitting next to him was a turbaned octogenarian dressed in an outfit that Margery McCullough had worn in the days when she'd worked for William Randolph Hearst.

"Aunt Marge!" she breathed, astonished beyond words.

Virgil uncorked his eye from the camera's eyepiece and grinned. "I was wonderin' when you'd notice your aunt was here. Now I see why you're such a slave driver," he whispered hoarsely. "Chip off the old block, huh?"

"What's she doing sitting next to *King*?" Corlis whispered.

"She asked to sit there," Virgil said with a faint shrug, and returned to his eyepiece. "Shh . . . the testimony's startin' from the good guys."

What followed was King Duvallon's well-orchestrated presentation by the coalition of community leaders who vehemently opposed the Del Mar project. Slated to speak first was professor of black history Barry Jefferson, a veteran of the Korean War and Purple Heart recipient. The conservatively attired academic rose from his seat and strode confidently to the podium carrying a leather-bound volume in his right hand. He smiled pleasantly at the city council members seated before him.

"These eleven buildings you're proposing to tear down represent a golden age in this town when *real* diversity existed in New Orleans," he began, gesturing with his pen at the easel on which stood the rendering of the Selwyn block as it had looked in the mid-nineteenth century. "The year was 1842. I have submitted, to the council's secretary, copies of census documents that *prove* that forty-five percent of African Americans in this city were *Free* Men and Women of Color," he reminded the black majority sitting on the dais. "That's right, Mr. Council President . . . a proud time in our people's history when we have solid evidence that almost *half* of us were free before the Civil War. *Not* slaves!"

Shouts and whistles erupted spontaneously from the audience.

"Order! Order!" Council President Dumas shouted above the tumult, hammering his gavel. "We *will* have order in these chambers! This is testimony we have already heard, Professor Jefferson. If you have nothing new to enlighten us about—"

Barry Jefferson's booming voice soared over the heads of his audience. "And two of those free African men, Messieurs Colvis and Dumas, *were among the owners* of these historic buildings whose fate is being decided by you today," he declared, making a jabbing motion with his pen toward the second of the two easels. "I beg you on the council to consider this: Today, *not one* building on this city's main thoroughfare is owned by a black citizen, even though we make up seventy-two percent of the city's population. *Not one!*"

Boos and catcalls greeted this announcement. The historian leaned over the podium and glared at the members of the city council. "Do you mean to tell me that this governmental body is even *considering* tearing down any one of these national treasures?" he demanded acidly. "Especially the two priceless, historic buildings owned by tailors Colvis and Dumas? Beautiful Greek Revival structures here in our city that these amazing gentlemen built and owned at a time when the majority of our enslaved black brothers and sisters in the South were not allowed, by order of the Black Code, to own *anything*, including the shirts on their backs."

More boos and rude noises burst forth on all sides of the auditorium, prompting President Dumas to bang his gavel repeatedly.

"We will have order!" Edgar Dumas shouted angrily.

Corlis glanced over at King, who was ignoring the uproar and instead was scribbling energetically on a notepad he held in his lap. Dr. Jefferson's basso profundo rose above even Edgar Dumas's stentorian roar.

"Do you city council people really intend to destroy this tangible evidence of our people's history?" he asked again. "Do you really want to erase from the face of the earth our *struggle* and our *triumph* over the evils of slavery? You're really gonna *do* that?" he reproached his listeners. "By destroying these buildings, you're not going to allow the black and white children of this town to know that—once upon a time in New Orleans—there was a whole city block that had buildings constructed by these two gentlemen right here," he said, pointing to the antique portraits of Colvis and Dumas displayed on the easel, "who, with their partners, owned 'em and rented some of the space to several *white* merchants, mind you. And not only that," Jefferson declared, thumping the podium like a Sunday preacher, "their neighbors and co-owners on the block included Paul Tulane and other Scots-Irish, French, and English people—

and that the very land on which these buildings stand was owned by an *unmarried* Free Woman of Color named Martine Fouché LaCroix!"

"Yay!" burst out Althea LaCroix. Sitting next to her, Dylan Fouché began to clap wildly.

"Professor Jefferson, your time is up!" Edgar Dumas declared rudely, banging his gavel.

Ignoring him, Jefferson narrowed his focus to the two female council members. "I should think the *feminists* should get exercised about something like this being bulldozed by greedy developers who won't be giving many *ladies* construction jobs on this new high-rise hotel project!"

A burst of laughter rippled throughout the auditorium like a drumroll.

Well, glory be, Corlis thought. A word in favor of feminists. Was this the New South she'd been told about but had yet to see?

Dumas pounded his gavel once more. "Now settle down, everyone! Professor Jeff—"

Jefferson abruptly turned his back on the city council members and made a sweeping gesture that embraced the entire hall. "There's something precious for every single citizen—black or white, man or woman—in the city of New Orleans that is contained in these buildings that the *men in gray suits* at the back of this chamber want to turn into rubble," he declared, his voice dripping with righteous sarcasm. "It's our *history*! Our collective history. It belongs to each and every one of us . . . and it should be a tangible reminder to us that we're *all* in this together— especially *you*, Edgar Dumas!"

Expert showman that he was, Professor Jefferson abruptly turned to face the dais again. With a dramatic flourish, he seized the tattered, leather-bound volume that he had placed on top of the podium. He banged the brown cover with his fist while casting a piercing look directly at the city council president.

"Your time is *up*!" Edgar Dumas declared firmly.

"I know that," the historian acknowledged, shifting his tone to one that was pleasant and cordial.

King rose from his seat and approached the podium. Corlis glanced to the back of the auditorium in time to witness Grover

Jeffries's expression of astonishment turn to red-faced fury. It was obvious that the developer hadn't caught sight of his adversary in the standing-room-only auditorium—until now.

Professor Jefferson continued talking. "Kingsbury Duvallon has just been handed a diary that was written in the eighteen thirties and forties by the *wife* of one of the white contractors hired by the Canal Street Consortium, as they called themselves, to erect the buildings that, for the moment, at least," he added with heavy emphasis, "are still standing."

Professor Jefferson ceremoniously handed his coconspirator the diary. Then he neatly stepped to one side to allow the younger man to take his place at the microphone. King glanced sideways across the packed audience until his gaze came to rest on the roped-off area assigned to the media. He flashed a triumphant grin in Corlis's direction and then looked down at the leather-bound volume in his hand.

"This family treasure," King began conversationally, "has come to us all the way from California, where it has been in the custody of a woman kind enough to fly to New Orleans—at her own expense, mind you—when she heard that y'all were considerin' demolishin' the buildings." A smattering of applause greeted this aside. "The diary—which we will allow the Historic New Orleans Collection archivist to authenticate to your satisfaction," King continued, "gives a fascinatin' account of the amazin' mix of people who were involved in the buildin' project back in the eighteen forties. However, one passage, in particular, I want y'all to hear."

"I will ask you to make this *extremely* brief, Mr. Duvallon," Dumas intervened caustically.

King opened the volume to a page marked with a paper bookmark, and began to read:

I paid a melancholy call on tailors Colvis and Dumas this morning, to inform them of the tragic passing of their partner, Julien LaCroix, of yellow fever yesterday. Unfortunately, Mr. Joseph Dumas was not in his shop, having been summoned to the carré de la ville *to conduct a fitting for one of his roster of distinguished clients. However, his son, Edgar . . .*

King paused dramatically, and smiled at city council president Edgar Dumas.

> . . . *his son, Edgar, treated me most kindly, indeed, while I recited my distressing news about the death of poor Mr. LaCroix. Young Edgar Dumas, who has become a close friend of my Warren, served me a goodly cup of very hot, very strong coffee.* . . .

King looked up.

"The diarist makes specific mention of Joseph Dumas's *son*," King said, speaking forcefully into the podium's microphone while pointing at the engraving of the long-deceased tailor. "She speaks of this man's son—*Edgar Dumas,*" he added emphatically.

King then addressed the city council president directly.

"Your family, Mr. Dumas, like mine—the Kingsburys and Duvallons—has been in New Orleans for at least two hundred years, isn't that so?" Edgar Dumas didn't answer, nor did he interrupt the speaker or tell him to take his seat. "So, it is *possible*, isn't it," King continued in a friendly tone of voice, "that this kindly, courtly, exemplary young black man . . . this *Edgar Dumas* . . . whose father, Joseph Dumas, *owned* one of these buildin's you propose to destroy . . . may very well . . . be *your* direct ancestor?"

The council president appeared greatly taken aback by this assertion and by the sudden attention of all eyes in the council chamber. His gaze drifted to the easel, where he studied the engraving of Joseph Dumas with evident interest.

"Now tell me, President Dumas," King demanded, his voice shaking with intensity, "as a distinguished public servant—and perhaps a *direct descendant* of the celebrated Joseph Dumas and his son, Edgar—are *you* gonna be able to *live* with yourself if you vote to allow a bunch of bulldozers to demolish these national treasures whose architectural beauty survives *behind* the ugly metal screen you see here?" He pointed dramatically to a photographic blow-up of the site on Canal Street.

Edgar Dumas shifted uncomfortably in his seat and cast an

unsettled glance at his colleague in the next chair. He opened his mouth as if to speak and closed it again. King smiled faintly and continued in a conciliatory tone.

"Do you want to be known as the president of this august body who led his fellow public servants into *history* as the folks who turned into ruins a heritage that belongs to *every single person* in this country—and most especially, *yourself?*"

"No!" someone shouted from the back of the hall.

"No! No! No!" echoed a chorus suddenly swelling throughout the council chamber.

Corlis regarded Edgar Dumas, whose startled expression conveyed his apparent belief that forces greater than his were at work in the council chambers. He sat speechless, his hand draped limply around the handle of his gavel as King Duvallon abruptly retired to his seat next to Marge McCullough amid thunderous applause.

As if on cue, black investment banker George Barrett, a colleague of architect Keith LaCroix, rose from his seat in the second row and walked briskly toward the podium while the clapping continued at a deafening roar. Once he leaned toward the mike to speak, however, the audience grew silent.

"Tearing these buildings down is ludicrous from an *economic* standpoint," emphasized the young African-American banker, also dressed conservatively in a three-piece suit.

Corlis had read George Barrett's résumé. The businessman had attended a Catholic high school in New Orleans, then Yale on a full scholarship, graduating magna cum laude, and then had worked his way through Harvard Business School. He returned to New Orleans and started a small fund that invested in black-owned businesses.

"I have received commitments from private investors, architects, and loan officers," Barrett declared, "who firmly believe that the buildings can be adaptively re-used and put to good purpose, leaving their historic facades intact." He swiftly pulled the historic rendering of the city block off the easel. Behind it was a modern architectural drawing of the same scene with a modest hotel tower designed in a style compatible with the existing buildings.

Corlis looked at King. She'd bet her cell phone that one of

Barrett's silent "private investors" was none other than the Hero of New Orleans! Meanwhile, the investment banker declared earnestly to a rapt audience, "You could have, say, a *twelve*-story hotel instead of a twenty-eight-story steel-and-glass monstrosity, and still make a decent—but not obscene—profit. *And*," he continued with rising passion, "I propose the Colvis and Dumas tailor shops, themselves, become a museum dedicated to the unique history of black entrepreneurship in this city!"

Wild cheers from the audience greeted this proposal, including—Corlis noticed—enthusiastic applause from several uniformed security guards. As the rhythmic clapping increased, the side exit suddenly opened and the entire LaCroix Jazz Ensemble stood in the doorway. Althea jumped to her feet and shouted at her fellow musicians, "And a one . . . and a two . . . and a three!"

A maximum-strength arrangement of "When the Saints Go Marching In" reverberated loudly in the hearing room, drowning out Edgar Dumas's half-hearted attempts to gavel the impromptu jazz band into silence. Marching in front was Althea's brother Eldon, blowing on his clarinet. Her youngest brother, Julien, pumped a slide trombone. Beside him stood patriarch Louis LaCroix wailing on his tenor sax, while son Rufus—magically plugged into a battery-powered amplifier—strolled into the hall twanging on a bass guitar, accompanied by his twin brother, Ronald, whose soaring trumpet blasted holes in the walls.

Althea reached under her seat and pulled forth a small electric keyboard, connected by a long black cord that ran along the carpet floor and plugged into the wall next to Manny's sound equipment. She slapped it onto her knees and pounded on the keys.

Within seconds the majority of the audience rose from their seats and began swaying to the infectious beat. A spontaneous conga line formed at the back of the hall and snaked down both aisles of the auditorium. Soon it wound its way around the raised dais where the members of the governing body of the city of New Orleans sat, trapped and impotent, in their high-backed leather chairs.

When the musicians concluded their first selection, they immediately swung into the tune that had become an anthem in the Big Easy: Dr. John's "Goin' Back to New Orleans." Virgil had lifted his camcorder off its tripod and switched his gear over to his battery pack. Next thing she knew, he and Manny joined the conga line as it swung past their media outpost.

"Oh, what the hell," she muttered, falling in line behind her soundman. There was no other way to cover this story, she reasoned, as she swayed to the hypnotic beat.

"That's it, boss lady," Virgil called over his shoulder. "Get *down*, baby. Just let the good times roll!"

She glanced over at King. Cindy Lou and her mother had jumped to their feet and were both dancing in the aisle with the man of the hour.

As for the elected officials, they had two choices: They could look like stiffs and frown disapprovingly at the merrymakers dancing in the hall, or they could become part of a world-class photo op and cheer on the historic preservationists. At least four uniformed security guards were gyrating in the crowd, along with everyone else.

Corlis could see, over the bobbing heads of the impromptu chorus line, that Grover Jeffries, along with the flock of lawyers and representatives of the Del Mar Corporation, had gathered in an emergency huddle at the back of the room. Jeffries frequently glanced over his shoulder nervously at King and then shouted something at one of his lawyers.

To Corlis's astonishment, King abandoned Cindy Lou and raced up the aisle in the direction of Grover's legal team—and Lafayette Marchand. When the music finally came to its tumultuous conclusion, a virtual bedlam of clapping and cheering erupted on all sides. Mopping his brow, Edgar Dumas shouted into the microphone, "This meetin' will stand in recess for ten minutes!" He didn't even call for seconds to his proposal but merely banged his gavel and retired swiftly through a door in the paneled wall behind his chair.

Corlis tapped Virgil on the shoulder and shouted, "Wait here, but *watch* me. If I give you the high sign, beat feet *fast* to the back of the hall!"

Chapter Twenty-nine

June 1

Corlis pushed her way through the gyrating melee engulfing the New Orleans City Council chambers, arriving in time to hear Lafayette Marchand address Grover Jeffries and his battalion of advisers.

"I do believe, gentlemen, that you've reached the end of the road, as far as this hotel buildin' project is concerned." While Grover Jeffries's frown deepened, his public relations consultant pointed to a sheaf of papers that King, who stood within their tight little circle, held in his hand. "Mr. Duvallon has just shown me a memo that has recently come to the attention of the preservationists."

Corlis noticed that Jeffries's florid jowls blanched chalk white. Lafayette continued to speak in a pleasant, even tone of voice.

"As you no doubt remember, Grover, on this particular memo are your comments regardin' my summation of the Canal Street hotel proposal, along with your instructions to your accountant—scribbled on the page in your handwritin', need I remind you—to disburse certain ah ... *questionable contributions* to the campaign war chests of sittin' city council members who just so happen to be votin' on the Selwyn measure today."

"What the devil?" Jeffries growled, his nervousness at seeing King giving way to belligerence.

"The point is, Mr. Jeffries," King interrupted with a grim smile, "our side has a copy of that incriminating memo. And

423

now we have *two hundred* copies that we've run off." He nodded faintly as he acknowledged Corlis's presence on the periphery of their group. "I assure you, sir, we are prepared to distribute each and every one of them to the audience here, includin' the media."

Corlis could hardly believe that she was staring over King's shoulder at a copy of the memo she'd seen in Grover's home office the night of the costume ball. Earlier in the week somebody had leaked word to the *Times-Picayune* about the existence of this damning document. But who had later *given* the document to King and his troops? The same thing had happened with Jack Ebert's invoice for his writing services. A copy of it had obviously been leaked to King as well. But by *whom*?

King caught and held Corlis's gaze. With a sly smile he made a gesture as if he were prepared to hand the memo over to her. "I'm sure that television stations like WJAZ would be very interested to see this. The same probably goes for those few members of the city council who were *not* slated to receive any soft money from your coffers."

"Give me that!" Grover snarled, snatching the memo from King's fingers. His eyes swiftly scanned the first page. "Why, this is privileged information! It must've been stolen!" He glared at King. "One of those buildin' huggers of yours broke into my office. I'll have your organization brought up on—"

"Charges?" King scoffed with a bitter laugh. "I don't think so." He nodded at Corlis. "Do you know, Mr. Jeffries, that there exists, as of today, a very fascinatin' videotape showin' Jack Ebert doin' your dirty work at Lafayette Cemetery?"

"What in blazes are you talkin' 'bout, boy?" Jeffries blustered. "This is gettin' ridiculous!"

"The tape shows Jack openin' the padlock to one of those marble crypts out there," King continued smoothly, "in order to let me *out* of the tomb he'd locked me *into* last night."

Lafayette reached in his suit jacket pocket and pulled out a black plastic videocassette. "That's right, Grover. A copy of that tape has come into my possession. On it, Jack says *you* were the one who put him up to kidnappin' Mr. Duvallon to keep him from testifyin' at today's hearing. That was a very unwise move on your part, and one—as your adviser—I never would have countenanced."

The men in the gray suits exchanged worried looks. One of the lawyers representing the Del Mar contingent pointed a fore-finger and demanded of Jeffries, "Wait a minute . . . wait a minute. Are you telling me, Grover, that you had the *leader* of the preservationists in New Orleans kidnapped and locked in a graveyard tomb prior to this hearing?"

Grover's complexion suddenly appeared so pallid, he seemed a likely candidate for cardiac arrest. "A . . . videotape?" he re-peated, his voice faltering.

"Yes," Marchand confirmed. "As it happened, a TV crew was in the vicinity when Mr. Duvallon, here, was found in the ceme-tery, and the entire event got recorded," he added, tapping the plastic cassette for emphasis.

"Even *you* must know that kidnappin' and obstructin' justice are federal offenses," King commented coolly.

Grover remained silent.

"When I became aware Mr. Duvallon was taken against his will," Marchand explained to his client, "I naturally worried that he might think I approved of such tactics . . . or worse yet, that I had been a party to them. Fortunately, someone directly involved was kind enough to make me a cassette of what hap-pened at Lafayette Number 1 to show to my attorney."

"Me, too," King said, pulling a duplicate cassette from his jacket pocket and waving it in front of Grover's face.

Grover turned to glare at Corlis.

"You're in league with 'em," he hissed. "You've been spreadin' your le—"

"I'm *not* in league with them," Corlis interrupted coldly, "and I didn't give either of these men copies of that video-cassette *or* steal any memos." She glared at the developer and added, "May I advise you, Mr. Jeffries, to watch that foul mouth of yours. There are witnesses here, and I won't hesitate to call on them if you or Jack Ebert make any further attempts to de-fame me."

Grover looked from Corlis to King and back to Corlis again. His shoulders sagged and he remained mute.

"Well, gentlemen," Lafayette addressed Jeffries's associates. "What do you say y'all fold your tents with a little dignity?"

"This project's dead as fish on a Friday," the Del Mar lawyer pronounced flatly.

Lafayette Marchand glanced sharply at King and put forth a startling proposal. "Of course . . . there's always room for compromise."

Grover's eyes narrowed and he barked, "What *sort* of compromise?"

Marchand cocked his head in King's direction and said, "Mr. Duvallon, what would you say to the idea of Mr. Jeffries withdrawin' his plan for the twenty-eight-story high-rise, along with any other plan that requires demolition of the Selwyn buildin's? Would you then agree not to press charges?"

Corlis watched with astonishment while King appeared to mull over the proposition. The buildings would be saved—but then so would Grover Jeffries's reputation, leaving him free to demolish other historic buildings on another day.

Much to Corlis's amazement, King said to Grover, "I might . . . consider it." He turned to confront the developer head-on. "But only *if* you agree to build the complex that George Barrett's architect, Keith LaCroix, designed, down to every lintel and cornice in his plan."

"It's a stupid plan!" retorted Jeffries. "Fixin' up those worthless buildin's—"

"Grover?" Lafayette said, a stern note of warning edging his voice. "It's an *alternative*."

"The design calls for only a *twelve*-story hotel tower," Jeffries exclaimed contemptuously. "There's no decent money in that!"

"Then there's no deal," King snapped. "Let's just call for a vote." He looked over his shoulder at the council members, who were wandering back to the dais.

The chief negotiator for the Del Mar hotel chain put a restraining hand on Jeffries's sleeve.

"After the little floor show these folks put on here today," the lawyer cautioned, "the chance of getting these city politicians to let us demolish those buildings and put up a twenty-eight-story tower in a historic district are exactly zero. Grover, if you're not willing to do business with these folks, that's your call, but either way, we're outta here. What time is the last plane to Saint Louis, Jim?" he asked his colleague.

"Nine-thirty tonight, sir."

"Please tell Edgar Dumas that Del Mar, at least, is no longer part of Mr. Jeffries's project. It's not gonna get approved, but our company doesn't need the bad publicity if, by some miracle, it *does*."

"Wait!" Jeffries cried. He swallowed hard and turned to face King. "Okay. I'll build Keith LaCroix's plan, if George Barrett'll raise all the funds." Then he stared suspiciously at Corlis. "But who's to prevent this broad from airin' *her* video—despite our deal?"

"I am," King said calmly.

"King!" Corlis exclaimed. Her heart was pounding in her chest. "You can't simply order me not to air that tape. You cannot *do* this kind of thing."

"What kind of thing, sugar?" King said solicitously. "All I'm sayin' is that after Virgil made me a copy and made one for Lafayette, here, to give to his lawyer, somethin' terrible happened to the original tape," he added with an innocent air. "On the way over here, Virgil's duplicatin' equipment in the news van seized up somethin' fierce. Fried everything, he told me. He had some technical term for what happened. You'd probably know, if he told you what it was."

Corlis closed her eyes and counted to ten.

Yeah . . . sure . . . a media meltdown. Happens every day to the city's top video technician!

"Well, since you and Mr. Marchand both have copies, one of you can make a new one for *me*," she insisted. "Just the way Virgil did for *you*."

"Yeah," Grover said. "What about that?"

"I'd love to make you a copy, sugar, but I'm afraid I can't do that," King declared solemnly. *"My* lawyer says it's evidence now . . . part of a case that may go to litigation if Mr. Jeffries and I don't strike a deal today. And wouldn't you know?" he added, nodding at his erstwhile godfather. "He's got the very same problem."

"Who's your lawyer?" Corlis demanded of King, already knowing the answer.

"Why, my godfather, Mr. Marchand, here," King drawled. "He's still licensed to practice law in Louisiana, so we're dealin' with close family ties and that lawyer-client privilege thing, y'know what I mean? It'd be one of those conflicts-of-interest deals you're always tellin' me about. Surely you, of all people, Ms. McCullough, realize that it really wouldn't be the right thing for *either* Mr. Marchand or me to provide copies of this tape to you at this time."

Then Lafayette Marchand made another startling proposal. "May I suggest, Grover, that you announce to everybody, right here and now, that *you've* agreed to put up . . . ah . . . let's make it forty-nine percent of the funds for the Selwyn project, to be run by that articulate young investment banker and designed by Keith LaCroix? If you do that, why I think you'll come out lookin' like a hero—'specially to the African-American community."

Jeffries pursed his lips and remained silent for a long moment before saying, gruffly, "Here's the deal: I want *physical possession* of the WJAZ tapes you two got right there and *all* two hundred copies of the memo with my handwritin' on it, plus the one leaked to you—or forget it."

"*If* I should agree to that," King bartered, "you have to sign a letter of agreement to everything Lafayette, here, just proposed, and *after* you sign the big check, you then agree in *writin'* to stay out of the deal entirely till the project's completely finished. How 'bout it?"

"Yeah . . . ?" Grover retorted, a bullying edge to his voice. "Well, you'll have to sign an affidavit sayin' that you won't press charges against me—ever."

Like a player in a tennis match, King lobbed one final volley over the net. "I'll sign an affidavit sayin' I won't press charges against you for havin' me locked up all night in the cemetery— but that's all. Who knows what *else* you'll try to pull at some time in the future? I reserve my right to sue if you—"

"Jesus, Duvallon!" Grover exploded.

Corlis held her breath while the two adversaries glared at each other, each refusing to give ground. Grover Jeffries blinked first.

"If you agree to do everythin' *you* just said," he announced grudgingly, "I'll sign."

Everyone waited.

With a faint nod of his head, King echoed, "If you'll put in writin', right now, everything *you* just agreed to—I'll sign, too. You can pledge the money in an affidavit tomorrow."

After a long pause Lafayette inquired, "Well, Grover . . . shall I inform Edgar Dumas of your decision about the buildin's, or do you want to do it?"

"You do it," Grover said truculently.

"Happy to oblige," the handsome, silver-haired PR man said with a broad smile in King's direction. "Give me a sec and I'll write up the agreement. You can sign before you leave the auditorium tonight. Consider it my last duty under your employ." Marchand quickly drew a legal pad out of his briefcase and wrote furiously for a few minutes. "There," he said, sounding pleased with himself. "That's the gist of it. I can put in all the lawyer language later. Sign here, Grover."

Everyone watched in silence while Jeffries scrawled his signature at the bottom.

"Done," he grunted, handing pen and pad back to Marchand. "Are ya happy?" He put out his hand and said, "Okay. Gimme those two tapes and the memos."

King and Lafayette complied with his request. Then Jeffries turned to the Del Mar contingent and said, "Before y'all go back to Saint Louis, do you guys wanna talk about that piece of land over near Lake Pontchartrain? I hear there might be an Indian casino goin' up near there."

The chief negotiator for the hotel chain consulted briefly with his colleagues. "Sure, Grover. . . . Why the hell not? Seeing as we're already down here."

Corlis watched, nonplussed, as five men in gray suits, including King's nemesis, strode out of the hearing room. Just then Edgar Dumas banged his gavel, calling for order. Lafayette Marchand put a hand on King's shoulder and said, "After this vote, I'd like to buy you a drink. How 'bout goin' with me to the Old Absinthe House in the Quarter?"

"I thought we had our little horse-tradin' talk in the news van earlier?"

Marchand paused and said, "This is on a different subject. I've got somethin' personal I'd like to talk to you about."

King gave him a measured look and shrugged. "Sure. Why not?" He turned to Corlis and said, "I expect you've spotted your aunt by now."

"I did," she replied. "I'm going to take her home to Julia Street to get some rest."

"What about your deadline?" Lafayette asked, concerned. "Did you get enough tape for your broadcast tonight?"

Corlis shrugged, feeling totally spent. "I think so. Virgil shot some great stuff during the meeting. I'll do a few people-on-the-street sound bites and hightail it back to the station. Somehow, by the time we go on the air tonight, I hope I can make sense out of what happened here today." She regarded Lafayette Marchand closely. Grover Jeffries's former PR man had made an invaluable contribution toward shaping the compromise to which both sides of this heated controversy had just agreed. And most important, the Selwyn buildings were saved. "Good-bye, Mr. Marchand," she added, extending her hand. "All the best."

"Good-bye, Miz McCullough, and thank you for . . . showin' such professionalism and grace under fire here today. I admire you greatly, my dear."

"Why, thank you," she said, touched by his compliment. "Thank you for noticing." As for King, she merely offered a brief nod and then strode down the aisle, summoning the energy to officially welcome Aunt Marge to the Big Easy. The story was over. Her relationship with King was over. And as usual, she was left with her job. Well, at least, she thought, waving to her aunt, *that* was something.

But, in the immortal words of Peggy Lee . . . "Is that all there is?"

"Are you feeling okay?" Corlis asked her aunt anxiously as she slid behind the wheel of her Lexus. "It's been a long day, and you're in a different time zone, you poor thing."

"I'm a little tired," Margery McCullough admitted, leaning back in the passenger seat and smiling faintly. "Don't you find this heat terribly oppressive?"

"You get used to it," Corlis replied, inserting her key into the ignition.

"You're right," Marge said with a laugh. "All those people you just interviewed on the street didn't seem to notice how hot it is."

"The locals? They've got different DNA, I think," Corlis said as she flipped the air-conditioning to its highest setting. "The car'll cool down in a sec, and Julia Street will be like an ice box."

"My stars," Marge declared with a happy sigh, "wasn't that city council meeting *exciting*? The right side won for a change."

Corlis arched an eyebrow at her aunt's uncharacteristic show of partisanship. "I'm not supposed to agree with you, am I?" she replied with an ironic, sidelong glance. She put her car in gear, adding, "Aren't I required to remain strictly neutral till I've filed my last dispatch on the subject of the Selwyn buildings?"

"Technically, yes," Marge said with a little laugh. "But when a jazz band plays right in the middle of a political showdown inside a public building, well . . . it's rather difficult not to show your feelings and tap your toes, if you know what I mean."

"I know what you mean," Corlis repeated.

Exhaustion was invading every pore, but she tried to ignore it. She'd filed a "live" stand-up in front of city hall and one outside the Selwyn buildings. Now she had only three hours remaining before the late news began in which to write and edit the full story on the day's events. She nosed her car out of her parking place and headed for the exit.

"Is your arm hurting you, Aunt Marge?" she asked.

"Not much, but you'd better get me home so you can meet your deadline, dear."

"And *you'd* better take a nap. Promise?"

Corlis felt her aunt scrutinizing her from the passenger seat. Suddenly she said, "Kingsbury Duvallon is a fine young man, you know. He handled himself wonderfully today, don't you agree?" Corlis nodded, but didn't reply. "Why didn't you congratulate him, then? That tall redhead and her mother certainly did. When we were all standing at the front of the auditorium, I noticed that you two didn't exchange a word."

"I'll tell you about it when there's time," Corlis replied,

making an attempt to sound casual. Then she exclaimed impulsively, "Remember the conflict-of-interest problems between King and me that I e-mailed you about last week?" Her aunt nodded solemnly. "Well, the whole thing basically blew up in my face today. I don't think King and I will be seeing each other anymore . . . other than just as acquaintances." And maybe not even that, she thought morosely, turning down Julia Street. As she pulled up in front of the entrance to her brick apartment, Aunt Marge put a soothing hand on her arm.

"Corlis, dear, this story will be over soon. Don't make the mistake I did years ago."

Corlis looked at her, puzzled. "What do you mean?"

"In a situation like the one you've just experienced, sweetheart, there are journalistic ethics to be careful about, to be sure," she said thoughtfully. "And then there's one's *damnable* pride. If you'd like to reconcile the two, it might be wise to try to figure out which is which," she suggested with a sad smile. "Believe me, I knew a man once very much like your King Duvallon. I'm extremely sorry, now, that I let him walk away and called it professionalism." She patted her niece's arm. "I'll grant you, it's not an easy thing to reason through. Just try to decide if the other person, at heart, can be counted on to wish you well. Have King's intentions toward his work and toward *you* always been honorable? If the answer is yes, then consider your responses to the conflicts facing you both *very* carefully—and while you're at it, don't forget to consider your own well-being. You have a right to do that, you know. It's probably not healthy to turn over every aspect of yourself to journalism, the way I did. I may have used it as an *excuse* not to live a real life."

Corlis gazed soberly across the car's interior but remained silent. Aunt Marge turned toward the passenger door and gingerly opened it with her good arm.

"Whoa there! Wait," Corlis exclaimed, scrambling out from the driver's side. "Let me help you, sweetie pie."

"If you'll just carry my suitcase upstairs," Marge assured her niece, "you can be on your way. I'm looking forward to taking a nice nap in your elegant plantation bed. Then I'll watch you on TV."

* * *

"Is a beer okay for you, King, or do you want somethin' stronger?" asked Lafayette Marchand. The two men walked to a round table in a secluded corner of the famous plastered brick building on Bourbon Street, known for nearly two hundred years as the Old Absinthe House.

"A Dixie's fine," he said to the waiter.

"I'll have a bourbon," Marchand announced. "Straight up."

"Hard day?" King asked blandly.

A long silence ensued.

"Very . . ." Marchand exhaled finally. "I . . . uh . . . imagine you're wonderin' why I . . . was the one who recruited Corlis McCullough and her TV crew to help find you at the cemetery this mornin'?"

"Actually," King responded coolly, "I'm more interested in findin' out how long *after* you knew Grover was gonna have me kidnapped it took you to initiate damage control."

"About ten minutes," Lafayette replied. "This mornin', Jack Ebert bragged about what he'd done last night. I . . . I about leapt through the phone to kick the bastard in the balls."

"And why would a man like you, familiar with every venal, self-servin' thing that guy has done in this town the last ten years, be surprised he and Grover'd pull a stunt like that?" King asked.

"I *wasn't* surprised, but this time it hit close to home."

"I seem to remember relievin' you of your godfatherly duties some time ago."

"There are certain family ties that simply cannot be severed, and you and I share one of them." Marchand leaned forward slightly. "King . . . I've wanted to . . . to tell you somethin' for a very long time."

The two men stared across the table at each other for a moment. Finally King said, "Look, Laf . . ." He hesitated and then continued, "Let me spare you somethin'. I already know."

"Know what?" Marchand asked cautiously.

"I've known for at least ten years that you fathered me. And that you wouldn't marry my mother."

Marchand stared across the table in astonishment. "*How* did you know?" he demanded, losing his customary unflappable demeanor. "Did Antoinette tell you? Our agreement was that she'd never *do* that. . . . She'd let me stay reasonably close to you, posin' as your godfather, and—"

"No . . . Mother wasn't the one who told me," King interrupted. "She doesn't know that I learned the truth. It was Grandfather Kingsbury."

"Ah . . . the vengeful almost-father-in-law," said Lafayette, a bitter edge to his voice.

"It wasn't like that," King said calmly. "I'd just come back from the marines, and he wanted to be sure Waylon didn't get his hands on the bonds you'd given me at my birth. He gave me the key to a safe-deposit box and said not to open it till after he was buried. Told me that I'd understand everythin', once I saw what was locked away at the Whitney Bank."

"And what, exactly, *did* you understand?" Lafayette asked quietly. "What had that old reprobate put inside the safe-deposit vault?"

"The bonds," King replied with a shrug. "And a short, pithy explanation in his handwritin' sayin' that you and my mother were in the same Mardi Gras court in 1962 . . . that you'd played duke to her queen. That you had sex with her and—I was the result. That was about it."

"No context. Typical of him. André Kingsbury liked to keep things simple. It was either black or white, right or wrong. No subtleties for old André—'specially when it came to understandin' the differences between his two daughters."

"Bethany and Antoinette . . ." King murmured thoughtfully. "Hard to believe they're from the same parents, isn't it?"

Lafayette absently traced his forefinger around the rim of his highball glass. "I am ashamed even to speak of what happened between your mother and me—mostly because I caused an unforgivable injury to Bethany."

"Ah . . . Aunt Bethany," King said. "Her voice always gets breathless whenever your name comes up, and then her face has this incredibly sad look."

Lafayette inhaled sharply, as if suddenly assaulted.

"Since we were practically in kindergarten, she and I . . . had an understanding. As soon as I finished law school, we were goin' to get married, despite my parents' objections that the Kingsburys had . . ." He faltered.

"Had made a colossal series of stupid financial decisions and lost all their money?" King supplied bluntly.

"My father's words, precisely," Laf said bitterly. "Well . . . that year of Mardi Gras, 1962, I was your basic hot-blooded, arrogant southern white boy of twenty-five. Not that that excuses anything . . . but perhaps it explains things a bit. Well . . . anyway, I got roarin' drunk on the night of Fat Tuesday, like everyone else in New Orleans, and I let myself be—" He stopped short and then selected his next words with extreme care.

"Just say it," King said impatiently.

"Antoinette . . . your mother . . . as you might have concluded by now, is a very willful, very persuasive woman and she . . . well, I knew she'd always been jealous of her older sister. We were thrown together so much that year. She flattered me and played up to me in a major way, 'specially that night, and I did what stupid, arrogant, intoxicated males are wont to do."

"In the words of André Kingsbury, you 'had sex,' " King said coolly.

Marchand nodded. "The next mornin' . . . not only did I have the mother of all hangovers, I quickly realized that I'd been idiotic and would have done *anything* to turn back the clock. However, as Antoinette soon revealed to me, she got pregnant as a result of that one wild night."

"And accordin' to Grandfather, you flatly refused to marry her," King said, as if he were talking about people he barely knew.

"No!" he said sharply. "I told Antoinette that I thought it was wrong to marry her if I still loved her sister and didn't love her. I promised her, though, that I'd pay for everything. See her through her pregnancy, if that was her choice. I'd agreed to place the baby for adoption, if that was what she wanted." Marchand stared across the table at King, his eyes suddenly moist. "Jesus, King! It's hard, now, to think I'd never have known you. Up until you went into the marines, I at least had those years as your godfather . . . doin' things with you when you were a boy . . . tryin' to *be* there for you, as best I could."

"Amazin', isn't it, how everybody kept those secrets, avoidin' a scandal," King said with the first hint of bitterness. "And nobody ever mentioned that I shot up to six-foot-one and my father was barely five-ten. Waylon used to call me 'the Stranger.' Didn't *he* know for sure that I wasn't his?"

"This may sound crazy," Lafayette said, "but I have no idea. Antoinette . . . your mother . . . immediately turned around and married Waylon to save face."

"At least he was *willin'* to marry her," King said.

"Not quite," Marchand corrected. "Since tonight is truth-tellin' time, the fact is—not to put too fine a point on it—she trapped Waylon into marryin' her, sleepin' with him real fast and makin' him think she was pregnant by *him*. Of course, she passed off your early birth as premature . . . but as you began to grow up, Waylon must have noticed how unalike you and he were."

"He knows . . ." King mused, almost to himself, "even if he *doesn't* know."

"Antoinette agreed to name me godfather, if I'd put some money away for your future—which I *wanted* to do, by the way," Marchand added parenthetically. "The other reason she went along with it was to put her own friends and Waylon's family off the scent of possible scandal. I mean," he added with an ironic smile, "who'd have the *gall* to name me, in church, before God, as your godparent, if the whispered rumors were true? But then you fired me from the job . . . and now I know why, after all these years. That note you found in the safe-deposit box must have hurt."

"Grandfather's note wasn't the reason I fired you," King said. "I ended our relationship because you went to work for Jeffries. In my eyes, you were no longer an honorable man." Hearing this, Marchand visibly winced. King continued in a steady voice. "You signed on as the man behind the scenes for a person whose values I despise, orchestratin' public opinion so that everyone would think Grover Jeffries was God's gift to philanthropy. It made me sick to see it was *you* doin' the fixin'.' "

"It didn't start that way," Lafayette said heavily. " 'Bout ten years ago, soon after you got out of the service, my life just seemed to hit a brick wall. I got pretty deeply in debt. I like goin' to the race track, and—well . . . I used to play for some pretty high stakes back in those days . . . and I got to like those gamblin' boats Grover had goin' for a while. When he wanted me to work off what I owed, doin' public relations for the proposed Good Times Shoppin' Plaza, I—"

"Accepted an offer you couldn't refuse."

"That about describes it. I hated myself even more than *you* did when I handled damage control for that fiasco. But when the Selwyn buildin' project first started, I thought that Grover had finally gotten hold of somethin' that would benefit the city. I had no idea those beautiful Greek Revivals were behind that ol' screen."

"I didn't notice you advisin' Grover to give up his hotel project, even when you *did* find out about them," King reminded him.

"No. Unlike you, son . . . I didn't have the guts. I couldn't kick ass and take names until the moment I thought you had been left in one of those mausoleums to suffocate. When I heard what Grover had done, I kinda went insane, you know? You're my *son*! You could have died, and I . . ." Marchand's sentence trailed off. Horror and self-loathing distorted his handsome face. "If anything had happened to you, I don't think I could have—"

"Well," King intervened swiftly, "you picked the right reporter to search for me. How much does Corlis McCullough know about all this?"

"Everything. Time was short. I had to tell her the truth so she'd trust me and help me find you."

"What about Manny and Virgil?"

"They don't know I'm your father."

"Well . . . Corlis kept your confidence. She didn't tell me a thing."

"She's quite a woman, King. But then, I suspect you already realize that."

"She's no magnolia, that's for sure. With Ace McCullough, you know just where you stand." King took a long draught on his bottle of Dixie. He set it on the table with a thump and abruptly asked, "Why didn't you ever marry?"

"I didn't *want* anyone but Bethany. And if I'd married someone else, just to keep up appearances, I honestly think that I would've probably put a bullet in my head . . . or Bethany might have."

"You broke Bethany's heart anyway, didn't you?" King pronounced, taking another long draught of beer.

"That, of course, has been my punishment all these years," Marchand's voice suddenly cracked. "After Bethany got over her initial shock, that dear lady was relentlessly civil to me on those few occasions when we'd meet," he continued, "but she wouldn't have anything to do with me."

"No . . . she wouldn't," King agreed quietly.

Lafayette turned slightly and gazed over King's head through the windows overlooking Bourbon Street. "Bethany told me a few years later that she'd forgiven me for what happened, but she wouldn't accept any of my invitations to see one another. The only way to protect the family honor, she said, was to"—he raised a hand to his forehead, as if he had a migraine—"was to keep a polite distance. I'd created the disaster in our lives, so all these years, I've honored her wishes."

King's father stared fixedly at his amber glass of bourbon and shook his head. "Not marryin' at *all* was lonely, but it was also liberating. As a matter of fact, my refusin' to marry some uptown magnolia, just to make it up to my daddy for dishonorin' the family name, was the thing I'm proudest of . . . except, of course, for what *you've* done, takin' on the establishment in this town, savin' buildin's that preserve the historic character of New Orleans."

"Thank you," was all King said.

Pain etched Marchand's eyes. "I asked you to meet me here tonight because I can't go on livin' this lie. I am your *father*! And I'm glad you know it. And I need to ask . . . not for your forgiveness, I guess, because you probably can't give it, after what I've done. But because *I* just want you to know I've always recognized you as the son of my heart. That I've always *loved* you as my son, and worried about your welfare and—"

"I'm grateful for those times we had together when I was a boy," King interrupted gently. "They were among the few bright spots of my childhood. I do forgive you, Laf. And it helps to know the truth about why you wouldn't marry my mother. I thank you for tellin' me 'bout that. Another thing." Lafayette lifted his eyes from his highball glass and met King's gaze head-on. "I have a lot of admiration for what you did today. A lot."

"What do you mean?" Lafayette asked with a baffled expression.

"Standing up to Grover Jeffries like that today took a lot of guts. You risked virtually everythin', but you took him to the mat anyway. You were an unbelievably skilled negotiator, wrestlin' with a real viper. And so, I just want you to know . . . I *do* respect you. Now."

There was a long silence. Then Lafayette leaned across the table, covered one of King's hands with his own, and said in a voice choked with emotion, "Thank you . . . for sayin' that, son."

"So," King declared. He set his glass of beer hard on the table, like a period at the end of a sentence. "I think it's time I reinstated you as my godfather. That is, if you're willin' to take on the assignment again."

Lafayette Marchand raised his chin, with its distinctive cleft, and squared his shoulders. "It's a start. . . . It surely is a start."

Chapter Thirty

June 1

"McCullough!" barked a disembodied voice over the newsroom intercom. "You're wanted in Zamora's office. Pronto!"

"Jeez Louise, *now* what?" she exclaimed to the walls of her reporter's cubicle. She rose, exhausted, from her chair and pushed it to her desk. The last three hours had been a blur of activity. By some miracle she'd managed to meet her broadcast deadline with only two minutes to spare before the program went on the air.

"Good job, Corlis," director Bernard Sinclair said, patting her back as he emerged from the control room. "Your piece tonight actually made me care about a *buildin'*!" he added, laughing. "My mother's mother was a Colvis, y'know." Then he grinned. "Half the Colvises you meet round here are *black*. My mama's family had some ol' plantation upriver that they lost after the Civil War."

"Really?" she replied. Then something about Sinclair's dark blond hair caught her attention. Its texture was rather coarse, and it had a distinct wave to it.

Passé blanc . . .

"Yeah," Bernie replied. "I'm Scots-Irish on my dad's side, way, way back." He gave her a friendly salute. "Anyway . . . it's been a great series. See ya."

In fact, nearly everyone at the station had congratulated her on the Selwyn story tonight. However, Corlis felt utterly drained—and depressed. She'd half expected a call from King when the broadcast concluded, but she'd heard nothing.

440

Oh well, she sighed. She imagined him sitting with Lafayette Marchand at a small table at the Old Absinthe House bar, listening to revelations that were bound to turn his world upside down. Wearily she made her way to the station owner's office. Inside, Marvin Glimp was standing beside Andy Zamora, who sat behind his desk.

"You did a great job," her boss declared.

"Well . . . thanks," Corlis replied, surprised by Andy's unqualified compliment. "Manny and Virgil deserve a lot of credit. The pictures really told the story." There was no point in repeating tales about Virgil making King an unauthorized duplicate tape and then destroying the master. The buildings were saved, and the story was finally at an end.

Zamora patted her on the hand. "Yeah, but you were the one to decide where to point the camera and you told 'em to keep rollin'," Andy insisted. "And one more thing . . ."

"Yes?" Corlis said. *Here it comes,* she thought grimly.

"I wanted Marvin to be here when I apologize to you for even suspectin' that you might have leaked the Jack Ebert invoice to King Duvallon's crowd."

Corlis shrugged. She didn't care anymore *who* leaked the invoice.

"How do you know I didn't?"

" 'Cause Virgil came in tonight and told me that *he* did."

"*Virgil* leaked the Ebert invoice?" Corlis replied, amazed. "Wow."

"And he thinks that mentionin' to another cameraman at a bar last week that he got a shot of Grover's campaign contributions memo on videotape tipped off the *Times-Picayune* reporter that such a memo existed."

" 'Loose lips sink ships,' as my great-aunt Marge is fond of saying," Corlis said blandly.

But why was she surprised? she asked herself. Virgil was a cameraman, not a reporter. He had no scruples about giving his friend King a little boost by getting him a copy of Ebert's invoice off the videotape and dubbing an extra copy of the cemetery tape when he made one for Lafayette Marchand. Like Althea LaCroix, Dylan Fouché—even Cindy Lou Mallory— longtime New Orleanian Virgil Johnson obviously cared passionately about the fate of the Selwyn buildings and had done what he could to help save them.

Zamora laughed and said, "By the way, Virgil told me how you saved the day at Lafayette Number 1."

"That stuff's strictly off the record," Corlis said, alarmed that Marchand's confidentiality had been breached.

"Our lips are sealed, right Marvin?" Zamora said. The lawyer nodded.

"I promised Marchand certain conditions in exchange for getting information about what Jeffries was doing behind the scenes today." How *much* of the story did Virgil tell Andy? she worried. Then she had another terrible thought. "Did you fire him? Virgil, I mean?"

"I suspended him for two weeks. I told him to use his vacation time and get the hell out of town for a while."

"Boy . . . are you tough," Corlis replied dryly. She held up her hands in front of her face. "I know. . . . I know. . . . This is New Orleans."

Marvin Glimp spoke up for the first time. "Tell me something, Corlis. How did Grover Jeffries ever come around to agreeing to revitalize those derelict old buildings? My sister told me that Grover said he'd go to jail before he'd ever let those building-huggers tell him what he could do with his property."

"Sorry, Marvin . . ." Corlis replied with a certain amount of relish. "I *do* happen to know why Jeffries agreed to save the buildings, but that's part of the story I agreed to embargo, so I can't divulge what I learned from my sources." Then she suddenly wondered: Who leaked the actual memo to King with Jeffries's handwritten instructions? King had somehow been given *that* little bombshell before the city council meeting in time to make two hundred copies to wave in Grover's face.

As Aunt Marge taught her, when there's a leak, ask yourself who had immediate *access* to the document in question.

Only Grover and Lafayette Marchand had physical access. At WJAZ we didn't realize we had the Grover-Marchand memo on tape until much later. The tape editor couldn't have cared less. Virgil only blabbed about it, and I certainly didn't hand it over to King.

Corlis judged that Jeffries wouldn't have been the one to give it to him. That left Lafayette Marchand. She'd bet her breakfast beignets that when Lafayette got wind that Grover had King kidnapped, he took action that would insure his son's cause would triumph in the end and slipped the incriminating memo under the door at the Preservation Resource Center. After all, blood was thicker than water, wasn't it? Especially in New Orleans.

What a day, she groaned silently, turning to leave her boss's office.

"Take a week off, McCullough," Zamora suggested. "Since your cameraman's on suspension, you might as well take advantage of it."

"Thanks, I will," she replied. "My eighty-three-year-old great-aunt's in town. It'll give me a chance to show her around."

"Gonna take her to the Mid-City Rock-N-Bowl?" Zamora teased.

Corlis smiled at the mention of the celebrated bowling alley on Carrollton Avenue where patrons not only slung balls at ten pins, they danced the night away to a pulsating zydeco band.

"If only you knew Margery McCullough, you'd realize that's a very good suggestion. See ya."

"Hey, Corlis!" Zamora called after her. "If you wanna take King Duvallon along on your little sight-seeing junkets—it's okay now. Virgil said you two behaved yourselves the whole time," he added with a sly smile.

Well, not quite . . .

"Gee, thanks," she replied, and rolled her eyes.

She walked down the corridor toward the newsroom attempting to put her boss's quip out of her mind. She sat down at her desk in a mood of free-floating melancholy. All the places around New Orleans that she wanted to cast before her aunt like precious pearls were the spots she'd also love to see with Kingsbury Duvallon. By all rights, she and King should be out celebrating tonight.

Corlis stared at the clock in her cubicle. It was a few minutes after 11 P.M. No light blinked on her voice mail. King hadn't called, and from the looks of it, he wouldn't. He could be as stubborn as she was about digging in his heels. He judged that she'd let him down as a friend—never mind, as a lover—when the fur was flying, and that probably ended it as far as their relationship was concerned.

Just then the phone on her desk rang, startling her from woeful thoughts. Her heart racing with hopeful anticipation, she picked up the receiver.

"Hello?"

"Corlis? Good! You're still there."

"Hi, Dylan."

"Great job on the ol' tube tonight, sweetheart. I watched from my office."

"Thanks," she said, trying to keep the fatigue and disappointment out of her voice.

"You comin' to Café LaCroix tonight?" he asked.

"First I heard of it. Why?"

"Didn't you know? The preservation guerrillas are celebratin', sugar! Won't be any fun if you and your aunt Marge aren't there. Althea told me to make sure you'd come."

King would be there. And probably Cindy Lou. Corlis couldn't face it.

"I'm just dead," she temporized, "and I expect my aunt is pretty jet-lagged."

"She's rarin' to go," countered Dylan with enthusiasm. "Had a nice little nap. I just talked to her, tryin' to track you down."

"Oh, Dylan . . . I dunno. . . ."

"Hey, babycakes . . . what's the matter?" Dylan said quietly. Corlis suddenly felt a lump rise in her throat and couldn't speak. "You havin' the postpartum blues, sugar, now that the Selwyn story is over?"

"It doesn't *feel* over," Corlis said bleakly. "I never did find out if Julien LaCroix's will stood up in court . . . or if Joseph Dumas's son Edgar married Lisette, or if Martine got to keep her property and pass it along to her son Julien—"

"Corlis!" Dylan said insistently. "The story's *over*. *The buildin's are saved.*"

"But I never learned if my namesake, Corlis Bell McCullough, left her rotten husband."

"*That's* not why you're feelin' so blue, is it?" Dylan intervened abruptly. "You don't want to come to the party because . . . what? You and King have a fight or somethin'?"

"I guess it falls into the 'or something' category," Corlis said morosely, amazed, as always, that Dylan seemed to be able to read her mind. "Before the city council meeting today, King wanted me to reveal what I knew from my sources, so he'd be prepared for what Jeffries and his goons were going to sling at him. But I couldn't . . . I *wouldn't* tell him because of a professional conflict of interest. Now he's . . . he's . . ."

"He's *what*?" Dylan asked impatiently.

"Cool. Preoccupied . . ." she said obliquely.

"Have you talked to him since the city council voted?" Dylan demanded.

"No . . ." Corlis admitted, "he never called me. Look, Dylan . . . I have a long history of misunderstandings with the man. Let's just leave it at that."

An idea was forming in her mind. A wild, insane, crazy idea prompted both by her conversation with Dylan Fouché and her fervent desire to do something that was totally absorbing to take her mind off the victory party.

"C'mon, Corlis! It won't be a party without *you*. Promise you'll drop by Café LaCroix later," Dylan insisted. "It's gonna go *real* late, I guarantee. Promise?"

"Maybe later," she said noncommittally. "I have to check out something first."

There was a pause on the phone. Then Dylan announced, "You're gonna try to do your flip-back thing tonight to find out what happened, aren't you, girl? You won't be satisfied till you've tied up all the loose ends on this story. Well, that's *not* a good idea right now," he said flatly.

Wow! This guy was scary!

"It'd take my mind off my troubles," she suggested, tongue in cheek.

"Don't," Dylan said shortly. "I very nearly couldn't get you to come back to consciousness last time you visited another century. Doin' it on your own . . . you could get into serious trouble."

"You mean *permanently* lose my mind? How inconvenient," she responded. "Well, then, would you consider meeting me at the Selwyn buildings? Right now. Before we go to Café LaCroix?" she asked, making an abrupt decision. She'd make a deal with him. She'd go to the victory party if he'd help her find out what ultimately befell Martine, the other Corlis McCullough, and the original Lafayette Marchand. "I want to try something . . . but I agree with you. I don't think I should do it alone."

"Absolutely not," Dylan said emphatically. "You're tired. You're depressed about King. Don't risk it right now."

"I'm *fine*."

"I don't think so," he pronounced sternly. "Listen, sugar . . . I'll be glad to help you answer any questions still plaguin' you, but let's wait till you're rested. Till you're not so stressed out, y'hear what I'm sayin'? Maybe one day next week."

But I want to know now! *I have to know what happened to Corlis Bell McCullough and why the women in my family always have so much trouble with the men in their lives. Maybe it's in our genes?*

Even steady, sensible Aunt Marge had never had a sustainable relationship with a man. Lovers aplenty, and someone very special, from what she'd disclosed today . . . but never a partnership that lasted in the face of driving ambition. And the same was true for Corlis herself. Was it the men, or was it the McCullough women? If Dylan wouldn't help her find out tonight why this was so, she'd just hazard it on her own.

"Okay, Dylan," she agreed calmly. "Will you do me a favor? Will you go pick up Aunt Marge on Julia Street while I finish up a few things here? Then I'll meet you both at Café LaCroix in about an hour, okay?"

"Okay," Dylan replied doubtfully.

"My other phone's ringing," she fibbed. "Gotta go. See you later."

It was a few minutes after midnight when Corlis parked her car on Common Street next to the entrance to the old LaCroix & Company brick warehouse. She turned off the headlights and scanned the buildings on either side. Architect Keith LaCroix's rendering of the old site had identified the third entrance from the corner as the probable location of Joseph Dumas's tailor shop. Colvis, his competitor, had had a similar establishment facing Canal Street. Dumas's business was just a few doors down from the back entrance to Martine Fouché's former town house, located above the shop where her sister Annette had once sewn gowns for the city's elite.

She locked the door to her Lexus and dug inside her voluminous shoulder bag for the item she'd purchased at the all-night supermarket. The box of children's drawing chalk was not precisely the kind tailors used to mark alterations on clothing, but Corlis hoped it would produce the desired result.

She felt slightly ludicrous as she withdrew her heavy black police-style flashlight from the car trunk and glanced up and down the street to be certain there was no one in sight. Fortunately the massive aluminum three-story screen did not extend around to Common Street, so she located the door to Dumas's old shop with relative ease. One of its hinges had broken off, and in a few seconds she was inside the former tailor's establishment, shining the broad beam around the deserted interior space.

The shop's most recent incarnation had been as a tax preparer's storefront office. Outdated IRS manuals and a smattering of tax forms lay strewn about the floor. Otherwise the space was empty. Corlis trod gingerly around the debris and made her way toward the rear of the space, attempting to imagine the place as a nineteenth-century haberdashery. Had Joseph Dumas and his son, Edgar, actually occupied these very rooms? she wondered. Had her namesake, Corlis Bell McCullough, truly sipped a cup of coffee here, as described in her diary?

She aimed her flashlight's powerful beam into a small room at the back. Toward the rear wall stood a scarred desk and wooden chair where some benighted soul had toted up the taxes for citizens too weary or too confused by the complicated federal regulations to figure out the forms by themselves.

Despite the dust, she sat down in the straight-backed chair and piled her leather purse and flashlight onto the desk's scratched surface. Warily she extracted a piece of blue chalk from the box. With determination she lifted it to her nose and inhaled deeply. The dry, cretaceous smell made her want to sneeze, and for an instant she thought she might be transported to her first-grade school room at El Rodeo, K through 8, on Whittier Drive, in Beverly Hills. She could picture Miss

Bettelheim standing at the blackboard in a room where chalk dust blended with the fragrance of macaroni-and-cheese drifting down the corridor from the nearby cafeteria.

Corlis wistfully pushed this memory aside and deliberately began to take deep, measured breaths, just as Dylan had instructed her in her bedroom on Julia Street. She envisioned a shield of white light encasing the battered old desk like a bell jar and protecting her from forces unknown.

Inhale . . . exhale. Inhale . . . exhale.

She allowed her mind to empty of all other thoughts and instead concentrated on the sound of her slow, even breathing and the dusty, powdery aroma of chalk. A sensation of deep relaxation began to flow through her body. How pleasant this exercise was, she mused. It felt wonderful to release the tensions of this tumultuous day . . . to allow all thoughts to drift . . . to merely drink in sensations . . . to imagine someone sketching quick, bright blue lines down a piece of finely woven wool . . . light black wool of the sort that fine clothes were made . . . clothes to be worn on important occasions like . . . like a *wedding*. Oh, yes a wedding! It would be a ceremony that the man, whose trousers were being so deftly marked by blue chalk, hoped would surely be the most joyous occasion of his life.

Chapter Thirty-one

May 12, 1852

"You *will* come to our wedding, Mrs. Mac?" Edgar Dumas asked, standing on the small rounded dais where his father's many clients had their clothing tailored to precision.

Corlis Bell McCullough noted that Edgar was staring past the rather rakish straw hat she'd donned today. The groom-to-be gazed out of the shop's window onto Common Street as a large wagon, pulled by a team of gargantuan workhorses, lumbered by. Edgar's father, Joseph, squatted on his knees, chalk in hand, putting the final touches on his son's wedding suit.

"At our nuptials," Edgar continued, resuming his attention to his visitor, "Lisette has decreed there shall be an orchestra and that I'm to play my violin and she the pianoforte!"

"Ah . . . but what a wonderful treat for all your guests," Corlis replied, smiling. "You both have such a talent for music, Edgar, as does Lisette's mother, Martine. My wish is for any children you and Lisette may have together to be blessed with her beauty and your shared artistic ability."

Corlis knew that young Edgar would cheerfully give up the tailoring business entirely to pursue his dream of playing professionally, if only his father would permit it. The senior Dumas never would, of course. Even the younger man could see that it would be very imprudent to exchange such a thriving business for the uncertainties of playing violin in an orchestra or string ensemble.

Corlis took an appreciative sip from the cup of rich chicory coffee that the Dumases always had brewing on the hob for the patrons who called at their popular shop. However, Mrs. Mac, as Edgar and his father had come to call her over the years of their acquaintance, was more than just a neighbor—she was also their bookkeeper. And as was her habit, she arrived at the end of the business day, on Tuesdays, to deliver an updated record of the shop's accounts.

"I wouldn't miss the marriage of Edgar to Lisette for the world," Corlis warmly assured them, "although one of the reasons I came to see you today was to tell you that I shall be leaving New Orleans very soon."

"My dear madam, we are so sorry to hear this," the elder Dumas declared. "Of course, we understand such a decision on your part," he added with the diplomacy that had made him the confidant of his many clients, black and white. The Dumases realized, given the mysterious disappearance of Mr. McCullough, that his abandoned wife could neither mourn a deceased spouse nor divorce a live one. Her only solution was to depart for foreign territories where no one knew her and there, assume the role of bereaved widow. "But where will you be going?" Joseph asked.

"My son Warren has written from California that there are wonderful holdings we can homestead just outside the capital in Monterey. That's south of San Francisco, on the sea," she explained.

"What an adventure for such a young man," Joseph exclaimed, and cast a protective look at his own son. "And only seventeen," he murmured. "He's a credit to you, Mrs. Mac."

"I was worried sick about him when he stowed away, till I heard of his safe arrival," Corlis nodded. "I've determined to leave on the fifth of June, on a sailing ship from New Orleans down to Panama, and then take a mule train across that narrow isthmus that separates the two oceans."

"Isn't that an awfully perilous journey?" Joseph asked, concerned.

"Perhaps," Corlis replied, "but I've already had yellow fever and feel equal to the challenge of tramping through a jungle." She heaved a sigh. "I must admit I *am* concerned for young Webb. I do hope he'll be all right."

"Webster's grown strong as an ox, Mrs. Mac," Edgar assured. "Mr. Bates says he's the best stable boy he's got!"

It had been nearly a decade since Corlis's husband, Randall McCullough, had abruptly disappeared, along with his erstwhile partner, Ian Jeffries. Speculation was that they had escaped into the wilds of Texas, where bank examiners could not scrutinize their many past-due accounts. She'd been too proud to request charity from her banker father in Pennsylvania. Rather, her two young boys had each sought employment, and she had kept her small family together through the use of arithmetic skills she'd absorbed at Enoch Bell's knee.

"Well, I certainly hope the very best for you and the boys," Joseph declared sincerely. With practiced hands the tailor smoothed the frock coat's fabric over Edgar's broad shoulders, marking wherever he thought a slight tuck was needed to make the jacket fit to perfection.

Corlis sighed and dabbed her damp brow with a lace handkerchief. She was happy, finally, to be leaving this ghastly swamp, but it would take a long time to find friends as loyal as the Dumases and Martine Fouché LaCroix—as Martine had styled herself in the wake of Julien LaCroix's death and his generous bequest to her and her children.

"Webster and I shall miss you all dreadfully," Corlis said soberly, "and Martine and her children, of course. However, I would be lying if I said I shall miss this horrid heat and humidity."

Just then the door burst open, and a gangly youth with coffee-colored skin and straight black hair raced into the fitting room, followed by Webster McCullough, flushed of face and panting to keep up.

"Julien LaCroix!" scolded Joseph. "Does your mama know you're tearin' round the block like this?"

"And you, Webb," Corlis admonished. She frowned at her son, as well as at Julien, the product of the liaison between Julien and Martine. "You two boys are supposed to be doing your sums and preparing for the spelling test I shall be giving you tomorrow. Now, *where* have you been, and what mischief have you been getting into?"

"My mama's gettin' dressed for the big ball," Julien

announced with a sullen expression. "Grandmama Althea don't want us botherin' her."

"*Doesn't* want you bothering her," Corlis corrected him. "Your mama and I want you two boys to learn to speak English correctly."

"Right, Miz McCullough," Julien agreed emphatically. "Grandmama Althea . . . she say 'y'all run along and play.' So, we's *playin'*."

And with that the two boisterous youths raced out the shop's back entrance, slamming the door behind them.

Corlis sighed once more. Over the years she had grown very fond of Martine, although her mother, Althea, had proved to be as cold and as calculating a woman as Corlis had ever known. Martine Fouché LaCroix remained just as kindhearted and beautiful as ever, blessed with a voluptuousness that graces some women as they mature. She was now a woman of at least forty years old, although Corlis didn't know her exact age. The stunning-looking quadroon was as much sought after as ever—both by Free Men of Color and by white Creoles. However, Martine had removed herself from the Salle d'Orleans and the Quadroon Balls to look after her two children, Lisette and Julien, and to supervise her holdings on Canal Street.

Corlis rose from her chair and drifted, cup in hand, to the shop window. A shining black carriage was pulling up alongside the *banquette*. Its pair of sleek roan horses pawed the ground and shook their handsome heads, jangling their polished harnesses. The cab door opened, and out stepped a tall, extraordinarily elegant man, impeccably dressed in white tie, black broadcloth tailcoat and trousers, top hat, and a magnificent black cape.

"My stars," Corlis exclaimed, looking back over her shoulder at the Dumases. "That's Lafayette Marchand, isn't it? The late Adelaide LaCroix's brother." Marchand had received quite a fine inheritance from his sister—as well as his brother-in-law—when poor Adelaide had fallen from her horse the same day her husband had died, struck down by yellow fever before she could ever reach New Orleans.

Young Edgar Dumas had stepped behind a screen in order to don his normal working attire. "Is Mr. Marchand expected here for a fitting?" she inquired. "Though why the man would be out-fitted so formally on such an errand is a mystery," she added.

Joseph Dumas nervously peered into his appointment book and declared in a relieved tone of voice, "*Mais, non* . . . he's not scheduled. Ah! Look!" he exclaimed. "He's headed for a door down the block."

Corlis's eyes narrowed thoughtfully as she watched the dashing Lafayette Marchand saunter toward the back entrance to Martine's flat above her sister Annette's dressmaker's shop.

"Why would he enter by the back door to Martine's?" Corlis wondered aloud.

But the answer was obvious, she surmised with a start. The young lawyer who had inherited Julien LaCroix's first-rate stable of horseflesh and won several rich purses this year at Metairie Race Course was probably secretly courting his brother-in-law's former paramour. If Martine's mother had anything to say about it, this blossoming liaison would cost the man a pretty picayune.

Would Martine Fouché LaCroix accept a steady patron for the third time in her life? Did she need or want a man to support her in a sumptuous fashion, in exchange for her . . . favors? Corlis was fully aware—as per Julien's stated wishes in his will—that her friend was planning to host the finest wedding for her daughter, Lisette, and Edgar Dumas that the Free People of Color in New Orleans had ever witnessed. It was to be an expensive affair, an extravagance heaped on top of the cost of recently sending Lisette to France for a year of schooling—not to mention the price of outfitting her golden-skinned daughter in the best clothes Paris had to offer.

And now there was young Julien's future for Martine to consider. The boy, whom Julien LaCroix had named heir to his Canal Street holdings, must be properly educated to be able to take over from his mother the running of this residential and commercial block of buildings. Martine was, to be sure, a woman of substance. However, considering her recent expenses, the upkeep of the slaves she owned, and her sumptuous manner of living, Corlis knew only too well that her friend was relatively cash poor.

But would it be prudent for Martine to replenish her coffers through a relationship with *Lafayette Marchand*, of all people—a man infamous for wagering on horseflesh? And people still whispered about the shocking revelation that the notorious Mademoiselle Fouché had had intimate relations with the LaCroixs—father *and* son—and had borne a child by each of them. What a time the gossips would have had if the beautiful quadroon, with her pressing financial responsibilities, accepted Julien's despised brother-in-law as her new patron.

Ah . . . these Frenchies! Corlis thought, wondering what her strict, Scots-Presbyterian banker father would say if he knew the company she kept down here in the swamps of Louisiana. Who could fathom the mysterious ways of these native New Orleanians?

"Well . . . thank you for the coffee," Corlis said cordially, setting her cup on the table where the latest journals were laid out for the perusal of the Dumases' customers. "I've put your week's accounts on the desk in your office, Joseph," she said. "I hope you will find them satisfactory."

"As always," Joseph said with a slight bow, "I'm sure I will, Mrs. Mac. Good day to you."

Corlis stepped outside the shop and felt the full force of the rising heat. Just then Lafayette Marchand turned from Martine's door and their eyes met. Corlis recalled the day, so many years ago, when they had witnessed, together, Julien's torturous demise in the second-floor bedchamber of her former house on Julia Street—that same, terrible week André Duvallon fired a bullet into his brain.

She paused to open her ruffled parasol beside the busy thoroughfare as an omnibus rolled past, its team of horses kicking up clods of dirt in the dusty street.

"Good day to you, Mrs. McCullough," Marchand said.

"And to you," Corlis replied, prepared to resume her passage down the street. Martine's slave Elfie, stooped now with arthritis, opened the door. As Lafayette inclined his head politely, the man at least had the grace to flush with embarrassment. "Enjoy the ball, Monsieur Marchand," Corlis couldn't resist adding.

And who knew? she reflected with a suppressed smile, continuing down the street. Perhaps one day there would be a child of Martine and Lafayette's who would bear the name Marchand. Then again, Monsieur Marchand might well marry among his own set, and *those* children would be the progeny to carry on his line. With these Frenchies, who could predict *what* would happen?

My stars, she thought, chuckling to herself as she rounded the corner to Canal Street and her gaze glided from granite column to column along the grand block of buildings that came as close to a Greek temple as anything that Corlis Bell McCullough was likely to see. There was certainly *one* thing she had learned during her eighteen years in the Crescent City.

In New Orleans everybody who was anybody was related to *everyone else*!

In California, she prayed, life was bound to be different.

Chapter Thirty-two

June 2

Dylan and King peered cautiously into the deserted commercial space and called out, "Hello! Anyone in here?"

An eerie silence greeted them, along with the sight of light illuminating the rear of the empty office. The pair slowly moved farther into the room, sweeping the beam of their flashlight across the walls. Then Dylan said in a whisper, "Uh . . . oh . . . there she is. In the back . . . see?"

Corlis sat slumped over an old desk. Her eyes were closed and her breathing shallow.

"Well, what do we do *now*?" King asked worriedly.

"Shhh . . . Let's wait a few minutes and see if she comes out of it."

"Out of it?" King demanded in a hoarse whisper. "What's *it*?"

"A self-induced trance."

A half hour earlier, Corlis's great-aunt and her escort, Dylan Fouché, had grown alarmed when they hadn't spotted her among the noisy, rambunctious throng celebrating at Café LaCroix. Dylan hailed King, who walked into the smoke-wreathed music club with Lafayette Marchand. King had immediately introduced the visiting Californian to his older companion.

"I'm delighted to meet you, Mr. Marchand," Margery said, extending her good arm in a firm handshake. The elderly lady was still attired in her tight-waisted suit and matching velvet turban. She peered through the haze of cigarette smoke to scrutinize Kingsbury Duvallon and asked abruptly, "Where do you

456

suppose my niece could be, Mr. Duvallon—and why aren't you two celebrating this victory together? The story's over now. Where do you suppose that girl's got to?"

King had glanced briefly at Lafayette and explained with a pained expression, "Well, it's kinda a long story, Miz McCullough." Then he shot a glance at Dylan and asked, "You got any ideas where Corlis could be?"

Dylan paused, scanning the darkened club, hoping to catch sight of her. "Yeah," he drawled. "I 'spect I do."

Leaving Margery in Lafayette's care, the two men then set out to find Corlis. Dylan immediately suggested they head straight for the Selwyn buildings. Once they arrived at the 600 block of Canal Street, they made several wrong turns before they spotted Corlis's car and an unlocked door. Advancing toward the rear of the building, they found her with her head cradled in her arms. She appeared fast asleep. A piece of blue chalk rested in her right hand, and her ubiquitous shoulder bag lay at her left elbow. Dylan put two fingers at the pulse point on her neck.

"It's steady," he pronounced.

"Well, that's somethin', " King said worriedly. "Whad'ya think? Maybe we should call a doctor."

Dylan remained silent, staring down at the woman whose countenance in repose was so unlike her animated appearance on television. Then he said abruptly, "I think you should kiss her."

"Do *what*?"

Dylan flashed a sly grin. "Ask her permission to *kiss* her," he repeated. "Tell her that if she's ready, she will begin to become aware of her surroundin's . . . the sounds on the street . . . the temperature of the room, and so on. Then say that you and I are here, waitin' for her to come back to normal consciousness . . . and that you love her very much and want to show her so by kissin' her."

"Dylan!" King exclaimed. "You're a little crazy, you know that?" He glanced down at Corlis with a troubled frown. "Look, *you're* supposed to be the expert. What if I hurt her in some way? I want *you* to bring her out of this."

"No . . . *you* should," Dylan considered with a thoughtful expression. "She'll respond better to you. Now do as I say."

"But—"

"This is serious stuff, King," he said. "Corlis wanted to find out the fate of her namesake. She didn't give me any details, but I also think she was extremely upset about whatever happened between you two earlier today. I don't know what that was, mind you, but I sensed when I spoke with her on the phone tonight that she felt terribly conflicted . . . because she *cares* about you, boy!"

"But that can't be the reason she won't wake up," King protested.

"Ah . . . but I think she may be stayin' in the trance because she's exhausted by everything that's happened. It's a form of escape."

"What if I can't bring her out of it?" King asked soberly.

Dylan turned toward the shop door with an impatient wave.

"Look, now. Gimme your car keys. I'm gonna risk my life and go sit in that hideous claptrap of yours parked out front. Why you never drive that Jaguar of yours round town is beyond lil' ol' *me*." He pointed at his watch. "If you two don't come out in ten minutes, I'll go for help."

King nodded in agreement and cast the flashlight's beam toward the door that opened onto the street, providing a pathway for Dylan's departure. Then he devoted his full attention to Corlis, who remained motionless, her head still cradled in her arms.

He bent forward, his hands resting on the desk. "Darlin'?" he ventured awkwardly, feeling both foolish and afraid. "Corlis . . . ? Dylan says it's time to become aware of where you are, sugar."

He waited. Nothing happened.

He bent closer and whispered, "Take your time, baby, but . . . I want you to know that you're safe here with us. Start to become aware of the room . . . the temperature in here. The sounds of traffic outside."

Corlis didn't respond.

"Sweetheart," he urged, attempting to keep the desperation out of his voice, "I'm here baby. Wake up. Please."

King thought he detected the slightest flicker beneath her closed eyes. There! He *definitely* saw a movement.

"I'm here, darlin'," he whispered. "When you're ready . . . you can open your eyes. *Please* open your eyes . . . so I know you're all right. We have to talk. . . . Please, Corlis . . . come back. . . ."

A lump had suddenly grown in his throat. What if he couldn't rouse her? What if he'd hurt her so much this afternoon that—?

Just at that moment she inhaled deeply and allowed her breath to escape in a long, even exhalation.

"That's right, baby . . ." he pleaded. "You gotta know how sorry I am for the way I acted toward you today. You behaved honorably in every way. You were *right* to wait till Marchand—" His words suddenly stuck in his throat. It was his turn to inhale deeply. Then he continued. "To wait till my *father* finally told me the truth. He trusted you to help him get me outta that crypt. He said tonight that he'd known from the very first that you were a woman of integrity, just like I did. That you were a person he could count on to do the right thing."

Very gently he covered one of her hands lying on the desk with his own and was reassured to feel its warmth. He bent even closer and whispered into her ear, "I am so sorry that my tunnel vision made me so blind. I should have trusted that you only had my best interests at heart. But you see . . . it's been so long since I felt that anyone *did*. Have my interests at heart, I mean."

Corlis seemed to have settled back into complete unconsciousness. He stared at her immobile features and felt the beginning of panic.

"You *have* to wake up, Corlis," he demanded roughly. "I'm here. . . . It's King. . . . It's truly *me* . . . maybe for the first time in my life."

Instead of kissing her cheek gently, as he knew Dylan would have advised, he impulsively scooped Corlis into his arms, sat down on the chair himself, and cradled her in his lap.

"Please, baby . . . please be here with me," he crooned, rocking her gently in his arms. "*Please!* I want you to be part of my life . . . for the *rest* of my life!" he whispered fiercely, kissing her forehead, her cheeks, her closed eyes. "I've known it for a long, long time. Long before I took you to the fishin' cabin and we made love. But then the fight to save the buildin's got in the middle of everything. You didn't agree with me 'bout some things . . . or see everything *my* way, so I . . . I got frustrated, you know?" He was kissing her hair now, brushing a tendril away from her brow. "I'm not used to bein' round a woman like you. Smart. Sassy. Real uppity. Too many magnolias in my past, I guess. I pushed away what I wanted for myself and focused everythin' on just tryin' to keep those buildin's from being bull-dozed. You were right . . . I saw everything as either black or white."

Corlis heaved another sigh . . . as if she agreed with his self-assessment, but still she remained inert in his arms.

"I'm *glad* they're saved . . . those buildin's . . . but I've spent most of my life rescuin' ruins. . . . Now I've got to start buildin' something, and you and I—"

"King?"

Corlis's eyes were now open, and she peered up at him sleepily.

"I'm baaa-ck," she whispered with a crooked smile.

He pulled her hard against his chest, fighting a swell of emotion.

"Well, it's about time!" he whispered hoarsely. Then in a more normal voice he added, "You had me scared half to death, sugar."

"Say that part again," she murmured.

"What part? That I was scared?"

"The 'please be with me, I want you to be part of my life' part. . . ."

"You heard that, huh, baby?" he said, hugging her close.

"And the part about too many magnolias in your life." She stared up at him, her gaze troubled. "Is that really true?"

"You mean like Cindy Lou?" He brushed his lips against hers and murmured, "You may be a helluva feminist, but, boy, do you get jealous for no reason. I was happy the Mallorys supported the cause and wrote a few checks, but you should know by now that I'm a lot like you. Cross me once, and you're off my list."

"Well . . . *I* crossed you," Corlis said quietly. "I wouldn't give you information that you felt was due you. I certainly felt scratched off your list today."

He seized her right hand and brought it to his lips. "I had no right to judge you at all. . . ." He gently stroked the backs of her fingers against his chin. "I am *really* sorry for what I said earlier today . . . and for goin' off in a huff. Can you forgive me for that?"

She closed her eyes briefly, as if warding off the memory.

At length she said in a husky voice, "It's all right, King. Believe me, I've done the same thing myself, many a time. All my life, in fact. I've been the queen of getting mad and then taking a powder."

"Well, you've got company there, Ace," he said, kissing her on the nose.

"Making judgments is a big part of my job," she said thoughtfully, gazing up at him, "but sometimes I'd do a lot better if I'd just keep the focus on my *own* behavior and made sure to keep *my* side of the street clean."

"Your behavior has been just fine," he reassured her. "But like those lady marines told me, *I* still need a little attitude adjustment."

"Not too much," she said smiling. "As long as you show up when I conk out like this, and then tell me you need me around for the rest of your life."

"Were you playin' possum just now?" he demanded, chucking her lightly on the cheek.

"Sort of. I was in such a relaxed state . . . I wanted to stay like that forever and just listen to the sound of your voice."

"Speakin' of that little journey you took yourself on tonight . . . do you mind tellin' me where you've been?"

"Oh boy," she said, struggling to sit up within the circle of his arms. "For a person who likes to deal in hard facts, I honestly don't know where to begin."

"Well . . . you can take as much time as you need," he replied, bending forward to kiss her again on the nose, "but someday I want to hear all about the things you haven't told me. And I promise . . . we'll keep it strictly off the record," he teased.

She abruptly sat bolt upright.

"Oh . . . my God!" she exclaimed. "With all this woo-woo stuff, I completely forgot Lafayette Marchand!" she said, her expression full of loving concern. "Did he . . . ?"

"Yes," King replied simply. "Yes, he did. In true southern style, over drinks at the Old Absinthe House bar, he filled me in on the last thirty-five years of his life. Then we walked through the Quarter to Café LaCroix, where we've been waitin' for you ever since."

"And?" Corlis asked softly.

"I have to give the guy credit. He didn't spare himself at all. He was decent about everythin'. I'd say things between us went 'bout as well as they possibly could. We both agreed to unravel this thing slowly . . . and keep our expectations under control."

"Oh, King . . . I'm so glad that he . . . that he told you the truth," she said at length. She leaned back, her eyes moist with compassion. "He risked everything, you know, to get you out of that crypt in time for the city council meeting. I expect that none of what you talked about tonight was easy for him to say . . . *or* for you to hear, for that matter."

"And as you so candidly pointed out to me today, I haven't been a great one for waitin' to get all the facts before makin' up my mind about some things," he reflected, staring off into space.

"But sometimes there just wasn't time, or the building would be rubble, just like you've said," she protested. "I think everything you did was brave and solidly thought out and—"

King grinned. "Why thank you, Ace. Comin' from you, I consider that high praise."

"I bet *now* your dean at the architecture school is going to have to show some appreciation for what you've done."

"He already has," King said with a short laugh. "I checked my voice mail before I went to Café LaCroix. The little twit is recommendin' me highly for tenure, he says. I think I see the hand of Lafayette Marchand at work on this one."

"Maybe your father is attempting to make up for his boss trying to pressure the university to fire you."

"Well . . . speakin' of all that," he said seriously, "I have another question."

"And that is?"

"Can we be *seen* together, now? In public? As a goddamned couple, I mean?" Corlis smiled faintly and nodded. "And how 'bout maybe drinkin' a *beer* in public?" he demanded.

"Tonight?" she asked with a mischievous smile. "I'm off duty . . . so, sure. Besides, we have a lot to celebrate."

King flashed her a lecherous grin. "Oh, believe me, I know *just* how I want to celebrate. How 'bout your place? It's close by," he proposed, gently pinching her fanny.

"Can't be *my* place."

"Why not?"

"Do you want to give an eighty-three-year-old woman cardiac arrest?"

King looked at her, puzzled. Then he burst out laughing. "Oh, I forgot. Aunt Marge is now in residence. For a second I thought you were pullin' a magnolia. . . ."

However, Corlis wasn't listening. "Oh, my stars," she gasped. "Where's Aunt Marge right *now*? It must be one A.M."

"Don't worry, sugar. Half the preservation guerrillas are drinkin' with her at the bar at Café LaCroix." King stood up and gently settled Corlis on her feet. Then he put his arms around her once more. "As for later tonight, smart folks like us can surely figure out the logistics."

"Well, there's always the fishing cabin," she proposed, arching one cyebrow suggestively.

"You know somethin'? You are one uppity woman."

"You betcha."

King cast a faintly salacious gaze in the direction of her legs. "And you know what else?"

"What?"

"The thing I continue to find truly amazin' about you, Ace, is that regardless of what century you might be in," he pronounced solemnly, "you've got—without a doubt—the greatest pair of legs in Louisiana."

"And what *you've* got, Mr. Preservation," she whispered softly, moving her hips against his midsection, "I consider a national treasure."

King's swift intake of breath was followed by the husky sound of his voice. "You are one lucky lady that this dusty ol' tax office is the most uninvitin' place for a tryst I've ever seen."

"Later, *monsieur* . . ." she said with a throaty laugh.

For a long, quiet moment they stood silently with their arms wrapped around each other in the darkened room that had once been a tailor's shop. Then King murmured into her hair, "I am so damned relieved . . . you came back."

"Me, too. And I don't need to go there again."

King took a step back and said, "Well, then . . . come on, baby. Let's go *dancin'*!"

Long after midnight, Café LaCroix was packed to the rafters with members of the preservationist community, along with family, friends, and scores of supporters who had departed city hall and headed directly for the Decatur Street music club to raise a toast to the winning side. By the time Corlis and King arrived, bystanders from the neighborhood, who merely wanted to be part of the triumphant celebration, had joined in as well.

At the front of the hall, the band was wailing rock 'n' roll and Dixieland favorites in response to requests shouted from dancers crowding the floor. A security guard, late of the New Orleans City Council chambers, danced in and around the swaying couples, waving a confiscated SAVE OUR SELWYNS! picket sign like a giant fan. Aunt Marge and the preservation guerrillas jammed around a clutch of small cocktail tables, drinking beer and rehashing their triumph.

"It is *so* sweet!" chortled King, tipping his brown bottle in a salute that enveloped the entire room. "This victory is 'bout as sweet as it gets!" he added as he and Corlis gyrated on the dance floor to loud and seriously funky music. Then he raised his Dixie once again and declared, "To the gang who *could* shoot straight!"

"You betcha," seconded Virgil nearby, with a tip of his beer bottle in Corlis's direction. He had stopped off at the party prior to his impending "vacation," which she had ribbed him about unmercifully for a good ten minutes. Earlier he had asked King, "Are you tellin' me that nothin' nasty's gonna happen to Jack Ebert, that little creep?"

"I don't think we'll have any more trouble from him. Jack's just grateful he's not in prison on federal kidnappin' charges."

"Yeah," Corlis noted sourly, "but that still leaves him free to wield a poison pen again."

"Oh, Jack'll stay in line," King guaranteed. "In Lafayette's employment settlement with Jeffries, our PR czar's acquirin' *Arts This Week.*"

"Lafayette Marchand is a regular horse trader," Corlis commented dryly. She looked for King's father. "Where is he, anyway?"

King pointed to the doorway at the back of the club where his father had just reappeared with Bethany Kingsbury on his arm. Before Corlis could react, however, the noise level in the small, crowded café grew even more deafening as Althea LaCroix's youngest brother, Julien, banged on the drums and cymbals to get everybody's attention. When the throng had substantially quieted down, Althea leaned toward her microphone mounted on the piano.

"Parrrr-teee!" she shouted in her distinctive husky style, and received a roar of approval from the rowdy gathering.

Corlis surveyed the mass of acquaintances, colleagues, and news sources, each of which had played some part in the day's momentous events. A year ago she hadn't known any of these people—except for King. Now she counted many of them among her closest friends.

Althea held up her hands and called for quiet amid piercing wolf whistles and catcalls.

"Ladies and gentlemen," she shouted into her microphone. "We have a surprise for everyone tonight. It's only two A.M.! A little more jammin' is in order, don'tcha think?"

The crowd went wild with delirious applause as patrons in the middle of the café took several steps backward, forming an aisle in the sea of revelers. Approaching the bandstand was a bear of a man dressed in black T-shirt and black pants, with a black mustache and beard to match, and sporting a red bandanna rolled into a 70s-style headband.

"Joinin' us tonight," purred Althea's sexy voice over the club's state-of-the-art sound system, "by special arrangement with Café LaCroix . . . is none other than . . ."

The crowd roared back in one voice, *"Doctor John!"*

The jazz legend approached Althea, who graciously slid to the end of the piano bench. He extended his fellow pianist a high-five greeting and pointed to an electric keyboard nearby, pantomiming that he wanted Althea to play along.

Then, to hoarse cheers from the assembled crowd, Dr. John laid his big, beefy paws on the piano's keys. Within seconds he and all six members of the LaCroix family swung into the raucous, howling tune everybody was waiting to hear: "Goin' Back to New Orleans."

Nearly everyone was on the dance floor. Horns wailing, drums beating, Corlis whirled under King's arm. She lowered her lids and cast her dance partner a distinctly vampish, come-hither glance, stomping her feet and rotating her hips with heathen abandon.

"Ace, you're gonna pay for that later, big-time," King shouted with an appreciative smirk.

Goin' *back* to New Orleans? Corlis thought joyfully.

How could a person ever really leave?

Author's Note and Acknowledgments

This is a work of fiction, first page to last.

However, much of the story has been inspired by the passion, knowledge, and perseverance of a host of people dedicated to preserving our nation's architectural heritage and culture.

My undying thanks and appreciation go to reference librarian Pamela D. Arceneaux at the incomparable Historic New Orleans Collection, the researchers and historians at Louisiana State University's sugarcane archive, the Louisiana Historical Society, the Louisiana Landmarks Society, the National Trust for Historic Preservation, the National Association for African-American Heritage Preservation, and the other institutions and organizations that make up America's preservation community. After some four months spent in New Orleans in 1996, I realized that most Americans have no idea of the debt we owe these guardians of our country's historic buildings, artifacts, and written history.

Among the "preservation guerrillas" I particularly wish to thank are historians Sally K. and William D. Reeves, the staff and executive director, Patricia H. Gay, of the Preservation Resource Center of New Orleans (as noted in the novel, headquartered on Julia Street), and the thousands who support the preservation movement in Louisiana and across the nation. I am deeply grateful to PRC member extraordinaire Jeannette Bell. During a week when her daughter was graduating from law school, she was kind enough to read a late draft of the manuscript for accuracy regarding the Free People of Color and the role African Americans have played in building and preserving many of New Orleans' historic structures.

My sincere appreciation is due, also, to William E. Borah, attorney, architectural historian, and seasoned trench fighter who—along with his childhood friend and colleague the late Richard O. Baumbach—wrote the seminal work *The Second Battle of New Orleans: A History of the Vieux Carré Riverfront Expressway Controversy* (University of Alabama Press). Together, Borah and Baumbach led a ten-year battle to save the French Quarter from a six-lane elevated highway that would have destroyed forever a national treasure. Counselor Borah, whose family is one of those "livin' in New Orleans since the Year One" clans, was at the forefront of a more recent skirmish to rescue from the wrecking ball a block of Greek Revival buildings in the downtown business district. One of these days, the New Orleans politicians should give him a big gold key to the city in appreciation of his stewardship in a town where the tourists *don't* come to gaze in awe at glass-and-steel high-rises.

Fellow writer Michael Llewellyn, author of the historical novel *Twelfth Night* (Kensington Publishers)—a work set in New Orleans ten years after the historical portion of *Midnight on Julia Street*—has also earned the title "preservationist," in my opinion, for his ability to describe and animate a world long past. He is a master of the telling detail, and I doubt very much I could have completed my novel without his knowledge, wisdom, treasured friendship, culinary mastery—and those Welsh curses he is apt to cast when provoked. His boundless hospitality on Dauphine Street proved both a refuge and the inspiration for Kingsbury Duvallon's wonderful living quarters.

A partial list of the outstanding resources and books I consulted includes: *New Orleans: Elegance and Decadence* by Richard Sexton and Randolph Delehanty (Chronicle Books); *Classic New Orleans* by William R. Mitchell, Jr., photography by James R. Lockhart (Martin-St. Martin Publishing Company); *New Orleans Interiors* by Mary Louise Christovich, photography by N. Jane Iseley (published by Friends of the Cabildo, Louisiana State Museum, and The Historic New Orleans Collection); *The French Quarter* by Herbert Asbury (1938 edition, Garden City Publishing Company); *The Free People of*

Color of New Orleans by Mary Gehman (published by Margaret Media, Inc., New Orleans); *Louisiana's Plantation Homes: The Grace and Grandeur* by Joseph Arrigo, photography by Dick Dietrich (Voyageur Press). The Huntington Library in San Marino, California, where I have been a reader in eighteenth- and nineteenth-century European and American studies since 1983, proved to have its usual treasure trove of historical documents and secondary texts.

I also wish to pay homage to the raft of hardworking, ethical, and often courageous electronic and print reporters I've known and worked with during my years as a radio and television broadcaster. These journalists continue (despite unholy pressure from some of the "suits" upstairs) to get their facts straight and their sentences parsed correctly. Thanks especially to the "top news hens," my buddies Suzanne LaCock, Peggy Holter, and Mary Murphy for adding to my own storehouse of dopey decisions made in the executive suites of the nation's news organizations.

Friends who served virtually as my guardian angels during the time it took to create this novel cannot all be thanked here, but you know who you are. The ones with double halos include: Carol Adams, Tamara Asseyev, Barbara Babcock, Dorian M. Bennett, Margery Bernard, Michi Blake, Ellie Cabot, Colin and Louise Campbell, Cover to Cover Books owner Mary Lou England, in Natchez, Shea Dixon and harpist Rachel Van Voorhees, Mary and Edmund Fry, Jan Gough and Seamus Malin, John and Linda Grenner, Tom and Alayna Grey, Taylor Hackford and Helen Mirren, Diane Hister, Ann James, Anthony and Susanna Jennens, Wendy Kout and Dennis Koenig, Brianne Leary, Nicki and Michael McMahan, Terry Cagney Morrison, Joanne Forbes Nelson and Dale Nelson, Paul Nevski of Le Monde Créole, Elberta Pate, Dan and the Rev. Diana Phillips, Meryl Sawyer, Jackie and Dean Stolber, Barbara and Andy Thornburg, Garden District Book Shop's Britton Trice and Deb Wehmeir, the late Catherine Turney, Gayle and Wayne Van Dyck, Nancy Wagner, my ace editorial assistant Beth Wellington, C.K. and Mary Williams, Elizabeth Booth, John Woodward, Michael and Diane Worthington, Cynthia Wright and Jim Hunt, Marilee and Al Zdenek, and the Montecito Monday Noontimers.

At The Ballantine Publishing Group, I am thankful for the talent and high-level skills of publicists Jennifer Richards and Marie Coolman, cover whiz Carlos Beltrán, sales maven George Fisher, and a publishing executive who is no relation—though I wish she were—my wonderful editor, Elisa Wares. Thanks, too, to Carolyn Nichols, who brought me into the Random House family where my father, the late Harlan Ware, published a novel a half century ago. Jane Chelius knows all the reasons she's my respected friend and a great agent.

And then, of course, there is my family, without whom the publication of *Midnight on Julia Street* wouldn't mean what it does at this time in my life: my dearest (and only!) sister, Joy Ware Hollien, who walked the walk with me on this one; my wonderful son, cinematographer (and soon-to-be major motion picture director, I'm sure) Jamie Ware Billett; my amazing cousin, Alison Thayer Harris, R.N., her husband, David, and her parents, Charles and Liz Ware Thayer; the Cook clan; and, finally, the Miracle Man of this and any century, my beloved husband Tony Cook—all of you are part of my psyche and my heart.

And, of course, my humble thanks to the late, great Cagney Cat. His paw prints are everywhere on this novel.

Ciji Ware
San Francisco

A COTTAGE BY THE SEA

by Ciji Ware

After a scandalous Hollywood divorce, Blythe Stowe needs to get away from the pain and the humiliation of the tabloids that shout the details of her husband dumping her for her own sister. She goes to the wild coast of Cornwall and a cottage by the sea that her Wyoming grandmother claimed had been the home of her ancestors.

But Blythe encounters more than just a quaint retreat nestled amid vivid skies and gorgeous ocean. She has the odd sensation that her handsome neighbor Lucas Teague is more than a British gentleman going broke. He might be her destiny. . . .

Published by Fawcett Books.
Available at bookstores everywhere.

LORD OF VENGEANCE

by Tina St. John

Set in majestic medieval England, this is the story of two valiant people who struggle with the sins of the past to forge a love as turbulent as the land they live in. Devilishly handsome Gunnar Rutledge has spent years plotting against the man who nearly destroyed his life. He seeks the ultimate vengeance on Raina d'Bussy—his enemy's daughter—a proud beauty who will be slave to no man. Gunnar sets out to break Raina's glorious spirit but instead finds himself bewitched by her goodness and strength.

Published by Fawcett Books.
Available at bookstores everywhere.